TEMPTING
A
SINNER

Books by Kate Pearce

The House of Pleasure Series

SIMPLY SEXUAL
SIMPLY SINFUL
SIMPLY SHAMELESS
SIMPLY WICKED
SIMPLY INSATIABLE
SIMPLY FORBIDDEN
SIMPLY CARNAL
SIMPLY VORACIOUS
SIMPLY SCANDALOUS

The Sinners Club Series

THE SINNERS CLUB
TEMPTING A SINNER

Single Titles

RAW DESIRE

Anthologies

SOME LIKE IT ROUGH
LORDS OF PASSION

Published by Kensington Publishing Corporation

TEMPTING
A
SINNER

KATE
PEARCE

APHRODISIA
KENSINGTON PUBLISHING CORP.
www.kensingtonbooks.com

eISBN-13: 978-0-7582-9020-5
eISBN-10: 0-7582-9020-9
First Kensington Electronic Edition: August 2014

ISBN-13: 978-0-7582-9019-9
ISBN-10: 0-7582-9019-5
First Kensington Trade Paperback Printing: August 2014

10 9 8 7 6 5 4 3 2 1

Printed in the United States of America

TEMPTING
A
SINNER

1

County of Lincolnshire, 1827

Benedict, Lord Keyes, drew his horse to a halt in front of the dilapidated gates of Alford Park, his ancestral home, and considered his options. He wasn't quite sure why he was here, but the unsigned letter from a well-wisher had sparked his interest. In his profession, once he was on the trail of something, he never gave up until he'd achieved his goal, or caught his man. Or in this case—possibly his woman.

As he turned into the overgrown drive, he noticed smoke belching out of one of the lopsided Elizabethan chimneys. So his source had been correct about one thing. The ramshackle house was definitely inhabited. He doubted his father had forsaken his mansion in Mayfair and decided to take up residence in the county of Lincolnshire. There was no political advantage to be gained here, or anyone to bully. But if his mother's latest missive was correct, and not merely a ploy to force him home, the current Marquis of Alford was suffering from a mysterious ailment that kept him tied to his bed.

From what he remembered of the family history drummed into him as a boy, this decaying manor house had once been the seat of his family's power when trade was with Europe and wool was king. In truth, it resembled a castle rather than a house, ready to repel marauders with its stone towers and partially filled-in moat. The locale was desolate now, and from his observations as he rode north, the population scarce.

The faint sounds of a barking dog reached him from inside the house. He straightened in the saddle and checked that his pistol was primed and ready. This might be his home, but it always paid to be careful. The noise increased in volume as he made his way along the main façade of the timber-and-stone house toward the stables at the rear.

A window swung open above him. He swiveled in the saddle toward the sound, bringing his hand up as the sun struck the multifaceted panes and reflected right back in his eyes. The *crack* of a rifle shot came a second later. Still blinded by the sun, he could do nothing to stop the shock of pain and the blackness of unconsciousness slamming into him and sending him pitching forward onto the ground.

"Oh my goodness, Mally! You've *killed* him!"

Malinda lowered the shotgun and took a deep, steadying breath. Despite the fact that she was trembling like a willow tree, she'd enjoyed aiming at the man coming down the drive as if he owned the place. Even though, officially, he and his family did.

"I aimed at his shoulder, not his heart, Doris. I've merely incapacitated him." She handed the gun over to Jim, the stable hand, and observed the man on the ground. "He'll get up in a moment, I'm sure of it."

She advanced a step, her sister on her heels.

"He's not moving. What have you done?" Doris whispered.

Malinda walked right up to the apparently unconscious figure and used the tip of her riding boot to roll him onto his back. Even in repose, he was still a handsome devil. Blood stained the upper left side of his immaculately fitted blue coat and was spreading rapidly. His hat had fallen off to reveal the thick corn blond of his hair.

"He's alive. Otherwise he wouldn't be bleeding."

"You're so callous!" Doris moaned and fell to her knees beside the unconscious man. She drew out her lace handkerchief and dabbed ineffectually at his shoulder. "Perhaps he hit his head when he fell."

"That's very likely." Malinda looked behind her at the small audience now gathered by the side door into the hall. "The window distracted him perfectly, Gwen. Will you take the horse around to the stables, and ask Mr. McFadden to take care of it, but keep it hidden?"

"Yes, Malinda." Unlike her sister, her cousin, Gwen, showed no signs of squeamishness as she stepped over the unconscious man and took hold of the horse's slack reins. "Do you want me to help carry him inside when I come back?"

"No, Jim and Malcolm can take him upstairs before he wakes. You can meet me there." Malinda glanced back at the two men. "Bring him up to the crimson bedchamber, please." She raised her voice. "And remember, if anyone asks if we've seen him, we have not."

Doris moaned again, but she didn't say anything. That was all Malinda could hope for at this particular moment. She knew her sister didn't like her plans for Lord Keyes, but when challenged had been unable to come up with anything better. Justice would be served and Benedict, Lord Keyes, would pay for his sins and the sins of his father whether he liked it or not.

By the time the men carried Keyes up to the already prepared crimson bedchamber, he was stirring. She instructed them to lay him on the large four-poster bed, and dismissed them to their usual duties. As soon as the door closed behind Jim, she lifted the red velvet bedcovers, withdrew an iron shackle, and locked it securely around Keyes's right ankle. She hoped it would hold him. The chain was old and looked rather rusty in places. It was the best she could manage without going into the village and asking the blacksmith to make her something he would probably wonder why she needed.

She checked his pockets and retrieved a pocketknife, a dagger, his purse, and a very handsome and very lethal pistol.

As soon as his eyes fluttered open and fixed on hers, she raised the pistol. He blinked at her very slowly and licked his lips.

"Where am I?"

"You fell from your horse."

His right hand came up to his left shoulder and he groaned. "There's no need to point a gun at me. I'm scarcely in a position to hurt you."

"So you say."

His head fell back onto the pillow and she wondered if he'd swooned again. Without opening his eyes, he murmured, "I promise not to hurt you if you do me a favor in return."

"You're scarcely in a position to bargain, sir, are you?"

"Oh, this is quite an easy favor."

"I doubt it." Malinda tightened her grip on the pistol, but her captive made no effort to reclaim his weapon.

His blue eyes opened, and she tensed.

"Am I considered dangerous?"

"Quite possibly."

His brow creased. "What am I supposed to have done?"

"That's a question for your conscience, sir. None of us are without sin."

"But I'm trying to understand why I'm bleeding, and why you're holding me at gunpoint. Have we met before?"

Oh, she wanted to shoot him now. "What do you think?"

"That's the problem." His smile was charming. "I can't seem to think of anything at all."

She scowled at him. "Don't try your tricks on me."

His hand moved gingerly up toward his head. "I'm not." He

winced. "Damnation, this is ridiculous. I can't even remember who I am."

Malinda stared at him for a long moment, but he closed his eyes and appeared to lose consciousness again. The door behind her opened. Gwen came in carrying a basin of water and Malinda's medicinal supplies.

"How is our patient?"

Malinda waved at Gwen to speak softly. "He says he doesn't know who he is."

Gwen came to stand alongside her and stared down at the quiet face. "He *did* hit his head. Perhaps he really doesn't remember anything." She glanced at Melinda. "Does that make our task easier or harder?"

"It depends on whether he's lying or not." Malinda rolled up her sleeves. "Let's attend to his wound, and make sure he doesn't die before we have a chance to confront him with his misdeeds."

"How are we going to get him out of that coat?" Gwen stroked the sleeve. "It is beautifully made, and clings to him like a second skin."

Malinda smiled and produced the knife she'd just taken from Lord Keyes. "I think we're going to have to cut him out of *everything*, don't you?"

"The poor man will be quite naked."

"And thus unable to run away."

Malinda slit his right sleeve and soon had him out of his shirt, waistcoat, and coat. She was gentle as she moved across to his left side and eased the blood-soaked garments away from his skin. He stirred in his sleep but didn't awaken. She paused to examine the wound that marred the perfection of his upper arm. From what she could see, the bullet hadn't lodged in his flesh, but had passed through, not hitting the bone, and exited through the muscle at the rear. She would have to make sure no strands of fabric remained in the wound, but otherwise it looked as if he would survive.

"I told you I was a good shot."

"I never doubted it," Gwen said. "After all, you practiced enough."

"As I said, I didn't want to kill him, merely *incapacitate* him a little."

"Then I think you succeeded in your aim—unless he really doesn't know who he is."

Malinda concentrated on washing out the wound and patting some basilicum powder onto the skin. She accepted the bandage Gwen offered her and slowly wound it around Keyes's upper arm and shoulder. Now that his injury had been satisfactorily attended to, she couldn't help but notice how well he'd grown into his frame and how little weight he carried around his middle. He reminded her of one of the king's racehorses, all fine bone and fast thoroughbred mettle.

"Should we take off his boots and breeches?"

Malinda tore her gaze away from the interesting contours of Keyes's abdomen. "Yes, we should."

Gwen paused as she noticed the shackle around Keyes's ankle. "Is that really necessary at this point?"

Malinda's sense of well-being dissipated. "Trust me. He's as slippery as an adder and twice as dangerous." She turned to Gwen. "Don't let his good looks and pleasant manners deceive you. This man is a survivor. He and his loathsome family will stop anyone or anything that gets in their way."

Gwen touched her hand. "It's all right, Malinda, I won't let you down."

She tried to smile at her favorite cousin. "Then don't let your guard slip for a moment. I'll sit by him until he wakes up, and see if his 'memory' has returned. If it has, he should have no difficulty recognizing me this time."

"Are you sure?" Gwen picked up the bowl of water and the bloodstained clothes.

Malinda smoothed down the unbecoming folds of her oldest brown dress. Had she changed that much? If she had, it was Keyes and his damned family who'd caused it. At some level she'd imagined that the moment he locked gazes with her he'd remember her, he'd remember it all. . . .

"Malinda?"

She shook off the old memories and concentrated on the present. She held Lord Keyes captive in his own family home. This time, the odds were in her favor, and she intended to win.

Keyes came awake into a haze of pain and darkness and immediately knew he wasn't safe and that someone was watching him. Had he been captured again? He inhaled the scent of lavender and his confusion increased. A soft hand touched his forehead and then withdrew to be replaced by the blessed coldness of a wet cloth. He sighed and attempted to open his eyes. Something was very wrong, and he didn't know what it was. Instinct told him to remain silent, but he couldn't remember why.

"Where am I?"

"You're quite safe."

He knew that sultry, low-pitched voice, but when had he last heard it? Yesterday, today, ten years ago?

"Where am I?" He repeated his question.

"In bed. You fell from your horse and damaged your shoulder and head. Are you in pain?"

He choked back a laugh. Was he in pain? How could she even ask him that when he was shivering and whimpering like a child?

"I have laudanum to give you."

Thank God. He hated the stuff, but he was beyond that now as agony sliced through his shoulder. He moved restlessly against his pillows eager to dissipate the pain but just made it worse. The woman raised his head so that he could drink the laudanum from a spoon. He took it gratefully, murmuring his thanks and allowed her to settle him back on his pillows.

Heat flared through his fingers and burned down his spine and he moaned as sweat gathered on his brow. Her hands on him again, stripping back the covers and pressing cold, dripping sponges against his burning skin. He no longer had a sense of time, only that he had to survive this agony because if he died now, he'd die not knowing who he was, or how he'd ended up in this place, and that was simply unacceptable.

The voices changed and he could no longer sense if that was due to his fever, or that more than one woman was caring for him. Only one of them was distinct, she held him to life, her voice a puzzle he needed to solve.

He woke into darkness, the soft glow of candlelight and the crackle of a wood-burning fire. With some difficulty, he turned his head on his pillow, and spotted a small dark-haired woman sitting beside the bed. She was reading something, her shoulder turned to the light, and her spectacles perched at the end of her nose. He must have made a sound because she looked up, a smile breaking out on her pleasant face.

"You are awake! Are you thirsty, sir?"

Without waiting for him to answer, she came over, picked up the mug beside his bed, and offered it to him. He managed to grasp the cup with his right hand. To his chagrin, it proved impossible to gather the strength to raise it to his lips. With a soft sound, the woman helped him, wrapping one arm around his shoulders and her hand around his and the cup.

"There you are, sir. Drink as much as you need."

He discovered he was extremely thirsty and gulped down the entire cup. She refilled it and he drank more until, with a sigh, he sank back onto his pillows.

"Thank you."

His voice sounded rusty with misuse. How long had he lain in this unfamiliar bed?

"How long have I been here?"

"About a week. You fell from your horse and developed a fever from your injuries." His helper put the cup down and fussed with his bedcovers and pillows.

"But why—?"

She smiled at him and hurried toward the door. "I must tell the others that you are feeling better!"

With that, she escaped, leaving him to the comforting crackle of the fire. He looked around the room, noticing the closed red velvet curtains and the matching hangings on the four-poster bed. It was obviously a fairly wealthy household; the ceilings were high and the furniture ornate. There was also a sense of disuse—as if time had stood still and the trappings of a previous generation's grandeur had never been replaced. Something nagged at his brain, something familiar, but the thought vanished before he could latch on to it.

Tentatively, he sat up, wincing as his fingers grazed the goose egg on the side of his head just above his ear. He'd definitely fallen from his horse. His fingers found the edge of a bandage, and he inhaled sharply and studied his shoulder and upper left arm. He recognized the hot, tearing sensation of a bullet wound beneath the bandages.

But why had he been shot?

He took another look around the room. He wasn't on the Continent. He had a vague sense that England was no longer overtly at war with France, so this wasn't the result of a battle. The woman who'd tended him had also been English. Anxiety tightened his gut. He attempted to swing his legs out of the bed only to realize he couldn't. With all his remaining strength he threw back the heavy covers and discovered he was completely naked apart from the shackle on his right leg.

With a groan, he fell back against the mound of pillows. He

didn't even have the energy to test the strength of the metal. A soft *click* announced the opening of the door and the return of the woman who'd helped him drink the water.

"Oh, dear, sir, you must be cold!" She drew the covers back over him. "Please try not to set back your recovery with such foolish tricks."

"Where am I?"

She looked at him, her gaze attentive. "Don't you know?"

"Ma'am, at this point in my existence, I don't remember anything."

She cocked her head to one side. "Not even your name?"

He considered that. "No."

"You did bang your head quite badly." She was all sympathy. "My cousin is going to bring you up some nice broth."

"But—"

"Ah, here she is now."

The door opened again, and he stopped speaking as a tall auburn-haired woman entered carrying a tray. She bore herself like a queen and had a certain air of authority that made him think she was the mistress of the house, and potentially the one who'd planned to keep him chained to his bed. Or was it her bed?

She placed the tray carefully on the table and smiled at the other woman. "Go and have your dinner, Gwen, dear. Jim is outside the door if I need him."

He waited until she finally looked at him, her gaze as searching as his own.

"Do you remember me, sir?"

Another wisp of thought, this time even fainter.

"I assume you are the woman who shot me?"

She slowly blinked at him. "What else was I to do?"

"Ask my name and business like any other civilized human being?"

"Ah, but I'm not civilized, and I wasn't expecting visitors."

She raised her chin. "I have a right to be wary. The last man who came here tried to force me out of my home."

"Did I look that threatening?"

"Sir, you had a loaded pistol in your hand. I couldn't take the chance that you might be an enemy."

There was no apology in her tone, which might have amused him if he hadn't been her intended victim. She leaned forward and offered him a spoon of gruel, the lavender scent of her soap enfolding him. She wore a thin gold band on her finger and he wondered where her husband was and whether he was aware of his wife's machinations. It seemed unlikely. He was too hungry not to eat and sipped gratefully at the fragrant broth until he'd emptied the bowl.

"Thank you."

She took the bowl away and sat back to study him.

"Are you quite certain you don't know who I am?"

He focused his gaze on her interesting face. She'd never be called beautiful. She was all sharp angles, pale porcelain skin, and ruthless determination. "There is something familiar about you, but I just can't remember what it is."

Her lips thinned. "And what is your name?"

"I can't remember that either."

"Why should I believe you?"

His strength deserted him. "You don't have to believe any-thing. You have me at a disadvantage, chained to my bed. Was that *necessary*?"

"You were delirious, sir. We were worried that you might hurt one of us, or try to get up and wander about before you were well enough."

"And now?"

She rose from her seat. "You're getting better. Isn't that enough?"

"Which is no answer at all." He closed his eyes. "Good

night, ma'am. Thank you for your care. I promise not to try to escape tonight."

"That's very good of you, but Jim will be here just in case. Good night, sir."

"Do you know my name?"

She paused at the door and looked back at him. "Does that distress you? Not knowing who you are, and what you've done?"

"Yes." He forced the word out.

"One would think it might be a blessing."

She swept through the door. He distinctly heard the sound of a key in the lock and the low murmur of voices before her footsteps died away.

He closed his eyes, flooded by a terrible wave of helplessness, and cursed in several languages he didn't even know he knew. *Distressed?* He was bloody terrified and she knew it. He took several deep breaths and forced himself to calm down. She knew who he was; he'd wager money on it. Now he just had to find a way to make her tell him.

2

"I really don't know whether he's telling the truth or not," Malinda concluded her story and studied the rapt faces of her audience. They'd assembled in the kitchen after dinner to hear what she had to say. "Is it possible that he really has lost his memory?"

"It might be true," Jim said doubtfully. "My brother fell out of the hay cart once, and was unconscious for days. When he woke up, he couldn't remember a thing about what happened on that day. He never could."

"Lord Keyes remembered being shot." Malinda shuddered. "I'm just not sure if he's lying about losing his memory. It would be rather convenient. Remember, he is the head of a spying network and probably knows every trick there is. He could just be pretending."

Yet, she'd sensed his bewilderment and the fear he'd been unable to conceal.

"What are we going to do?" Doris wailed. "This isn't working out how we anticipated at all. I told you it was a ridiculous idea, Mally."

Malinda shot her sister a severe look. "We will continue with our plan, and assume that at some point Lord Keyes will either stop playacting, or regain his memory."

"What if he doesn't?"

"He will, Doris, he can't afford to languish here forever."

"And what if someone comes looking for him?"

"If they do, we'll simply say we've never seen him."

"But what—?"

"Doris, will you please try to be positive? If Keyes sent that obnoxious man to drive us out of our home, he deserves to suffer. And he must have done so, because he is the only person who knew I was here."

Doris looked unconvinced so Malinda continued. "Don't forget, he arrived with his pistol at the ready. I really had no choice but to shoot him. If we hold him captive he'll *have* to agree to let us stay at Alford Park."

"But what if he *doesn't?*"

"He will. He thinks he's far too important to the running of our nation for it to manage without him. He'll *have* to capitulate eventually."

And when she had guaranteed the safety of Doris and Gwen at Alford Park, she'd embark on the second part of her plan—to use Keyes to get to his father, the Marquis of Alford. She'd promised her mother revenge on the Keyes family, and if she had to use Benedict to get it, she would.

Malinda gave Doris an encouraging smile. "I have an idea to test whether Lord Keyes is pretending or not." Doris wouldn't like her new idea either, but as far as Malinda was concerned, it was an excellent notion. "I'll speak to him in the morning and see how he reacts."

Jim, Malcolm, and the cook dispersed to continue their various tasks, and Doris went to the stillroom to brew some more witch hazel for their patient's many bruises. Malinda sat across from Gwen and poured them both some more tea from the large brown earthenware pot.

"What exactly are you intending to do to our reluctant guest, Malinda?" Gwen asked.

"I'm going to construct him an alternative identity so scandalous that if he's pretending, he'll choose to regain his senses in a second." She smiled at her cousin. "I might need your help."

"With something scandalous?" Gwen leaned in and touched the rim of her mug to Malinda's. "I can't wait."

He'd woken from his troubled sleep when a maid had opened the curtains and re-laid his fire. The sky outside was leaden and gray and didn't help raise his spirits. Benedict glanced down at his right ankle. Even if he did get the shackle off, where would he go? His clothes and pistol had disappeared, and he had no idea where he was, or even his own name. Running into the nearest village, stark-naked and babbling, would simply result in him being taken off to the nearest madhouse, which would solve nothing. At least here he was comfortable and slowly regaining his strength.

The man named Jim came in with a bowl of water and a towel over his arm.

"Good morning, sir. I'll help you wash if you'll sit up."

"I'm not a child." He favored Jim with his most disdainful glare. "I'm old enough to piss by myself, and shave too."

"The pissing part I can help you with, sir." Jim used the toe of his boot to nudge a potty out from under the bed. "The razor, not until my mistress says so."

Benedict managed to maneuver his shackled leg well enough to use the pot, and allowed Jim to hand him a sponge to wash with and then a towel to dry himself.

"It's damned chilly in here. Any chance of my clothes being returned to me?" he asked.

"I think they're still in the wash, sir." Jim eyed him speculatively. "I'd give you one of my nightshirts, but you'd burst it at the seams."

"Thanks for the offer." He sank back onto the mattress, exhausted by even such small measures of independence.

"You're welcome, sir. Now just bide quietly for a bit, and my Ellen will be bringing you up a nice bowl of porridge for your breakfast."

He ate the porridge, which was remarkably good and served with thick cream and honey, sipped at his tea, and felt his energy returning. Ellen removed the tray and he contemplated his first full day of lying in bed doing nothing. . . .

"Is your mistress about?"

"Oh, there it is, can't having you lying on that now, can we?" Ellen retrieved his spoon, which he'd tried to hide under the edge of his pillow. "She'll be up to see you soon, sir. She told me to tell you so."

He realized there wasn't a clock in the room and waited impatiently for any sign of his hostess for what felt like hours. When she did appear, she wore a high-waisted gown made of the thin patterned Indian muslin popular ten years ago. Her dark auburn hair was braided and coiled on her head apart from two curls that fell over her ears. She should've looked dowdy, but somehow her elegance made everything she wore seem interesting and fashionable.

"Good morning, sir."

"Ma'am."

She drew a chair beside the bed and sat down. She produced a leather wallet and a money bag that clinked when she laid it on the covers. "Today is laundry day, and when we were trying to discover whether any of your clothes were salvageable, Ellen thought to check the pockets for any valuables or identifying marks."

"What a shame that no one thought to do that when I first arrived. Did you discover who I am?"

She unfolded a piece of paper and looked up at him, a slight blush reddening her cheeks. "Actually, it is rather embarrassing."

"In what way?"

"The thing is, I probably shouldn't have shot you after all." She bit her lip. "It never occurred to me that Madame Helene would respond so promptly, or that she would actually send a"—her gaze swept over him—"a man such as you. I was expecting someone of lower class, of more *earthy* appetites."

"Madam, I have no idea what you are talking about."

She sighed. "I suppose I'll have to tell you the whole story."

"That would be helpful."

She sat up straight, giving him an excellent view of her rounded bosom, which was on level with the side of the bed. "I am a widow of several years, but like most women who have experienced the *pleasures* of the marriage bed, I found myself *lacking* something." She blinked at him. "If you understand me, sir."

"I believe I do, but I'm not sure what—"

She rushed on. "I have an acquaintance in London who put me in touch with a Madame Helene Delornay, who occasionally helps ladies like myself find that which they are missing." She held out the letter to him. "I found this in your coat. I can only apologize for the misunderstanding, Ben."

Ben?

It sounded almost right; he tested it in his mind, and focused on the letter. The closely written words floated across his eyes, and he shook his head.

"I can't decipher this scrawl with a headache and without my spectacles. Can you read it for me?"

"Yes, of course." She took the letter back and cleared her throat. "My dear madam, please let me introduce Ben to you. He is proportioned exactly as you required (fair-haired, muscled, and tall with a goodly sized rod), and is as lusty as a stallion. Please enjoy him, and send him back to me only when you are *completely satisfied*. He is extremely biddable, and well worth the money. Best wishes, Helene Delornay."

He let out a long, slow breath. "You are suggesting you bought my *stud services?*"

She had the grace to look guilty. "It appears so."

"I'm a *prostitute?*"

"I have to admit that when I saw you, the idea never crossed my mind." Her smile was hesitant. "But thinking about it now, and considering how much I had to pay for you, perhaps you are very sought after, and can live like the gentleman you so obviously are." She patted his hand. "One might ask how a man such as yourself became involved in such a trade, but I wouldn't want to be insensitive."

He simply stared at her as his mind cartwheeled around seeking a sense of truth, of something in her outrageous claim that resonated within him. Nothing surfaced except a distinct conviction that he had played many parts. Perhaps this was why. Did he spend his life acting out women's fantasies?

She was still holding his hand, her thumb rubbing back and forth across his, her beautiful hazel eyes full of shy hope. Damnation, was she expecting him to admit it? To throw back the covers and invite her to inspect her purchase? To touch his goodly sized rod that was stirring to life at such a bizarre idea.

She rose to her feet and kissed his cheek. "I'm so sorry, Ben. I will, of course, offer you compensation for my appalling mistake. I hope you will consider staying here until you are well enough to return to London and the bosom of Madame Helene's pleasure house."

He couldn't think of a single word to say as she brought his hand to her lips and tenderly kissed it before escaping through the door.

* * *

Once outside his door, Malinda stuffed her fist into her mouth to stop herself from laughing. She'd leave Lord Keyes alone for a few hours, and see whether he preferred to be a male prostitute or a peer of the realm. From the horrified look on his face, she was going to assume his memory would come flooding back. It was almost a pity, though; she'd fantasized about having him doing her sexual bidding many times over the past years. . . .

Gwen met her on the stairs and Malinda took her aside to tell her what she'd done. Soon her cousin was laughing too.

"Oh my goodness, I almost hope he believes you so that I can pretend to be another grieving deprived widow too!" Gwen touched Malinda's arm. "Not that I'd actually want him to—"

"It's all right, in the current circumstances I'd be quite happy to line up all the staff and insist he service each one."

"Men as well?"

"Why not? He went to Eton. I've heard he's not averse to male companionship."

Ben . . .

No, that wasn't it.

Benjamin?

No.

His headache worsened as though his mind protested being made to function normally. He let out his breath and concentrated on breathing regularly, ignoring the pain, a survival technique that had come back to him with such ease he suspected he'd been badly injured, or in danger on more than one occasion.

Benedict . . .

He opened his eyes, aware of a vast surge of relief. He had a name. Now what? Nothing else surfaced from the murky depths of his muddied thoughts, but it was a start. He contemplated his joined hands, turning them over to examine the palms.

There were a few calluses, but he obviously wasn't a manual laborer. He spoke like a gentleman. Was he, in fact, this "Ben" the madam had offered her client? Why else would he have had the letter in his possession if he weren't that man?

Because he played many parts.

Because his captor was a consummate liar.

Was he an actor, then? Perhaps an actor who supplemented his income by playing the whore? It was a possibility, although it didn't feel quite right. He slid a hand beneath the sheets and cupped his balls. If he was Ben, was he willing to fulfill his part of the contract if it meant his captor would eventually release him? His cock stirred. All he had to do was "completely satisfy her," and that wouldn't be a hardship. He ran his thumb up the side of his cock.

Another day or two of good food, and he'd at least be able to lie back and let her have her way with him. Would she like that? His fingers curled as he imagined thrusting a hand into her thick, unbound hair as she rode him to a climax. . . . He gently rubbed his shaft. He was trapped in bed, so why not be agreeable? He could play the part fate had assigned to him, and gradually gain her trust. Women always confused the physical act of sex with emotion. If he pleased her, she'd be clay in his hands.

For the first time in days Benedict smiled and contemplated a far more agreeable future.

With a huff of annoyance, Malinda contemplated her sleeping patient. For the last three days all he'd done was eat everything offered to him, and sleep. Jim reported that he'd barely managed to rouse him long enough to help him wash. Tentatively she placed her hand on his forehead. His skin was cool to the touch, and his cheeks were slightly flushed beneath the faint fair stubble on his chin.

A beautiful boy, and now a handsome man with more than a

hint of ruthlessness around the eyes and the mouth. But she could scarcely say she'd stayed the same either. Life had a way of imprinting itself on a person's face, and from the look of it, neither she nor Lord Keyes had enjoyed an untroubled existence. That comforted her somehow. She'd always feared he would move on to the leisurely life of an aristocrat and forget his past, but he certainly hadn't taken that easier route. The work he did to protect the British nation required steely courage and a devious brain.

She stroked his blond hair away from his brow.

"Don't stop," he murmured.

She snatched her hand away as he opened his eyes and she stared down into their intriguing blue depths.

"Ben."

He smiled at her.

The shock of it made her smile back. She set the candle beside the bed and turned to him. "Are you feeling any better?"

"A lot better, ma'am, thank you." He stretched carefully, displacing the covers and displaying the muscled beauty of his upper body. "Even my shoulder has stopped hurting."

"I'm very pleased to hear it." She fought to keep her gaze on his face as he rubbed a casual hand over his chest. "Have you remembered anything else about yourself since we last spoke?"

He frowned and shoved his fingers through his already disordered hair. "I'm not sure my name is Ben."

"Oh, really?"

"I think it might be Benedict."

Her heart gave a little jump, but when he didn't immediately denounce her, she continued to look interested. "Well, Ben is a derivative of that name." She hesitated. "Perhaps you only use Ben for your *professional* activities."

"That might be true." He sighed. "I haven't remembered anything else yet."

He was either a skilled liar, or truly at a loss. "I'm sure you will." She leaned over him and checked the bandage on his shoulder. "Your wound appears to be healing quite well now. In another week or so, you should be healthy enough to leave." She straightened. "I will send you on your way with as much money as I can muster." She heaved a martyred sigh. "Although it won't be a large sum, as I'd already devoted rather too much to my original investment."

"Why choose this route? Why haven't you remarried?"

"I've never met another man who matches up to my husband." She met his gaze and realized that was the truth. How humiliating to discover that fact right now. "And this region doesn't exactly overflow with wealthy men."

"Then why don't you move?"

"This is my home." She summoned another smile. "I don't have the funds to set myself up in style in London and chase after the eligible bachelors."

He shifted back on the pillows, his face positively angelic in the candlelight with his high cheekbones, blue eyes, and the glints of gold in his ash-blond hair. But his eyes were cold. At least she knew the truth. The beautiful façade concealed a devious mind. His long fingers toyed with the covers as he surveyed her.

"What time is it?"

"Just after midnight, why?"

"I thought the house was quiet."

"This is the first moment I've had to visit you all day. It's harvesttime. I've been busy putting apples away for the winter."

He picked up her hand and brought it to his face. "That explains why you smell so sweet." She shivered as he turned her palm upward and kissed it. "I *am* willing to fulfill my part of the bargain, ma'am."

"I beg your pardon?"

He kissed each of her fingers and drew her thumb into his mouth. "I'm offering you my . . . services."

"But you're still unwell and you don't think your name is Ben and—" Her knees wobbled as he kissed his way up to her wrist. Damnation, he'd called her bluff. Why was she stopping him? Did she really *want* him to remember who she was and end everything? Doris would say she should stick with the plan; her traitorous body yearned to find out exactly *how* Lord Keyes intended to service her.

He let go of her hand and pushed back the covers, displaying himself to her gaze. His cock was already erect and was, indeed, a goodly size. He wrapped his hand around it and stroked himself.

"You're not well." She sounded far too unsure for her own liking.

He smiled at her. "I'm well enough to lie on my back while you ride me and take your pleasure. I'd hate to be considered a waste of money."

Malinda couldn't stop staring at his cock, her own sex softening and throbbing as a glint of pre-cum appeared on the tip of his crown. He gathered it on his thumb and smoothed it over his swollen head, murmuring with pleasure.

"Please use me."

She took two steps toward him before she halted and considered what she was about to do. His right ankle was still tethered, and his left shoulder was vulnerable. If she *did* take up his invitation, would she be safe if he was pretending?

He groaned softly as wetness trickled down over his working fingers. With a deep, wrenching sigh, Malinda sat on the side of the bed.

"I think I should just watch you this first time—to see if you are well enough to perform without further injury to yourself."

He raised an eyebrow. "You want to watch me come?"

"Yes." She wanted to climb on him and ride him hard until he screamed, but that might happen later. She couldn't afford to ruin his recovery. Doris would be so proud.

"Then watch."

He eased his left hand down to cup his balls and used his right to play with his thick shaft. His fingers toyed with his crown, sliding through the gathering wetness, to push down his foreskin, circling and probing the slit until his back arched into each pull of his demanding hand. He planted his feet flat on the bed, freeing the motion of his hips, his buttocks clenching with every thrust.

It was like watching a scandalous nude Greek statue in motion. Malinda couldn't look away. She wished she was as naked as he was and could at least touch her needy sex and join him when he climaxed. He licked his lips and groaned with each stroke, his gaze now fixed on her as his hand moved faster and faster on his stiff shaft.

"Do I satisfy you, ma'am?" His words were guttural with lust. "Is my rod big enough for your pleasure? Will I fill you and make you scream?" His mouth twisted into a grimace. "Damnation, I want to please you. I want you to see this."

He closed his eyes as with one last savage yank on his cock he started to come in thick endless waves that drenched his hand and made Malinda want to lean forward and lick him clean. He subsided against the sheets, his breathing uneven, his gaze fastened on her.

Malinda offered him a tepid smile. "That was very pleasant to watch, Ben. Thank you." She went to get the jug of water and basin that stood next to the door. She soaked one of the cloths and rubbed it over his flat stomach, which was covered in his seed. His cock jerked as she washed him.

"Do you wish to finish cleaning yourself, or shall I continue?"

"Be my guest."

She carefully cleaned his half-erect cock and patted his balls dry before returning her attention to the rest of him.

"Is there any reason why you can't release me from my

9

shackles now, ma'am?" he murmured. "Surely I've proved I'm no danger to you or the inhabitants of this house?"

She continued drying his skin, her mind desperately seeking a way to deny his perfectly reasonable request.

"I'd rather you remain chained, Ben." She didn't need to fake her heightened color. "That was one of the original requests in my letter to Madame, that my lover wouldn't object to such a thing. I *assumed*—"

He tensed as the bedroom door opened. Malinda looked over her shoulder and smiled in relief to see her cousin.

"Ah, Gwen, you missed such a treat."

"And what was that?"

Gwen had already changed into her night robe and brushed out her hair.

"Ben is feeling much better and offered to provide his services to me." She turned back to her patient, who was lying motionless on the bed. "I think he is recovering quite nicely. Would you like to see?"

Benedict blinked as his captor cordially invited her cousin to view not only his naked body, but also the remains of his arousal. She was obviously a lot more clever than he'd anticipated. For a while there, he'd thought she was going to mount him, and he'd have her in more ways than one. But she'd proved her mettle and insisted on him proving his. The sight of her watching him pleasure himself had proven remarkably stimulating. Her refusal to release him from his chains only heightened his sense that all was not as it seemed.

He shifted on the bed. With two females now staring at his manly parts, it was no surprise that his cock started to grow again.

"Oh, he is rather large, isn't he?" Gwen whispered.

"He's not even fully erect yet." She studied his groin. "Wait until you see the rest of it."

He shivered as Gwen touched his cock and circled the wetness at the crown. "May I?" She leaned over him and licked him very delicately. His gaze flew to his tormentor, who was watching approvingly.

"Did I forget to mention that Gwen and I both paid for you? If you are well enough to service me, I hope you are well enough to help her too."

Gwen sighed and gave him one last, lingering kiss. "But probably not tonight. He needs to recover his strength. I'll make sure he gets a good breakfast so that he'll be ready and eager for more tomorrow night."

The women covered him up and tucked him in like a child. Gwen patted him on the head, and they both withdrew, leaving him without even the candle. He glared at the locked door, wondering desperately if he was still unconscious and merely dreaming he was in the middle of this rather ridiculous farce. The scent of sex and the slight soreness of his cock made it all too clear that he was awake. Anger battled amusement as he considered who else might have contributed to the fund for his prostitution skills. Would Jim be next, or Ellen, or the timid young woman who hadn't returned to his bedside since he'd woken up?

Exhaustion won out and he finally fell asleep.

3

Benedict opened his eyes to discover three women studying him. It was becoming quite usual to be gawped at as if he were an exhibit at the county fair. Two of them he recognized, the third looked very young and ready to burst into tears, her handkerchief clutched in her hand, her expression aghast.

"You can't be serious, Mally!"

His captor's name was *Mally?*

"I'm afraid that it's true. I shot the wrong man. This is Ben. He came highly recommended from Madame Delornay."

"That woman who runs a brothel?"

"It's not a brothel, Doris, it's a private club. And I believe, since her elevation by marriage to the peerage, her son Christian runs it now."

Benedict considered that information, which sounded vaguely familiar. An image of a supercilious blond flashed across the tatters of his memory. Had he met Christian Delornay? He had a suspicion that he had. Perhaps he really was a prostitute after all.

"You'll have to send him back."

"I can't send him anywhere at the moment; he's still recovering."

Was there a hint of amusement in his captor's voice? What had Doris called her? Mally? That was an unusual name. If he could recall Christian, why not the redheaded vixen who'd allegedly bought his services?

"Then send him by carriage!"

"Where? He can't remember anything except his first name. His calling card wasn't amongst his possessions. I can't send him out into the world like that." She finally looked down at him and smiled. "The *least* I can do is keep him comfortable until he remembers who he is, and can be returned safely home."

He didn't believe a word of it. She was still keeping him tethered to the bed like a wild animal.

They were talking about him as if he were a stray dog, or something that had no will of its own. Was that what they thought of him? That because they'd purchased his services, he was somehow beneath them—even lower than a servant? He wasn't even sure why he was so annoyed. Men treated whores like this all the time. Perhaps he hadn't expected women to be so callous.

He cleared his throat, and the smallest of the three women, Doris, gave a guilty start and started backing away from the bed.

"Oh my goodness, he's awake." She practically ran toward the door. "I'll go and check with Cook about dinner."

It was good to see that at least one of the inhabitants of his prison had some scruples. The other two harpies stayed put and continued to study him.

"I think you scared her off, Ben." Gwen smiled at him.

"I think that was me." Mally shrugged. "She insisted on knowing what was going on, and I had to tell her." She lit another candle and placed it on the right side of Ben's bed. "I knew she wouldn't like it. Her constitution is not as strong as mine."

"She seemed like a nice, virtuous young lady," Ben said.

"Are you implying that I'm not?"

He opened his eyes wide, his gaze lingering deliberately on her mouth. "Not at all, ma'am. Any woman who has the nerve to buy a man's services and then shoot him in her own drive-way has my admiration and respect."

The lies tripped easily off his tongue. Despite his inconvenient memory loss, he was good at this verbal fencing. It felt quite natural. Who *was* he?

She moved closer and he held his breath.

"I don't mind if you think I'm not ladylike, Ben. I certainly wasn't brought up to be a 'lady.' Perhaps it still shows." She glanced over at Gwen. "Shall we begin?"

He tensed as Gwen pulled the covers away from his naked form.

"Do you think we should make sure he's secured before we try anything?"

His tormentor studied him carefully. "He is rather big and strong." She touched his left shoulder, which was still bandaged. "Whatever we do, we'll have to be careful not to open up his old wound. What if we do this?"

She climbed onto the bed and made him sit forward. He didn't stop her, his mind at war with his body again. Should he play along? Was he even playing? Being naked and vulnerable in front of two women was curiously arousing. When was the last time he'd not been in control of a sexual encounter? He had a strange sense of freedom mingled with fear, which made him acutely aware of everything, the soft pulse at the base of his jailer's throat, Gwen's hand stroking his knee. . . .

"Do you have the silk scarves, Gwen?"

"Yes."

She took his hands and tied them together at the wrists, then gently eased him back onto the pillows stacked behind his head and shoulders. "I think this should suffice. Can you bring your hands up, Ben, or does it pain your shoulder too badly?"

"It's fine, ma'am."

She helped him raise his hands over his head. He was so intent on what she was trying to accomplish that he hardly noticed the jab of pain as the damaged muscle in his upper arm protested being moved at all. He cautiously relaxed his arms, and the pillows instantly supported them. She tied the ends of the scarves to the headboard without pulling on his wrists at all.

He looked down at his nakedness: the metal shackle on his right ankle and the already hard length of his erect cock. She touched his knee and he obediently spread his legs. Gwen climbed onto the bed, too, and stroked his hip.

"He is *so* beautiful, Mally."

"Let's just play with him for a while then, shall we?"

Her hands moved over his body as did Gwen's, touching and stroking every inch of him. He felt as if he was being devoured. She circled the base of his cock with her finger and thumb.

"He's so big, Gwen, I can barely grasp all of him."

Pride swelled in him along with his cock. If he was just a thing, a whore to be used, shouldn't he be gratified that he could satisfy them? Was he worth their money? Did he want to be? He groaned as Gwen licked his nipple and then sucked on it until it throbbed in time to the heat of his cock. He looked down over Gwen's head as something tickled the inside of his thigh. His chief tormentor was now between his thighs. Holding his gaze and still grasping his shaft, she lowered her head and licked a slow, circular path around the wet crown of his cock. The tip of her tongue flashed red as she probed his slit and then spread the wetness she found there all over his now throbbing head.

He groaned as she pursed her lips and hovered over him,

fighting not to lift his hips and press his aching cock against that slick warmth and beg to be let inside.

"Taste him, Mally," Gwen murmured and turned to watch. Benedict was simply grateful that she'd said it before he started to plead. His breath hissed out as she took him deep, the head of his cock hitting the back of her throat before she swallowed him even deeper.

"*God...*"

His hand fisted. He wanted to plunge his fingers into her hair to hold her exactly where she was now and keep her there forever. Sensation hummed through him as Gwen's clever fingers stroked his chest and hips and then pinched his nipples hard. He almost moaned when Mally released her ferocious grip on his cock, leaving him caught almost at climax, but not quite there.

"Please." This time he did beg.

Gwen took her place and started to suck him, shorter and harder pulls driving him higher until she, too, stopped, her fingers tight around the base of his cock.

"Both of us, Mal?"

They knelt on either side of his hips and leaned in, giving him the perfect view of their profiles. Two tongues on him now, his shaft wet, his balls tight and more than ready to come. He moaned as their lips met on his throbbing crown, moving over him, kissing his needy flesh, licking up his pre-cum, kissing each other. . . .

It was too much. He climaxed and as Gwen released her iron grip on the base of his shaft, his seed shot out of his beleaguered cock into the willing mouths of his seducers. He closed his eyes and just lay there, aware of the ache in his shoulder and the bite of the iron in his flesh.

Whoever he was, no man could've resisted that temptation. . . .

* * *

Even after watching Lord Keyes come like that, Malinda still shook with lust. She wanted that big cock inside her so badly. His body, bathed in a faint sheen of sweat, glowed in the candlelight. She wanted to lick him clean, keep him tied up, and convince him he was really Ben, her personal sex slave.

She looked over at Gwen, who was panting and had one hand down the front of her bodice, her fingers moving over her nipple.

"More, Gwen?"

She reached over Benedict's body and cupped Gwen's breast until it flowed over the top of her corset. With a soft sound she sucked Gwen's nipple into her mouth, felt her cousin shudder. She slid her hand beneath the hem of Gwen's nightgown and found her way to the apex of her thighs and her wet, throbbing sex. As she continued to suck on her nipple, she slid two fingers inside and pumped them slowly back and forth.

"Oh, God," Gwen breathed. "Don't stop, Mally, please, I—"

Malinda looked from her cousin to her captive, whose gaze was fixed on the movement of her hand. With deliberate slowness, she pulled Gwen's nightgown over her head, leaving her naked, and angled her slightly toward Benedict.

"Look, Gwen, he's watching me have you. Do you like that, Ben? Is she not beautiful?"

He licked his lips as Malinda thrust another finger into Gwen, her thumb pressing on her cousin's clit with every inward stroke.

"Would you like to see my mouth on her?"

His body stiffened, his cock rising.

"Oh yes, I think he'd like to see that very much." Malinda smiled at Gwen. "Would you like that, love?" Gwen nodded. She arranged Benedict's legs so that his knees were drawn up and helped Gwen straddle him and lean back against his knees, facing him, her legs spread, her sex on view.

For a few moments, she just used her fingers, drawing them

in and out of Gwen's throbbing wetness until her cousin was moaning for release. Kneeling beside Benedict's hips, she added her tongue to her fingers, flicking Gwen's clit to a tight, throbbing bud until she was climaxing hard.

She looked at Benedict. "Do you want to lick me while I finish Gwen?"

He nodded once and she straddled his chest, raising her bottom until her sex was level with his face and pushing back until she found his mouth and the press of his tongue and teeth against her softness. Reaching forward, she held Gwen's hips and brought her mouth to her cousin's cunt and thrust her tongue deep.

God, she wanted to scream as he pleasured her, his mouth everywhere, the rasp of his teeth, the way he sucked her clit hard into his mouth. Gwen bucked her hips and climaxed with a cry and Malinda followed her, undulating her hips against Benedict's working mouth until she'd probably drowned him.

When they'd both recovered and climbed off him, they studied their wounded captive, who had his eyes closed, his breathing as harried as theirs. His face was wet with Malinda's juices and his cock was already showing signs of recovery.

"He looks capable," Gwen murmured. "But we don't want to tire him out."

A muscle twitched in his cheek. Malinda guessed the mighty Lord Keyes didn't appreciate being talked about as though he wasn't there. Even though he claimed not to know who he was, arrogance was bred into his very bones. For an aristocrat, it was probably a new experience to be treated as nothing. She couldn't help but enjoy it.

"I'll leave him to you, Mally, and take myself off to bed." Gwen crawled toward the edge of the bed.

"Are you sure?"

Gwen's amused brown eyes met hers. "He's all yours, love. When we can trust him enough to use his hands on us, I'll be back." She blew them both a kiss. "Thank you, Ben. You are definitely worth the money, I'll make sure to write a hearty recommendation to Madame Helene to take with you when you leave."

Malinda followed Gwen to the door, kissed her cheek, and ushered her out. Jim was asleep in a chair against the wall and snoring loudly. She could only hope he'd wake if she screamed for help. She went back into the crimson bedchamber, locked the door behind her, and leaned against it. Bathed in candlelight, Lord Keyes was sprawled on the bed, his wrists tied over his head and his legs spread to reveal his thick cock. Still watching him, she reached behind her back to loosen the buttons of her gown and wiggled her way out of it. She also removed her petticoats and returned to him dressed only in her stockings, corset, and thin undershift.

She sensed he was observing her through his lowered eyes, so she took her time climbing onto the bed and knelt between his thighs.

"Madame Helene said you bed men. Is that true?" She cupped his balls and slid her finger behind them to stroke the soft skin of his taint. Tension shuddered through him as she played with him.

"I—I don't remember."

She leaned forward, easing her finger toward the pucker of his arsehole, watching the surge of his cock and the flush of renewed arousal on his face.

"You seem to like this."

He swallowed hard and moved restlessly against her. "I—don't know."

She removed her hand and licked her middle finger. His gaze fixed on her hand as she returned to cupping his balls, her thumb at the base of his cock, her longest finger now pressing for admittance against his hole. His cock was fully erect now, and she licked at it, sucking him occasionally as she pushed deeper, watching him as she did it for signs of discomfort. But there were none. Whatever Lord Keyes did in his private life, he was no stranger to another man's cock, but then any aristocrat who'd attended one of the great public schools could claim the same.

She pulled back and simply studied him, the lean muscle at his hips, the intriguing lines down to his groin, and the fair thatch of hair between his legs. Careful not to jog his shoulder she climbed over his hips and sat on his stomach, his cock settled behind her buttocks.

"When you are well, I'm going to take you in the arse while you fuck me. I'm not sure what I'll use, but something nice and wide and . . ." She undulated her hips and felt her own arousal slide against his skin. "Rigid, harder than a cock, and I'll make you take all of it until you beg me not to stop."

She rose up onto her knees and placed her hand on the top of the headboard bringing her breasts close to his face. With her other hand, she pushed her loosened corset down, cupped her breast, and brought it to his mouth.

"Kiss me here."

With a helpless sound, he opened his mouth and started to suck and lick her nipple. Desire coursed through her and she thrust her fingers into her sex to the rhythm of his sucking until she was so close to coming she shook with it. His cock thrust against her buttocks, wet now and as hot as she was.

"Look at me," she ordered, and he obeyed, his eyes narrowed with lust. "Watch me take you."

She shifted down and lifted herself over him, one hand holding his cock upright. With a soft moan, she used him to rub her clit and then around her aching, needy sex.

"Take me." His words were less of a command and more of a desperate plea. She liked that.

She lowered herself over the first inch of him and then off and then took a little more. The sensation of fullness was exquisite. The third time she took all of him, her greedy moan joining his as she rocked against him straining to take every bit of his impressive shaft. She touched her clit and circled the now swollen bud, let him watch her use him as she wanted for her own pleasure. He was trapped beneath her, his cock at her bidding, his beautiful body straining to give her what she wanted.

She should have felt triumphant. But he didn't know who she was. . . .

"Set me free, damn you." His hoarse words broke the spell. "Let me touch you."

The thought of his hands on her . . . She climaxed and barely held on to her ability to breathe, let alone contemplate untying him. Did he think her vulnerable now; did he truly think he could make demands of her?

She rocked against him, driving herself toward another peak, using his stiff cock as it was meant to be used, for *her* pleasure, not his, never his.

"God, I need to come, I—"

Before he even finished speaking, she pulled away from him and watched as he climaxed, his seed soaking the sheets between his thighs. It was an impressive sight. This time, when he slumped back against the pillows, he truly did look exhausted. Malinda suffered a slight pang of remorse. She needed him to recover. She'd allowed her emotions to override the success of her overall plan. It was imperative that she didn't let that happen again.

Damn her.

He'd wanted to come inside her. Wanted her to know what it was like to be filled with his seed. Wanted to see her lose control as she'd made him lose control. But she'd moved off him, leaving his cock suddenly cold and vulnerable and watched him come as though he were some kind of botanical project.

Perhaps she was keeping score of his prowess so that she

could report back to Madame Helene when she'd had enough of him.

Would he ever have enough of her?

She got off the bed and returned with a basin of water to wash him clean. It took quite a while. He submitted because he was exhausted and he had no other choice. When she'd dried him off, she came around to untie his wrists and helped him lower his arms. He winced as his left shoulder protested the change of position. She massaged his neck and shoulder until the ache eased sufficiently for him to relax into the pleasurable afterglow of sex.

"Thank you for attending to my shoulder."

"It was nothing."

"Nonsense. You could've left me tied up all night and walked away without a care in the world."

She paused at the door to look back at him. "And damage the merchandise?"

His faint gratitude died an instant death. "I keep forgetting that I am nothing more than the equivalent of a lapdog or a stallion to you."

"You sound rather bitter." She raised her eyebrows, her face austere in the flicker of the candlelight. "Are you regretting your decision to fulfill your part of the bargain?"

"Regretting fornicating?" He gave her his best lazy smile. "I'm a man. I'll fuck anything that lies down with me."

"As long as you are paid."

He allowed his gaze to slide down over her body. "Sometimes even a man needs an incentive."

"Damn you to *hell*, Benedict."

She opened the door in a swirl of skirts and departed, banging it behind her. His smile died. Antagonizing the woman who held the key to his future recovery and freedom was hardly wise. If he was a prostitute, he was obviously an outrageous one. Had he hurt her with his last comment? It was impossible to tell. She guarded her expressions almost as well as he did.

She'd called him Benedict.

He sighed and cupped his still-throbbing cock and balls. He was starting to lose track of what was real and what wasn't. Her sexual appetite was certainly unusual for a lady, but had she really brought a prostitute into her home to satisfy her needs? She struck him as an intensely private person. Perhaps she believed she had no other option. And if he was Ben, and she was a lonely, deprived widow, he'd just as good as told her that the only reason he was touching her was for money . . . not the best way to win a lady's trust.

The sound of Jim's snoring filtered through the thickness of the door, and Benedict reached over to blow out the candle. As he lay back down, a sense of conviction flooded over him. He wasn't Ben, and she wasn't a frustrated widow. It was as if he was punching blindfolded in the dark. Eventually he was bound to connect with something. Therefore, anything he said was acceptable in the uneven battle of wills they were currently engaged in. When he did remember exactly who he was, nothing would stand in his way, and he would continue to use any weapons at his disposal.

He imagined her tied to *his* bed, her legs spread wide, and her sex open to his gaze, begging him to fill her with his cock. His shaft twitched. She must never know that if their positions were reversed, he'd willingly pay for her touch for the rest of his life.

4

"Hold still, sir."

Jim staggered as Benedict deliberately leaned most of his weight on the smaller man. In an effort to stop him from falling, Jim rocked back and forth, his feet planted wide, but it was no use. His legs gave way like a toppling tree, bringing them both down to the wooden floorboards. Jim's breath whooshed out as Benedict landed squarely on top of him.

He pretended to scrabble for purchase, and eventually managed to roll away.

"I'm sorry, Jim. I'm obviously weaker than I thought." He got back into bed wincing with pain. "Are you all right?"

Jim sat up, too, his expression aggrieved. "I'm fine now that your huge carcass isn't crushing the life out of me. You weigh as much as one of those elephants from India!"

"I'm sorry." Benedict lay back and closed his eyes. "I won't try to do that again today, I promise."

Jim harrumphed, gathered up the discarded towels and soapy water, and departed, with his nose in the air.

After counting to a thousand, Benedict opened his hand to

reveal the bone handle of the pocketknife he'd taken from Jim's coat pocket. With one eye on the door, he pulled back the sheets and studied the shackle around his ankle and the chain that connected it to the bed. There'd been no sign of Mally for the last three days, but Gwen had come to see him regularly, as had the most timid of the three, Miss Doris. When Benedict asked after their intimidating leader, he'd been informed that it was quarter day week, and she was busy paying wages, settling disputes between farmers, and organizing the disposal of the crops brought in from various outlying orchards and fields.

Somehow, he understood the needs of a country estate, and had no problem accepting the answer—even though he assumed she was avoiding him too. Every day meant a growth in his strength and a new revelation about who he might be. The idea of stealing the knife had come to him from nowhere, but had been incredibly easy to orchestrate.

He bent closer to examine the metal. The band around his ankle looked very solid, and he doubted the puny knife would have any impact on it. The chain was older and rusting in places. It looked as if it had been attached to the iron in something of a hurry. He carefully checked each individual link and then the final link that was attached to the shackle. Using the tip of the knife, he found a weak spot in the weld, inserted the blade into the tiny gap, and, careful not to break off the tip, wiggled it back and forth. He breathed a sigh of thanks as he felt the metal give very slightly. It was highly possible that he could detach the shackle from the chain.

The sound of voices at the door gave him just enough time to rearrange the covers and slip the knife under his pillow. He was sitting up when Miss Doris came into the room carrying a tray. She smiled hesitantly at him.

"Good morning, sir."

"Miss Doris." He inclined his head respectfully.

"I've brought you some chicken soup. Cook says there is more if you require it."

"That is very good of her, and it is very kind of you to bring it up for me."

She settled the tray on his lap and handed him a spoon. Her eyes were a cornflower blue that reminded him forcibly of someone else. "You are most welcome. Everyone is rather busy today. I was worried that you might be overlooked."

"I understand that your sister is running the house by herself?"

"When we arrived here from the Continent, there was no staff and the place was a shambles. Mally had to arrange everything." She sighed. "She is a remarkably competent woman."

"So I understand." He sipped at his soup. If he wasn't mistaken, this was the first time Miss Doris had visited him by herself. Did they think she wasn't to be trusted, or was she simply indiscreet? He gave her his warmest smile and she blushed.

"Miss Mally is lucky to have such devoted helpers as you and Miss Gwen. I'm sure you both take on much of the burden of running a large household."

"We do our best, but Mally oversees everything."

He continued to sip his soup. "It must be difficult to get staff in this part of the country."

"It is, indeed. Lindsey St. Joan is close by, but most of the inhabitants prefer to go and work on the fishing fleet rather than into service." She sighed. "And this house isn't the most convenient of locations. The rooms have been added over centuries. The kitchens are at one end of the house, the dining room the other, and the remains of the medieval hall plonked right in between them! The food is always cold by the time it reaches your plate. That's why we've ended up eating in the kitchen."

He concentrated on finishing his food, using his bread to

mop up the last of the delicious broth. Miss Doris watched him approvingly.

"Would you like some more, sir?"

He pushed the tray away. "No, I thank you. That was excellent." He dropped his napkin on the tray, concealing the contents, and handed the whole thing back to her. He yawned and covered his mouth. "Excuse me. After that excellent repast, I think I'll take a nap."

"Then I'll make sure that no one disturbs you."

Her smile reminded him of her sister, but there the likeness ended. Where Doris was petite and fair, Mally was built like a queen, her hair the dark auburn of an autumn leaf. He guessed Doris was considerably younger than her sister, or had been protected sufficiently for her beauty to survive. Doris was sweetly pretty. Mally was *formidable*. He preferred the latter. It was more of a challenge.

"Miss Doris, did you say you had lived abroad? I've always wanted to travel."

"Yes, indeed. Our mother was married twice to military men, so we traveled all over Europe."

"How exciting."

Her ready smile wavered. "Sometimes it was exciting, but most of the time it was quite frightening. If it hadn't have been for Mally, I don't think I would've survived." She glanced down at the tray. "I must be getting this back to the kitchen."

Benedict let her go, aware that if they realized she'd been alone with him, she'd probably be interrogated by her sister or Gwen. He pondered what she'd revealed. He was in an old house, near the coast, and in a desolate area. The name of the village was familiar to him, and the description of the house had resonated too. The problem was, the harder he tried to pin something down—the more it dissipated into nothingness. The memories emerged randomly and at their own pace. It was quite infuriating.

With a sigh, he retrieved his latest acquisition and focused on what he could control. He'd managed to steal his spoon, which could be used as a bigger wedge to separate the link of the chain.

He set to work on the metal, easing the knife into the weld and cleaning out the rusted parts, shoving the thicker part of the blade ever deeper until he could finally wedge the end of the spoon in there. The link started to distort and he renewed his efforts, his fingers aching with the strain as he wrestled with the intractable metal. He had to find a way to detach it from the rest of the chain but also be able to put it back, at least temporarily, until he was ready to leave.

He cursed as his fingers slipped and he scraped his knuckles. Wiping his sweating hand on the sheets, he assessed his work, took a deep breath, and managed to twist the link free. He listened intently but there was no sound of an imminent interruption, so he detached the link, leaving his ankle still enclosed in the metal band. At least he could now move off the bed. He placed his right foot on the floor and then the other and stood up. For a second, the room dipped and swayed, and he took a deep, shuddering breath.

He'd been in bed for at least two weeks, maybe even three, and had lost both weight and strength. Instinct made him take two stumbling steps toward the door, before he forced himself to stop. There was no need to leave until his memory returned or he gained a sense of where to go. If he could recover his mobility without the ladies realizing it, he would be in a better position to run when the occasion arose.

By God, it was good simply to be free. He took a moment to stretch his cramped muscles and then crawled back into bed. His energy was low and he was afraid he'd be discovered before he worked out how to reattach the chain. It took him a while, but he eventually lay back down, his chest heaving as though he'd run a mile. He allowed his thoughts to wander as to what

Mally would do when she discovered he could overpower her with ease . . . well, perhaps not with ease, she had shot him in cold blood after all, and he still didn't really know why.

He heard Jim's low voice out in the corridor and the higher-pitched tones of a flustered Doris. He found the spoon, laid it on the bedside table, and closed his eyes.

Doris crept up to the side of the bed and he heard the soft *clang* as she picked up the spoon.

"Oh, thank goodness," she whispered. "As if you would be able to use such a thing as a weapon. Mally's imagination is really too wild sometimes."

She retreated with a soft rustle of petticoats until he heard the door open. This time Benedict really did fall asleep, only to be awakened by the sound of raised voices outside his window.

Heart beating wildly, he removed the chain and hobbled over to the nearest open window that looked down onto the side of the house and the stables beyond. Below him stood Mally, with a shotgun aimed at two strangers who were wisely holding their hands up. One of the men was a redhead; the other had crow-black hair and was dressed like a fashionable country gentleman. He was the one doing all the talking. Despite his charming smile, Benedict could've told him he'd get nowhere with his hostess.

He couldn't hear what they were talking about. The fact that Mally considered them a threat might mean anything. She guarded her home with the ferocity of a mother bear. Should he call out? If he did so, would they hear him, or even know who he was? And what if Mally shot them both because of him? While he was frozen with indecision, the men began to back away and disappeared into the undergrowth that choked the once-formal gardens and the long drive.

Mally whistled once and the household dogs emerged from all directions and set off in pursuit of the two hapless men, barking loudly. Whoever they were, he hoped they made it safely over the high wall that surrounded the estate and also had the means to get away. He leaned against the windowsill and studied the terrain. How had he known the estate was walled? Had he ridden up that driveway?

He touched his still-bandaged shoulder. He must have done so to fall far enough from his horse to lose consciousness. Where was his horse now? If it was in the stables, he had the opportunity of retrieving it when he made his escape. His gaze came to rest on a stone fountain on the edge of the driveway facing the front of the house. Its classical lines were covered with ivy, but he remembered it flowing with water, the naked goddess pouring water from a large urn at the center.

Alford Park.

He smiled.

Mally stared at the door to the crimson bedchamber. She supposed it was time to check on her patient, but she was increasingly reluctant to do so. On the last occasion she'd seen him, he'd given her immense pleasure and then deliberately insulted her. She sensed the latter had more to do with his loss of control than his true feelings about the sex they'd shared. It had been quite extraordinary, after all.

She squared her shoulders and went in. Perhaps it was time to end the charade. She could hardly keep him chained up forever, and she had *questions* for him. The visit from the two men had shaken her resolve. The one who claimed to be a secretary to the Honorable John Lennox had asked for her by *name*. She'd hoped that no one apart from Benedict knew she was even in the country, let alone at Alford Park.

Had the men really come in search of Lord Keyes, or was their mission more sinister? Whom would he have told that he was coming to Alford Park, and when would his friends and associates start getting worried about his non-return? After the visitors today, it was possible that they already had . . . She'd been a fool to capture him. Lord Keyes wasn't exactly a nonentity. As keeper of the nation's secrets, he was far too valuable to lose.

She summoned a smile. "Good evening, Benedict."

"I thought you preferred me to be Ben."

He turned his head toward her as she crossed the carpet to sit beside his bed.

"Benedict suits you."

"I have to agree." He hesitated. "You look tired."

"I've been rather busy."

"So I heard." He smoothed his hand over the covers. "Whom did you set the dogs on this afternoon?"

"I beg your pardon?"

"I heard a commotion outside, and Jim muttered something about intruders. Were you in danger?"

"Hardly. I persuaded them to leave quite quickly."

"You didn't shoot them? Was the thought of being the warden of three wounded men too much for you?"

"Being your captor is quite enough, thank you." She frowned at him. "I'm beginning to suspect you are more trouble than you are worth."

He wrapped his fingers around her wrist. "Then why capture me in the first place?"

"I've already explained that."

His grip tightened and she was drawn inexorably toward him. "And I don't believe a word of it."

She met his searching blue gaze, her nose almost touching his. "You are not in your right mind, sir, you don't count."

Incredibly he smiled. "Then why am I worth anything to you at all?"

"As I said, you have caused me nothing but trouble. I hardly expected you to lose your memory!"

"Then why not tell me who I am, and have done with this farce?"

She tried to shake off his hand but he wouldn't release her, and instead yanked hard and pulled her half over him on the bed.

"Let me *go!*"

He slid one arm around her waist and dumped her unceremoniously in his lap, her back to his chest. "Didn't you promise to fuck my arse as I fucked you?"

"I . . ."

She wiggled to get free, and his hand slid lower, pushing her hips back until she could feel the heated rod of his cock against her buttocks. He nipped her ear, and then her throat and her body was instantly on fire.

"I was about to suggest that—"

"*Suggest?* You usually order me around like a servant. Do you want me to undress you?" His fingers started working on the back of her dress. "I'd like to see you as naked as I am."

"But you don't need to do that. I came to tell you—" She gasped as he made short work of the three buttons on the back of her dress and started on her corset. She tried to get away from him again, but he held her securely with his right arm and used his left to relieve her of her clothing.

"But what if I like being Ben, lying here chained and naked, just waiting for you to come to me so that I can give you pleasure?" He bit her exposed shoulder. "It does have a certain charm to it. I have nothing to do but think of ways of pleasing you so that when you send me back to Madame Helene, you can honestly say that you were completely satisfied."

She opened her mouth to tell him that he wasn't Ben, and then sighed instead as he shoved down the bodice of her dress and tossed her unlaced corset to the floor. His hand cupped her breast and then he lifted her again, turning her around until her petticoats and skirts were drawn away from her legs leaving her in just her shift. He dispensed of that in a flash and she was naked, his hands now all over her, her breasts pressed to his chest and her core to his cock.

Perhaps she should tell him *after* he'd pleasured her. A man never took well to being interrupted while in rut, and he would be far more malleable afterward.

With a groan, he dipped his head to her breasts and suckled her, his palm spread over her buttocks, rubbing her against his already wet shaft. She grabbed his shoulder for support as he continued to suck, his teeth grazing her nipple until a shudder of sensation slid straight down to her sex. Her hand fisted in his hair, forcing his head up to meet her mouth so that she could kiss him.

God, if she raised her hips just a little, he'd be inside her rather than rubbing against her already swollen bud. She tried to accomplish her desire, but he wouldn't let her, his cock a tantalizing inch away from penetrating her fully. With a frustrated sound, she bit his lip. He laughed and continued to slide his cock over her mound, his wet finger now circling her arse as she had done to him on their previous encounter.

He bent his head to her breasts again and eased the tip of his finger inside her arse. She bucked against him. Could a woman come like this? She realized she'd answered her own question as her body clenched around nothing, and she wailed with need.

With a rough sound, he rolled them over and rose over her, his expression savage, and shoved his cock deep with one single thrust. She screamed and he muffled the sound with his mouth as he moved over her, his movements powerful, his body a dominant instrument of pleasure that pumped into her without pause. It was too much, it was too hard, it was—she climaxed again. He drew back long enough to lock her legs over his hips and kept going.

She held on to his shoulders and simply endured the pounding, her body accepting his dominance without question as he filled needs she'd forgotten in her fear and anger and grief.

"Do I please you?"

She opened her eyes to see him staring down at her, his blue eyes narrowed with lust and something else. Something far more dangerous. He drew back his hips and plunged into her again.

"Will you be able to tell Madame that you have been completely satisfied?"

He reached between them and touched her clit, making her move uneasily against him.

"Don't, I can't . . ."

"Then you consider yourself completely satisfied?"

She risked a glance down over his body and realized what she should have noticed straight away. He was over her, and the shackle on his right ankle was no longer attached to the chain. She pushed hard on his chest.

"Yes, I'm satisfied, now get off me."

His smile made her go still.

"Now, why would I do that when I've finally got you under me?"

She opened her mouth to scream for Jim, but his hand was quicker. She bit him and it made no difference. With all her strength, she made a fist and tried to punch him in his wounded shoulder, which he'd anticipated, because he avoided her blow with ease.

He was still throbbing inside her, pinning her to the bed, his weight preventing her from moving anywhere.

"What's my name?"

She swallowed hard. "It's Benedict. Now let me loose."

"Don't be ridiculous." He rocked his hips and she shivered. "Why would I do that? Who else has more right to be here and fill you with seed than I do?"

"Don't!"

He slowly withdrew until his cock was almost free and looked down at where they were joined. "No pleading? Is that because you know I'm right?"

"I'll beg if you want, I swear it."

"It's too late for that, Malinda, my sweet, my *wife*, don't you think?"

Holding her gaze he slowly pushed himself home, and with a sigh started to come deep inside her, each hot pulse making her already sensitive flesh quiver anew. He collapsed over her, and she could do nothing but lie still and try to breathe beneath his considerable weight.

Now she knew what she'd seen in his eyes.

Vengeance.

It seemed hours before he finally found the energy to stir and roll off her. Before she could gather her senses, he put his hand over her mouth and then replaced it with a gag made from her thin shift. He looped the shortened chain around her ankle and tied it closed with a strip torn from her petticoat. Sliding from the bed, he stared down at her.

She looked furious. Her thick auburn hair framed her face and her pale skin was flushed with arousal. He couldn't resist running his hand down her long flank to the nest of red curls now damp from his seed at the apex of her thighs. She tried to close her knees, but he was quicker, his palm cupping her heat and wetness until she quivered and pushed up into his hand.

Lust roared through him again, and he bent his head and licked his way around the swollen lips of her sex and the raised bud of her clit. His tongue slid easily inside her now. He moved it back and forth until she started to cry out behind her gag, her body tensing in the throes of imminent pleasure.

He continued his exploration, gathering up moisture on his longest finger and sliding it deep into her arse until she bucked against his mouth. His thumb penetrated her cunt and he set his teeth delicately on her clit. She climaxed and he stuffed his other fingers inside her and felt her clench and writhe around him.

He left her on the tangled sheets and went to jam a chair

under the latch of the door before lighting more candles and bringing them back to the bed. She kicked out at him as he climbed onto the bed, but he straddled her and held her still. Using his teeth and hands, he tore her petticoat into long strips and, reversing his position, tied her ankles to the posts at the corners of his bed.

When he turned back to her and took hold of her wrists, she tried to punch his wounded shoulder again, the blow glancing off his chest. It hurt, but he ignored the pain. He captured her wrists, bound them together, and tied the ends of the muslin to the headboard. She spluttered something behind her gag. He found himself smiling as he rearranged the pillows so that her head and arse were supported.

He liked seeing her tied up and wished he had the energy to fuck her again. That would have to wait until more important matters had been solved to his satisfaction. Straddling her stomach again, he untied the gag, pressing his hand over her mouth as she tried to screech something. He found Jim's pocketknife and laid the edge of the sharp blade against her throat.

"If I take my hand away, you must agree not to call for help, or I'll slit your throat."

She went still, her furious gaze locked with his. She inclined her head an awkward inch.

"Good girl." He slowly took away his hand from her mouth. She glared back at him and licked her lips.

"Where did you get that knife?"

"Jim gave it to me."

"As if he would betray *me*."

"I forgot you're the only person who's allowed to do that, aren't you?" He pressed the tip of the blade against her skin. "Why did you invite me here?"

"To kill you, of course. Unfortunately, I'm an extremely bad shot."

"If you'd wanted me to die, you would've left me on the driveway to bleed to death."

"Perhaps I didn't fancy watching the crows pick at your corpse from my window."

"From the regretful tone of your voice, I think you would've been out there selling tickets. What do you want from me?"

"I didn't want you to fall off your horse and lose your memory." She had the audacity to scowl at him. "What an inconsiderate thing to do, but then, when have you ever been anything but?"

"It was not intentional, I assure you. Being trapped in bed and given a false identity was not part of my agenda either."

"But you were good at being Ben. Perhaps you missed your true career."

"Perhaps not. I'm used to playing a part, Malinda. You of all people should know that. What do you want?"

"I've changed my mind. I came here this evening to tell you that you were free to go."

"Did those men today scare you?"

"Did you know them?"

He frowned. "One of them, I think. Is that what sparked your sudden desire to set me free? Were they looking for me?"

"No. They were looking for me." She sighed. "Which means I will have to be leaving this place myself."

He contemplated her for a long moment, all his instincts alert. "Who wants you?"

"Obviously, not you." She favored him with a dismissive glance. "If you let me go, I'll return what remains of your clothes and money. You can leave tonight."

"But you asked me to come here."

"As I said, I was mistaken. I thought—" She briefly closed her eyes. "It doesn't matter anymore. If I have to go, I can't leave you here alone, can I?"

"You're currently tied to my bed. You aren't going anywhere without my cooperation. What are you afraid of?"

"Nothing!"

"Don't lie to me." He caught her chin in his hand and made her look at him. "You've been at Alford for quite a while."

"Yes. No one else seemed to need it. I told the villagers I had your permission to open the house again."

"And you have made it a profitable enterprise, according to Doris and Jim. Is Doris truly your sister?"

"She's my half sister. My mother married again." She hesitated. "I don't care what happens to me, but I have to protect her and Gwen. Can you at least promise me that no harm will come to anyone here because of what I've done to you?"

No harm . . . There was much he wanted to say about that, but this wasn't the time or the place. Ruthlessly he concentrated on the matter at hand.

"Malinda, if you felt the need to contact me, a man whom I'm fairly certain you hate, loathe, and despise, things must be pretty dire, indeed."

She didn't reply, her lips set in a thin, stubborn line that he was all too familiar with.

"If I promise to help the occupants of this place, I need to know whom I am dealing with."

"I thought it was you."

"What do you mean?"

"I was told the threat came from you—that you wanted me dead."

"Why on earth would you think that?"

"Because I am a part of your past that you probably regret and wish to have removed. A man in your position can easily get rid of such a person."

"You're my bloody *wife.*"

"That's not correct." She glared back at him. "Your father arranged an annulment."

"My father . . ." He shook his head. "You'll have to come back to London with me."

"Don't be ridiculous! I'll let you go; we'll leave within a few days. You can tell your father that I swear never to break my promise and return to England again."

Every time she spoke, she led him further into a version of the past he didn't understand. He hated that. His whole life was spent understanding the schemes and plots of others. He couldn't bear the thought that his own past was a lie. All he knew was that if he let her escape, he'd never be at peace with himself.

"I still don't understand why you want to kill me. What did I do to you? You are the one who left *me*."

Her expression turned mulish. "There are good reasons why I left."

"But what do they have to do with the present? Damn it, Malinda, you didn't even give me a chance!"

"I wanted to get your attention. I knew the best way to do so would be to slightly inconvenience you, and—"

"*Slightly?* Devil take it, woman, you could've murdered me!"

"As I'm an excellent shot, sir, that is extremely unlikely. I simply needed your complete attention and cooperation."

"You wanted to see me bleeding and in pain?"

"No." She sighed. "Why did you send that man to threaten me if you came in peace?"

"What man?"

"The thug who threatened to throw us out of the house on the orders of the Keyes family."

"I didn't send anyone. I prefer to deal with such matters myself."

"But you arrived brandishing a pistol!"

"I inhabit a dangerous world. I came armed because I wanted to make certain the information I'd received was truly from you and not a trap." He fixed her with his most penetrating stare. "And this is irrelevant, Malinda. You had already decided to shoot me on sight. I don't understand why you hate me."

She raised her chin. "Your family destroyed mine, isn't that enough?"

"Mally—" Damn it, she was exasperating, and he was too mentally exhausted to think clearly. "You are coming to London with me." She opened her mouth to argue, but he kept talking. "If you agree, I'll get trained men up here to protect your family and your staff from any interference from my father or anyone else. If you don't come willingly, I'll take you anyway, and leave them to fend for themselves."

"I won't leave until those men are in place."

"Agreed. It should only take a few days to arrange. Ask Jim and that other servant of yours to come up and see me. I'm sure they'll know who is trustworthy around here. I'll pay the locals well until I can supplement them with my own men."

"And you must agree not to travel until I say your shoulder is sufficiently healed to withstand the journey."

"I'll stay as long as it takes for the men to settle in and no longer."

She considered him, her teeth biting into her lower lip.

"Do we have an agreement, Malinda?"

"Why would you do this after everything that has happened? Why would you offer to help me?"

He bent down and kissed her stubborn mouth. "Because you are as devious as a fox, and I hate to be beaten." He kissed her again, his tongue probing between her lips to tangle with hers. "In a little while, I'll untie you and you can go and tell your sister and staff that you are coming with me and that they will be safe until you return."

She tugged impatiently at her bounds. "Untie me right now, and I'll accept your offer."

"You've already accepted it. One thing I do know, is that you are a pragmatist." He moved down to the space between her spread thighs and smiled at her. "So I'm sure you'll understand that having you bound hand and foot in my bed is too good an opportunity to miss exploiting."

"You wouldn't *dare*."

He crawled up to her shoulder, his cock and balls cupped in his hand. "Oh, I dare, and, by God, by the end of it, when I've had my cock in your mouth, your cunt, and your arse, you'll be screaming my name, I swear it." He rubbed the wet crown of his cock against her luscious mouth and prayed she wouldn't bite.

5

Malinda glanced over at her companion. He rode with his pistol in his right hand, and his left loosely holding the horse's reins. The terrain they were passing through seemed deserted, but he hadn't relaxed his guard since they'd left the house. His complexion was pale, and there were dark shadows under his eyes. If she was very lucky, he'd overestimated his strength and would soon succumb to exhaustion. Then she would be free to leave.

But where would she go? When she'd contacted him, she'd known he was her last chance of survival. If he couldn't protect her from her enemies, then no one could. And if he was in league with those she feared? Then her death would be unavoidable. It wasn't the first time she'd had to face such uncomfortable facts, but now she had less youthful optimism that she'd somehow survive.

He'd helped her survive the first time as well. ....

It started to rain and she cursed the heavy fabric of her riding habit, which would soak up the water and weigh her down even more.

"We'll stop at the next inn."

When he spoke, he barely glanced at her, but she knew he'd been aware of her position for the entire journey. When she nodded, water tipped off her hat and down her neck, making her shiver. There were faint lights in the distance, and she hoped it was the inn he'd mentioned. They'd been traveling since dawn and had barely stopped all day. Gwen and Doris hadn't wanted her to leave, but she'd explained that in order to carry out the remainder of her plan, she had to go with Lord Keyes. She'd tried to sound more confident than she felt and they seemed to understand. She only hoped she'd see them again. Nothing was certain anymore.

"Malinda?"

He reached across to grab her reins and guided her down a short slope to the welcoming lights of a small inn. He dismounted in the small stable yard and turned to help her down. She all but fell into his arms. He winced as he bore her weight down to the muddy cobblestones.

"I'm sorry," she murmured.

He took her elbow and led her into the inn. It was warm inside and smelled of peat smoke and beer. A small woman came toward them and Benedict bowed.

"Good evening, ma'am. I'm Mr. Benedict of Crouch End. My wife and I were caught in the storm. Do you have a room available for the night?"

"Yes, sir, I do. I'm Mrs. Goodman. Will you be wanting dinner?"

He gave her a grateful smile. "Perhaps you could bring something up to us on a tray? I suspect my wife is longing for her bed."

"Aye, 'tis a nasty night out there, sir. Now, follow me." She started up the stairs and Malinda obediently walked behind her. "Lizzy will bring you up some nice hot water in just a moment."

"Thank you, ma'am."

Even his voice and mannerisms sounded different. Gone were the aristocratic tones of privilege, replaced by the more humble accent of a county gentleman of no particular interest at all. He'd claimed he was used to acting a part. Now she believed him. She tripped over the long hem of her skirt and his hand was immediately there to steady her.

"Here you are, sir, ma'am." Mrs. Goodman opened the door into a low-ceilinged room with curved oak beams stretching down to the windows. There was a large bed under the eaves that drew Malinda's longing gaze. She couldn't wait to close her eyes and sleep.

With Benedict, Lord Keyes.

If he'd let her sleep.

She was still sore from their previous encounter where he'd been true to his word and had her in every possible way he could until she screamed his name and begged him. Her knees went weak at the memory, and she grabbed hold of the back of the nearest chair. At this point she didn't care if he bedded her or not. She'd probably sleep through it, which would be a just revenge.

Mrs. Goodman left after banking up the fire, and Benedict closed the door behind her. He immediately crossed to Malinda's side and started working on the buttons and ties of her riding habit.

"You're soaked through."

"I know."

He raised his head to stare into her eyes. "Then help me get you out of these clothes."

She unpinned her hat and laid it on the chair while he stripped off her jacket and undid her skirt. His hands were fast but impersonal, and she was grateful for his help. If it had been left to her, she'd probably have fallen into bed fully dressed and died of a chill by the next morning. He stripped off his heavy, many-caped driving coat and eased himself out of his waistcoat. He'd had to borrow a shirt and coat to replace the ones Malinda had cut off him. There was no sign of any blood oozing from the wound on his shoulder, which made her feel slightly better.

A knock on the door heralded the arrival of Lizzy with a bowl of hot water and soap, which Benedict took from her with thanks. Malinda stepped out of her skirt and petticoats and Lizzy gathered them up to take down to the kitchen to brush off the mud and air the damp out of them. With a sound of distaste, Malinda plucked at her corset.

"Let me." He turned her away from him and spent a few moments battling with the damp lacing before he managed to ease her out of the contraption. "Now sit."

She scowled up at him. "You are extremely dictatorial, sir."

"I'm trying to stop you dying of a chill."

"Why bother?" She shivered as he washed her face with the warm water.

"Because I want the pleasure of killing you myself? You of all people should understand that." He washed her throat and then down her arms and over her hands. "I'll wager you enjoyed putting a bullet in me."

She didn't deign to reply as he crouched in front of her and washed her fingers. He reached the cloth toward her breasts and she grabbed his wrist.

"I can do that part, thank you."

She squeaked as he squeezed the cloth and water ran out, soaking her shift and making it transparent. With a soft sound, he leaned closer and licked her nipple through the muslin. His other hand cupped her between the legs.

"Should I wash you here, instead?"

Her heart was pounding, which was ridiculous because she was too tired to care what he did. She stared down at his blond head, at his hand buried between her thighs. It didn't matter what she told herself. She'd never forgotten him. Perhaps it was true that the first man who took you was always the one you remembered.

His fingers curled inward, stroking and tempting her to relax into his caress. His hot mouth drifted over her taut nipple, his tongue flicking out to circle her plump flesh. She could do nothing but watch him, her senses too fraught to either stop him or offer him encouragement. Goodness, this would never do. She slid a hand into his hair and yanked hard.

"Ouch."

"Our dinner will be here in a moment."

"I know." He pulled out of her determined hold. "Which leaves me just a few moments to complete my task."

He retrieved the washcloth and brought it between her thighs, patting and parting her folds, his mouth following the path of the cloth, and his fingers. She moaned when he licked her clit, her hips bucking to meet his waiting hand. The cloth felt rough on her tender flesh as he continued to clean and arouse her at the same time.

Eventually, when she was on the brink of a climax, he stood up and stripped off the remainder of his garments. Holding her gaze, he washed himself, the water running down in soapy rivulets over his chest and stomach, catching in the dense hair of his groin and dripping off his erect cock. He rubbed the cloth over his shaft and balls and groaned.

"I want you."

She raised her eyebrows. "But I'm not tied up."

"That could be arranged."

"You overestimate your charms, sir."

"You underestimate yours." He leaned over the chair, caging her in. "You're wet and wanting. When I thrust inside you, you'll come so hard you'll beg me never to stop."

"As I said, arrogant and deluded as well."

"Do you want to wager on it? I managed quite well the other night."

"I want my dinner, and then I want to go to bed and sleep for all eternity."

He moved away from her, his hands raised palms up. "Then get into bed."

Eyeing him suspiciously, she scrambled out of the chair and headed for the bed, turning her back on him to climb up the high side. She realized her mistake as he caught her around the hips, lifted her buttocks, and slid his cock home in her cunt. And God, he was right, she was climaxing within a minute as his fingers closed on her clit and he rubbed her in time to his pounding.

In five more thrusts he was coming, too, filling her with his hot seed, making her climax again with the sheer power of his need. A knock on the door had him expertly sliding her between the sheets and covering himself with the topmost quilt.

"Come in."

She bolted upright, quivering with a combination of satisfied desire and a reluctant admiration for his tactics and his ability to appear so normal. But he was the great deceiver. Why should she expect anything else?

Lizzy brought in a large tray and set it beside the fire, modestly averting her gaze from Benedict's exposed chest.

"Here you are, sir. There's soup and roast lamb and some potatoes."

"Thank you."

Lizzy picked up the bowl of water and the rest of the clothes scattered on the floor and left closing the door firmly behind her.

"Do you wish to eat in bed, or come closer to the fire?"

She glared at him. "*You* are not a gentleman."

"No, I'm an aristocrat. As you've always been fond of telling me."

"Only to remind you of why we wouldn't suit."

His gaze dropped to her breasts and became heavy. "We suit very well."

"Only in bed." She drew her knees up to conceal her chest. "Once I'm over this inconvenient ... *lust* for you, we'll have nothing more to say to each other."

"I doubt that." He expertly fixed her a plate of food and brought it over to the bed. "Don't throw it at me, or I'll be forced to lick you clean."

She snatched the plate from him and balanced it on her lap. "You forget, I'm not quite such a hoyden anymore."

"Only in bed."

"Will you *stop?*"

"But you make it so easy." He cut into his lamb. "Did you really ask Madame Helene to find you a male prostitute?"

"No, I made it all up."

"For my benefit?"

She shrugged. "You were the one who lost your memory. I merely wanted to see if you were faking."

"By telling me you'd bought my sexual services and that my name was Ben?"

"I thought it might shock you into regaining your memory."

"Liar, you enjoyed it immensely."

"It was rather fun." She sighed. "I wish I'd had a few more nights to use you as I wished, though."

"You can have as many nights as you want. Consider me entirely at your disposal."

"What about your wife? Won't she object? You do have one now, don't you?"

He regarded her steadily. "How could I have a wife when you are still alive?"

She waved away his reply. "We've already discussed that."

"Then why haven't you married again?"

"Because—" She returned her attention to her food. "This lamb smells excellent."

For a while there was a blessed silence as they both concentrated on their food. Malinda found her appetite lagging and soon set the plate to one side. She was not getting out of bed and displaying herself to the man again.

He seemed oblivious to her regard, but she knew differently. He was as aware of her as she was of him. It was rather infuriating. She'd hoped that when she saw him again, all the inconvenient lust she'd felt for him as a young girl would dissipate in disgust at what he and his family had done to hers. The strange thing was, they'd also slipped back into their old combative friendship without a second thought. But she needed his compliance if her schemes were to come to fruition.

"Don't sigh like that."

He really did know her far too well. She met his gaze. "I'm tired."

"No, you're thinking too hard. Would you like to share your concerns with me?"

"The man who's forcing me to accompany him to London?"

"I'm not forcing you." His gaze swept over her. "I haven't chained you to the bed."

"Coerced, then."

He put his plate back on the tray. "Malinda, don't treat me like a fool. We both know that if you hadn't wanted to come with me, I'd have had the devil's own job making you."

There was a hardness to him now that made her doubt that statement was true. Even though he smiled and appeared to be at ease, she sensed the tension vibrating through him like a fine wire. What would happen if he did lose his temper? She didn't think she wanted to find out. When it became inevitable, she would have to make sure she was as far away from him as possible.

"What do you expect me to do in London, anyway?"

"Identify those who threaten you and let me deal with them."

"I can deal with them myself."

He stretched out his legs. "That's obviously not true, as you've asked for my help. Is it my father?"

She froze. "Why would you think that?"

"Because he is a manipulative old bastard and has no cause to love you. You openly challenged him and he never forgets an insult." He paused. "I don't see much of him myself these days."

"Why is that?"

"Because for one thing, he doesn't approve of me working for the government. He considers it beneath a Keyes to work for anyone."

"Which is why he hated me, the daughter of his own regimental sergeant who forgot her position in life and married above herself."

"That's certainly one of the reasons. Do you think he wants you dead?"

Damn, he was quick to make connections.

"Why would I think that?"

"Because you asked for my help. I'm probably the only man who *can* protect you from him."

She forced a tremulous smile and leaned forward, clasping her hands together on her lap. "Yes, that's it. That's exactly why I wanted your help."

Benedict rose to his feet, gathered up the supper dishes, and piled them on the tray. "I'll take these down to the kitchen and get us both a glass of brandy. I think we need something to warm us up while we talk."

From her startled expression he guessed she hadn't expected him not to pounce on her confession immediately. But he needed a moment to think. He took the tray down and received the thanks of Lizzy and Mrs. Goodman, who gave him a whole bottle of brandy and two glasses to take back upstairs with him.

He didn't doubt that his father was involved in some way, but why had she admitted it so easily? What was he missing?

He paused outside the bedroom door, aware of his headache returning and the stiffness in his wounded shoulder. Despite being able to ride, he still wasn't at his best either mentally or physically, and he needed to be at the top of his game with Malinda. She'd always been as sharp as a pin. It was one of the reasons why he'd spent so much time with her when they were both children following the army. His father hadn't liked it, but Benedict had felt more at home with Sergeant Rowland and his family than with his own.

He'd missed her.

He'd pushed her memory ruthlessly to the back of his mind because it hurt too much to think about what he'd done, and how he'd allowed himself to be manipulated by the man who was supposed to have his best interests at heart. But he supposed his father would argue that he'd done what he needed to extract his son from a scandal. And Malinda hadn't helped. She'd seemed equally determined to get rid of him.

He pushed open the door to discover that she'd fallen asleep in the bed, one arm pressed over her eyes, curled up like a child. He removed his shirt and breeches and hung them close to the fire to air. Perhaps this was for the best. Tomorrow they'd reach London, and all the resources of his personal empire would be available to him. He'd be able to keep her more at a distance and use his mind instead of his cock to make the decisions that needed to be made. He'd never had to make that distinction before. But she was the first woman he'd ever made love to. He hadn't realized until she'd left him and he'd embarked on his years of debauchery how unusual the connection they'd shared had been.

It seemed that time hadn't changed that at all. She was fire in his arms, and he was incapable of denying his lust for her. But hadn't that been his downfall the first time around? His inability to separate his emotions from the facts? Whatever he felt for Malinda, he had to remember who he was now, and the painful process he'd embarked upon to rid himself of such weaknesses in his personality. It shouldn't be too difficult. He was nothing like his younger self and was known as a cold-blooded bastard. If Malinda thought to manipulate him, she'd soon learn her mistake.

He uncorked the brandy bottle and took a long slug. It would help ward off the pain of his injuries while he tried to get some sleep. He drew the covers over Malinda and climbed into bed beside her. It felt surprisingly right to sleep next to her. It always had. With a sigh, Benedict checked that his knife and pistol were close by and went to sleep.

6

_____

"I hope you don't expect me to stay at Alford House."

"As I don't live there myself, it's highly unlikely." Benedict turned briefly to look at her as they waited for a heavily laden cart to pass across the junction. They'd left their weary horses at one of the many inns, and were continuing in a hackney cab.

London seemed twice as grim and three times as crowded since the last time she'd ventured into the city. Malinda hated the smells, the filth of the streets, and most of all, the beggars who hung around every corner or followed you, tugging at your skirt or sleeve. It wasn't the beggars themselves she disliked—God knows, she could've easily become one herself—but the sheer number of them, and the sense that she'd never be able to help them all overwhelmed her.

"Do you have your own house?"

"I do. I also have lodgings at my place of business."

"Otherwise known as the Sinners Club?"

He glanced at her again. "You seem remarkably well informed. Who told you about the Sinners?"

"I can't quite remember. So you have an office there?"

"Yes." He hesitated. "I also have a more 'official' place of work on Whitehall, but I tend to conduct most of my business from the Sinners."

"Why is that?"

"Because most of the people I associate with have no wish to be seen anywhere near a government building. They prefer to remain anonymous."

"That makes perfect sense. Where do you intend to leave me?"

"I'm not sure."

"It's most unlike you." She studied his unsmiling profile. "To be so indecisive."

"We'll go to the Sinners first, and speak to my partner. I'm sure he's been wondering where I've been."

"Do you think he's the one who sent those men?"

"It's possible. But I thought you said they asked for you by name."

"That's true." She frowned. "And he is hardly likely to know about me, is he?"

"You'd be surprised what Adam Fisher knows."

Before she could ask him to explain that dry comment, the hackney drew up outside a very respectable-looking white-stucco town house in a pleasant square. Benedict stepped out of the cab and paid the driver before offering her his hand. They ascended the steps of the house together. The door was flung open by a liveried footman.

"Lord Keyes! Good morning, my lord!"

"Good morning." Benedict kept moving. "Devil take it, I should have used the back entrance. I don't wish to advertise my presence to the masses. Is Mr. Fisher in his office?"

"I'm sorry, my lord." The footman looked crestfallen. "I was just surprised to see you. I'll ask Mr. Maddon if Mr. Fisher is here."

As he apologized, the servant tried to keep up with Benedict, who was walking rather too fast for Malinda's comfort.

Intrigued by her first glimpse of the inner workings of a gentlemen's club, she tried to slow her steps so that she could take in the lofty ceilings, the dark-paneled walls, and the austere portraits.

Benedict didn't alter his pace at all and swept her along, her arm tucked securely in his. The footman opened a door at the end of the long corridor and ushered them into a pleasant, well-lit room lined with bookshelves and a handsome walnut desk.

"I'll bring you some refreshment, sir, and send Mr. Maddon to you at once."

"Thank you."

Malinda took a seat by the fire as Benedict paced the hearthrug, his hands folded behind his back, his expression inscrutable. Although the desk was piled high with documents and leather-covered books, there was a sense of emptiness about it. The fire was out and the desk so tidy that she had to imagine the occupant of the office was absent.

The door opened and a stately older man came in and bowed to Benedict.

"My lord, it's a pleasure to have you back." He gestured at the footman who hovered in the doorway behind him. "Bring in the refreshments, James." He bowed again in Malinda's direction. "I took the liberty of ordering some tea for you, ma'am. Cook will be sending up some cakes and other delicacies momentarily."

"Thank you," Malinda said.

"Where is Mr. Fisher, Maddon?" Benedict asked abruptly.

"I believe he has gone into the country, my lord."

"Leaving the Sinners unattended?"

"Oh no, my lord. He established Mr. Lennox upstairs in the vacant apartment next to yours to oversee matters while he was gone."

A muscle flicked in Benedict's cheek. Gone was the charming man Malinda shared her bed with, replaced by an autocrat who reminded her all too forcibly of his father. She'd do well to remember that. The Marquis of Alford could be charming too. He'd certainly deceived her and her father.

"Do you wish me to open up your apartment, my lord? It will need airing and the fires haven't been lit." Maddon cleared his throat. "I must apologize. We were unsure of the expected date of your return."

"No, we won't stay here." He accepted the cup of tea Malinda offered him with a curt nod. "As soon as Mr. Fisher returns, ask him to contact me at my other address."

"I will do so, sir." Maddon paused. "Do you intend to come in and oversee activities while Mr. Fisher is away? If so, I can inform Mr. Lennox that his help is no longer required."

"I'll definitely pop in and keep an eye on the place, but Mr. Lennox is welcome to be in charge for as long as he likes. And by the way, I don't want him to know I'm back. In fact I'd rather we kept that information to the fewest number of people we can."

"I understand perfectly, my lord." Maddon paused. "There is an entertainment scheduled for the upcoming Friday—a troupe of exotic dancers from India. I don't imagine you will need to be involved. Lady Westbrook has been coordinating affairs with the help of Mr. Lennox."

"That's fine by me, Maddon. You may, of course, inform her ladyship that I am back in Town. Naturally, if she wishes to speak to me, I am always at her disposal."

In one indignant gulp, Malinda swallowed too much tea and scalded her lip. He'd said there was no other woman in his life. Yet, he professed undying loyalty to the unknown Lady Westbrook, who was obviously married, and presumably untroubled by that to inspire such devotion in the cold heart of Lord Keyes.

"Did you say something, my dear?"

She smiled sweetly at him. "I was merely blowing on my tea, my lord."

The door opened again, and the footman returned with a tray of delicacies that he placed on the small table directly in front of Malinda. With a contented sigh, she ignored her former husband and helped herself to a plateful of beautifully prepared food.

"If that will be all, my lord?"

"For the moment, thank you, Maddon. Unless there is anything else you think I should know about?"

Maddon considered, his expression grave. "Most of the recent activity has centered around Mr. Lennox and the Dowager Countess of Storr."

"I didn't know there was a dowager countess. Isn't that the title Jack's in line for?" Benedict asked.

Malinda stopped chewing.

"I believe it is, sir. From what I understand from Mr. Theale, who has been doing some investigating for Mr. Lennox, there appears to be some confusion over whether the previous earl's marriage was legal."

"All the more reason to stay away from the Sinners until Jack sorts himself out. I have a suspicion he'll manage it eventually, but he certainly won't welcome my interference or advice."

Maddon bowed to them both and withdrew, leaving Malinda staring at Benedict, whose mind appeared to be elsewhere.

"Jack Lennox?"

"Yes."

"Is he by any chance related to the man who turned up on my doorstep a week or so ago?"

"Black-haired, blue-eyed, and persuasive enough to charm the birds from the trees?"

"That's the one." She glared at him. "So he *was* after you after all. But how did he know my name?"

Benedict glanced at the empty desk. "I suspect someone told him."

"And how would Mr. Fisher come by that information?"

"That's the part that's worrying me. What exactly did Jack say to you?"

"He said that he was the personal secretary of a Mr. John Lennox, and that his solicitors were searching for a Malinda Keyes with news of a small legacy that was due to her. Am I to understand that Jack is actually his own employer?"

"Yes, I have no idea what that was all about." He frowned. "But then, Jack has always enjoyed playing games."

She put down her cup. "He did seem rather surprised that I was the woman he sought."

"But he didn't mention my name in conjunction with yours?"

"No."

"I wonder what Adam told Jack to persuade him to visit Alford Park? Possibly some version of the truth that didn't reveal our connection."

"Perhaps it was a coincidence. Maybe there really is a legacy due to me."

"How likely is that?" His narrowed blue gaze landed on her and stayed put. "Why all this sudden interest in you, my love?"

"Don't call me that." She scowled at him. "And as I said, I'm not supposed to set foot in England. That's why."

"According to my father's wishes."

"Yes."

"Why would you do anything my father asked you to? You dislike him intensely."

She met his gaze. "Perhaps that's why I came back after all."

He stared at her for so long that she had to drop her gaze and fiddle with her napkin and tea plate.

"Malinda, what aren't you telling me?"

"I don't know what you mean. I thought I'd explained. I came to you to stop your father forcing me from England again."

"But why was it important for you to come back after all this time?"

She shrugged. "Doris needed a home, and I knew Alford Park would provide us with one if I could just keep out of your father's orbit."

That piece at least was true. She hoped he'd remember that after she was gone, and honor his promise to protect her family. "Are we not staying here, then?"

"I don't believe it would be wise to advertise our presence in London too widely." He leaned one elbow against the mantelpiece and stared down into the empty fireplace. "I do have another place for us to stay."

"So you said." She heaved an exaggerated sigh. "I suppose that means I won't be invited to the entertainment on Friday."

He looked up, a hint of amusement returning to his expression. "I can only apologize. Even in such a discreet environment, your presence would be noted, as would mine."

"Is it usual for a gentlemen's club to offer such scandalous . . . entertainment?"

"It's not your usual type of club."

"In what way?"

"It was founded by a married couple whose aim was to provide a safe haven and support for those who served the government and their nation in less public ways. Men and women who risked their lives extracting royalists from the French Terror, or who spied on Napoleon's army. Those whose sacrifice was often immense and yet were left destitute or unrecognized by their nation."

"That was a very praiseworthy endeavor. I can quite understand how you became involved in it."

"You can?"

"You've always been an honorable man, my lord."

"Don't talk rot."

She raised her eyebrows as he scowled at her. "I've known you since you were twelve. You were always honorable. For God's sake, Benedict, you married me!"

"And that worked out so well that you ran away from me as fast as you could."

"I didn't run, I—" She rose to her feet. "Shouldn't we be going?"

He stalked over to her. "You ran away from me, and now you're trying to do exactly the same thing again."

She shoved at his chest. "It's not the same at all. You're the one who said we shouldn't stay here in case we were recognized!"

"You ran because my father gave you money." He wrapped his hand around her throat. "He showed me the promissory note with your signature on it."

She slowly raised her head to stare into his intimidating blue glare. "That's not true."

"Are you suggesting he lied to me?"

She wanted to look away, but there, deep within his gaze, was her friend, the person she'd hurt so desperately in her panic to escape.

"Benedict, I swear, he didn't give me any money."

His fingers tightened around her neck. "Then why did you run?"

"Because it was the only thing I could do for you," she blurted out.

"What the devil does that mean?"

"I didn't want to ruin the rest of your life with my presence."

"So that's how he did it." He briefly closed his eyes. "He played on your conscience, didn't he? Suggested that I'd regretted marrying you and was desperate enough to ask him to help me find a way out." He stepped away from her. "God damn him to hell."

She took two unobtrusive steps toward the door. "He was right, though, wasn't he? You didn't ask me to stay. We'd never have survived society's scrutiny."

"Do you think I cared about that?" he demanded.

"I cared." She met his gaze. "I think we should go now." She turned toward the door. "Is there a less public exit?"

She didn't wait for his reply, just turned toward the least or-nate door that she guessed would lead into the servants' do-main. It opened onto a small stairway, beyond which was a maze of rooms and a hallway that led to what looked like a door to the outside.

He caught up with her in the corridor, his hand firm on her elbow, and pressed her back against the wall.

"You don't know where you're going."

"I never do. But I always get where I want to in the end."

She glared up at him and, with a stifled curse, he bent his head and kissed her until she had to kiss him back. When he fi-nally raised his head, she was still trapped against him and very aware that he was aroused, his shaft hard against the softness of her belly.

"My father has a lot to answer for." His breathing was as ragged as hers.

He had no idea. She reached up and cupped his cheek. "He did what he thought was right. If it makes you feel any better, my mother was equally adamant that I should leave you. She was as horrified by our marriage as your father was."

He turned his head so that his lips brushed her fingers. "They should not have interfered in a matter that was ours alone to resolve."

"We were children."

"We were old enough to be wedded and bedded." He rested

his forehead against hers. "I don't understand why I'm behaving like this. I don't lose my temper with *anyone*."

"I've always been a thorn in your side, don't you remember?"

"But I've changed. I've learned to control myself."

She couldn't stand this. Couldn't let herself weaken. Why couldn't he be the coldhearted bastard he obviously thought he was with her? She needed to hate him and yet it was proving impossible. In the end, she supposed it didn't matter. He'd learn to hate her again soon.

"Which perhaps explains why it was better that we were separated. You wouldn't have achieved such success in your career if you hadn't learned to put your emotions aside." She spoke briskly, pushing on his chest until he took an involuntary step back. This time he stayed put and let her move off the wall.

He held out his hand. "If we continue down this way, we'll come out in the kitchen garden. We can walk the rest of the way from there."

7

Benedict reviewed the day's events as he walked with Malinda through the ancient back streets that surrounded the newly built London squares. Adam had disappeared into the country-side, possibly to avoid him, Jack Lennox was in charge at the Sinners, and he himself was currently in a state about his wife. He was never in a state. He was a cool, logical thinker with an outstanding ability to make connections, lead men, and discern the truth at a single glance.

Apart from when dealing with Malinda, who brought out a version of himself he no longer recognized, a lust-crazed emotional wreck of a man who couldn't tell when she was lying or telling the truth. He had to bring himself under control. Kissing her had been a mistake; so had touching her. His cock twitched as he thought of that kiss and he tried to ignore it.

Perhaps he should leave Malinda at his lodgings and go back alone to the Sinners. But what if her enemies came after her and she was unprotected? He could hire men to guard her, of course, but no one would be as good at it as he would be. And then there were all the contradictions between her version of the past and his that he needed to sort out. . . .

He was a doomed man. He couldn't leave her alone, and his desire to know the truth would force him to stay close until he knew all. He retained enough intelligence to realize that she wasn't telling him everything. If there truly was that much interest in her from more than one party, then the stakes were considerably higher than perhaps even she realized.

What to do?

He halted in front of his inconspicuous house in Maddox Street. He owned the whole property, but lived in the upper floor and rented out the lower. He patted his pockets and realized he didn't have the key. The curtain of one of the front windows twitched and within moments a small boy flung the door open.

"Where have you been?" he demanded loudly. "You've been gone for weeks!"

"And you don't need to announce that fact to the entire neighborhood."

The boy's face fell as Benedict went through the door, his hand still gripping Malinda's.

"But you said you'd take me and Michael to see the balloon ascension, you *promised* and—"

"Jason." A quiet voice came from the now-open door to the lower apartment and the boy looked stricken. "Come away, and leave his lordship be."

"It's all right, Mrs. Jones. He does have a point." Benedict bowed. "I did go back on my promise." He crouched down in front of Jason. "If you let me know when the next balloon ascension is planned, I will do my best to take you and your brother and make up for my appalling lack of manners."

"Really?"

"Yes." He stood up and smiled at Mrs. Jones. "I mean it. Please keep me informed."

"Oh, I will, my lord, or else I'll never hear the end of it either." She came forward and put her hand on her son's shoulder. "Say thank you to his lordship, Jason."

Benedict held out his hand and Jason obediently shook it.

Mrs. Jones glanced at Malinda and then at Benedict. "I've kept your rooms aired and ready for use, my lord. The fires are laid so you just need to light them. I've just baked a nice chicken pie so I'll bring you up some of that later for your supper—if you're staying."

"We are." He reclaimed Malinda's hand. "Do you have a spare set of keys? I seem to have mislaid mine."

She touched Jason's hair. "Go into the scullery, fetch me the keys hanging on the hook there, and bring them up to his lordship."

"Thank you, Jenny."

"You're welcome, my lord." She dipped a curtsy. "It is good to see you back. We were beginning to get a little worried."

"I was detained in Lincolnshire for a few weeks while I sorted out some family issues." Malinda shifted slightly behind him, trying to pull away from his grasp. He urged her forward. "I had to reclaim my wife."

Jenny's mouth formed a perfect O. "Your wife?"

"Don't tell anyone, will you?" Benedict winked. "I'm only mentioning it so that you won't think I've started bringing women of ill repute into your home."

"As if you would, sir." Jenny chuckled. "It's a pleasure to meet you, my lady. If there's anything you need, you just come and ask me."

"Thank you." Malinda smiled.

He led the way up the stairs, pausing at the locked door to wait for Jason to come thundering up behind them with the key. He thanked the boy, gave him a coin, and sent him back down to his mother. What would Malinda think of his living arrangements and the very modest apartment he inhabited? He tried to view it through a stranger's eyes and realized there was nothing of worth or value to draw the eye, nothing out of place, and nothing of himself there. He'd wanted it like that and now he wondered why. Even watching his wife move through the space made him yearn for something more. Something she alone had ever given him.

"It's a very nice set of rooms, Benedict." She moved toward the closed door. "Is this your bedroom?"

She opened the door and went through. It was a large room spanning the entire width of the back of the house and contained his one luxury, a bed fit for a king. She turned to look at him and took off her bonnet.

"You don't bring women here?"

"Apart from you? No."

"Why is that?"

He shrugged, defenses in place again, amiable smile at the ready. "Because if I want sex I can go to the Sinners, or the Delornay pleasure house, or any brothel I choose. I could even set my mistress up in a discreet house somewhere in the city and visit her there when I felt like it."

"And have you a mistress?"

"Not at the moment."

"How nice to have so many choices."

"Whereas you had to write to Madame Helene to engage the services of one measly prostitute. How do you know Madame, anyway?"

She frowned at him. "I told you, I didn't engage a prostitute."

He stripped off his gloves and took off his hat and tossed them onto the nearest chair. "Don't avoid the question. How did you know about the house of pleasure?"

She opened her eyes wide at him. "I can't remember."

"I was the one who hit my head, not you. With whom do you correspond?"

"You are relentless. It must prove very useful in your chosen profession. But as far as I'm aware, I'm not under investigation."

"But you will understand that I'll continue to ask until you tell me what I want to know."

"Why does it matter?"

"Because *everything* matters. Something that seems small and insignificant when placed within context can suddenly become extremely meaningful."

"There speaks the spymaster." She sighed and stretched her arms up over her head. "Do you mind if I take a nap? I'm dreadfully tired."

"Are you trying to distract me?"

She undid the buttons of her jacket to reveal the creamy skin of her throat and he instinctively moved to help her.

"You'll need new clothes," he murmured as he unpinned the back of her skirt.

"Why?"

"You can't walk around in this all the time. I'll ask Jenny to arrange for a dressmaker to call on you."

"I don't need—" She gasped as he nipped her ear. "That hurt!"

"It was meant to. You are infuriating."

"I don't have any money to pay for fripperies."

"Clothes aren't fripperies; they are armor. You need to be prepared if we have to confront my father." She shivered and he nuzzled her throat, inhaling her unique scent. "And I'm rich enough to pay for a few damn gowns."

"I don't expect you to pay for anything." She stepped out of her heavy skirts and folded her arms across her chest. "When will you get it into your thick head that we aren't married, and that you are not financially responsible for me?"

A strand of her long red hair had escaped her coronet and

curled provocatively over her breast. Benedict leaned in, wrapped the curl around his finger, and tugged hard.

"Do you want help getting out of your corset, or will you sleep in it?"

His fingers dipped lower, playing with the edge of her corset and stroking the softness concealed within its well-boned shell.

"Perhaps you could just loosen it a little."

"Of course. Turn around."

He untied the laces at the bottom of the stays and spent quite a while easing the ties free, a complicated process with a spiral-bound corset.

"Why do women wear such ridiculous garments?" He kissed her shoulder.

"As armor against men?"

"Possibly." He buried his face in the crook of her neck. "Are you sure you don't want me to take it off completely for you?" Even as he spoke he realized he was falling under her spell again. She arched her back, pushing her pert bottom against the swell of his cock.

Probably quite deliberately.

He still didn't know whom she corresponded with at the pleasure house.

He forced himself to let her go and watched as she sauntered over to the bed, her hips swaying in a languid invitation that perhaps only he could appreciate.

"So if you didn't need a prostitute, how have you satisfied your needs in the last few years?"

She climbed onto the bed. "That is none of your business."

"You jest." He closed in on her. "I'm your husband."

Her eyes sparked with fury. "Benedict . . ."

He stroked her knee. "Tell me who you know at the pleasure house." He spread his fingers wide, sliding his thumb between her thighs. Her hand came to rest on his shoulder and she relaxed against him. It was impossible to miss her quick smile of satisfaction. She was beginning to believe she could lead him around by the cock. He'd given her no reason to think otherwise. He eased his hand higher until his thumb circled her clit. She made a soft sound of approval as he played with her.

"Who, Malinda?" he whispered against her ear as he continued to stroke her.

"Are you still asking about my lovers?"

His thumb stilled. "No."

"Because I could tell you some stories about them." She sighed and moved luxuriously against him. "The Russian count, the French émigré . . ."

He changed the position of his hand so that he could slide a finger into her gathering wetness. "You can tell me about them when I'm inside you, tell me every filthy, little thing they did to make you come so that I can do it to you again and do it better."

"You are *so* competitive."

"If you want to know exactly how competitive I can be, you'll need to oblige me first."

"How?" Her skin was flushed now, her body undulating beneath his fingers, seeking release.

"By telling me whom you know at the pleasure house."

She went still. "Go to the devil."

"If that's what you wish, my love." He forced himself to remove his fingers and very slowly licked them clean. "Enjoy your nap. I'll wake you in time for supper."

He left her sitting there in furious outrage and shut the door, leaning against it until he could breathe without inhaling the scent of her arousal. When he had composed himself, he lit the fire, sat down with the brandy decanter, and stared into the flames. Absentmindedly he brought his glass to his lips and smelled her on his fingers.

With a soft curse, he unbuttoned his breeches, wrapped his hand around his aching cock, and pleasured himself to a quick and deeply unsatisfying climax. His cock knew better now, and found this solitary exercise as lacking as Benedict did, but he refused to go back in there and let her dictate to him. A man had to have some standards.

When Jenny arrived with the pie and other savory items for their supper, he was sitting in his chair reading the newspaper that Jason had thoughtfully slid under the door. After thanking Jenny, he placed the food on the table and went through to his bedroom, knocking politely on the door before entering.

Malinda lay on her back, the covers kicked away. One of her knees was bent, giving him an excellent view of her sex and the sight of her fingers pleasuring herself. Her eyes were closed and she was making those little whimpers of pleasure that meant she was close to climaxing. He was immediately as hard as stone again. With all the composure he could gather, he set his jaw, walked over to the bed, and cleared his throat.

Her eyes flew open. "Oh my goodness, I didn't realize you were there, I—"

He patted her cheek. "I just wanted you to know that supper is on the table. Please feel free to join me when you're done."

He bowed and went out, his cock aching like a toothache. She'd done that quite deliberately. He wanted to go back in there, spank her, and then fuck her so hard that she wouldn't be able to walk or argue with him for a week.

"Are you all right, Benedict?" He jumped as he noticed Adam Fisher sitting in the chair by the fire he had so recently vacated.

"How did you get in here?"

"You know I can get in anywhere." Adam shrugged. "I heard you wanted to speak to me urgently, so I came as soon as I could." His gaze dropped to the huge bulge in Benedict's breeches. "Did I catch you at a difficult moment?"

"Don't try to distract me." Benedict snapped. "Perhaps you'd like to explain why you sent me off to find my wife?"

"Oh, that." Adam waved a careless hand. "I merely thought it was time you reclaimed her."

"She doesn't consider herself my responsibility. She says that my father legally dissolved the marriage."

"Did he?"

"Why didn't you just tell me that she'd returned to England?"

"What would the fun have been in that? I simply decided to allow the letter she'd sent you to get through."

"Where did you acquire the information?"

"From a mutual acquaintance at the pleasure house."

"Who?"

"So many questions," Adam murmured. "It was one of the French women who works there. I believe she met your lovely wife when they were both following the army. They've kept in contact for years."

"That explains a lot." He fixed Adam with a fulminating glare. "It does not, however, excuse your behavior. What in the devil were you thinking, sending me up there to deal with a madwoman? Didn't you know we parted on extremely bad terms?"

"One had to assume so, seeing as you haven't seen or spoken to each other for over eighteen years."

Benedict jabbed his shoulder and then regretted it. "She shot me and chained me to her bed!"

"What an enterprising woman. I can't wait to meet her." His gaze strayed to the bedroom door. "I assume she is the reason you are in such a state?"

"I am not in a state. And even if I was, you would be partially responsible for it."

"I apologize if I am *de trop*." Adam smiled sweetly. "If I interrupted you, please go back and attend to your wife. I'll wait." He stretched out his legs and crossed them at the ankles.

"I am not—" Benedict paused and cupped the still-urgent swell of his cock. "She—"

"She is what?"

"She's sleeping."

"And you don't wish to wake her with your inconvenient desire?" Adam shook his head. "What a considerate lover you are."

Behind him, Benedict heard the faintest of sounds and the *click* of the bedroom door latch. Perhaps Malinda needed to understand that she wasn't the only one who could play games.

He advanced toward Adam and unbuttoned his breeches to reveal the thrust of his cock. His friend's gaze fixed on his arousal and Adam purred like a cat.

Malinda climaxed with a delicious shudder, let out her breath, and stretched luxuriously. It was amusing teasing Benedict. She hadn't anticipated having any fun with him at all. But his relentless need to know everything had to be controlled and checked before he uncovered all her secrets. His ability to focus on what he wanted was legendary and, in this instance, worked in her favor because he wanted her. But that lust was combined with a ruthless intellect that secretly intimidated her. Even as a young man of eighteen he'd shown signs of it. The fact that he'd organized their marriage and made everything legal should have warned her that, when he wanted to achieve something, he would do anything to accomplish his goal.

One thing was becoming clear. He wasn't as involved with his father as she'd originally believed. She was beginning to doubt that he had any idea what the Marquis of Alford had done to her father, or why she'd had to return to England. Could she trust him with the full sum of her story? It would be difficult for her to accept that anyone who bore the name Keyes was less than the devil incarnate. But it was tempting. . . .

She stilled as she thought she heard voices. Was young Jason back in the apartment, or was it someone else? She crept toward the door and eased the latch free. Benedict was standing near the fireplace talking to a man she'd never seen before. There was nothing remarkable about his face, or his form, but his smile was quite lovely.

"Put your mouth on me."

Melinda gasped and took an instinctive step into the room. Benedict didn't turn around. "Ah, my dear, your supper is on the table. I'll join you when I'm done."

She stormed over to him, her hands on her hips, hair streaming down her back. Her corset was now almost falling off.

"What on earth are you doing?"

Adam grinned and leaned forward to lick a drop of pre-cum from Benedict's crown. "I understood that you were asleep, my lady. I'd be more than happy to relinquish my place to you."

She gathered herself and gave him her most charming smile. "Oh no, please go ahead! Ben told me that he never brought women to this place. I should've realized he only had his *men* here."

"Malinda—"

She ignored him and held out her hand. "I assume you must be Adam Fisher."

"I am." He kissed her proffered hand. "It is a pleasure to finally meet you, my lady, although I am slightly embarrassed at being found about to suck your husband's cock."

"Be my guest," Malinda said. "As long as you don't mind if I watch, of course?"

"I'd be honored."

She studied Benedict's cock. "He is rather tempting, isn't he?"

"He is, indeed." Adam took a long, slow, salacious lick around the head of the crown. "Mmm . . ."

Benedict stirred. "There is no need to talk about me as if I wasn't here."

Malinda caught Adam's eye. "Please go ahead. I've never seen two men together before. It will be *quite* educational."

"I don't think this is the time, or—" Benedict groaned as Adam took him deep, his lips tightening around his shaft, one hand wrapped around the base. He sucked hard, his cheeks hollowing with every pull of his mouth.

Malinda watched closely. "It appears that your friend can suck you quite a lot harder than I can. Do you like it?"

Benedict didn't reply, his gaze lowered to Adam's head, his hands clenched into fists at his side.

"I wish I could suck you like that."

She angled her body against his so that she could rub herself against his thigh and slid her hand beneath his balls and cupped them. His hips were moving now, pushing himself deeper into Adam's willing mouth, forcing the pace. She stroked him between the legs and his strokes became faster until he lost his smooth rhythm and simply hammered his cock down the other man's throat.

He climaxed with a curse, and she smiled against his coat. It had, indeed, been educational to see him with another man. Now all she had to do was work out what they meant to each other, and how she could use that to her advantage.

She waited until Adam released Benedict's cock and sat back before crossing over to the small dining table in the bay window.

"I hope you are going to stay and share our supper with us, Mr. Fisher. I'm sure Benedict needs to unburden himself of his concerns."

"I'd be delighted to stay." Adam stood up and bowed. "But please, call me Adam. I imagine we will become very well acquainted in the future."

Not if she had her way. She suspected that despite his benign exterior, he was even more dangerous than Benedict.

"We have a mutual acquaintance already, my lady."

"Apart from Lord Keyes?" Malinda sat down and Adam joined her.

"Yes, Charlotte Delamere from the pleasure house." He

considered the contents of the tray. "That's how I knew you were seeking news of Keyes."

Benedict sat down too. "I told you he knew everything."

Adam looked pained. "I didn't know you would be shot, Keyes. I didn't think you so crass as to invite such a response from the bosom of your family."

"He rode up the driveway as if he owned the place." Malinda fought a smile. "I really had no alternative."

"But to shoot me and chain me to your bed?" Benedict demanded.

"That is all in the past. What I want to know is why Adam has been reading my private correspondence to Charlotte."

Adam's gaze was cool. "For the security of our great nation, I am prepared to overlook the social niceties."

"What does my relationship with Lord Keyes have to do with that?"

"Your husband is a very important man."

"I know, but he's no longer my husband."

"You are still connected to him." He sat back and studied her. "I understand that your mother died last year."

She inclined her head a stiff inch. "So?"

"I just wished to offer my condolences."

"Thank you."

Benedict reached across and took her hand. "Why didn't you tell me? Your mother was very kind to me when we were children."

Malinda swallowed hard. "She was very fond of you, too, until you decided to marry me."

"I'd forgotten you met as children," Adam commented.

She forced her gaze back to Adam, aware that she had to be careful of every word. Why had he brought up her mother? "Yes, my father was a sergeant in the regiment the marquis raised. When he traveled with us, Benedict often came too."

"How romantic."

"Hardly."

"May I ask what drew you back to England if not the wish to reconcile with your husband?"

"I wanted a home for my family. I asked to see Benedict to get his permission for us to live quietly at Alford Park."

Would Benedict correct her? She refused to allow her gaze to stray away from Adam's. "As you might imagine, the Marquis of Alford is not very fond of me at all."

"But you thought the man you married at seventeen, and then abandoned, might be fond enough of you to help instead?"

"Yes." She took a deep, calming breath. "I hoped he would stand my friend."

"So you shot him."

"I didn't want him to escape me again. But what does all of this have to do with you? All you have told me so far is that Benedict is an important man. He's made that very clear to me himself."

"Yes," Benedict spoke up. "What relevance does my wife have to your concerns?"

"Anything that makes you appear vulnerable is a problem, you know that."

"I am not a problem, and I am not his wife," Malinda said strongly. "I just wish to stay at Alford Park."

"But no one will let you do that, least of all your husband, and certainly not the Marquis of Alford."

"Then perhaps I can persuade Benedict to give me an allowance. I'll return to France and everyone will be happy."

"It's too late for that, my lady." Adam sighed. "I'm not the only man who knows that you've returned to England. The marquis is well aware of it too."

After Adam had left, Malinda returned to the bedroom and spent a few moments brushing her tangled hair. She'd had supper with two men in her undergarments and neither of them had mentioned it. Had Adam come to warn Benedict about his father's involvement, or simply to meet and assess her? Probably both.

Benedict spoke from behind her. "Did you really come here to extract an allowance out of me?"

She saw his reflection in the glass. He leaned negligently against the door frame, his tall, elegant frame displayed to advantage.

"It's definitely an idea." She sighed. "I only wish I'd been thinking more clearly when I had you tied up. Instead of using you for sexual pleasure, I should've been extorting money from you."

"I've always paid you an allowance."

She put down the brush and turned to face him.

He half-smiled, but his gaze was searching. "I sent it to your mother and told her it was part of your father's pension. She knew you'd never accept it otherwise. I wonder what happened to it after your mother's death?"

She briefly closed her eyes. If he was telling the truth, then his money had helped keep them safe in France during the long years of the war.

"I also wonder whether it was your mother's demise that triggered your desire to return to England."

She raised her head. "It certainly was a factor in my decision. I assumed your father was paying the entire pension, and that on her death the money would cease. That proved to be correct. I knew we wouldn't survive on the Continent, so I decided we stood a better chance in England."

"Did you perhaps consider approaching my father and asking for the continuance of the allowance?"

She shuddered. "Not for an instant. If he even caught a glimpse of me, he'd—"

"He'd what?" He stood over her, his blue gaze far too piercing. "If we are divorced, and he no longer feels obliged to support you financially, why would he still hate you that much? He'd be far more likely to forget your existence and never think of you again."

"One might think so, but the aristocracy doesn't always behave as they ought."

"Don't blame this on *class*. There must be another reason."

"Why? As far as your father is concerned, I ruined you. You said yourself that you rarely see him. He has every reason to blame that on me."

"*I* don't blame you."

She met his gaze. "You should."

"Your decision to leave me and my father's response to it shaped the man I became. I can't regret that."

"A man known for his ability to destroy people's lives and crush resistance, a cold man with the ability to play many parts."

His gaze hardened. "For my country's sake, yes."

"And at what cost?" She shook her head. "You've allowed yourself to become as cold and unfeeling as an iceberg."

"You of all people know that isn't true, my love."

"But I'm the exception, aren't I?" She turned her back on him. "Can you untie me?"

He worked her laces free. "You're done with this line of interrogation?"

"I'm not interrogating you. I'm just trying to understand what's going on. I refuse to be manipulated."

"As you were by my father?"

"He manipulates everyone and everything he touches. It is all a game to him—other people's lives."

"You sound bitter." He kissed her shoulder. "Do you regret running away from me, then?"

"I regret hurting you, but I still had to go." She crossed over to her side of the bed. Would he admit that she'd hurt him? What would she do if he did?

He stayed where he was and started to remove his clothes.

"As soon as you are decently clothed in the latest fashions, we will pay my father a visit."

"We will not." She tried for a lighter tone. "You, of course, may do as you like, but I see no reason to stir the flames of his resentment even further."

He smiled at her. "Sometimes it pays to confront an aggressor. If he sees us together, he might have to rethink his strategy."

He sat to remove his boots and took off his breeches and then his shirt. His body gleamed so enticingly in the candlelight that Malinda had to look away. He climbed into bed beside her and blew out the candle.

"Tomorrow we should look for a maid for you."

"Are you tired of having to deal with my corset?"

"No, I can't say that will ever become a chore."

She stared up at the canopy above their heads. "I cannot afford a maid."

He sighed. "Let's not argue about this again. You sought my protection, and I need you to look respectable. Having me as your ladies' maid will not suffice."

"I'm perfectly capable of looking after myself."

"I know that. But you aren't used to London society."

She snorted. "You're afraid I'll show you up."

He moved so suddenly that she found herself underneath him. "Your inferiority complex is showing."

"Which is why we would never have succeeded as a married couple. Society will *never* accept a peer married to a common sergeant's daughter."

"Good Lord, you sound just like my father." He gave her a tiny shake. "Peers have married actresses and known whores. The entire royal family is a scandal. No one would give a damn. The only person who cares about it is you."

"Go *away*, Benedict."

"You don't think you are good enough."

She tried to punch him in the shoulder. "I'm not!"

"You're a survivor, Malinda. How do you think the aristocracy attained their positions? By trampling over everyone else, that's how." He rolled away from her. "You're afraid. You're afraid that you'd fit in too well."

She decided not to dignify his ridiculous remarks with an answer, and resolutely closed her eyes. Unfortunately he kept talking.

"I'll speak to Jenny tomorrow about the maid, and consult with Lady Westbrook about the modiste. She's sure to know who is currently in vogue with the ladies of the *ton*."

She pressed her lips together and prayed for patience.

"You'll like Lady Westbrook. She reminds me of you."

Which explained a lot. Malinda turned onto her side away from her tormentor and sighed heavily.

"If I know Adam, he's probably told her all about you." He paused, but not for long. "What did you think of Adam?"

She flopped onto her back. "Are you ever going to stop talking?"

"Probably not. I do some of my best thinking just before I fall asleep."

"This isn't 'thinking'; it's rambling."

He nudged her arm. "But did you like him?"

"Oh, for goodness' sake, what's not to like in a man who is willing to suck one's husband's cock?"

"You enjoyed that?"

"Did you enjoy watching Gwen and me pleasuring each other?"

He shivered, took her hand, and brought it down to his cock. "Immensely."

"Then, of course I enjoyed it." She left her hand where he placed it. "It was interesting to see how roughly he treated you."

"Men tend to know how much another man can stand."

"Do you do that to him?"

"Sometimes."

"Are you in love with him?"

"With Adam?" He sighed as she stroked his cock. "No, we just share a similar pleasure in exploring the full extent of our sexual natures."

"Hmph."

"Adam is more inclined toward men than I am. He prefers to be fucked by a man, whereas I still prefer a woman."

"Even though we aren't as strong?"

His hand curved around her neck, his thumb rubbing gently, mimicking the motion of her fingers on his cock. "That's the best part. Caring for you, giving you as much pleasure as you can take without hurting you." She gripped his cock hard and he shuddered. "Although women are often stronger than they look."

He urged her closer until she was on her side, half-lying across him, her fingers still working his shaft.

"Do you remember the first time we tried this?"

She smiled against his shoulder. "I was torn between horror at the monstrous thing you expected me to hold and curiosity to touch you and see what you felt like. Curiosity won, and then I realized that for a few moments you were totally in my power. I learned to appreciate that."

The low rumble of his laugh surprised her. "And then you asked if you could lick me just to see how I tasted, and I came all over your hand."

"And my dress." She sighed. "I had to go down to the river and try to wash out the stain before my mother saw me." She squeezed his shaft. "But when I did finally get you in my mouth, I enjoyed it immensely. Did you like me watching you with Adam?"

"Yes." His breathing hitched, and he pushed into her hand.

"I'd like to see you on your knees in front of him one day sucking his cock."

His hips bucked as he thrust against her tightening grip. "Yes."

"Is he big?"

"*Yes.*"

"Oh, good." He started to come, and she let him slide through the tight grip of her fist, wet and slick and hard, until he climaxed. She unwrapped her fingers and patted his lean, muscled chest. "Good night, Benedict."

He sighed, turned onto his side, and finally stopped talking. Malinda smiled into the darkness. It seemed he still was in her power when she had her hand around his cock. . . . Some things would never change.

8

"Here we are."

Benedict took a firm grip on Malinda's arm as he helped her out of the hackney cab in front of his parents' mansion in Mayfair. He'd have to thank the Countess of Westbrook. Malinda had decided to wear the gown the countess had sent her and was dressed in a very becoming lavender-colored pelisse with lace at the throat. A pattern of satin leaves went around the hem and marched up the beribboned front. Her bonnet was feathered with an open straw brim drawn back to show her beautifully austere face.

"I still don't think this is a good idea," Malinda muttered.

He paid off the hackney driver and patted her gloved hand. "All you have to do is smile. I'll do the rest."

The look she shot him was positively murderous. "I'm perfectly capable of engaging in a conversation with your father."

"I don't doubt that for one minute." He stopped at the top of the steps and looked down at her. "I only ask one thing. Don't let him make you angry."

"Why not? I'd love to fling my teacup in his face."

He was beginning to see that not all the animosity in the relationship between his father and his wife sprang from his father. As he doubted either of them were telling him the complete truth, bringing them together might help him understand what the hell was going on—or at least clear the air.

"Please try to restrain yourself." He raised his hand to the door knocker.

She grabbed his arm. "Benedict, a few days before you arrived at Alford Park, a man turned up claiming he was your father's land agent and that he represented you. He threatened to give information to the local magistrate and have me evicted if I didn't leave within a week."

"So you said. Did he give you his name?"

"I believe it was Spoors."

"That *is* the name of my father's premier land agent, an unpleasant bully and one I will have great satisfaction in firing when I inherit the title." He glared at her. "I repeat, I had no idea about this before you mentioned it. Why are you bringing it up now?"

"Because I thought you were involved and I didn't think you'd be so foolhardy as to drag me to see your father!" she snapped. "When you turned up, I wasn't sure if you'd come in response to my letter to Charlotte, or as your father's representative."

"Which I suppose you think justifies shooting me?"

"Naturally." She tried to pull free of his arm. "Now, will you reconsider this stupid notion? If you didn't send Spoors, it must mean that your father did."

Drawing her tight against his side, he rapped hard on the door. "Which makes it even more imperative that we confront him."

Her uncomplimentary diatribe about his character was cut short when a butler in the Alford livery opened the door.

"Master Benedict!"

"Crawley." Benedict stepped inside. "Is my father receiving visitors?"

"Well, not really, sir. He's been quite poorly, but I'm sure he'll make an exception in your case." The butler nodded at the staircase. "He's in his suite. If you wish to visit with the marchioness first, I'll go and see if the master is awake."

"Don't trouble yourself, Crawley." Benedict took Malinda's hand and headed up the stairs. "We can find our own way. I promise I won't keep him long."

He ascended the wide, shallow staircase at some speed, hoping the butler would delay sharing news of his arrival with his mother for as long as possible. He couldn't bear her weeping over him and demanding things he was incapable of giving her.

"Benedict."

"What now?"

"This house is . . . *immense.*"

"Well, get used to it. One day it will all be mine." He focused his gaze on the door that led to his father's suite of rooms. Malinda slowed her steps.

"Is this a portrait of your mother?"

He barely glanced up at the enormous painting. "Yes."

"She is very beautiful."

"That's not why my father married her. He coveted her excellent lineage and large dowry."

"You are terribly cynical."

"I have a right to be. They're my parents, not yours. They barely spoke to each other, let alone to me."

He was aware that he was being rather short with her, but facing his father was never easy. He halted in front of the walnut and cherry double doors and took a deep breath. Cupping Malinda's face in his hands, he gave her a quick, hard kiss.

"The dragon awaits us."

He gave a perfunctory knock on the door and went in. The room was in half-darkness but he could clearly make out the upright figure in the bed, eating his breakfast and perusing the morning newspaper.

"Good morning, Father."

His father's hand paused momentarily and replaced his cup on the tray. "Kesteven."

Benedict came forward and inclined his head an inch. "Do you mind if I open the curtains a little more?"

"Be my guest."

There was no inflection in the marquis's voice, but that wasn't unusual. Benedict had spent his entire childhood trying to earn a note of approval from his father and never succeeded. He drew back one of the heavy curtains, turned back to the bed, and experienced a sick feeling as if he'd been punched in the gut. In the stark morning light, his father did indeed appear gaunt and thin. Despite his mother's letters, he hadn't expected that.

Malinda remained by the door, her expression calm, her gaze fixed on him. He walked over, took her hand, and brought her closer to the bed.

"I'm sure you remember my wife, sir."

"The sergeant's daughter."

"My wife." He met his father's gaze. "I have given her permission to reside at Alford Park. I do not expect her to be troubled by you, or your underlings, in the future. Am I making myself clear?"

The marquis looked at Malinda. "You agreed not to come back to England."

"That was many years ago, and the decision of a frightened child."

"So you decided to come back and try your luck with my son again, did you?" The marquis's laugh was dry. "I should've known a woman of your class wouldn't understand the concept of honoring her promises."

"But the promise was extracted under duress and by using false information. I fail to see the honor in that."

"Yet instead of coming to see me and bringing this matter of 'honor' up, you chose to involve my son."

Benedict gave a short laugh. "Trust me, she didn't want to involve me, sir. But when you sent Spoors to threaten her, you made it my business."

"I assumed you'd be grateful for my help. It wouldn't be the first time I'd had to step in and save you from your infantile infatuation with her, would it?"

"I certainly didn't ask you to do anything of the kind then, or now."

The marquis snorted. "You didn't need to ask. I know my duty. You need to marry and get an heir."

"I am married."

"You are a fool."

"You are entitled to your opinion, sir, but I repeat, none of this is your business. I'm no longer a child or a young man. You may safely leave the management of my affairs to me."

"Your life *is* my business, Kesteven. I own you. You are my heir."

"That last part is true, but I don't need to dance to your tune anymore."

"I'll cut off your allowance if you take up with her again."

"That's your choice. I don't need your money."

"Because you work for your damned living like a peasant." The marquis shook his head. "I suppose it isn't surprising that you choose your women from the gutter as well."

"You may insult me all you like, sir, but please refrain from speaking of my wife in those terms."

"She took money from me and ran away."

Benedict stared steadily at his father. "I don't believe that's true. She left because you tried your hardest to destroy everything that was between us."

"You're such a romantic fool. Marriage isn't about *love*."

The marquis made an impatient gesture with his hand. "There was nothing between you. Any man of your class should've known that all she was worth was a quick tumble in the hay and a penny for her trouble."

Benedict took a step forward, but Malinda put her hand on his arm.

"Your son is the most honorable man I've ever met."

"And the biggest fool." The marquis sighed. "You haven't told him the truth, have you?"

"And which truth would that be, my lord?"

"The reason you left."

Malinda went still, and Benedict watched a triumphant smile grow on his father's haggard face. He stepped in front of her.

"What truth?"

"The fact that her mother was my mistress, and that your darling Malinda is my bastard, and therefore your half sister?"

"Really, sir? If that is the case, surely the shame lies with you?" Benedict bowed. "I reiterate. Malinda is living at Alford Park under my protection. You will leave her in peace. Good day."

He maneuvered an unprotesting Malinda out of the door. In the hallway she grabbed his sleeve, her face white, her expression anguished.

"Benedict—"

"Don't speak." He marched her along the corridor and opened a door into one of the many guest bedchambers, shutting it behind them. He leaned against the door, preventing her escape, and took a long, slow breath as she paced the carpet, her hands clenched together at her waist.

"Please—"

He held up his hand. "Don't start defending yourself."

"But I have to explain . . ."

"Give me some credit, Malinda. If you were my half sister, you would *never* have gotten back into bed with me. When did you discover my father had lied to you?"

"When my mother was dying." She hesitated. "I asked her if it was true."

"Which explains why you finally thought it was safe to come back to England."

She nodded. "My mother wrote a journal, which she gave me on her deathbed. After her death, I was able to work out when I was conceived, and ascertain that the marquis was not with the regiment at all that summer so he couldn't be my father." She shuddered. "It was something of a relief. I even found my original birth certificate, signed by the army chaplain."

He tried to imagine how it must have felt for her to be confronted with such a monstrous lie at the age of seventeen.

"I wish you'd told me."

"How could I? I didn't want you to know."

"I could've—"

"You could've done nothing but ruin yourself and run away with me. That I could not allow."

"So you and my father concocted a plan to make it seem as though you'd been bought off. Did you actually take his money as well?"

"No!" She came toward him. "I decided to leave of my own accord. The fact that my mother supported my decision made me think there might be a kernel of truth in what the marquis told me." She cupped his chin. "I would *never* conspire with your father against you."

Despite the firmness of her voice, her lips were trembling. He barely resisted the urge to take her mouth in a savage kiss. Instead he eased out of her grasp.

"We'd better get moving."

"Yes."

Malinda retied the ribbons of her bonnet and fought to compose her expression. Her whole body was shaking and she felt cold to her bones. Benedict had believed her. She hadn't expected that. Had expected to have to argue her case and convince him, but he'd simply accepted what she'd said.

He held open the door for her.

Apart from that slight moment, when he'd asked in that incredibly calm voice if she'd conspired with his father, he'd remained in total control. She'd wanted to console him so badly because this, at least, she could say, hand on heart, was false. *This* part of the tangle was a figment of his father's distorted lies. The rest? She wasn't ready to share her suspicions about that with anyone yet.

It had taken all her resolve to stand there and not pull Benedict's dueling pistol from his pocket and fire it straight at the marquis's sneering face. He shared one thing with his son, the ability to hide his emotions behind an autocratic mask.

"Devil take it," Benedict muttered.

Coming along the corridor toward them was an angelic, blond woman clutching a lace handkerchief in one hand.

"Oh, Benedict! How could you upset your father so, by bringing *that woman* to the house!"

"Good morning, Mother." Benedict bowed. "May I present my wife, Malinda? I don't believe you've met." He turned slightly toward her. "Malinda, may I present my mother, Beatrice, the Marchioness of Alford."

Malinda curtsied. "My lady."

She'd guessed who the woman was immediately. The marchioness ignored her and stared straight at her son. "I asked you to come home, but not in this manner!"

"Then rest assured, we will not trouble you again." He kissed his mother's slack fingers. "Good day."

"Benedict!" Malinda winced as the marchioness's voice rose two octaves. "This is not acceptable! What am I to tell my friends? Why are you doing this to me?"

He kept moving, his hand firmly in the small of Malinda's back until they swept through the front door the butler held open for them and out onto the street. He hailed a passing hackney cab and had her installed in the seat. Within seconds they were pulling away and turning out of the square.

Malinda turned to study his stern profile.

"Your mother is still very beautiful. You look a lot like her."

"So I've been told."

She reached for his gloved hand and found it clenched into a fist.

"It's all right."

"No, it isn't. They both behaved appallingly."

She tried to think of a more neutral topic. It was imperative that she keep him from thinking about anything to do with her or his father. "Why did your father call you Kesteven?"

"It's my courtesy title. I don't bother to use it."

"Why do you need another title?"

His hand relaxed against hers. "Viscount Kesteven is one of my family's lesser titles. One my ancestors achieved on their relentless drive to the top of the pile and discarded when my grandfather became the Marquis of Alford. As my father's eldest son and heir apparent, I'm granted the use of his next-highest-ranked title. When I become the marquis, my eldest son will become Kesteven."

"Ah." She continued to hold his hand. "That makes sense, although it does seem a little greedy of your family to hoard so many honors."

"My father considers it his duty to keep as much wealth and privilege as he can to himself."

"But you prefer to be simply Lord Keyes."

"Officially, I'm Kesteven. At this moment, I'd prefer to be Ben, the well-paid prostitute."

She slid her hand around the back of his neck and brought his head down for a kiss. "How much are your rates?"

He half-smiled against her mouth. "For you? Less than my father considered you were worth. Let's say, a farthing?"

"As that is all I have in the world, I consider it money well spent." She licked a sultry line between his lips. "But only if you let me tell you what to do."

He caught her lower lip between his teeth. "I think I can manage that."

The hackney stopped outside the house in Maddox Street, and Benedict paid the driver and walked with her up the stairs to the apartment. Jenny had been in to set the rooms to rights. The fires were banked; a fresh newspaper lay on the table beside a bunch of wildflowers tied with a ribbon in a jar.

"I believe you have made a conquest," Benedict said. "Jason never used to leave me flowers."

"He is a very sweet boy."

"He's a rascal. His father was a friend of mine. When he was killed in France, I made sure that Jenny and his two sons were taken care of."

Malinda took off her bonnet and pelisse and laid them carefully over the back of the chair. "I did wonder."

"Whether the boys were mine?"

"They could have been." She shrugged. "Not that I would have minded. I've had lovers myself in the past."

"And carried their children?"

"No. There are ways to prevent conception if one is careful." She hesitated. "Not that any method is completely safe." She studied him carefully. "Aren't you going to undress?"

"I was waiting to be told what I was supposed to do."

She sighed. "I don't really want to own you right now, Benedict, I just want—" She gasped as he swooped down on her, picked her up, and walked her into the bedroom. He laid her on the bed, pushed up her voluminous skirts, and climbed on top of her. Making short work of his trouser buttons, he shoved them down and thrust his cock deep inside her.

"Oh yes—" she breathed. "That's exactly what I wanted."

She wasn't quite ready for him, but she didn't care. He made himself at home, stretching her to accommodate him as if it was his right. And God, it felt right. It always had. The slam of his groin against her, and the urgency of his need, made her wet for him. Her climax built slowly along with his, and soon she was gripping him with her arms and legs and tilting her hips to allow him access to the deepest, neediest parts of her.

"*Oh, God...*" She gasped as the long, slow waves of a climax rolled over her and he went still, holding himself deep inside, impaling her on his thick length. "*Benedict.*"

He levered himself up on his hands and stared down at her, his expression impassive, only his cock and lower body still entangled with hers. She tried to bring him back down to her but he shook his head and pulled out.

"No, don't—"

He reversed his direction, his cock now positioned over her head and his mouth on her cunt.

"Suck my cock."

She reached for him and brought him down between her lips as his mouth met her clit and the empty, throbbing place where his cock had just filled her. He crammed four fingers inside her, his thumb in her arse, his mouth on her clit, and she screamed around his stiff cock, making him groan.

Now all she could think of was pleasuring his cock, of taking him as deep as he was taking her, of giving him everything he wanted. He groaned against her sex, the vibrations making her climax, and he thrust strongly into her mouth and released his come in thick waves that she swallowed because he was so deep.

Within a moment he rolled off her and drew her against his side. All she could do was lie next to him and breathe. After a while, he stripped off her clothing and his own and pulled the covers over them.

"It's only midday," Malinda murmured.

"After the morning we've had, there's nothing wrong with enjoying a short nap."

"I suppose not." She sighed and rubbed her cheek against his bare chest. "Thank you for supporting me."

"It was my pleasure."

"I can go back to Alford Park now, and live there in peace."

Beneath her his body tensed. "Perhaps not *quite* yet."

She opened her eyes. "Why not?"

"Because I don't trust my father."

"If you send me back with some of your trained personnel, I'll be fine."

"I'm sure you will, eventually. But I'd prefer you to wait until I can accompany you and make sure the security arrangements are to my satisfaction."

She came up on one elbow and glared down at his calm face. "Why can't you come with me tomorrow?"

"Because I've been away from my place of work for almost a month, which, by the way, is entirely your fault. I need to catch up."

"And what am I supposed to do in the meantime?"

"Enjoy London?"

"You are *impossible*."

"You put me in this situation." His blue-eyed gaze was far too innocent for her liking. "The least you can do is be patient for a week or so."

She lay back down again with a thump and stared up at the canopy of the vast bed. "Go back to work, then. I don't care what you do."

"Thank you, I will."

"Good. I'm sure I can find many things to amuse me."

"I'm sure you can. In fact, the Countess of Westbrook would probably be delighted to take you around with her."

"She's the woman who sent me my new dress, isn't she? I

have no idea who she is." Malinda was aware that she sounded rather like a sulky schoolgirl, but she was too tired to care.

"She's one of the founding members of the Sinners Club. You'll like her."

"We'll see."

He stroked her cheek. "There is one more thing."

"What now?"

"I would appreciate it if you are known as my wife, Lady Keyes, or if you prefer it, the Viscountess of Kesteven."

"That's ridiculous on so many levels."

"Why?"

"Why is it important for you to maintain this fiction? Announcing to the *ton* that you've had an unsuitable wife stashed away for eighteen years will invite just the kind of gossip and scandal you abhor."

"I'm not ashamed to be married to you." There was an obstinate note in his pleasant reply that she knew rather too well. "Being known as my wife will keep you safe."

"From what?" This time she sat up. "Do you imagine your father is going to have me murdered?"

He stared up at her, one hand beneath his head, his blond hair disordered on the pillow. "It's an interesting thought."

"I was jesting!" She blinked at him. "You wish to use me as *bait*?"

He raised his eyebrows. "There's no need to get so agitated. I'm used to considering the best and worst of every situation and attempting to manipulate the best possible outcome."

"Why would he want to kill me?"

His smile was devastating. "Don't treat me like a fool, Malinda. My father went to great lengths to scare you away at seventeen and he's completely failed to detach you from me. Do you really think he'll meekly accept my command and leave you in peace?"

She swallowed hard. "Now you are wandering off into the

realm of fantasy. He's obviously a sick man who simply wants
to see his son marry well and produce an heir. Once he under-
stands that I'll stay quietly in Alford Park and never ask for
anything from the Keyes family again, he'll calm down."

He didn't say anything, his far-too-acute gaze fastened on
her face, a hint of a question forming in his eyes.

"What else are you afraid of?"

"That you'll never stop pestering me for information?"

"At Alford Park you mentioned that you were fearful and
needed my help."

"With your father, which you have provided for me."

"I suspect there is more to it than that."

She forced a smile and bent to kiss him full on the mouth.

"Do we actually have to nap?"

He kissed her back. "No."

"Oh, good." She ran her hand down over his stomach and
cupped his balls. His fingers closed around her wrist with surprising strength.

"Don't do this."

"What, touch you?"

"Distract me."

"Why would I?"

"That, my dear, I would love to know." He drew her hand
away and threw back the covers.

"You're leaving?"

"I think it best, don't you?" He picked up his discarded
shirt and breeches and put them on, his movements jerky, his
back turned to the bed.

For a moment, Malinda glared at his tense shoulders and
fought an absurd desire to cry.

"Oh well."

She closed her eyes and listened to him finish dressing, her
thoughts in turmoil.

"I'll return for supper."

She waved a careless hand at him. "Don't bother on my account. I'm sure you're very busy."

He paused at the door. "Malinda . . ."

"What?" She pretended to yawn.

"If you go out, would you inform Jenny?"

"If you wish."

He bowed. "Thank you."

She didn't bother to open her eyes. He sighed and left, closing the door softly behind him. Before the outer door slammed, she turned her face into her pillow and silently wept. She couldn't tell him about her other fears. Dealing with his father would have to come first. If things were as she expected, all her other worries would mean nothing and Benedict wouldn't have to worry about *her* ever again.

9

Benedict ignored the slight drizzle of rain and decided to walk to the Sinners. He needed to think and the exercise would do him good. Malinda continued to confound all he believed he knew about himself simply by existing. It was quite unfair. Getting out of a bed with her still in it had proved almost impossible. But why wasn't he satisfied with the outcome of his meeting with his father? He'd stood up for his wife, warned his father off, and ignored the old man's attempts to sully the waters with his claims of being Malinda's father.

Crossing the road, he tossed a coin to the small boy sweeping the pavement and angled his hat against the bite of the wind. Something was wrong; every instinct he possessed was screaming, and he'd learned to trust those instincts. He kept walking and entered the Sinners through the rear of the building. One of the footmen rose from the kitchen table and bowed to him.

"May I help you, Lord Keyes?"

"Good afternoon, William. Is the Countess of Westbrook here today?"

"I believe she is, my lord."

"Will you go and ascertain if she will receive me?"

Benedict sat down at the kitchen table and took the hot mug of tea Cook offered him with gratitude. He was halfway down its steamy, reviving depths when the footman returned.

"My lady awaits you in her study."

"Thank you, William. I'll take myself up."

Benedict used the backstairs and made his way to the second level of the house where the Westbrooks still kept their apartment and an office. Officially, they'd handed over the running of the club to Benedict and Adam, but they were still much involved. Their knowledge of the underworld of spies, traitors, and the inconsistencies of monarchs was too invaluable to lose.

He knocked and went in. Lady Westbrook was sitting in a chair by the fire. She wore her usual exquisitely fashionable gown, and her hair was drawn up into a braided coronet on the top of her head. She'd never be called a beauty, but there was something arresting about her face that had always reminded him of Malinda. Her expression brightened when he came across to kiss her hand.

"Benedict, how nice to see you. I understand you've been having quite an adventure."

"That's an understatement. I've been shot at, chained to a bed, lost my memory due to a fever, and been given a new identity as a prostitute."

"A *prostitute?*"

He took the chair opposite the countess. "My captor had the enterprising idea of forcing me to regain my memory by offering me an alternate persona that she assumed I'd be shocked enough to repudiate immediately."

"And did it work?"

"No, because I really had lost my memory. For a few days I started to believe she might be right." He sighed. "I suspect I've spent too many years playing a part to even recognize the difference."

"Yet everything worked out well in the end, didn't it? I understand you found your wife, and united with her to confront your father."

"News does travel fast." He sat back. "I was hoping to engage your help."

"In what way?"

"I want Malinda to stay in London for a few weeks while I catch up on my work here at the Sinners and on Whitehall." He hesitated. "She'd prefer to leave immediately for Lincolnshire. I've persuaded her that it would be in her best interests to wait until I can return with her."

The countess was watching him intently. "What do you fear?"

"I don't know." He shoved his fingers through his hair. "I just want to ensure that while she is in London she is safe. I can't think of anyone who could keep her safer than you."

"I'll certainly do my best. Do you want me to take her about with me and help her rejoin society as your wife?"

"She never 'joined' in the first place. Her father was the sergeant in my father's regiment. We met when we were children and became friends." He paused. "Of course, you probably know all this."

"Some of it. When we were considering whom we trusted to continue our work at the Sinners, we had to be sure that our candidates' backgrounds were acceptable."

"And you discovered I married a seventeen-year-old commoner."

"You were only eighteen yourself, I believe."

"And a fool, if you listen to my father. Malinda's father was killed during an ambush. She and her mother were left destitute. My father wanted to abandon them. I refused to allow him to do that."

He wasn't sure even now where he'd found the courage to stand up to his terrifying father, but he had. "I married Malinda in secret and presented my father with what I thought was a *fait accompli*. Of course, it didn't quite work out like that. The next thing I knew, Malinda was gone, paid off by my father, and her mother had remarried an old friend and gone to another regiment stationed nearby."

"And yet you still want to keep her safe."

He shrugged. "We were friends before we were anything else. Why would I not help her? I recently found out that my father lied to both of us. She ran because he told her he was her mother's lover and that she was, in fact, my half sister. He told *me* that she'd accepted a large sum of money to renounce me because that was what she'd been after all the time." His mouth twisted. "What a charming father I have."

"One wonders why he had to go to such lengths to keep you apart."

Benedict frowned. "With all due respect, why are you still so interested in my personal life?"

"Because I want you to be happy?"

He smiled. "I'm sure you do, but I sense this isn't just about me. What is your interest in Malinda?"

"She is a fascinating woman. The mere fact that no one knew about her for years makes her an object of curiosity, wouldn't you say?"

"I'll pray you're wrong about that. Her wish is to return to Alford Park and live quietly there. My purpose in visiting my father with her today was to gain his promise that he would not interfere with her decision to remain in England and to demonstrate that she had my protection. Hopefully, that's an end to it."

"Oh, dear."

Unease prickled over his skin. "What's wrong?"

The countess shifted in her chair and rang the bell. "Do you mind if I ask my husband to join us? He has some interesting information he wants to share with you."

Benedict rose from his seat when the Earl of Westbrook came into the room and held out his hand.

"It is good to see you again, my lord."

"Always a pleasure, Keyes." The earl drew up a chair and sat next to his wife. He took her hand and kissed it. "My love."

Benedict had always envied the couple opposite him for their obvious deep affection for each other. Their love had defied society's expectation that the "savage" Anglo-Indian rake would ever stay faithful to the intellectual bluestocking he'd married. But they were still married, had founded the Sinners together, and owned it equally.

"There is one thing I need to ask before we go any further, Keyes."

"And what is that, sir?"

The earl fixed his gaze on Benedict. "Are you willing to listen to the information I want to give you without allowing your emotions to cloud your judgment?"

"I've never done so before."

"But this is different. This concerns members of your family."

"All I can say is that I will do my best to remain impartial."

"I suppose that's the best I can hope for."

"I also promise that I won't take out my vengeance on the messenger."

The earl gave him a slight smile and settled back in his chair, his hand still clasped in his wife's.

"In the summer of 1810, you were traveling with the regiment your father raised."

"That's correct. We were heading back toward France after a spell on the Peninsula."

"I understand that your wife's father was killed during an ambush."

"Yes. There were no survivors."

"Who raised the alert when the soldiers failed to return?"

"I did."

"Why?"

"Because Malinda's mother, who also traveled with the army, was worried about her husband. I offered to carry her concerns to my father."

"And he organized a search party."

"No. He told me to go away and stop being a nuisance. He returned to finish his dinner."

"And, being an obedient son, you did what he told you."

Benedict smiled. "I gathered a few of the men and we went out ourselves."

"And what did you find?"

He briefly closed his eyes against the horrors. "Dead bodies, and dead horses, in a narrow gully halfway up the mountain. Vultures of both the human and animal kind picking over the remains." He shuddered.

"Did you know what the men carried?"

"The usual, I expect. A mixture of supplies and information, orders from the battalion commanders, letters from home." He paused. "What did I miss?"

"From what I've discovered, they also carried the payroll."

Benedict stared into the earl's impassive face. "Which I suppose explains why they were attacked in the first place."

"Indeed. You said there were no survivors."

"There weren't. I knew the three men and they were all accounted for."

"The men, yes."

"What are you suggesting?"

"Do you remember where Malinda was that night?"

"Her mother said she was sick and had stayed in their tent. That's why I went down there in the first place—to see how she was—and found out that the men were missing." He shrugged. "I had no reason to disbelieve her mother."

"Sources who met Sergeant Rowland and his party when he picked up the supplies on the other side of the mountain range say there were three men and a boy in the company."

"That can't be right."

"The boy was described as having freckles and the red hair of a fox."

Benedict took a long, slow breath. "You're assuming it was Malinda."

"It's possible."

"She would *never* have run away and left her father to die."

"What if she had no choice?"

"I suppose that's a possibility." He frowned. "But why didn't she tell me about it afterward? It makes no sense."

Silence fell and he slowly raised his head. The countess was looking anxious, her husband merely interested.

"Are you suggesting Malinda was involved in the robbery?"

"Is it possible?"

"I—" He stared at them. "No. It's unthinkable."

"Then we must consider other scenarios." The earl leaned forward. "If she was there, and she witnessed the attack, perhaps she saw the murderers. It is interesting that she didn't mention it to you, or to anyone else."

He forced himself to think carefully about the aftermath of the discovery of the ambush.

"I didn't see her for at least two days. My father had me flogged for daring to ignore his instructions. When I did see her, she was distraught. She and her mother were about to be thrown out of their tent and sent back to England." He paused. "I spent the next few days arranging for us to be married. Once that was accomplished, I gave her mother what remained of my savings, and prepared to face my father. Within another day, Malinda fled. I was sent home and deposited at my school, where I remained incarcerated for the rest of the year."

"Oh my goodness." Lady Westbrook sighed. "What a horrible situation."

Benedict turned back to the earl. "Does Malinda's return to England mean she might be in danger?"

"If you don't believe she was involved in the original crime, then yes, I think that's a reasonable possibility."

"Then you assume that whoever took that payroll stole from his *compatriots?*"

The earl nodded. "It also begs the question of what prompted your wife to return after eighteen years."

"Her mother died, and the allowance from my father was cut off. She said she wanted to stay at Alford Park with her half sister and cousin and that she needed my help to do so. That's why I insisted on taking her to meet with my father. She was extremely reluctant to see him." He stopped. "I knew there was something more to it! Damnation, my father's been preventing her from returning to England all along."

"Don't jump to conclusions, Benedict," the countess said. "It's not like you."

"Oh, don't worry, I won't." He set his jaw. "I just need to have a conversation with my wife before I do anything else at all."

"Don't judge her yet, either, Keyes." The earl hesitated. "I wonder if I might make a suggestion?"

"Be my guest."

"Perhaps we can utilize your original proposal, that my wife keeps an eye on yours while you work. If she is the target of unwanted attention, it will soon become apparent."

"And she might be dead."

"You know we won't allow that to happen."

"That's an impossible promise to keep."

The countess sighed. "Benedict, I know this is hard for you, but—"

That brought him to his senses. "I'm prepared to do whatever is necessary to find out what is going on. If either my wife or my father is involved in the murder of innocent men, I would hope I'd have the courage to charge them with their crimes."

"Then shall we proceed as planned? Let Malinda stay in London under my wife's sponsorship and we'll all keep a very close eye on her. We might be wrong, of course, and this is just a coincidence."

Somehow Benedict doubted that. "I appreciate you telling me all this."

The earl raised an eyebrow. "I'd hardly keep you in the dark, now, would I? I trust you implicitly."

More fool him. Benedict stood and bowed. "Where would you prefer to meet Malinda, my lady?"

"Perhaps at your house in Maddox Street? I doubt she'd feel comfortable coming here."

"She would love to visit the Sinners. She is already highly curious about the place."

"Then perhaps I'll bring her here after Jack Lennox sorts out his affairs."

"And when will that be?"

"I'm anticipating the announcement of his marriage to the Dowager Countess of Storr within a week or so."

Benedict paused as he pulled on his gloves. "You sound very confident."

She opened her eyes wide. "Of course I am! She is the perfect match for him." She came across to kiss him on the cheek. "Shall we say tomorrow at ten?"

"That will be fine."

"Then I will see you tomorrow."

Benedict nodded at the earl and headed for the door. "Is Jack around at the moment?"

"No, he's out."

"Then I'll take advantage of his absence and talk to my staff." He closed the door behind him and walked down the backstairs and through the maze of the servants' quarters to his office.

Maddon appeared almost instantly and offered him refreshments, which he accepted. After the butler departed with a new set of instructions, Benedict sat at his desk and studied the pile of correspondence that had accumulated in his absence. He needed to employ a secretary, but he'd never been able to trust anyone sufficiently to offer them the job.

He never trusted anyone.

He put his head in his hands and stared blindly down at the blotter on his desk. Why had Malinda come back? How much did she know about what really happened during the ambush? He'd believed her when she'd insisted she just wanted a home for her family, but was there more to it than that? Despite his smiling assurances of restraint to the Earl and Countess of Westbrook, he wanted to grab hold of her and shake some answers out of her. He felt like his eighteen-year-old self again, full of hope for the future with his chosen bride only to be told that she'd left him.

Damnation, he couldn't allow himself to feel that hurt again. Hadn't he learned anything? He let out a long, slow breath. From this moment he'd be on his guard at all times. Part of him yearned to tell her what the earl had told him, but there was too much at stake. This was the time for him to use his skills to keep her alive until the issue was resolved one way or another.

He groaned. He had no idea what his father was up to either. Had he really wanted to keep Malinda out of the country just to stop her reconnecting with his son, or was there more to it?

He picked up his pen and took out a sheet of writing paper. He'd attend to his correspondence first. Hadn't Adam made a list of several possible secretaries for him and left it on his desk somewhere? He'd read through it and ask some of them in for an interview. Moving a pile of letters, he spied something written in Adam's hand at the bottom and drew the single sheet of paper toward him. Maybe the task would deaden his passions sufficiently so that he lost the urge to put his stubborn wife over his knee and spank her until her teeth rattled.

10

Malinda ate her way through the enormous breakfast Jenny brought up for her and Benedict and steadfastly ignored his empty chair. He hadn't come back for supper last night. When she'd heard footsteps in the hall, she'd taken one of his pistols and peered through a crack in the door, only to see a strange man setting a chair out on the landing and sitting on it. When she'd emerged brandishing the pistol, he hadn't turned a hair, just politely informed her that he was from the Sinners, and that he would be guarding her door all night so she wasn't to worry about a thing.

She had to assume that Benedict had sent him. It had only dawned on her much later, when she had to wiggle out of her corset by herself, that he wasn't coming back at all. Her bad mood had worsened overnight and she'd woken up with all-too-familiar stomach cramps and the beginning of her menses. Relief at their appearance after her foolhardy risk-taking with Benedict had dissipated her concern over his whereabouts until now.

It took her a while to get dressed by herself and don the new morning dress Benedict had purchased for her. It was a soft green that complimented her unfortunate red hair and softened the hard lines of her sharp features. Once she was dressed, she went to check on her guard and found that he was still there, a plate of Jenny's finest cooking balanced on one knee.

He looked up as Malinda approached and smiled.

"Morning, my lady."

"Good morning." She paused. "What is your name?"

"It's Niall, my lady."

"Well, then, Niall. If I wish to leave the house, are you supposed to stop me, or accompany me?"

"His lordship said I was to be your shadow, so I reckon if you want to go out, I'll go with you. If you want to stay in, then I'll stay right here."

His accent held a slight hint of Ireland, which reminded her forcibly of her father.

"I might want to go out later. I'll let you know."

"Very good, my lady."

Malinda went back inside and considered what to do next. Her gaze caught on her old saddlebags, which she'd stuffed with a change of clothes and other personal items suitable for the journey on horseback with Benedict down to London. She had nothing of value in them, only her mother's journal, and the wedding ring her father had given his now-deceased wife.

If she was to continue with her plan, she should at least consider where to hide the journal. Benedict's father knew she was in London, and she would have to be more careful. After deliberating for several minutes, she placed the saddlebags in the corner cupboard, and then slid the slim journal inside the pages of a volume of parliamentary papers about the current composition of the army. She put the book back on the shelf in the living room and wondered why on earth Benedict bothered to read such things. But then, he would one day take his seat in the

House of Lords, so perhaps he considered such dull, worthy tomes a good preparation.

Damn him for making her stay in London at his beck and call. What made matters worse was that now, thanks to his warnings, *she* didn't feel safe when he wasn't with her. If she'd used her wits at Alford Park before leaving, she could've brought something to pawn or barter so she could afford a ticket on the stage back to Lincolnshire for herself. But Benedict had supervised her hurried packing and given her little time to do anything.

She glanced doubtfully down at her beautiful new dress and smoothed the skirt. She could sell the gown and wear her old riding habit, but that would necessitate a visit to a money-lender. She had to assume Niall would be reporting her movements back to someone at the Sinners, and that any suspicious activity would swiftly result in her not being allowed out at all.

She considered the furniture in the apartment and then delved deeper into the contents of the drawers and cupboards. To her disappointment, there was almost nothing of value to "borrow." Benedict didn't seem to keep a single pair of cuff links or a gold watch chain anywhere. Frustrated, she opened the chest of drawers next to the bed and smiled.

"What have we here?"

She drew out several elaborate oriental-style boxes and placed them carefully on the bed. Did Benedict collect porce-lain? It seemed unlikely. She opened the lid of the first box and studied the contents. Four beautifully carved jade phalluses of varying thicknesses and lengths were pillowed in red satin.

"Oh my," Malinda breathed.

A knock on the outer door had her shutting the lid and guiltily cramming all the boxes back into the drawers. She rushed back through into the living room and found herself confronting a stylishly dressed older woman with light brown hair and very blue eyes.

"You must be Malinda." The elegant woman held out her gloved hand. Malinda reckoned she was in her late thirties or forties. "I'm Faith, the Countess of Westbrook."

Malinda took the proffered hand and shook it. "Benedict mentioned you might be coming to see me."

"He is concerned that you will have nothing to do while he is busy solving the affairs of the nation."

"He is *concerned* that I might get up to mischief."

"And will you?"

"I haven't decided yet." She eyed the smiling woman in front of her. "You aren't how I pictured you at all."

"Good Lord." The countess raised her eyebrows. "What on earth did Benedict say about me?"

"That you had his devotion, and that you were extraordinary."

"That makes me sound far more impressive than I could ever be."

"I'm not sure. Any woman who cofounded a club for sinners *is* quite extraordinary."

"It was the only thing my husband could think of to get me to agree to marry him. I refused to be a conventional wife, and I insisted that we had to be partners in all things." She paused. "He had the good sense to realize I meant what I said, and came up with a plan that allowed us to be together."

"How romantic."

"It was, rather." The countess looked around the small room. "You must be bored witless sitting here by yourself."

"Oh, I am allowed to go out, if I take Niall with me." Malinda gestured at the chair closest to the fire. "Won't you sit down? I'll ask Jenny for some tea."

"That would be delightful."

Malinda saw Jason coming up the stairs and he frowned at her. "You don't have to come down. Mum said to ask you if you'd be wanting some refreshments."

"Your mother is a treasure. Yes, please."

He stomped back down and she returned to the apartment. She had to remember that behind her instant liking for the countess lurked other more serious matters. If Benedict was *truly* busy and not just avoiding her, Lady Westbrook was simply another watchdog like Niall—if a somewhat more engaging one.

She took the chair opposite the countess and watched as her guest unbuttoned her coat, took off her bonnet, and made herself at home.

"You are an intelligent woman, Malinda. We can sit here and talk about society and modistes and the latest scandal, or we can, as my husband would say, take the gloves off and have an honest conversation about the situation you face."

"You are remarkably direct."

The countess made a face. "I've never been very good at small talk. I'd rather we didn't waste our precious time fencing with each other, and simply got on with asking what we want to know."

Malinda's respect for the countess grew. "Then I'll start. Have you seen Benedict this morning, Lady Westbrook?"

The countess nodded. "Please call me Faith, I'd much prefer it. Benedict is at the Sinners. He was at his desk and busy with a mountain of correspondence that I am certain will give him a headache. He wasn't in a very *communicative* mood."

"Did you tell him you were coming to see me?"

"He arranged it himself yesterday, so there was no need to bother him." She paused. "Why? Did you need to speak to him urgently?"

"Oh no, not if he has the headache. He'd only snap at me."

"Benedict never snaps."

"Yes, he does. You simply have to know how to annoy him. I'm very good at it."

"He has seemed a trifle out of sorts since you returned."

"Good."

Jenny appeared with the tea tray and set it on the table beside Malinda, who thanked her. At the countess's nod, she poured a cup of tea and handed it to her.

"Thank you."

"You are welcome." Despite her large breakfast, Malinda helped herself to a piece of shortbread. "Did Benedict tell you that we met with his father?"

"I was aware of that."

"He thinks the marquis gave in too quickly, which is why he won't let me go back to Lincolnshire without him. He seems to forget that I am quite capable of looking after myself."

"I'm sure you are. You did shoot him, after all. Life traveling behind an army must breed resilience."

"And I am from peasant stock, which means my constitution is more suited to deprivation than your average aristocrat."

The countess smiled. "Are you trying to shock me into going away? It won't work, you know. I'm well aware of your background. You haven't spent your entire life trudging behind an army wagon. I believe you and your half sister were schooled at a French nunnery."

"None of which is your business," Malinda snapped.

"That depends on how you look at it."

"I pose no threat to this nation."

"But you are associated with a man who holds many of the secrets of that nation."

"I don't *want* to be associated with him. I want to go home. He is the one insisting I stay in London."

"Because he cares about you, and wants to keep you safe."

"It's not that simple. Benedict does what benefits him first, and the nation second. I am merely a small cog in some gigantic creation of his worst imaginings." She held up her hand. "I don't want to be involved. I want him to forget about me."

Even as she said the words, she wondered if she still meant them. Imagining a future without him suddenly seemed drab and pointless. He was the only person in the world who made her feel alive and passionate and . . .

"He feels responsible for you."

"He's a romantic fool. He always has been." Malinda sighed. "That's why he married me in the first place, although his father soon put a stop to that."

"So Benedict said. Do you no longer consider him your husband, then?"

"I was told the marriage was incestuous." She smiled. "I knew Benedict was his father's heir, but it never seemed important until the marquis spelled out exactly how I would ruin his son's life if I persisted in hanging on to him. I was seventeen and in love, and even then I knew I could never have him—that I'd never be considered good enough."

"So you didn't fight to stay with him."

"After his father told me he was my father too? No, that was enough to break me completely. Leaving him seemed the only fair thing to do because I knew he *would* fight to keep me, and that I was weak enough to let him."

"You were both very young."

"And easy to manipulate." Malinda drank her tea. "And this is all very much in the past, and not relevant to the situation today."

"I wonder if that's ever true? In my experience, the past always rises up when you least expect it."

"As poor Benedict discovered when I shot him."

"May I ask you something else?"

"Why not?" She wasn't telling Faith anything that Benedict didn't already know.

"Benedict asked me to take you out in society a little and present you as his wife. Would that distress you?"

"He says it will keep me safe—that as a peer's wife I'd be much more visible and harder to kill."

"He does have a point. But I refuse to do something you'll hate."

"If spending two weeks pretending to be Benedict's wife will allay his fears about his father, and allow me to go home at the end of it, then I suppose it's worth it."

It would also give her the opportunity to follow up on some investigations of her own.

Faith clapped her hands together. "Excellent. Now perhaps it's time to turn our attention to those fripperies I mentioned. Would you like to come out and visit my modiste?"

Benedict unclenched his fingers and rubbed his right wrist to try to ease the cramp. He'd been writing letters for at least four hours, and he wasn't even halfway through his correspondence. His concentration was scattered as he wondered how Malinda was fairing with Lady Westbrook and whether she'd missed his presence in her bed. He'd missed her, had woken far too many times and reached for her only to discover he was alone.

But he had to stop thinking with his cock and use his brain. A knock on the door made him look up as Maddon came into the room.

"I have a Mr. Maclean here to see you, my lord. Do you wish to speak with him?"

"Yes, please, send him in."

"I also have a message from Mr. Fisher. He would like you to meet him at the Queen's Head in Holborn."

"When?"

"Whenever it is convenient."

"Which usually means immediately," Benedict muttered. He stretched his shoulders. "I'll walk over there after I've finished with Mr. Maclean. If anyone asks for me, I'll return within an hour or so."

"Yes, my lord." Maddon bowed.

He came back within minutes with a tall man with auburn hair who instantly reminded Benedict of Malinda. Despite his comparative youth, his visitor walked with a cane, and had a pronounced limp.

"Lord Keyes."

Benedict gestured at the chair in front of his desk. "Good morning, Mr. Maclean, and thank you for replying to my letter so promptly. Please sit down."

"Thank you, my lord. I hoped that a man seeking a secretary would appreciate being attended to promptly."

There was a hint of Scotland in Mr. Maclean's low-pitched voice, as well as an edge of good humor.

"You were recommended to me by Mr. Adam Fisher. How do you know him?"

"Mr. Fisher is a . . . friend of my younger brother, Harry. I believe they were at school together."

There was a slight hesitation in Mr. Maclean's reply that Benedict couldn't fail to notice.

"Are you surprised that Mr. Fisher recommended you?"

He smiled. "To be honest, yes. I didn't think he and my brother were on very good terms these days. But it is to Mr. Fisher's credit that he didn't allow that to influence his endorsement. I, for one, appreciate it."

"I understand you were in the military, Mr. Maclean?"

"Yes, I was invalided out after the peninsular campaign."

"And what made you decide to take the position of a gentleman's secretary?"

Mr. Maclean's smile was wry. "Lack of funds, my lord. The English Crown beggared my family estate after the last Stuart risings, and my father's gambling finished it off. I had to find a way to support my mother and my siblings."

"Which was highly commendable of you."

He shrugged. "I never saw it as a choice. We abandoned the castle and made our home in one of the cottages on the estate. It is far cheaper to run, and we do very well there on my salary and my mother's pension."

"I should imagine." Benedict sat back. "Do you harbor any ill will toward the English for the state your family was reduced to?"

"You mean, am I likely to abscond with all your secrets to France? No, my family had a genius for picking the wrong sides in every conflict, even the internal Scottish ones. I don't blame anyone but ourselves."

"I deal with very complex matters of state, Mr. Maclean. I need someone who is completely trustworthy to work for me."

"I understand that, my lord." Mr. Maclean raised his gaze to meet Benedict's. "All I can say is that I will be the best damned secretary you have ever had."

Benedict held his gaze. "I'll need to see your references, and speak to Mr. Fisher."

"Of course, my lord." Mr. Maclean handed over a bundle of letters. "I have letters of recommendation for you here, and the addresses of all my previous employers so that you can contact them yourself."

"Thank you, Mr. Maclean."

"You're welcome, my lord." His potential employee rose and bowed. "Thank you for seeing me."

Benedict stood and held out his hand, saw the flicker of surprise in Mr. Maclean's green eyes before he shook it. "I will be in contact with you shortly."

"Thank you."

As if by magic, Maddon appeared at the door and looked inquiringly at Benedict. "Shall I see Mr. Maclean out, my lord?"

"Yes, please."

Even though he knew Adam was waiting for him, he took a moment to peruse the references Maclean had brought with him and raised his eyebrows. There was no reason to worry about his potential secretary's ability to keep a secret. He'd worked with two former members of the government and a retired general. The general had recently died, leaving his secretary to seek a new position.

For some reason, Benedict felt that Mr. Maclean would suit him perfectly. He'd have to check with Adam first, though. He didn't wish there to be tension between the two men. He had a suspicion that the younger Maclean had been more than an old school friend to Adam.

Maddon returned and Benedict abandoned his desk and walked toward him.

"Have you heard from Lady Westbrook?"

"I understand she went out to visit Lady Benedict Keyes at your other address."

"And she hasn't returned yet?"

"Not as far as I know, sir. Do you wish to be informed when she does?"

"No, I'm sure she'll come and find me if she has anything to say." He accompanied Maddon out into the kitchens, recovered his hat, gloves, and heavier coat, and headed out into the brisk morning sunlight.

It didn't take long to reach the Queen's Head and discover Adam tucked away in one of the private rooms enjoying a tankard of ale and a large breakfast.

"Good morning, Benedict." Adam gestured at the groaning table. "Help yourself. You look exhausted."

"I missed a lot of work. I'm still trying to catch up." Benedict picked up a plate. "I just interviewed a potential secretary, a Mr. Maclean."

Adam put his tankard down. "Which one? The elder son, Alistair, has an ancient Scottish title that he doesn't use, and the younger, Harry, is an acquaintance of mine."

"So the elder Mr. Maclean told me." Benedict observed his partner carefully. "Would it trouble you if I employed Alistair Maclean? I liked him."

"He would make an exemplary secretary, and one I heartily recommend to you, even though his brother has proven . . . less satisfactory in many ways."

There was an unusual hint of reserve in Adam's voice.

"I won't employ him if it means you are brought into contact with a family you are at odds with."

Adam sighed. "We're not at odds. Harry has just . . . moved on to other things. It's not an issue, Benedict, and certainly unlikely to cause me any problems at the Sinners."

"You're sure about that?"

"Yes." Adam smiled and refilled his tankard. "Now, how is your lovely wife?"

"My wife is currently with Lady Westbrook."

"I can't imagine a more dangerous pair. But you never know, Lady Westbrook might be more successful at finding out the truth than you or I could ever be."

Benedict filled his plate and realized he was starving. "I assume the earl told you everything."

"He did." Adam hesitated. "I don't think your wife was involved in the robbery either."

"Thanks for that." Benedict sat down and concentrated on eating.

Adam refilled his plate and sat opposite him. "Then what's your plan?"

"I'm supposed to have a plan?"

"You usually do."

"But I've never had to investigate my father and my wife before."

"If it is too personal, I'm quite prepared to deal with it for you."

Benedict pointed his knife at Adam. "Thank you, but you are not to go anywhere near my wife."

"Did I offend her in some way?"

"No. She rather liked you."

Adam's smile was full of satisfaction. "I knew she was a woman after my own heart."

"And she's my wife."

"She doesn't even seem to agree with you about that."

"She doesn't agree with me about anything on principle. It is her life's purpose to make my life as difficult as possible."

Adam grinned. "She really does have you in a tangle, doesn't she?"

Benedict took refuge in his ale and finished his food. "Lady Westbrook is going to take her under her wing and introduce her into society. Hopefully if someone *is* interested in her, it will draw him or her out."

"Does your wife know about this?"

"She keeps telling me that the danger stems solely from my father, and is willing to go along with my request that she stay in London until I can escort her to Lincolnshire."

Adam drained his tankard. "I don't believe that for a second."

Benedict sighed. "Neither do I. She's like my father; she *never* does what I ask her. She never has."

"At least you know that."

"True. Can you find out about the other men who died in that ambush? I'm also interested in any member of the regiment who left the army and suddenly came into wealth."

"I'll check, but it will be difficult because of the time that has passed."

"Someone must have benefited from stealing that payroll, someone who knew exactly when and where to stage that ambush." Benedict pushed his plate away. "It's a shame that Malinda's mother died. She was a great one for gossip, and knew everything that went on in our camp, sometimes even before the participants themselves."

"Did she stay with the army after Malinda left?"

"In a fashion. She quickly remarried a man she'd known for many years. He'd just bought a promotion, so she followed him into his new regiment. She reunited with Malinda and she had another child, Doris, whom I also met at Alford Park. When the fighting grew more intense, she boarded Malinda and the baby at one of the French nunneries. They were quite safe throughout the rest of the war."

"So you kept track of her, then?"

"Of Malinda?" He shrugged. "When I had the resources to do so, of course I did."

"Even though your father said she'd married you for your money, and she left you?"

"Yes."

Adam shook his head. "I damn well hope she isn't involved in all this."

"Why?"

"Because I think it would break you."

"I doubt it." He managed to laugh. "I survived her betrayal at eighteen, and it taught me an important lesson about trusting anyone. I told you Malinda's mother died last year, didn't I?"

"Yes."

"And very soon after that, my wife started her preparations to come to England. What did she find out that made her decide to defy my father and come home? What else could her mother have told her?"

"The identities of the ambushers?"

"I'm not sure she'd know them." Benedict rose to his feet and started pacing. "It has to be something—something that made Malinda reassess the past and realize she had to confront it. That would be just like her."

"Then why didn't she tell you the whole story?"

"I don't know, but I'm going to do my damnedest to find out."

11

Malinda gave a happy sigh as she surveyed all the boxes and bags filled with her new clothes, hats, and slippers. The cost of all the items put together would surely send Benedict around to Maddox Street in a rage, and then she could sweetly remind him that he'd insisted he could afford it. Her smile disappeared. But he probably wasn't coming back. Having set Lady Westbrook on her, he'd probably think his responsibilities were at an end.

She picked up one of the new day dresses and held it against her. But wasn't his absence a good thing? It meant she could pursue her grudge against his father without him being present or involved. She shouldn't be feeling guilty for deceiving him when it was in his own best interests not to know what she suspected his father had done. She'd thought about the problem long and hard, and couldn't see another way around it. She'd needed him to gain access to his father but that was now accomplished. How could she expect him to believe her suspicions when she only had the minimum of proof? Even as a child, Benedict had hated conjecture and always wanted the facts.

If only she could force his father to confess to her. . . .

But how? He would laugh in her face.

There had to be a way, and she had very little time to achieve her aim before either the marquis took action against her or Benedict worked out what she was up to. And he would. She'd never been able to keep anything from him for long. Her gaze fell on the bedside table, and she considered the objects she'd found in the drawers—the jade phalluses, the silken cords, and other things she couldn't quite identify but was sure Benedict knew exactly what to do with for each and every piece. . . .

A knock on the outside door heralded the arrival of Jason with a folded sheet of paper for her.

"Message for you, my lady."

"Thank you, Jason. Will you wait a moment to see if I need to reply?"

He sat himself down by the fire and warmed his hands while she read the short note.

Regret I will be unable to join you for dinner tonight due to pressure of work. I remain, as always your faithful servant, Benedict, Lord Keyes.

This would be the third night he'd stayed away. With a snarl she screwed the note up into a ball and threw it in the direction of the fire. Jason ducked to avoid the missile hitting him on the head.

"What's wrong, my lady?"

"Your master is an inconsiderate pig."

Jason frowned. "What's he gone and done now?"

"He—" Malinda stared at the boy. "Jason, would you be willing to help me out with a little experiment?"

"What's that mean?"

"It's for a game I'd like to beat Lord Keyes at."

"Oh."

"I'd pay you for your trouble."

He jumped up. "What exactly do you want me to do?"

She nodded at the hallway. "You know that man out there?"

"Mr. Niall, you mean?"

"Do you think you could distract him long enough for me to get out of the house?"

"Why would you want to do that?"

"Just to see if I can. I promise I'll come back, and I won't tell anyone what you did to help me."

He folded his arms across his chest. "It sounds like a silly thing to do to me. Who will look after you when you're on the streets? It's dangerous out there at night for a lady. And I can't lie to Lord Keyes. My mum would kill me."

She stared at her ten-year-old inquisitor and sighed. "I suppose you're right."

"Why can't you just ask Mr. Niall to take you where you want to go?"

"Because he probably won't do it."

"But if you don't *ask* him, and simply start out the door, he'll have to come after you, won't he?"

His startling example of childish logic made her smile. "You're right."

"Then you don't need me, do you?"

She kissed the top of his head and he squirmed away, his cheeks red, and ran for the door.

It didn't take her long to change into one of her new gowns, fill her reticule, and return to the door. With a calm smile she started down the stairs.

"Good evening, Niall."

"My lady, what—"

She was almost at the bottom of the stairs when she heard

him start down them, calling her name, and was on the pavement outside before he finally caught up with her.

"My lady, you . . ." He was breathing hard.

"I'm going out, Niall. You can come with me, or you can go back inside." As he showed no signs of moving, she continued, "Do you want to call a hackney, or shall we walk?"

Niall escorted her to the back of the Sinners and knocked until one of the staff came to unlock the door and let them inside. Malinda put on her sweetest smile and looked up at the surprised footman.

"It's James, isn't it?" She lowered her voice. "Can you help me get upstairs to my husband's bedchamber without being seen by anyone else?" She gave him a brief glimpse of the note in Benedict's handwriting she'd retrieved and uncrumpled from the floor. "He said I should be *discreet*."

James went red but nodded manfully. "Yes, my lady. You can use the backstairs."

"Thank you."

She followed him up several flights of steep, narrow stairs and emerged puffing on a small landing that contained three other doors.

"This is Lord Keyes's apartment, my lady."

"Is he there?"

"I believe he's still working, my lady. Do you want me to let him know you've arrived?"

"Oh no, I don't wish to disturb him. I'll wait for him to come upstairs." She nodded at the door. "Can you let me in? I don't have my key."

"Certainly, my lady."

Moments later she was on the other side of the door, and let out a quiet sigh of satisfaction. Niall was safely in the kitchen, and Benedict was trapped in his study. She had time to search the apartment to make certain he wasn't concealing anything important from her and mayhap play a little trick on him as well. . . .

After two hours of looking, she'd found out nothing of any importance except that Benedict liked to read, and had a wardrobe of extremely well-made clothes and polished boots, which were fashionable but not ostentatious or showy at all. She sank down on the side of the large bed and kicked off her shoes.

Would it be better to simply leave before he knew she'd even been there? She shook her head. Niall's presence in the kitchen would draw comment, and Benedict would know something was up. She didn't want to draw his attention in the wrong way. It would be much better if she could go on convincing him that she was simply too besotted to leave him alone and was happy to leave all other matters in his capable hands. With that thought, she opened up her reticule and started to unpack.

"Here you are, sir."

Benedict looked up to see James bending over him, with a tray holding a pot of fresh coffee in his gloved hands.

"Thank you."

James put the tray down and hesitated. "Mr. Maddon said to tell you that it is getting late, my lord."

"So?"

"And that you shouldn't strain yourself."

Benedict unconsciously eased his throbbing shoulder. "I think it's too late for that."

"Then perhaps, my lord, you should stop for the night and, well . . ."

"And, well, what?" He could've sworn James winked at him.

"You know, sir." James definitely winked. "Your lady." He raised his eyebrows heavenward.

"Thank you, James. That will be all."

Before the door even closed behind the footman, Benedict

gulped down an entire cup of scalding coffee and shot to his feet. Even the mention of his wife made him nervous, and he had no idea what James was angling at. He refilled his cup and went out into the hallway. Everything seemed to be running normally, so he went down to the kitchens, only to be brought up short by the sight of Niall sitting at the table.

"What are you doing here?" Benedict demanded.

Niall rose to his feet. "Her ladyship went out."

"She did *what?*"

"She walked right past me all ready to go, so I grabbed my hat and followed her."

Benedict was aware of a sense of relief washing over him. "You did the right thing. Thank you."

Niall looked relieved. "She said she wanted to come here. I didn't think there could be any harm in that."

Poor sweet, deluded Niall. Benedict clapped the other man on the shoulder. "You did exactly as I would've wished. Where is she now?"

"I believe James took her upstairs, my lord."

"Then you continue to wait here, and when I've seen her, I'll bring her back down so you can escort her home."

"Yes, my lord." Niall sat down again.

Benedict finished his coffee and left the cup on the table. He turned on his heel and climbed up to the third-floor apartments, surprised there wasn't fire shooting out of his nostrils. Why couldn't she stay put? Why did she have to hound him like this?

He opened the door and went through into the living area, but there was no sign of her. His bedroom door was open, so he kept moving.

"Ah, there you are, Benedict."

He halted at the door and glared at his wife.

"What are you doing here? Didn't you get my note?"

She turned around and smiled at him. She wore a fashionable gown made in green silk with an extremely low bodice. "I did, thank you." She looked beautiful.

"Then what in God's name do you want?"

"I was worried about you."

"I'm perfectly fine."

She bit her lower lip and eyed him consideringly. "You look terrible."

"Thank you. As I said, I am extremely busy because you shot me and tied me to a bed for three weeks."

"I do wish you'd stop going on about that. I've explained what happened on several occasions. There is no need to bear a grudge."

He stared at her for a full minute as he fought to regain his temper. No one else in the world enraged him so quickly or so completely as Malinda. But she knew that, so what was she really after?

"I repeat. How may I assist you?"

"As I said, I was worried about you, alone in this place with no one to give you . . . comfort."

"By comfort, do you mean sex?"

She fluttered her eyelashes at him. "That is part of it."

"I told you. I can go downstairs and get that in an instant, or stroll around the corner to the Delornay pleasure house and get even more."

"Oh." She looked as if she might cry. "Then I suppose my journey was wasted." She turned away and bent to pick up her shoes.

He forced himself to speak. "I'm not bedding you, Malinda."

"I don't believe I asked you to."

"Why else would you be here?" He tried to soften his tone. "You must realize it would be a mistake for us to be too close at the moment."

She stiffened, her color high, and looked him right in the eye. "Please listen carefully. I am not a fool. I did not come here tonight to beg you to take me to bed. I was concerned that you might be missing your 'toys' and brought them to you, that is all."

"What toys?"

She moved to one side and pointed to the objects lined up neatly on the bed. "These."

As if in a trance, he walked over to the bed and opened the first box, which contained jade phalluses. A silk bag contained soft rope and scarves, and another smaller box held a set of silver cock rings.

"What exactly do you *do* with the rings?" Malinda spoke close to his ear, making him jump. She was incorrigible. She turned his brain to mush and made other parts of him as hard as steel. And she bloody well knew it. He was too tired to even fight with her. Perhaps it was time to call her bluff.

"Would you like me to show you?" He started to pull off his coat and tugged at his cravat until he was able to throw it to the floor. "My only condition is that you sit in that chair by the fire, and you do not move one damned inch unless I tell you to."

She sat down so quickly her petticoats rustled, and placed her hands in her lap.

He finished undressing and climbed up onto the bed, retrieved a bottle of oil from the bedside cabinet, and set it beside the other pleasure toys. Ignoring them for a moment, he faced Malinda and slowly ran his hands over his chest, down to his hips, and over his flat stomach. He repeated the motion, soothing his skin, petting himself, pinching his nipples between his finger and thumb until they ached and stayed hard.

He licked his fingers and touched his nipples again. She licked her lips and he pictured them hovering over his cock. Still holding her gaze, he cupped his balls and stroked himself until a thin bead of pre-cum emerged from his cock. He rubbed his thumb into the wetness, creating more, until his fingers were slick with it, and his shaft moved more easily through the clasp of his hand. She shivered and he smiled at her.

"How kind of you to bring me these gifts. How noble and self-sacrificing of you."

"It was the least I could do." She tensed as he got off the bed and walked toward her, one hand concealed behind his back.

"Normally the scarves would be to hold me in place for another man to fuck me, but tonight I think I'll use them to restrain you." Before she could react, he wound one of the silk scarves around her right wrist and trapped her hand against the arm of the chair. He did the same to her left hand and then considered her mouth.

"I could gag you, but then I wouldn't be able to do this." He rubbed his sticky cum-laden fingers over her lips and she moaned something that might have been his name. He pressed his thumb into her mouth, mimicking the motion of his cock, and she sucked on him until he pulled free and returned to the bed, his shaft thickening with every second. Picking up the silver cock rings, he brought them back to show her.

"This is quite a complex pair. Some have no hinges, and the rings have to be put on before one's cock becomes too large." He unclipped the larger center ring and showed it to her before easing it around the base of his erection and fastening it. "I had these made to fit me."

He eased his balls through the smaller rings and let out his breath as the metal bit into his most tender flesh. His balls were now pulled up tight against his cock and his shaft was held away from his stomach by the thickness of the band. He stroked a finger through the gathering wetness and trailed it down his cock to the soft skin behind his balls.

"Does it hurt?" Malinda whispered.

"A little, but it is the pleasurable kind of hurt that you soon forget." He touched himself and shivered. "The bands prevent me from coming too soon and heighten my gratification."

He returned to pick up the bottle of oil and considered where best to display himself to her. He'd originally thought to stay on the bed, but he had a sudden urge to make it more close and personal. What would Ben the prostitute have done? He smiled.

"Sit back." He gently pushed on her shoulders until she sank into the chair, her bosom heaving with indignation, her breathing short, and her hands fisted against the silken bonds.

He stood in front of her and placed his left foot on the arm of her chair, perilously close to her hand, and eased his knee and thigh out to the side. Uncorking the oil, he anointed his finger and then placed the bottle between her breasts. Holding her gaze, he ran his finger down between his balls and stroked the skin behind them, back and forth, his fingertip moving ever closer to the pucker of his arse.

He added more oil, now warm from being cradled between her breasts, and played with his hole, rimming the skin, dipping inside until his cock started to ache and his hips angled forward wanting more. Her gaze had dropped to his groin and to what he was doing to himself. He pushed his finger deeper and worked it in and out in a slow regular motion that made him moan.

Eventually he had three fingers in himself, and every time he thrust them deep, his cock was pushed closer to her face.

"Do you like this?"

"Yes."

"Do you wish you could touch me? What a shame you can't."

She jerked forward and stuck out her tongue just catching the tip of his crown. He instantly moved away. "Perhaps I should gag you after all."

She snarled at him and he smiled. "Remember, you brought me the toys, not yourself."

He selected one of the jade phalluses and brought the whole box over and placed them on the floor. "I've picked the second biggest one. As you might imagine, I need to ready myself before I can fit something of this size and rigidity inside of me."

With the phallus in hand, he resumed his position and took a long time oiling the jade to his satisfaction. She was quiet now, her attention entirely focused on what he was about to do to himself. And he wanted her to see him fuck himself very badly, wanted her to understand that he didn't need anyone else in his bed at all.

He concentrated on letting out his breath as he broached his hole with the tapering head of the jade and eased it inside the tight ring of muscle. Forcing himself to keep breathing, he inched it farther in, the rough stone gripping onto his flesh, reluctant to let it go. It was like being fucked raw. But he was wet enough, and eventually he prevailed and the phallus slid home. He took a few moments to accustom himself to the feeling of being stuffed full, the throbbing tenderness of his stretched muscles, and the answering throb of excitement in his trapped cock.

Opening his eyes, he stared at Malinda, who was breathing as hard as he was.

"Do you want to watch me fuck myself on this phallus?"

"Oh, God, yes."

He braced himself and began moving his hand, bringing the jade in and out of his arse, each stroke as long as he could make it without the phallus coming out completely. And God, it was good, made even better by having Malinda watch.

"Are you wet for me?" he demanded hoarsely. "Do you wish you had your fingers stuffed in your cunt?"

She moaned and shifted restlessly in her seat, and he wanted to throw back her skirts and expose her to his gaze, to see all that wet welcome just for him. His balls tightened even more and he knew he was close. He wrapped one hand around his

cock and worked himself hard, ramming the jade deep and holding it there as he climaxed in long, shuddering waves of come.

When he could eventually breathe again, he smiled at her.

"You see? I don't really need to go anywhere. I'm perfectly
capable of pleasuring myself."

Malinda stared up at his smiling face and itched to slap him
so badly she had to dig her fingernails into her palms.

"It isn't anything to be proud of. All it means is that you
want to be in control of *everything*. It's what I'd expect of you."

Ignoring her, he eased the phallus out, laid it on the rug, and
set to work on the cock ring.

"All it *means,* Benedict, is that you're too afraid of having a
proper relationship."

He straightened up, his smile dying. "You are assuming I'd
know what a proper relationship is after being tied up with you."

"I make you lose control and you hate it."

He angled his head to one side and considered her, his blond
hair gleaming angelically in the candlelight, his blue eyes freezing.

"I'm definitely in control now. You're the one who's tied to
the chair."

"Then let me go. I think I've seen enough anyway." She
yawned. "I'm quite ready to return to Maddox Street and
sleep."

"There is the small matter of you trying to escape Niall and
rushing out into the night."

"Don't be ridiculous. I knew he'd follow me."

"And what if you'd been taken in those vital seconds when
he wasn't at your side?"

She raised her chin. "I would've thought you'd be quite glad
to have me taken off your hands."

"Well, there is that, but then you would present a danger
for me."

"Don't worry, I'd assure anyone who captured me that you would have no interest in having me back and that they should do away with me immediately." She tugged at the scarves. "Now, will you let me go?"

"But what will happen the next time you get it into your head that you have to go out without telling Niall?" He rubbed a casual hand over the faint golden stubble on his jawline. "What will prevent you repeating the same mistake again?"

She narrowed her eyes and thought lovingly of her shotgun at Alford Park.

"As your husband, I feel it is my duty to correct your behavior, don't you?"

He untied the scarf on her left wrist and she tried to punch him. He caught her fist and held on to it while he untied her other hand and then held them both in one easy grip. She kicked out at his shins but was hampered by her skirts.

"Don't you dare—" she gasped as she was picked up off her feet, swung around, and ended up over his lap with him now sitting in the chair. She tried to roll over, but he widened his stance and held her firm. The pins in her hair started to fall out onto the carpet, and she wriggled like a worm on a hook.

He rucked up her skirts and petticoats leaving her bottom bare to the elements. She went still when he laid one large, warm palm on her buttock.

"I've been wanting to put you over my knee since I woke up in that damned bed at Alford Park and finally realized who you were." His tone was light and conversational. "And, by God, I don't think anyone would deny I have the right."

"I do!"

He smacked her and she went rigid.

"That's better."

He smacked her again and this time it hurt. She bucked against him but it made no difference, she was trapped. She set herself to endure, but it was impossible as red-hot needles of pain skittered across her consciousness. His hand pressed down on her lower back.

"Be still."

She bit down on her lower lip as his fingers moved between her thighs, making a leisurely exploration of her sex.

"I knew you'd be wet for me." He penetrated her with one finger, and slid it easily in and out of her slick cunt. "Christ . . ." He dragged the wetness back, and eased his thumb into her arse. The only sound now was their ragged breathing and the wet slick of his working fingers.

She wasn't prepared for the quick smack of his palm on her already sensitive buttocks, or the way each stroke pushed her down onto his embedded fingers. Pain melted into something else, something dark and dangerous that she didn't want, but couldn't turn away from. She closed her eyes to let it overtake her, forgetting her outrage and the indignity of her position in pursuit of the sensation.

Lighter slaps now, but she was moving with him, not against him, her body no longer fighting him, but urging him on with every roll of her hips. Her climax hit her like a whirlwind, making her cry out and simply exist through the myriad of physical and emotional sensations.

With a savage sound he came down with her onto the rug in front of the fire, his fingers still inside her, his mouth now on hers as he kissed her.

"Don't fight me." He kneed her legs farther apart, and then she felt the cold slide of jade against her sex as he filled her with one of the phalluses from the box. He didn't stop there, but slid his oiled fingers inside her arsehole and then inserted the other piece of jade. She was coming before he'd finished sliding the second piece home.

And then he was moving again, reversing his position so that his cock was over her mouth, feeding it to her as he bent his head to her sex, his fingers busy on the phalluses, his tongue on her clit.

She had no more breath to think, just to experience the wholly physical sensation of being filled to bursting at his direction. His cock throbbed in her mouth, pushing farther down her throat as he increased the pace of his thrusts. She simply took him as he was taking her, owning every inch of her sex with his mouth and his hands. Would she survive the onslaught? Could she? With a muffled shout he climaxed and she swallowed everything he pumped into her as she came herself.

Benedict opened his eyes and carefully withdrew his cock from Malinda's mouth. He looked down at her. Her hair had escaped its pins and tumbled around her shoulders, her dress was rucked up to her waist, and, God, she still had the two jade phalluses inside her. She'd never looked more beautiful or more infuriating to him.

She slowly blinked at him. "You've ruined my new dress."

He bent to pick her up and deposited her on the side of his bed. Without asking for permission, he stripped her out of the crumpled garment and her corset and shift. He made the mistake of pausing to actually look at what he'd revealed and his heart nearly stopped. Stockings, garters, and nothing else but jade . . .

He placed his hands on either side of her flanks and kissed her breasts, licking and sucking her nipples into his mouth. She sighed and put her hand into his hair, her body languid and supple, moving into his as though she belonged there. He forced himself to stop kissing her and knelt to remove the jade from her cunt and her arse. She raised her hips slightly to help him, her breath hissing out as he finished the task. And then he just stared at her cunt, the swollen lips of her sex, the proud throb of her clit, and the wetness that enticed him to lean in and . . .

With an oath, he stood up. "You are the devil."

"I am sore."

"You deserve it."

She glared at him. "The toys were for you, not for me."

"I didn't notice you telling me to stop." He kissed her hard, nipping at her lower lip. "All I noticed was you coming hard and begging me for more."

She bit him back. "I did not beg!"

"You whimpered."

"So did you!"

"Men do not whimper." He was so close now he could see the flashes of green in her hazel eyes. "I was merely enjoying watching you squirm on my lap."

"And now I won't be able to sit down for a week!"

"Exactly my intention."

"You're a brute!"

He slid his cock inside her and started fucking her. "I know."

At the last moment possible, he pulled out and came against her belly, his face buried in the curve of her neck, his teeth grazing her throat.

"Do you want to go back to Maddox Street?"

"I want—"

"I think I know." He pulled away and studied her face. "I have the very thing."

She splayed her fingers against his chest. "Benedict, if you touch me again, I'll scream."

"And you think that will deter me? Wait here."

She fell back against the bed. "As if I can move at all . . ."

He went back into the living room and through the door into the shared bathroom. There was no one there, so he checked that the boiler had hot water and started to fill the bath. It was a newfangled invention, but one that he and Adam appreciated enormously. Being able to bathe without having to wait for the water to be boiled over the fire and brought up by the poor servants was a luxury he never failed to appreciate.

"Come on."

He scooped Malinda up in his arms, carried her into the bathroom, and set her down on the chair by the fire where he'd also spread the drying cloths to warm.

Returning his attention to the water, he checked the temperature, found a jar of soap and a natural sea sponge, and put them beside the bath. For once, his wife didn't question him as he picked her up again, stepped carefully over the side of the bath, and lowered them both into the warm water.

"Ah," he murmured, stretching out until his back rested against the head of the bath. "That's better."

He reached for the soap and the sponge and spent an enjoyable few minutes making sure Malinda was scrubbed clean. To his surprise, she didn't object and submitted to his ministrations with a quietness that eventually started to worry him.

"Are you all right?"

She blinked at him, and he carefully washed her face. His cock stirred against the curve of her arse and he winced.

"You're right, you know."

He paused, the sponge held in his hand. "I'm right about something? Are you sure?" He washed behind her ear, aware that the ends of her hair were now wet and had darkened to the color of mahogany.

"We shouldn't do this." She swallowed hard. "I shouldn't have come. I was just annoyed because you'd kept away from me."

He sighed. "And I should've sent you away instead of allowing you to provoke me."

She touched his cheek. "I don't want you to worry about me so much. Perhaps it would be better if I simply left for Alford Park."

His gut tightened. "I've already explained why I think that would be a bad idea."

"But I don't want you to be involved with any trouble between me and your father."

He frowned. "Do you really think he has the power to harm you? He's an old, sick man."

"He's . . ." She hesitated. "He's still your father, and even though you are estranged at present, blood is thicker than water."

"You think I'll eventually side with him against you?"

"You might have no choice."

"What are you planning?" He picked her up, displacing half the water, and turned her to face him.

"I'm not planning anything. How could I when you have Lady Westbrook and Niall monitor my every move?"

"Because I know you, and I know you are a tenacious creature who never gives up and can't be trusted."

"I am completely trustworthy!" she snapped.

"Not with me." He touched her cheek. "Did you expect me to come after you, when you told me to my face that you didn't love me and that our marriage had been a mistake?"

"You have it all the wrong way around. I told you that to make sure you didn't follow me. I thought we were *siblings*."

"So what is it? Perhaps you are the one who needs to let go of the past. Why can't you trust me now?"

Her smile made his heart hurt. "Because I know *you*, and I have to sort this out by myself."

"So there is something you're not telling me."

She put her hand over his mouth. "Stop this. Why can't we enjoy what we have?"

He bit her hard. "And just fuck each other?" He stood up and dumped her back into the bathwater, creating an almighty splash. "Why not? I'll go and tell Niall you're staying the night. I'm sure we can get in a few more tumbles before morning." He nodded at the fireplace. "There are warm towels over there."

He wrapped one of the towels around his waist and left the

bathroom before he either strangled her or got down on his knees and begged her to tell him what was going on. How *dare* she not trust him? He was one of the premier spymasters in England; thousands of people owed their lives to his integrity and ability to detect the traitors amongst them.

But, of course, Malinda wouldn't care about that. To her, he was always his stupid eighteen-year-old self.

"Benedict."

He turned and she was standing in the door, a towel clutched to her bosom. Her wet hair was over one shoulder. She reminded him of some exotic goddess with her endless legs and delicate bone structure.

"You aren't being fair."

"I'm simply trying to keep you alive and work out what is going on."

"Which is very kind of you, but quite unnecessary."

"It is necessary, I—"

She held up her hand. "If it truly is important to you, it begs the question of what you aren't telling me. Isn't it true that I'm not the only one keeping secrets, Benedict?"

"If I am forced to keep anything from you, it is because of the security of this nation."

"Which means there is something you're not telling *me*."

He slowly exhaled. "You're talking in circles."

"And you're not?" She walked toward the bedroom. "When you want to tell me the *truth,* Benedict, when you choose to value *me* more than your blasted country, then perhaps I'll be more inclined to be open with you."

Before he could answer, she slammed the bedroom door so hard behind her that it shook.

He contemplated following her and putting her over his knee again, but resisted. He'd actually gained some information. She was up to something, and it definitely concerned his father. Was she still aggrieved by his treatment of her all those years ago, or was there more? He had to remember that her father had *died* in that ambush, and that she might have seen the perpetrators. He also knew that *his* father had been in his tent all that day and evening, entertaining other officers from surrounding regiments. She couldn't have seen the marquis—could she?

12

Malinda woke up to the rattle of a maid pulling back the curtains and offering her breakfast in bed. There was no sign of Benedict, but she'd hardly expected to see him after he'd left in a huff the night before. She felt a twinge of remorse for using his own honorable nature against him and accusing him of putting his nation before her. But she'd achieved her aim and gotten away from him before she gave any more information away.

Once he thought about it, he'd realize what she'd done, and he wouldn't be happy. But she did have a point. He was obviously after *something* and hadn't bothered to tell her what it was. At least she had a *reason* for not telling him what she was up to. She was trying to save him.

After she'd eaten her breakfast, the maid returned and helped her into her clothes, miraculously producing a new day dress for her to wear while the other one was cleaned. She went down the backstairs and into the kitchen, hesitating when she saw Benedict sitting at the table reading a newspaper.

"Good morning. Where is Niall?"

Benedict looked at her over the top of the newspaper. "He hasn't come back. I'm going to escort you myself." He folded the paper and stood up. "Are you ready to leave?"

"Yes." She took his proffered arm and walked with him to the back door and out into the mews behind the Sinners. He was back to his usual stuffy self, which suited her perfectly.

It was a bright, crisp morning, and despite her silent companion, Malinda enjoyed the walk until they turned into Maddox Street and Niall came running toward them, his face blackened and the cuffs of his shirt singed.

"My lord!"

Benedict immediately pushed her behind him. "What happened?"

"The house was set on fire," Niall croaked. "Someone threw a burning brand through the upstairs window."

Malinda picked up her skirts and ran toward the smoke-damaged façade. A small crowd of people still stood around the building. Ignoring them, she looked desperately around. She gasped as someone caught her elbow in a hard grip.

"Don't run away from me."

"For God's sake, Benedict, let me go. Where is Jenny?" She tried to pull away from him. "Where are Michael and Jason?"

"They're fine. Niall got them out."

She stared up at him. "Oh, thank God. I—" She turned her face against his shoulder and his arms came around her. "I thought—"

"It's all right." He smoothed his hand over her back. "I'll make sure they aren't inconvenienced by this any more than they have to be."

She pulled away. "This is my fault, isn't it? Someone wanted to harm me."

"Or me." His face was calm, his blue eyes arctic. "It wouldn't be the first time I've been targeted. Jenny and the boys are at the inn at the corner of the street. We'll go and check on their well-being, and then I'll take you back to the Sinners. I know you'll be safe there."

The inn was busy, and it took a while to work their way through the crowd of passengers boarding the mail coach and into the low-set building of the Kings Arms. Benedict insisted that Malinda stay between him and Niall at all times, and for once, she was quite willing to oblige him. The shock of the smoke-damaged building was a stark reminder that all was not well, and that her very presence was endangering those she cared about.

Someone elbowed her in the back, and she stumbled and felt a slip of folded paper slide into her palm. Even as she righted herself with the help of Niall's hand, the crowd shifted again and she was moving into the shelter of the inn. She shoved the paper inside her glove and followed Benedict into a small parlor at the back of the inn where Jenny sat placidly drinking tea while the boys played.

"Oh, Jenny." Malinda rushed to embrace her. "I'm so sorry."

"Don't be silly, my lady. I'm just glad you weren't home!" She smiled up at Niall. "I'm glad Mr. Niall was, though. He got me and the boys out in a twinkling of an eye and then went back to get all the things he thought I'd need."

Niall was blushing and shifting from one foot to another.

"It was nothing, Mrs."

Jenny went over and kissed Niall on the cheek, which made him turn even redder. "You were wonderful."

"And he will be rewarded for his bravery," Benedict added. "Are you truly all right, ma'am?"

"Yes, my lord. The boys were coughing a bit from the smoke, but they both seem fine now."

"I wonder if you would like to leave London for a spell while the house is being restored?" He looked over at Malinda. "I believe you might be welcome at my country house, Alford Park."

Malinda nodded. "She would, indeed, be welcome, as would the boys."

Jenny sat down and lowered her voice. "Do you think it would be safer, sir?"

"I do. I'll hire a carriage, and Niall can escort you."

"Don't be silly, sir. We can go on the mail coach."

"No, I insist. It will be much quicker." He reached into his pocket and took out his purse. "Niall will take you all out to get the tickets, replace your clothes, and get some toys for the boys."

"You don't need to do that either, sir, I've got my savings."

"I don't need to do it, Jenny, but I want to. Consider it as a gift from your grateful government."

"Oh, all right, sir. But I'll pay you back eventually."

Benedict's smile was a thing of beauty. "Thank you, Jenny."

"If you need to go and arrange matters, my lord, I can remain here and write a note to my sister for Jenny to take with her." Malinda paused. "Unless you think I should go with them back to Lincolnshire?"

"I'd still rather you stayed in London." Benedict's gaze rested on her for just a moment too long for comfort. "You may remain with Jenny as long as Niall is with you."

She met his narrowed eyes and exuded trustworthiness. "I'll stay in the inn until you return for me."

He nodded and took off, leaving Jenny to offer Malinda and Niall some tea. After a moment, Malinda excused herself and went to the far end of the parlor where there was a writing desk. She removed her gloves, unfolded the small piece of paper, and read it.

I will be in the best parlor until two o'clock.

After checking the small clock on the mantelpiece for the correct time, Malinda opened the desk drawer, took out a sheet of paper, and found a pen. She concentrated on writing a short letter to Doris and Gwen, asking them to welcome Jenny and the boys. She didn't reveal much else. It was better for Doris not to know anything that might put her in a flutter, but it was hard not to confide in her cousin. She assumed Benedict would expect her to be discreet, and it was in her own best interests to keep everything to herself.

"Niall?"

"Yes, my lady?"

"Can you ask the landlord if he has any sealing wax? There doesn't appear to be any here in the desk."

"Yes, my lady."

While Niall was occupied, Malinda folded the letter and stood up. "I'll just use the necessary, Jenny. Tell Niall I'll be back in a moment."

Jenny was busy adjudicating in a brawl between her two sons and barely nodded, leaving Malinda free to slip out of the room and find her way to the best parlor, Benedict's purloined dagger tucked into the folds of her skirts. She knocked on the door and went in.

The woman sitting by the fire was heavily veiled, but there was no mistaking the gleam of her blond hair. Malinda sank into a curtsy.

"My lady."

She waited as the Marchioness of Alford lifted her veil to reveal her beautiful face and the trembling pout of her small, childish mouth.

"I have a message for you from my husband. He requests your presence at Alford House."

"And how does he expect me to honor his wishes when I am guarded by his son and the Countess of Westbrook?"

"I will send you an invitation to one of my 'at homes' this week. I will keep the countess occupied. You can speak to the marquis then."

"You can't want me in your house, and certainly not cluttering up your public drawing room."

"Unlike you, missy, I do what I am told by my husband, and this is what he wants. I have no idea why he insists on seeing you, and I have no interest in knowing."

Malinda took a step forward.

"Does it bother you that your husband told me that he was my father?"

The marchioness's eyelashes fluttered. "He would never do that."

"He did it to make me leave your son when I was seventeen."

She shrugged. "Needs must."

Malinda shook her head. "Poor Benedict. I would be happy to attend the marquis at your earliest convenience. Good day, my lady."

She removed herself from the room as quickly as possible and went back to find Jenny and Niall. It might be painful to have to agree to do anything her former in-laws wanted, but at least it gave her access to the very man she needed to see and in a way Benedict would never know about if she was careful.

Niall was standing in the doorway looking about him, his expression anxious.

"Oh, there you are, my lady."

Malinda smiled. "Did you find the wax? Thank you so much. Let me just seal up my letter, and we can be on our way."

It was only as she and Jenny shepherded the overexcited boys out into the street that it occurred to her to wonder how the marchioness had known she was at the inn at all.

*   *   *

"This is not acceptable!"

Benedict stared down at Adam, who, since the departure of Jack Lennox, was now restored to his office at the Sinners.

"I agree. How do you suggest we proceed?"

Benedict paced the hearthrug, his hands behind his back. "Tie her up? Shoot her and chain her to a bloody bed, and see how she likes it?"

"Actually, I was thinking more of how we could *protect* her, but I'm willing to listen to any suggestion you think might work." He paused. "I do wish you would sit down. You're wearing a hole in my rather expensive rug."

"I'm not in the mood to sit. Someone tried to kill my wife!"

"But they didn't succeed." Adam remained calm, his gray eyes steady and his posture relaxed. "And *because* they didn't succeed, they are going to have to try much harder next time."

"That's easy for you to say."

"Benedict, this isn't like you. We will utilize all the resources of the Sinners to keep your wife safe. Surely that is enough?"

He took a deep breath. Adam was staring at him as though he were a strange being from another world. And in truth, he was acting like one, but the thought of anyone hurting Malinda . . .

"I'm going to move her in here."

"That's an excellent idea. We'll increase the security around the perimeter and warn all our staff to be on their guard. Do we have any idea what the people who carried out this attack looked like?"

"I doubt it was my father throwing incendiary devices about, do you? Whoever is responsible probably hired some reprobates from the slums to do it for them."

"And if we're very lucky, we'll gather information as to exactly who that was and ask them a few questions."

Benedict took another hasty turn around the office. "Do you think I should confront my father?"

"With no proof of anything?"

"What if he wasn't in his tent all that day and night? What if he was the one who led the assault and Malinda saw him?"

"If she'd known he was the one who'd killed her father at the time, do you think she would've remained quiet about it?"

"No." Benedict sighed and sank into the nearest chair. "She would've gone for him immediately with no thought for her own safety or the consequences. She's always had a terrible temper."

"Then we can probably assume he wasn't actually there."

Benedict forced himself to speak. "But perhaps he orchestrated the whole thing?"

Adam sat forward. "Why would he need to do that? He was already a wealthy man. Why risk everything stealing that gold?"

"Even though the government started to take over the costs and the running of the regiment during the conflict, he'd already incurred heavy expenses." Benedict sighed. "Pure vanity, of course. What man really needs his own private army in this day and age?"

"So he might have considered the payroll his own private compensation."

"Yes."

Adam steepled his fingers and stared at them. "The more important question is whether your wife thinks it is true. Is it possible that something her mother revealed on her deathbed made Malinda believe your father was to blame?"

"It's possible, although I'm damned if I know what it might be."

"If Malinda believes your father is responsible, what will she do?"

"Well, she shot me for simply visiting." He groaned. "Perhaps we have this all the wrong way around and we shouldn't be worrying about who is trying to kill Malinda and worry more about whom she is trying to kill."

Malinda smiled at Lady Westbrook over the breakfast table. The gentlemen were nowhere in sight, and the servants had retreated to the kitchen, leaving the ladies to enjoy a leisurely repast.

"Faith, are you able to accompany me to the dressmaker's this morning?"

"I certainly am. I have a dress to try on myself." The countess took off her spectacles and tidied her vast heap of correspondence into a manageable pile. "Are you ready to go?"

"As soon as I've put on my bonnet."

"Then I'll meet you in the hallway."

Several hours later, the carriage was filled with parcels and the countess was complaining about her sore feet. Malinda was too tense to be tired, but managed to sympathize. As the horses slowed once more, she met Faith's questioning look with a calm smile.

"I hope you don't mind. I have one more call to make. You can stay in the carriage if you don't want to come in with me. I'll be as quick as I can."

The countess sat forward. "Where *are* we?"

"Alford House." Malinda opened the carriage door before the footman reached it. "I promised the marchioness I'd pop in for her 'at home.'"

"Malinda, wait—"

Without heeding her companion, Malinda ran up the steps and was admitted by the same elderly butler she'd seen on her last visit.

"Lady Benedict." He bowed. "A pleasure to see you again. I'll escort you upstairs. Her ladyship is expecting you."

Not pausing to see whether Faith was coming, because Malinda was fairly certain that she would be after her like a hound, she followed the butler up the stairs into the more formal apartments of the mansion.

"Lady Benedict, ma'am."

The marchioness rose and nodded as Malinda curtsied. There were three other ladies in the room and one gentleman, who were all staring at her with some degree of shock. She suspected she and Benedict would be the subject of much society gossip by nightfall.

"Where is Lady Westbrook?"

"She is just coming up the stairs, my lady."

"Then I shall await her arrival." The marchioness walked toward Malinda. As she passed her, she spoke in a low voice, "Take the door in the bookcase at the far end of this room, and you will find yourself in my husband's study."

"Thank you."

Hearing Faith come up the stairs, she picked up her skirts and, smiling graciously at the enthralled guests, went through the false door in the wall and into another room. It was quite different from the cold silver and white of the drawing room. The walls were paneled and the furniture the heavy oak and teak of the previous generation.

"Malinda."

She turned to see the Marquis of Alford sitting in one of the wing chairs by the fire. He had a cover over his knees and a walking stick by the side of his chair. It was strange to see him looking so small and old. In her imagination he was always huge and terrifying.

"Sit down."

She took the seat opposite him and clasped her hands on her lap before looking up at him. His eyes were the same bright blue as Benedict's. How could she have forgotten that?

"Why did you wish to see me, my lord?"

"To straighten out some matters between us without Benedict's interference." He studied her for a long moment. "Considering your parents, you've turned out quite well. You could almost be mistaken for a lady."

She raised her eyebrows at him. "As far as your son is concerned, I'm not only a *lady*, but a viscountess."

A muscle flicked in his wasted jaw. "Why did you come back to England?"

She met his gaze full-on. "To ask you why you killed my father."

"Why have you suddenly decided to confront me with something that happened years ago?"

"Because I have new evidence to support my claim." She paused. "Isn't that why you've been trying to kill me?"

"I haven't."

"I don't believe you."

He sat back. "Tell me what you think you know."

"Why should I?"

"You wanted this meeting as much as I did, my dear. You desperately want to convict me of this crime."

"You know I won't be able to do that officially. You're a peer of the realm and I'm . . . nothing. No one would take me seriously." She paused to gather her composure. "I just want to hear the truth."

He sighed. "I did not arrange that ambush."

"You must have done, my mother—"

"What exactly did she say? That she had suspicions of me? That she *saw* me? For God's sake, girl, ask anyone, ask *Benedict*, I was in my tent all that day and night." He paused and coughed into his handkerchief, the sound hollow. "Whatever your mother thought, I'm not the villain of the piece."

Malinda stood up, her legs trembling. "You aren't going to tell me the truth, are you? You're not capable of it. Dammit, I wish I was a man, and I could call you out."

"In truth, I wish you were a man. I'd much rather have my brains blown out than die like this."

"Everyone dies, my lord."

"Some of us more quickly than others." He stifled another cough. "I'm dying by inches, Malinda. I asked you here because someone *is* threatening your life, and it isn't me."

"Why do you care?"

"Because Benedict is involved. I can't have my heir being caught up in all this nonsense."

She stared down at him, wishing it didn't make a horrible kind of sense. "He doesn't have to be involved. We're no longer married, and I can simply walk away again."

"I don't think he'll let you."

"Maybe he'll have no choice. I managed to avoid him for over eighteen years. I can disappear again." She forced herself to meet his gaze. "I'll even take your money this time."

"Charming."

She spun around to see Benedict leaning against the secret door, his arms crossed over his chest, his expression bland.

"Selling me out again, my dear?"

She flattened her hand against her bosom. "How on earth did you know I was here?"

He came farther into the room and, before she realized his intent, grabbed hold of her and expertly removed the pistol from her pocket and confiscated her knife. Setting her free again, his cold gaze fixed on his father. "Are you still willing to help her, sir? Even though she came prepared to kill you? Why is that? What do you fear?"

"She's the one offering to take my money. I am, however, quite willing to accommodate her desires."

"So I've noticed. If the stick doesn't work, try the carrot."

"Good Lord, Benedict, don't you start." The marquis sounded incredibly weary. "I have no desire to murder your wife."

"What about her father? Did you choose to murder him instead?"

Malinda swung around to face Benedict. "He insists he had nothing to do with that either." She sighed. "And, as I'm fairly certain you will not allow me to force the truth out of him at gunpoint, perhaps we should just leave."

He held up his hand. "One moment, if you please. Why is my father so interested in talking to you if he has nothing to do with anything?"

She met his gaze. "Because he doesn't want you to be harmed. I told him that you are no longer responsible for my behavior, that we aren't married, were barely married in the first place, but—"

"We are married."

"I signed the papers releasing you before I left."

"I know."

"Then—"

His gaze flicked over her. "But I didn't sign anything. I refused, didn't I, Father?"

Malinda looked at the older man, who nodded. "That's the truth. I thought you a fool at the time, Benedict, but recently I have been applauding your foresight."

"What do you mean?"

"As your wife and a member of our illustrious family, she will never have her claims taken seriously, or be allowed to testify against you in court. In fact, if she keeps insisting I killed her father then, as the head of the family, I'll simply have her committed." His triumphant smile was ghastly as he turned his attention to Malinda. "That's what I've been trying to tell you. I don't need to have you done away with, girl. You are bound to us more completely by blood than you ever were before."

She turned and walked out, past her mother-in-law, past the Countess of Westbrook and the assorted visitors, and down into the great hall. She knew at some point that someone, probably Benedict, would stop her, but she couldn't abide the thought of remaining in Alford House for a moment longer. They were still *married*.

She couldn't even think about what that meant. It changed *everything*. She just couldn't. . . . There was something she had to do. She forced herself to concentrate on what was achievable instead.

A man she recognized from the Sinners appeared at her elbow. At least it wasn't Niall, who was on his way to Alford Park with Jenny and the boys. She ignored him and kept going. If he tried to stop her, she would damn well kick and scream and make such a fuss that he'd be forced to unhand her. But he merely kept pace with her, and she could just about bear that.

Maddox Street came into view, and she turned the corner and headed for the smoke-damaged house in the center of the row. Her guard hesitated on the pavement.

"My lady, the house probably isn't safe. Is there something you want in there? If you'll wait here, I'll go and retrieve it for you."

She shook her head and walked around to the back of the building. The kitchen door was open so she went inside. A dank smell of smoke and damp closed around her, and she held her handkerchief to her face. The stairwell was dark but she kept going until she reached the landing. There was no sign of her guard, although she was certain he was close. She went through into the living room, which appeared relatively un-scathed, and spent precious seconds locating the book where she'd hidden her mother's journal and then hiding it in her reticule.

She heard footsteps on the stairs, ran quickly into the bed-room, and pulled up short. Her hand covered her mouth. There was almost nothing left of the furnishings except blackened stumps. All her new clothes and shoes and hats were gone, fuel to the greedy flames that had destroyed half of the upper floor. If she'd been asleep in bed, would she have died surrounded by fire?

She turned, found her companion at the door, and summoned a smile.

"I just wanted to see if any of my new clothes had survived. It seems that everything was destroyed."

"Yes, my lady . . ." He hesitated. "Will you allow me to accompany you back to the Sinners Club now?"

"Certainly." She walked carefully down the stairs and out into the now-trampled vegetable garden behind the house. One of Jason's toy soldiers lay crushed on the path and she bent to pick it up, her throat aching with unshed tears.

"My lady? I have a carriage waiting on the back street."

She clutched the broken soldier to her chest and followed him into the carriage.

13

She should have realized that Benedict would not allow her to go upstairs at the Sinners without seeing him first. She was escorted to his office, which was next to Adam's, by her ever-helpful guard. Benedict sat behind his desk, his blond head bent, busy writing something.

"Sit down, my lady."

She sat because there was nothing else she could do.

"Benedict . . ."

He flicked a cool glance at her. "If you'll just give me a moment."

"But I—"

He finally put his pen down and sat back. "You are covered in soot."

"It's not soot. I went back to Maddox Street."

"Well, I suppose that's better than running to the nearest port."

"I needed to see what had survived."

"Don't worry. I'll replace all your garments. I'm sure you'll understand if I have the bills sent directly to me. I wouldn't want you having *too* much spare coin."

She briefly closed her eyes. He wasn't going to make this easy for her, and why should he? As far as he was concerned, she'd been bargaining with his father for money. God, she was tired of this, of the deceit, of hurting him, when that was the last thing she ever wanted to do again. . . .

"I didn't go to retrieve my clothes."

"How stupid of me. You didn't need them anyway—what with the money you were hoping to extort from my father."

"Your father asked to see me."

"And you *agreed.*"

"I was armed, you saw that."

He shrugged and rearranged the pens on his desk. "You would never have been able to kill him."

"Why not?"

"It's harder than you might imagine to kill someone face-to-face."

"I didn't think it would come to that. I just wanted to threaten him a little."

He looked up. "Never take a weapon into a situation where you are not prepared to use it."

"I thought I *was* prepared to use it."

He considered her. "Sometimes I don't understand you at all. Why didn't you tell me that you were going to see my father?"

She stood up. "I'm tired of repeating myself. I don't want you to be involved in this. Now, will you let me go upstairs and change out of these filthy clothes and enjoy your bathtub?"

He remained seated. "Do you have any idea what would have happened to you if you'd killed him?"

"I assume I would be tried and hung."

"And that doesn't bother you?"

She shrugged. "If he'd admitted to killing my father, I'm not sure I could've stopped myself, or whether I would've cared."

"How incredibly selfish of you." His expression hardened. "You did a stupid and dangerous thing."

"I had to try." She made a hopeless gesture. "Please, Benedict, will you let me go now? I promise I'll fight this out with you tomorrow, but at the moment, I just can't."

He didn't say anything for a long moment, and then he slowly exhaled. "What's wrong?"

"Nothing." God, he had no idea. And if she had her way, he never would.

"Go and have your bath, Malinda. I'll send one of the maids to assist you."

"Thank you, my lord."

She was halfway up the stairs before she realized she'd much rather he shake her and rage at her than sit behind his desk and judge her with that cool detachment. But perhaps he was as tired of the conflict as she was and had stopped caring. It was probably for the best. Tomorrow, when she could think more clearly, she would sit down with him and try to tell him the truth.

She was ripping him to pieces. Benedict put his face in his hands and contemplated the silence she'd left behind her. He hated that desolate note in her voice. She'd been vulnerable for the first time, and like a fool, he'd let her go, the thought of interrogating her too much for him to contemplate in his current state. He was still somewhere between reeling at her effrontery and yelling at her for being so careless with her own safety.

He sat up and stared at the dying fire. But did she now believe his father wasn't the man behind the ambush? Considering she hadn't grabbed the pistol from him and shot the marquis, he had to imagine that she had. He needed to talk to her about what had led her to the original conclusion that his father was responsible *and* what had dissuaded her in the end.

It was ironic that both of them claimed they didn't want him involved in their private war and had united to shut him out. His hand clenched into a fist. The idea of them as allies made him want to vomit. The shock of seeing them together haggling over him . . . they had no right to dictate his future between them. He'd allowed that to happen when he was eighteen, and he wasn't going to let it occur again.

Maybe it was time for him to be honest and tell Malinda what he knew, and hope and pray that she would offer him the same coin. If she didn't . . . He rose to his feet and headed toward the decanter of brandy. Then he'd have to pass the case over to Adam and stop pretending he was capable of dealing with it after all.

"Good morning, Lady Benedict."

Malinda smiled at Adam over the breakfast table as the footman settled her in her seat. Although his smile was full of charm, his face was unremarkable and would be easily forgotten, which in his profession was probably an asset. He wore his usual beautifully cut coat and sober waistcoat and would blend into any crowd of respectable gentlemen with consummate ease.

"Good morning, and please call me Malinda. Being referred to as anything to do with 'Benedict,' as if I have no identity of my own, is a rather sensitive matter at the moment."

"I can understand that." He concentrated on his plate.

"Where *is* Benedict? I haven't seen him for two days."

"He did leave in rather a hurry."

"Hmph." Malinda paused in the act of pouring her tea. "Coward."

"Benedict? I don't think so."

"I wanted to talk to him, and he knew it."

"I asked him to go, actually." Adam sounded apologetic.

"Why?"

"Because he was the only man capable of dealing with the situation I had at hand."

"Oh." She sighed. "I suppose I'm being selfish."

"You can always talk to me." His smile was a masterpiece of enchantment. "I'm fully up-to-date with what's happened. I made Benedict tell me everything before he left."

"I'm sure you did. But it's really quite simple. He was furious with me for going to see his father."

"Understandably."

"Of course, you're on his side, aren't you?"

He raised one eyebrow. "I didn't realize I was in the middle of a war."

"Well, that's where we differ. I've been living this battle for the last eighteen years."

"But which member of the Alford family are you at war with? Surely not all of them?"

"They've all had their moments." She slathered butter on her toast. "And now I find I'm still officially related to them. How could Benedict have been so *stupid*?"

"To insist on remaining married to you? There might be many reasons, the desire to infuriate his father, the need to offer you protection, the fact that once Benedict makes up his mind to something he never gives up."

She knew that far too well. "At least it gives me a valid reason to reside at Alford Park."

"That's true." Adam paused. "Would you like me to arrange your return there while Benedict is absent?"

"How very underhanded of you, Mr. Fisher. I'd prefer to remain here and finish things with Benedict first. He *is* coming back, isn't he?"

"I believe so."

"In the meantime, I will behave myself." She tried to look meek. "I will only go out with Lady Westbrook and never venture across the threshold of Alford House."

"If you do intend to stay, I would appreciate that. Perhaps I might offer my services to amuse you as well?"

An image of him sucking Benedict's cock flashed across her memory. "What kind of services?"

"Anything you wish, my lady."

She regarded him, her head on one side. "Will you let me see what goes on at one of the events on the second floor?"

He smiled slowly. "Now *that* would be my pleasure."

Three days and two nights chasing a rumor . . .

Had Adam sent him away deliberately? He certainly hadn't been at his best after his latest altercation with his wife. Benedict contemplated the pouring rain and the stables in front of him. He could take a room at the inn and return to London in the morning, or he could carry on and get soaked for his trouble. He looked back at the welcoming lights of the hostelry and inhaled the scent of roast beef and ale wafting through the door. At least he'd been well fed. A sense of disquiet kept him standing there on the threshold.

"Are we going, sir?"

He turned to see his groom, Tommy, hovering behind him.

"Yes. I'd like to push on to London."

He detected a faint sigh. "As you wish, sir. I'll go and see if I can find a pair of decent horses for us in the stables."

"Thank you."

He made a mental note to reward Tommy handsomely for his patience with his employer's whims. They were less than six miles from the Sinners, and as they approached the city, the quality of the roads would improve a little. He checked that his pistol was in his pocket, and that the powder wouldn't get damp, rammed his hat down further on his head, and walked back to the stables to find Tommy.

"Tonight is about fulfilling our members' fantasies," Adam murmured to Malinda as he led her down to the salon of the second floor of the Sinners. "You'll need to wear a mask or else Benedict will murder me."

"He can't do that if he doesn't return."

She resented his staying away from her more than she wanted to admit. It was typical of him to disappear just when she'd decided to make a clean breast of it.

"He'll be back, Malinda. I don't think anything could keep him away."

Adam steered her into a small anteroom off the main salon and opened one of the cabinets lining the wall. "Please help yourself to a mask."

She picked one at random and sat down so that he could tie the strings at the back of her head. "Don't you need one?"

"No, I'm the host this evening. We take turns."

"Even Benedict?"

"Naturally."

"I would've thought him too busy saving the country to engage in such licentiousness."

Adam chuckled. "Oh no, he always made time for his duties here."

"Are you trying to make me jealous?"

"No, I'm trying to incite you to rebellion. I want you to enjoy yourself this evening."

"With you?"

"With anyone you choose. Benedict can hardly object, can he?"

"Seeing as he isn't here, and when he *is* here he engages in such activities himself, how could he object?"

Adam bowed and held out his arm. "Shall we proceed?"

"What exactly do you want me to do?"

His smile was a challenge to misbehave. "Anything you desire, my lady, anything at all."

Malinda tucked her hand in his arm and allowed him to lead her through to the large gold and white salon. There were several couples dotted around the room, most of them clustered by the large buffet tables at the far end. A hum of conversation rose from the groups, and the occasional burst of laughter. To Malinda's eyes it all looked rather tame.

Adam glanced at her. "Don't worry. This isn't everything I have to show you, but it is the starting point. At the far end of this room is a corridor with six separate rooms leading off it, three on each side. Every month, we ask our members what sexual fantasies they would like to see reenacted or would like to take part in."

"They have a choice?"

"Some of our members, such as our founders, are married, or in long-term relationships. They will usually only engage in an activity if they are paired together. Sometimes they will suggest the fantasy, and allow others to watch them."

"And who determines which are chosen?"

"That happy task usually falls to me. I try to find a balance between members who want to participate and those who simply wish to observe." He pointed out a book that sat on a table near the buffet. "This is where you can write down your wishes for next month."

"I don't even know what they are, yet."

He studied her. "You've never imagined trying something out of the ordinary with Benedict?"

"Of course I have, but—" She frowned at him. "I am not going to tell you what that might be either."

"It's all right. You can write your requests down anonymously in the book. Now, shall we proceed?"

Malinda chose the first door on the left and slipped into the darkened room, Adam at her side. She turned to ask him a question, but he held his finger to his lips and nodded toward the front of the room.

She realized that something was already occurring in a circle of candlelight at the far end of the room. There was a woman leaning over a red velvet couch. Her face was hidden from view, her arms stretched out over the back of the couch gripping each corner. Her slippered feet were placed neatly together on the floor. As Malinda watched, a man came up behind her and stroked down her spine with his hand until she arched up against him. He slowly gathered her skirts and petticoats in his hand and drew them up to her waist to reveal her stockings, garters, and naked, rounded bottom.

For a moment, Malinda wished her cousin Gwen was with her. Gwen would probably appreciate the sight even more than she did. The man stood back to observe the woman, and then went down on his knees and pushed her feet apart until the audience could clearly see the swell of her sex. He started to play with her, sliding his fingers in and out of her cunt, rubbing her clit, and then bent to take her with his mouth until she visibly trembled.

Malinda raised her eyebrows at Adam. Was this the extent of it? The couple hadn't done anything that shocked her particularly. He simply smiled and gestured at the stage, where another man, this time a younger one, was approaching the woman. The first man moved around to the front of the couch and knelt on the seat, unfastening his trousers to expose the length of his cock to the woman.

As soon as she raised her head and took him into her mouth, the second man fell to his knees and began fingering and licking her sex. Malinda shivered, but not unpleasantly, and Adam bent close to whisper in her ear.

"The lady requires a lot of foreplay before her partner can penetrate her and she can climax."

"And he doesn't mind watching her with the others?"

"Why would he when the reward will be all his?" His mouth grazed her ear. "When she is ready for him, she'll signal, and he'll take over and fuck her properly."

"And how long will that take?"

"Quite a while." He regarded the woman, who was now getting ready to suck the second man's cock while a third waited behind her. "We can move on if you wish—unless you want to have a turn?"

"She takes women too?"

His smile was sweetly salacious. "She'll take anything she can."

"I think we should investigate the second room."

"As you wish."

They left as quietly as possible and went through the second door.

"Oh . . ." Malinda stopped so suddenly that Adam walked into her. His hands came to rest briefly on her hips, making her all too aware of his arousal before he released her.

The view was quite startling, and she sat down to consider the tableau in front of her more closely. One of the men was fully dressed, the other was naked and on his knees. A thick leather collar encircled the naked red-haired man's neck. There was a chain attached to it that was held in the hand of the man sitting in the chair.

"He looks like he is owned," she whispered to Adam.

"I believe he is."

"Why would anyone want that?"

"Watch and see."

When the man snapped his fingers, the redhead undid his companion's trousers. After a jerk on the chain, he lowered his head and started sucking his partner's cock, the sound loud in the silence of the watching and attentive room.

"Stop."

The cold command made Malinda jump almost as much as the naked man, who immediately paused, but remained in place.

"Up."

He stood and his partner maneuvered him backward using one hand on his hip, his other still wrapped around the base of his own shaft.

"Sit on my cock."

Malinda held her breath as, still facing them, the redhead did what he'd been commanded. It took quite a while for him to accept the man inside him. Malinda squirmed on her chair and felt every inch and thrust deep in her sex. Eventually, he was sitting astride his partner, facing the room, his feet planted on the seat on either side of the man's thighs. Despite the struggle to take his partner's cock, the man's expression remained serene, his eyes half-closed, his mouth relaxed. He was also aroused, but he made no move to touch himself, just waited, hands open on his thighs for the next order.

The seated man brought the chain leash around to the front and rubbed the metal links against the redhead's tight nipples and down over his stomach. Beside Malinda, Adam stirred, his hand briefly stroking himself as if rearranging the thrust of his own erection. She wanted to touch herself, aware of the slow throb of arousal settling low in her belly as she wondered what would happen next.

"Ah . . ." the redhead gasped as his partner wrapped the leash under his balls and drew them high and tight up against the stiff underside of his cock.

"Ride me."

He obeyed, rising and falling on the cock, his rhythm dictated by the subtle jerks of the leash. Candlelight gleamed on the wetness gathering on the crown of his cock as it slowly trickled down his shaft.

"Stop."

This time it was Adam who tensed, his gaze fixed on the naked man. Malinda wondered which man he would prefer to be—the one giving the orders, or the one obeying them?

"Who wants to lick his cock clean, but not make him come?"

Adam raised a leisurely hand. "I'll do it."

Malinda watched enthralled as her companion sauntered down to the stage area and crouched in front of the two men. He smiled up at them both, his gaze lingering on the redhead for rather a long time. Did they know each other? Malinda had a strange suspicion that they did.

Adam angled his body to one side so that the people watching could still see what he was doing. His touch was delicate, as if he were sampling a fine wine, or sipping at an ice from Gunters. Even so, the redhead shuddered, his hips bucking until the other man rebuked him with a jerk of the leash.

It seemed to take Adam a long time to finish the task, but that was probably because the more he licked, the more excited his companion became and the more pre-cum emerged.

"You may stop now."

Adam rose and stared down at the two men for a long moment before bending his head and brushing a kiss over the seated man's lips, and then gave a longer kiss to the redhead. He walked back toward Malinda, and for a moment, his charming mask slipped and she saw something close to despair in his eyes.

She rose to her feet and nodded at the door. Maybe he wanted to stay and watch, but she had a strange feeling that it would be difficult for him. He kept walking and opened the door for her, his smile back in place, his countenance untroubled.

"Room three?" she asked.

"Yes." He winked at her. "I think this one is *definitely* to your taste."

14

Benedict came into the kitchens of the Sinners and took off his sodden cloak and coat. There wasn't an inch of him that remained dry, and he was shivering with cold. If he wasn't careful, he'd go down with a chill, and it would be all Malinda's fault.

Maddon came toward him, his expression concerned.

"My lord! You should take yourself upstairs immediately and into a nice hot bath. I'll bring you a late supper." He paused. "Would you like some hot whiskey and ginger? Cook just made a batch."

"That would be much appreciated."

He stayed by the roaring warmth of the large kitchen fire, aware that he was spreading a pool of water on the flagstone floor, but too tired to move another inch. It was quiet in the kitchen, the usual bustle of the staff subdued. He searched his memory and recalled that there was an event on the second floor that night, which meant the majority of the staff was needed upstairs.

Maddon returned with the hot drink, and Benedict sipped it

gratefully until the warmth pooled in his stomach and settled comfortably into his bones.

"Ah, that's better."

"More, sir?"

He held out his cup and it was instantly refilled.

"Is Mr. Fisher officiating on the second floor?"

"He is, sir."

"And is my wife upstairs in my suite?"

Maddon hesitated. "She is definitely on the premises, my lord."

Benedict lowered the glass. "Where, exactly?"

"I believe she's with Mr. Fisher."

"On the second floor." He finished the scalding whiskey, slammed the glass down on the table, and headed for the door.

"Do you want me to start your bath, my lord?"

"Not yet." He kept going, tiredness forgotten as he forged up the main staircase toward the large gold salon on the second floor. It was hard to decide whose neck he was going to wring first, Adam's or Malinda's.

She wasn't in the main salon. Ignoring the other guests, he moved on to the smaller rooms at the far end of the space. She wasn't in the first four rooms, which left the two opposite each other at the end of the corridor. He chose the left, moved quietly into the room, and leaned against the wall.

Adam was sitting in the front row, but where was Malinda? A flash of auburn hair made him peer intently at the woman on the bed who was surrounded by three men who were . . .

Red fury colored his gaze, and he marched toward the group on the stage.

Languidly Malinda opened her eyes as she sensed something wasn't right and looked toward the door. Oh, good Lord. Benedict was furious, soaking wet, and heading straight for her. She did what any sensible woman would do, scrambled off the bed and ran through the door into the servants' stairs before doubling back into the main salon. He caught her there, grabbed her around the waist, and threw her over his shoulder.

"Put me down, you big oaf!"

She pummeled his back and tried to force him to stop. In reply, he slapped her so hard on the bottom that she almost screeched. Halfway up the stairs, she managed to get a hand into his hair and yanked as hard as she could. He stumbled, and they came down together on the steps, him twisting his body so that she fell on top. Even as she scrambled away, he caught her ankle and slowly, inexorably pulled her back toward him.

"Benedict, there are people watching!"

"And there weren't a moment ago?"

He hiked up her shift and shoved his cock deep inside her, pinning her on her hands and knees as he fucked her. The force of his thrusts made her bite her lip and start to come. Before she'd even finished, he pulled out, hauled her into his arms again, and marched back down the stairs, ignoring the grinning faces of the club members who'd emerged from the various rooms to see what all the fuss was about.

Aware that she was only in her shift and corset, Malinda buried her face in his shoulder, her cheeks flaming as he took her back into the salon. Adam stood by the far door and bowed.

"Do you want something, Benedict?"

"A room." He proffered her like a parcel. "Which one?"

"Take her into room three if you like. You scared everyone away, so you might as well provide the entertainment for the rest of the night."

"Thank you," Benedict growled. "And don't forget to come and be entertained yourself."

"I'll do that once I've settled everyone down again."

Benedict kicked open the door with his booted foot and slammed it shut behind them. Malinda closed her eyes as he threw her down onto the bed and stood over her, breathing hard.

"I wasn't—"

He leaned in close. "Be silent."

She surged upward. He placed a hand on her chest and pushed her none too gently back down again. "And stay put."

"I will not be—"

"You damn well will."

She gasped as he ripped off his cravat and gagged her with it. As she knelt up and frantically tugged at the knot behind her head, he left her and went across to the chest of drawers by the door. Before she could even think of getting off the bed, he was back with a fistful of silk scarves. She kicked out at him, but he tied her ankles to each bedpost. Straddling her, he removed her corset and shift, leaving her in just her stockings.

"That's better."

She glared at him behind her gag but he took no heed of her, securing her wrists together over her head and tying the silk to the headboard of the bed. He climbed off and studied her before sliding a pillow beneath her buttocks, raising her hips and spreading her legs.

"Now, where were we?"

He removed the gag and she hissed at him.

"What are you doing on the second floor, Malinda?"

"Enjoying myself?"

"Without me?"

She considered him for a long moment and then smiled. "I had Adam to entertain me instead."

"Adam."

"He offered to bring me down here."

"But you were the one who asked if you might come."

"I was bored. I promised not to leave the Sinners and I kept my word. I didn't know you were coming back."

He cupped her chin. "I'll always come back, don't you know that?"

She fought to ignore the sincerity edging his lighthearted tone. "I don't know anything about you, Benedict. We've been apart for eighteen years." And that was another lie. He hadn't changed at all. "I hardly thought you'd notice if I enjoyed the facilities. I understand that you do so yourself."

"But I'm a member of this club. I have a responsibility to my associates."

"To fuck them?"

"To make their visits here as pleasurable as I can."

"Then if you're allowed to have other lovers, why aren't I? You let Adam suck your cock right in front of me!" She widened her eyes. "And before you start being all ridiculously territorial, Benedict, I wasn't letting any of those men fuck me. I was merely—"

"—being pleasured, I saw that. What else did you and Adam do?"

"Why should I tell you?"

"Because if you wish to be untied at some point, you'll have to cooperate with me."

He sounded remarkably composed, which annoyed her immensely. She pretended to yawn.

"I'm bored of you tying me up, Benedict. It is extremely juvenile."

"Really? I believe you kept *me* chained up for weeks. Perhaps I consider this just retribution."

She said nothing and glared at him instead. It made no difference; he continued to regard her, his smile gentle, his angelic countenance serene.

"What did you do, Malinda?" He leaned close and fingered her nipple, drawing it into a tight peak before moving on to the other one. "What did you see?"

"Not much." She tried to wiggle away, but her bounds wouldn't let her.

He licked her nipple and then sucked it into his mouth. "What exactly?"

"A woman being pleasured by several men while her husband awaited his turn, and two men who—" She gasped as he stroked her mound, one finger sliding between her already slick folds to brush her clit.

"Two men who did what?"

"Fucked each other with a little help from Adam."

He raised his head to look at her, his blue gaze intent. "Adam touched another man in public? What did the man look like?"

"He was a redhead, why?"

"Good God." The good humor faded from his face. "I'll place a wager it was Harry Maclean."

"Do you know him?"

"Adam does."

"I thought he might. He seemed rather shaken by the whole incident." She pretended to hesitate. "Don't you think you should go and make sure he's all right?"

"Nice try, my love." He nipped her ear. "But I'm not going anywhere. What else did you see?"

"Nothing until we got to this room and I realized this was *quite suitable* for my purposes."

"Ah, now I understand. You thought it would be enough to annoy me, but not make me have to challenge all three of those men, those members of my *club*, to a duel?"

"You are so arrogant, Benedict. That's not what I meant. I had no idea you were even in London. I meant that I needed some *relief.*"

He looked sympathetic, the lying toad. "I can understand you missing my presence in your bed."

She glared at him. "I was missing sex, not you."

"And I'm more than willing to make that up to you." His finger slid deeper and then back and forth through the wetness of her arousal. "I would hate to think of you being unsatisfied."

She smiled sweetly. "Then why don't you take yourself off to bed, and leave me here to continue my evening without you?"

He pinched her clit hard. "I wouldn't dream of it. I'll give you one choice, though, seeing as I believe we should both have the same opportunities. You can have me, or you can have Adam and me. That's it."

"Did I hear my name?"

Malinda turned to the door where Adam stood, his smile lightening his countenance, his earlier mood seemingly quite forgotten. He strolled over to the bed and looked down at her.

"You are very beautiful, my lady."

Benedict caught her chin in his hand so that she could only look at him. "What is your decision? Does Adam stay or go?"

"He can stay if he *wishes* to, not because you command him. Despite appearances to the contrary, we are not all your subjects, Benedict."

"Says the woman who is tied to the bed." He kissed her with a rough possession that left her breathless and squirming against the sheets. "Do you care to stay, Adam?"

"Oh, yes please."

"Then make yourself useful. I believe my wife would like you to use your mouth on her."

"It would be a pleasure."

He moved to one side and Adam climbed up onto the large bed and crawled between her legs, his gaze fixed on the already aroused folds of her sex. He leaned even closer and Malinda shivered at the first delicate foray of his tongue across her swollen bud.

Benedict cupped her breast, and rolled her nipple between his thumb and forefinger. "That's nice, Adam. Give her more."

"Do you want me to make her come?"

Benedict turned back to Malinda. "Well?"

She tried to shrug as if she was used to having two men in her bed. "Adam made you come."

"Then he will do the same for you."

And then she forgot everything but Adam and Benedict's hands and mouths on her. . . .

Benedict studied Malinda's flushed face in the candlelight as Adam worked her with his tongue. Despite her easy acceptance of his offer for them both to pleasure her, it was obvious that this was a new experience for her. She writhed against the sheets, her hips lifting into each subtle stroke of Adam's tongue and slide of his long fingers. He knew she was close to coming. Seeing her like this without his own passion overwhelming him as he pleasured her was surprisingly erotic.

He leaned closer and licked her nipple and then found her mouth and kissed her thoroughly, his tongue using the same rhythm as Adam's. He wanted more, he wanted everything. . . .

Adam groaned and Benedict moved down the bed to observe his friend at closer quarters. He rested one hand on the curve of Adam's buttocks and stroked him, urging him forward until his lover arched his back and he slid his hand down further to cup his balls and erect cock. He eased Adam to one side so that he could add his fingers and mouth to Malinda's cunt and clit.

She screamed and lifted her hips into their dual touch and penetration as she climaxed. Adam's mouth met his over Malinda's swollen bud and they kissed, too, drawing her taut flesh into their mouths, taking turns sucking and licking and plundering her wetness. Two fingers each in her welcoming cunt now, widening her with every stroke. Benedict slid his wet thumb down to her arse and rimmed her puckered hole.

"Oil?" Adam murmured, before moving to one side and opening the bedside cabinet. He passed the bottle of oil back to

Benedict, who slicked his thumb with it and slid inside her. Adam came to help, his fingers dancing over Malinda's clit making her come again as Benedict added another finger and moved them back and forth in her arse.

Benedict looked up at Malinda. Her eyes were heavy-lidded, her beautiful mouth trembling with the passion they'd aroused in her.

"How do you want us, love?"

She licked her lips. "What?"

He guided Adam's fingers into her cunt. "You wanted us both, I believe?"

"You'd let him inside me?"

"He's already inside you. Where do you want his cock?"

"I—"

He smiled and looked down at their moving fingers. *His* cock was so hard that he wanted to rip off his trousers and shove himself deep inside whichever orifice she offered him.

"His fingers are in your cunt, mine are in your arse." He paused to make sure he had her full attention. "Would you like two cocks in there? Or would you prefer a different variation?" He ran his wet thumb down the front of Adam's straining trousers. "The possibilities are endless. You could have one of us in your mouth, or Adam could fuck you while I fuck him, or vice versa."

Still watching her, he leaned over and unbuttoned Adam's trousers and shoved them down to reveal the thick length of Adam's cock. He kissed the wet crown and Adam groaned.

"Do you want to taste him too?"

She gave only the smallest hint of acquiescence, but he saw it, and nodded for Adam to move closer to her head. Adam gripped his shaft around the base, drawing it away from his tight stomach and within distance of Malinda's tongue. Benedict shuddered as she reached out and licked his friend in a lazy, salacious circle around his straining crown. He ripped open his own trousers and crawled toward her, waiting until she turned to him and offered him the same sensual flick of her tongue.

"Where, Malinda?" he murmured. "Both in your mouth? Or do you want me to decide?"

She licked her own lips and he almost came. "I'm tied up and at your mercy. Surely I'll just have to . . . *endure?*"

He smiled at her. "Then perhaps you'd like to endure for a bit longer. Adam, come here."

He waited until his partner moved in front of him and then set about undressing him. He took his time, stroking Adam's skin as it was slowly revealed, running his hands over the other man's thighs and muscled chest, pinching his nipples until he moaned and his hips bucked against Benedict's hard cock.

Malinda watched, too, her avid gaze on Adam's slight frame as Benedict played with his cock and balls, sliding his wet finger up and down Adam's shaft until it was shining with pre-cum, and then down to the soft skin of his taint and the tight pucker of his arse.

"I almost wish I'd brought the jade with me, Malinda. While Adam and I have you, we could've been stuffed full of those cold, rigid lengths. If your hands were free, you could've held them deep inside us as we fucked you."

Her nipples drew tight, and as he bent to take one in his mouth, Adam followed suit. She was trembling now, her cunt open and wet for him, her body ready to accept exactly what he wanted to give her. He finally took off his own clothes, fully freeing his aching shaft from his trousers, and gave himself two hard yanks, which was enough to soak his hand with pre-cum.

Adam turned to him, a question in his gray eyes. "You are sure about this? You won't be demanding satisfaction at dawn?"

"Malinda wants you, and as I've already had you, it seems only fair."

"Then I'll do whatever she wants."

"Thank you. I'll need to untie her." He lowered his voice. "I don't think she'll run, but you never know."

He found the bottle of oil and slicked it over his cock, then nodded to Adam to untie Malinda's left ankle as he did the same to her right. To his relief she didn't even move, her gaze still fixed on her two naked lovers. He turned and quickly undid her hands before sliding behind her and settling her down on his lap facing outward toward Adam.

"Suck her breasts."

Adam obliged as Benedict, heart hammering, slid two oiled fingers into his wife's arse, and then, when he was certain she would accept him, started to lower her down onto his waiting cock. He took his time, playing with her clit, his fingers tangling with Adam's mouth as she climaxed and he was able to slide deeper with every spasm of her pleasure.

"*God . . .*" He breathed hard through his nose as the sensation of her tight passage clasping his oversensitive cock shuddered through him. He settled her back against his chest, her hips in his big hands, her knees spread wide over his. Adam's gaze lowered, and he reached out and circled where Benedict was joined to Malinda before dropping down on hands and knees and delicately licking his way up to her empty cunt, circling and sucking at her swollen lips before tonguing her clit.

"Please . . ." Malinda's voice was high and tight with need.

Benedict bit her shoulder. "What do you want, love?" Would she ask for Adam's cock, or would she expect Benedict to ask for her? At this point, if she didn't voice an opinion, he was going to. Even if it never happened again, he wanted her to experience this pleasure alongside him.

She shifted restlessly against him, making him rock his hips.

"I want Adam."

He smiled down at her head.

"Then have him."

Adam fitted himself between Benedict and Malinda's entwined legs and slid his cock deep, making them both cry out. He set a strong and regular pace, which Benedict picked up on, alternating his thrusts to his partner's to give his wife the most pleasure she had ever had in her life. Adam gripped hard on Benedict's shoulder, anchoring himself against Malinda's uncontrollable movements. She was lost in them now, her body pressed between them, her responses tuned to theirs, her pleasure theirs to amplify and make last forever.

But it couldn't last and as she kept climaxing, Benedict held on to his desire not to come less and less. His mind was caught between the urgent spasms of her sex and the driving thrust of Adam's cock through the thin wall that separated them. He winced as Adam's fingers dug into his wounded shoulder.

"I need to come, Benedict," Adam gasped. "I—"

He pulled out and rolled to one side, one hand wrapped around his pumping cock as he spilled his seed against the sheets. Malinda cried out, too, and Benedict came, jamming his fingers in her cunt as she climaxed around him in endless, shuddering waves.

After a quick nod in Benedict's direction, Adam climbed off the bed, picked up his clothes, and left the room. It was unlike him to be less than polite, but even through his own desires, Benedict had noticed his look of utter desolation, as he'd come helplessly into his own hand. He'd worry about Adam later; he had his hands full with his wife, who was slumped against him, her whole body vibrating.

He eased her off his lap and she collapsed onto the sheets with a faint moan. While she was quiet, he took the opportunity to get off the bed and go and thoroughly wash himself. He was bone-weary and shaking like a young child. He looked back at the bed, where Malinda hadn't stirred, and walked quietly over to her. She looked up at him and opened her mouth.

He gently covered it with his hand. "No. I can't." She kissed his palm and then tickled it with the tip of her tongue. "I just want to sleep beside you, and not wake up with a hatchet in my head, or to the sound of you scolding me about something. Is that possible?"

She nodded, and he wrapped the sheet around her and picked her up. For a second, his legs buckled and she caught at his shoulder, her long hair tickling his skin. He pushed open the door to the servants' stairs and took her up those to his suite of rooms. She rolled into bed; he pulled the covers over them and fell into a deep and dreamless sleep.

15

Of course Adam was the first person Malinda encountered in the breakfast room at the Sinners. He stood as she came into the room and hurried around to pull a chair out for her.

"Thank you." She tried not to look into his face as she gingerly sat down.

He returned to his seat opposite her and grimaced sympathetically. "Are you sore?"

"I'm quite well, thank you." She poured herself some tea. "I need to speak to Benedict. Is he in his office?"

"I believe so." She felt his gaze on her. "Malinda, are you *blushing?*"

"Not at all. I merely want to see my husband. There's something I wanted his advice about."

"I'm sure he'll be delighted that you are actively seeking him out." He hesitated. "It doesn't have anything to do with what happened last night, does it?"

She looked up then into his smiling eyes. "Why, are you worried he'll be angry with you?"

He brushed imaginary crumbs off his coat. "I hope not. But I did leave rather abruptly."

She smiled at him. "Did you? I can't say I noticed. I was too overwhelmed with all the pleasure you both gave me."

He winked at her. "Flatterer."

She shook her head and laughed. "I've realized it's pointless being embarrassed with you."

"There's really no need. I was glad to help out." He sighed. "To be honest, I was grateful for the distraction."

She studied his expression, but he seemed disinclined to elaborate. Even as she opened her mouth to explore her curiosity, he stiffened and looked toward the open door of the morning room.

"May I help you?"

A tall red-haired man came into the room and bowed. Something about the line of his jaw reminded Malinda of the naked man they'd seen the previous evening. Had Adam mistaken the object of his desire for this man? On closer examination, he was older and looked far less malleable than the other redhead.

"Mr. Fisher? I'm Alistair Maclean. You are acquainted with my brother, Harry. I believe I owe you my thanks for the recommendation for this post."

"Ah, yes." Adam stood and went around to shake the other man's hand. "Mr. Maclean. May I introduce you to Lady Benedict Keyes?"

Mr. Maclean turned his clear green gaze onto Malinda and bowed again. "My lady, it is a pleasure to meet you. I hope I can be of assistance to you as well as to his lordship."

Malinda looked inquiringly at Adam over the top of Mr. Maclean's auburn head.

"He's your husband's new secretary."

"Oh, I see." Malinda smiled. He *was* related to Harry, the

other Maclean Benedict had mentioned and Adam knew. "What an excellent idea. Is my husband at his desk at this moment?"

"He is, my lady. Do you wish to speak to him? He told me to help myself to some breakfast before we started on the next batch of correspondence." He looked back at the door. "But I am more than happy to accompany you back to his office."

She waved him into a seat. "I'm quite capable of finding him myself, Mr. Maclean. Please enjoy your breakfast. I'm sure Mr. Fisher will be delighted to keep you company."

She needed to speak to Benedict before he said or did something that distracted her into arguing with him again. Last night, when he'd let her enjoy the delights of the second floor, had been quite extraordinary. She wasn't certain if she would wish to *continue* such extravagances, but it was nice to know they existed, and that Benedict wouldn't deny her that knowledge.

She knocked on his door and went in. He was sitting at his desk, which appeared a lot less cluttered than it had been the week before. The wary look in his eye when he realized who it was made her hold up her hand.

"It's all right. I haven't come to annoy you."

He put down his pen. "That *would* make a pleasant change."

She sat on the chair in front of his desk and gripped her hands together.

"What's wrong?"

"Nothing. I'm just trying to find the right words."

"Are you sure you aren't annoyed about something? Last night, perhaps? When I forced another man on you?"

"You know quite well that you didn't force anything on me that I wasn't eager to sample."

"Are you sure?" He ran a hand through his blond hair. "I've been told I have a tendency to be a mite overbearing sometimes, especially when I lose my temper."

"Who would say that?"

"I believe it was you."

She slowly raised her head and met his innocent blue gaze. "I enjoyed every minute, and you damn well know it."

His smile was beautiful. "Well, good. Now, how can I help you?"

She drank in the smile, knowing that she'd probably not see another one for a while after she'd told him everything.

"It's about your father."

"Ah, about that—"

She kept speaking. "You wondered why I insisted on seeing him alone, and why I even agreed to come to London with you. Well, I *thought* there was a good reason, but now I'm not so sure."

His brow crinkled. "I'm not sure I understand you."

"I thought your father was behind my father's death."

"So I gathered." He glanced down at the letter he was writing, and set it carefully to one side. "You've changed your mind?"

She stared hopelessly at him. "I'd better start at the beginning, hadn't I?"

"That would be helpful."

She leapt to her feet and started to pace the carpet. "You probably don't remember this, but that last summer when we were both traveling with the regiment—"

"—and we fell in love."

"Yes, I suppose we did, but we also argued a lot."

The corner of his mouth quirked up. "We still do."

"There was one particular argument we kept having about the restrictions placed on females, and your assertion that because you were a man, you were stronger, wiser, and far more heroic than I could ever be."

"I *was* a year older," he murmured.

"I was determined to prove I was just as capable as you

were, so I decided to do something that in retrospect was stupid and reckless."

"Hindsight is a wonderful thing, love."

She swallowed hard and then blurted it out. "I pretended to be ill so that you wouldn't miss me, then I dressed up as a boy and accompanied my father and his troop to fetch the supplies from the main port on the other side of the mountain range."

He went still. "Go on."

"By the time my father realized I was following them, we were too far from the camp to send me back, so he was forced to bring me along." She shook her head. "It was quite an adventure until we were on the return journey, with the mules laden with supplies and—" She forced herself to go on. "You know what happened. We were attacked."

He shifted slightly in his seat. "You were there?"

"I—" She turned away from him as tears threatened. "I saw very little. As soon as my father realized what was happening, he set me on his horse and ordered me to go and get help. I tried to argue with him, but he walloped the horse hard enough to send it careening down the mountainside. It was all I could do to stay on." She bit her lip. "When the horse eventually slowed down, I was hopelessly lost, and it was eerily quiet. I knew that couldn't be good, but I dismounted and led the horse back up the trail until I found the way blocked with dead horses and mules, and . . . my father and his companions were all dead too."

She looked over her shoulder at him. He was sitting motionless at his desk, his expression curiously blank.

"I had to turn away and be sick." She took a deep, shuddering breath. "I'll never forget the smell of death."

"Neither will I." Their gazes met and held for a long moment. "What happened then?"

"I was about to go to my father, when I heard voices, so I hid in the rocks."

"That was very wise of you."

"At first I thought it was a rescue party, but then I realized the men were masked and that they were systematically stripping everything of value from the dead. I knew that if they heard me, they'd kill me, too, so I ran away."

There was a silence and she braced herself for his anger.

"May I ask you something?" His voice was incredibly gentle.

She instinctively straightened her spine like a soldier about to be flogged. "Why I was such a little coward?"

"No, why did you initially think the men were a rescue party, and not the same men who had carried out the ambush?"

She met his gaze. "Because they spoke English to each other."

"Ah." He nodded. "So you managed to get back to camp."

"Yes, only to find that I hadn't been missed at all because you'd already raised the alarm and set off with a search party to find the missing men. I crawled into bed and pretended that nothing had happened, that I'd dreamed it all, that my father—" She pressed her fist to her mouth.

"I wish you'd told me."

"How could I? I knew you'd be furious at me for doing something so ridiculous, and I couldn't bear for you to be right—that you would've been stronger and braver than me, that maybe you would've saved my father rather than run away like a child."

He sighed. "I wouldn't have done any better than you did, love. I probably would have stayed and been killed alongside those other brave men."

"You don't know that."

He rose from his chair and came around to stand next to her. "I do. I was just as reckless as you were in my own way."

"I did intend to tell you what had happened, but you didn't come to see me, and your father threatened to put us out of our tent, and then when you did appear, you'd decided to marry me and—"

"And everything changed, and you were thrust into another crisis of my making." He took her hand. "I do understand."

She wrenched her hand free and stepped away from him. "Don't be kind. I can't bear it."

"What do you want me to do, shout at you? Tell you that you failed your father in some way? Because I don't believe that. I don't believe he would've wanted you to die for a second."

"But I should've spoken up about what I'd seen."

"My father wouldn't have listened. He had no time for women in general, and in his eyes you were busy trying to ruin his son. He would *never* have believed you." He took her hand again, and this time she let him lead her over to the chairs by the fire. She sat down and he busied himself at the decanters, bringing a glass of brandy over to her.

"Drink this."

She obeyed and shuddered as the fiery spirit trickled down her throat. She handed him back the glass and he sat opposite her and finished the contents in one swallow.

"There's more," she said.

He nodded and put the glass down, his attention fixed on her face.

"When my mother was dying, she liked to talk about the past. I think she found it easier than contemplating the present. She talked about the days before she married George Makethorpe and how happy she'd been with my father. But as time passed, I sensed she was struggling whether to tell me something important about my father's death. One night, quite near the end of her life, I woke from a nap and found her clutching my hand and struggling to sit up. I soothed her as best I could. She whispered to me that she would never be able to rest in peace if she didn't confess."

Lost in the past, Malinda wrapped her arms around herself. "She told me that the night before my father was due to go and pick up the supplies, he went out drinking with some of his old friends in the regiment. She was woken up when he was escorted back to the tent by your father."

"*My* father?"

"From what she overheard, the marquis was furious with my father for getting drunk, and mayhap giving away their secret."

"And what secret was that?"

"She didn't know, only that the marquis said that if my father completed his part of the plan successfully, he would be well rewarded, and if he failed, he would suffer the consequences."

"Did she question him further when they were alone?"

"She tried, but he was still drunk and angry with her for eavesdropping. He told her that if she ever mentioned what she'd overheard, he would beat her. He said that they would be rich." Malinda twisted her hands together on her lap. "She was too afraid to argue with him. He'd never hit her before, not even once."

"And when he didn't return, what did she think?"

She raised her gaze to his. "That your father had reneged on the deal and somehow arranged for there to be no survivors. She begged me to find your father and take my revenge."

"That was a terrible burden to place on you and quite unwarranted."

"It was what she'd come to believe." She shrugged. "How could I argue with a dying woman? I promised to do my best."

Silence fell until she had to look away from Benedict's cool blue gaze.

"Is this another reason why you were angry with me? Did you think I had a hand in it?"

"Originally, yes, but I soon came to realize it was unlikely."

He raised an eyebrow. "It's a shame you didn't realize it until *after* you'd shot me and chained me up."

"All *right,* I know I should have talked to you first, but I was determined to get the upper hand."

"And shooting me gave you that advantage?"

She frowned at him. "Benedict, by all accounts, you are an extremely difficult man to pin down. I knew that if I stood any chance of convincing you of anything, I'd need to guarantee your full attention."

He shook his head as if trying to force his mind back to the problem at hand and took a deep breath.

"I assume that when you remembered that the men searching the bodies had been English, you immediately thought your mother could be right."

"Yes." For once she was grateful for his insistence on remaining unemotional.

He sat back in his chair and regarded her. "Did your father tell you what the mules were carrying as well as the usual supplies?"

"No."

"They carried gold to pay the soldiers."

She slowly brought her hand to her mouth.

"Is it possible that what your mother overheard was my father and yours discussing the fact that he would be bringing the payroll? Could that have been the 'secret' between them?"

Malinda tried to collect her addled wits. "I suppose that might be true. It would also explain why the marquis is so adamant that he had no hand in the ambush."

Benedict nodded. "If it is true, does it make you feel any better about your father's part in this?"

"But why did he say he was going to be rich?"

He shrugged. "Perhaps my father offered him a greater share of the gold if he brought it safely through the mountains."

His voice was matter-of-fact, as though they were discussing the weather rather than events that had shaped and distorted so

much of their lives. He also made a lot of sense. Something nig-
gled at the back of her mind, but she tried to focus on viewing
the events of the past differently.

"So if it wasn't a plot between our fathers, who were the
Englishmen I saw going through the baggage?"

"That is a very interesting question, my dear, and here's another one for you. If my father isn't trying to kill you—who is?"

Benedict waited as the shock of his question registered in
her wide hazel eyes and then watched as she struggled to dis-
semble. He'd *known* there was more to it and so, obviously,
had she. That was why she'd been afraid all along.

"I don't know. I'm not even sure someone *is* trying to kill
me. That might all be a product of your imagination."

"Someone tried to burn down the house you were known to
be staying in. Did that not convince you?"

She raised her chin. "You said it might have been aimed
at you."

"I was trying not to worry you."

"And now you are?"

"Yes, because knowing my father is your potential murderer
is far easier to deal with than not knowing whom the devil I
should be going after."

"You think someone is after me because I saw the ambush?
But no one else survived."

"The ambushers did, and they got away with the gold. And
if they were, indeed, British, then you are in danger."

"But why now?" She shook her head. "It was more than
eighteen years ago."

"Because you came back to England and you allied yourself
with me."

"Only as a means to get to your father."

He forced himself to ignore that jab and concentrated on the
problem at hand. "Unfortunately for you, I am known as a man

who investigates such matters of national security and duplicity. They might think you have finally decided to reveal what you know, and that makes you dangerous."

He was relieved to see that some color was returning to her cheeks and that she was no longer on the verge of tears. He wanted to pick her up and hold her close to his heart.

"Wait a minute."

He froze. Naturally, along with her recovery came her feisty nature and her desire to divert attention away from herself.

"You *knew*, didn't you?"

"About what?"

"Don't prevaricate, Benedict. You knew about the ambush."

"I was there, don't you remember? I was the one who led the search party to recover them."

"I mean about the gold. Did your father tell you?"

"No, he didn't. In fact he—"

"So when did you find out?"

He sighed. "Quite recently."

"Who told you?"

"I can't reveal that."

Her gaze narrowed. "That's why you've been guarding me so closely, isn't it?"

"Naturally." He held up his hand. "And before you start getting all self-righteous, I was going to tell you what I knew."

"When?"

"As soon as I realized you no longer believed my father was responsible." She opened her mouth and he kept talking. "Don't glare at me. I know that nothing I would've said when we first met would have made any difference. Once you get the bit between your teeth you're unstoppable. You had to come to your own conclusions and be ready to tell me the rest."

She slumped back in her seat. "I hate it when you're right."

"You're actually admitting that I might be?"

"I'm not stupid, Benedict. I understand that I put you in a

difficult situation with regard to your father, but you did *insist* on getting involved."

He realized he was clenching his jaw. "I did what I thought was necessary to keep two members of my family from killing each other."

She wagged an accusatory finger. "And because you wanted to see how far your father was implicated. In fact, I was a useful tool so that you didn't have to investigate him too closely yourself."

"You can't have it both ways, Malinda. When I interfered, you raked me over the coals, but when I *didn't,* you now insist I should have declared my interest. Which is it to be? I was quite prepared to do what was necessary."

He abruptly stood up and, needing to do something with his hands rather than wrap them around her pretty neck, helped himself to another glass of brandy.

"Then what are we going to do now?"

He turned to look at her. "We are going to continue to keep you well-guarded and hope that your aggressor will show himself."

"You propose using me as bait?"

"In the meantime, we'll consult with Adam and pool our knowledge so that we can try and figure out exactly who might have known you witnessed that ambush." He crossed the room to the fire and came down on one knee in front of her. She let him take her hand but looked wary.

"Promise me something."

"It depends what it is."

"Promise me that you will abide by my decisions regarding your safety."

She stared into his eyes, her head angled to one side. "All right."

"And if you think of anything else, anything at all that

might help us discover who might want to kill you, tell me or Adam immediately."

"I will—as long as you both do the same."

"Agreed." He kissed her hand and slowly rose to his feet. "How are you feeling now?"

"I need to think." She rubbed her forehead and stood up. "I have a headache."

"I'm not surprised." He leaned in and kissed her parted lips. "Thank you."

"For what?"

"For trusting me enough to tell me the truth."

"I've always trusted you."

He kissed her again just because he could, and because he didn't have the words to tell her how much that trust meant to him, how he'd die for her, how . . .

"Malinda—"

"Yes?"

"Remember to let someone know if you wish to go out."

Her smile died and she patted his cheek and stepped out of his reach. "I think I'll go back upstairs and sleep for a while."

He watched her leave, her head high and her gaze sure, aware in the pit of his stomach that he'd failed her in some subtle way—that he should have spoken up. He hadn't told her he trusted her. He didn't trust anyone, but the fact that she'd noticed his lack of reply and withdrawn from him hurt far more than he had anticipated.

16

"So you knew about this too?" Malinda stared down at Faith as she took a seat in Adam's office.

The countess smiled. "Of course I did."

Malinda made a huffing sound. "It seems I'm the only one who's been kept in ignorance."

"You didn't exactly share what you knew either."

"I suppose that's true." She poured herself some coffee from the tray the estimable Mr. Maclean had left on the table and added a large helping of cream.

"The aim now is to move forward and make sure you are kept safe, and that whoever is responsible for this terrible crime is apprehended." Faith sipped at her tea, her expression thoughtful. "I wonder if Adam has found out anything new? He met with Nicodemus Theale this morning."

"Who is Nicodemus Theale?"

"He is a gatherer of interesting information. You'll like him."

"Yet another man who knows all my secrets," Malinda grumbled.

"Oh, I hope not."

"What do you mean?" Despite everything, Malinda knew she sounded defensive.

"Just that you are used to being the strong member of the family, the holder of the secrets, not the one who needs help. It must be hard for you to relinquish control."

"Indeed." Malinda tried to relax and picked up her cup. "Especially to Benedict."

Faith chuckled. "Who finds it equally difficult."

The door opened and Adam came in, accompanied by Benedict and Mr. Maclean, who paused to shut the door and then bowed to the two ladies. Benedict looked calm as usual, Adam even more so.

Adam took the seat at the head of the table. "Alistair will take notes if that's all right with everyone."

The secretary took the seat to Malinda's left and placed a bottle of ink and a spare pen on the table in front of him.

"Now, let's summarize," Adam said. "We know that a large sum of gold was stolen during the ambush that killed Malinda's father. Despite earlier suspicions, the Marquis of Alford denies ordering the attack."

Malinda gave a reluctant nod.

"We also know that Malinda witnessed the ambush and its aftermath, and confirmed that those who carried it out appeared to be English. Her recent reappearance at Benedict's side and her reluctant acceptance by the Keyes family must have alarmed the perpetrators enough to consider killing her."

"You believe there is more than one?"

"It's possible." Adam shrugged.

"So do you have any new information for us?" Benedict asked.

"Nicodemus is currently trying to trace the man who set fire to your house in Maddox Street. He believes he is close to discovering him."

"And what about that other matter I asked about?"

"Information about the men who died in the ambush? I have that." Adam sorted through a pile of papers on his desk and brought a single sheet back to the table. "Two of the men had families back in England, the third was unmarried and lived with his parents. None of the families received more than the usual military payoff, and none of them appear to be living in great style."

"Which probably means they didn't benefit from the ambush."

"One must assume so." Adam sighed. "Then who else knew they carried that gold?"

"We always come back to the Marquis of Alford," Malinda said. Opposite her, Benedict stiffened.

"But would he steal his own money?" Adam asked.

"What do you mean?"

"I understand that the majority of the gold was actually the marquis's own. Apparently he was unhappy with the delays in paying his troops by the Crown and decided to supplement the payments himself. It wasn't an entirely altruistic gesture; I saw a letter he wrote to the paymaster general in which he informed them that he intended to call in the debt when the Crown provided their usual promissory bank notes and coin."

"Perhaps he decided he'd rather keep it *all* for himself." Ignoring the frown on Benedict's face, Malinda continued, "That might also explain why he wanted the matter to be a secret between him and my father."

"She does have a point, Adam," Faith said.

"But why go to all that bother to bring the gold to Portugal and then steal it?" Benedict demanded. "And I can swear to you that none of it came home with me, or my father. The last thing I did before he took me back to school in England was pack up our tent and belongings, and there was no gold."

"Of course there wasn't. Don't be dull-witted, Benedict. The gold was taken away by his accomplices."

He looked down his aristocratic nose at her, his eyes frosty. "I thought we'd established that my father was no longer a suspect."

"But that was before Adam told us who owned the gold."

"I fail to see—"

"If I may intervene for a moment?" Adam said smoothly. "We should certainly keep the marquis in mind, but we must also consider who else might have known about the gold. Your party was not unobserved on the coast, my lady. That's how we found out that you were with them. It's possible that someone who loaded those mules and knew what they carried followed you back and took what they wanted."

"I suppose that's possible," Malinda reluctantly agreed. "My father tried to keep all the men close by and wouldn't allow any of them to wander off and enjoy the pleasures of the city. But I'm not sure if he was entirely successful."

"You had no sense of being observed or of being followed?"

"None at all." She shivered. "The ambush came out of nowhere."

"Which indicates a well-planned attack in the most dangerous of places. It hardly sounds like an adventurous thief or two."

"But for all that gold . . ." Faith breathed and then promptly became more businesslike. "Would you like me to go and visit the Marquis of Alford? I can acquaint him with our new knowledge of his ownership of the gold and see if it changes his mind about what he wants to share with us."

"If you would, my lady, that would be most helpful. I think we should keep Benedict and Malinda away from him at present." Adam bowed. "I'd also like to widen the search to other members of the regiment, especially those who were friends of your father, Malinda."

"I can make you a list," Malinda offered. She paused to take her mother's journal out of her pocket. "I also have this. My mother didn't write a lot, but it is very interesting."

"Your mother wrote a journal?" Faith smiled. "How fascinating. Would it pain you to read out what she thought about the night of the ambush?"

"If you think it might help." Malinda cleared her throat, found the correct page, and steeled herself to read.

" 'Mally says she is sick. I think she's sulking again over a fight with the young lord. It's quite late now, I can barely see to write, but Patrick hasn't returned yet, and I'm worried something might have befallen him, especially since that business with the marquis. I pray God will keep him safe.' "

Malinda swallowed hard and looked up. "There's nothing more on that night or for a few days afterward."

"Is there anything in the journal that you think is important?" Adam asked.

"I don't know. The more I read it, the less clear it all becomes. She writes about the men who attended his funeral, and then there's another big gap because that's when she met up with George, her second husband, and she went off with him within a week or so."

Faith held out her hand. "May I read it?"

Malinda looked down at the battered journal, which was almost all that she had left of her mother. "Yes, of course."

"I promise I'll take great care of it."

"I know you will." She passed it across to Faith. "Perhaps you'll see something I've missed."

"Even if your mother's journal doesn't hold any clues to the mystery, it is still a useful tool."

She looked up at Adam. "In what way?"

"We can *pretend* it does. Any self-respecting murderer would want to get his hands on it then."

"And how are we supposed to accomplish that? Should I wander through the hallways and ballrooms of London reading it out loud?"

"Oh, there are much easier ways of spreading information

than that." Adam smiled. "We are fairly good at it here at the Sinners."

He rose to his feet and studied them all. "Is there anything else we need to discuss at this point?" No one answered him. "Then let's carry on gathering as much information as we can and entice this murdering bastard out into the open."

Faith stood and slipped the journal into her reticule. "I have to go. Ian wants me to accompany him to an exhibit at Somerset House."

"I'll escort you upstairs, my lady." Adam offered his arm and they left together, followed by a silent Mr. Maclean.

Malinda remained at the table, her hands joined in front of her.

"It will be all right, Malinda."

She looked up to see that Benedict had also stayed in his seat. He wore a navy blue coat that darkened the color of his eyes and set off his blond coloring to advantage. He seemed relaxed and rather distant. It wasn't hard to guess why.

"I suppose you are annoyed with me."

"Why would you think that?"

"Because I can't let go of the notion that your father is somehow behind all of this."

He shrugged one elegant shoulder. "As I mentioned before, there isn't a lot I can do about it, is there? When you get an idea in your head, it is impossible to reason with you."

She shot to her feet. "So I'm the one who is at fault here? It isn't that you are still so mired in loyalty to your father that you can't see him for what he truly is?"

He stretched out his legs and leaned back to look up at her, his face expressionless, his mouth a hard line. "I might say the same about you."

"My father is *dead*."

"And mine soon will be."

"So he still deserves your respect, your sympathy, and your protection, is that it?"

"I don't know what he deserves, which is why I'm trying to keep an open mind and not allow myself to become bogged down in emotions."

"Like I am."

"I didn't say that." He hesitated. "Malinda, he might be my father, but I am perfectly capable of believing he might have lied. No one is perfect, especially those we love."

"I don't believe that you are able to detach yourself so easily from this particular set of circumstances. This isn't just another case. It involves your *family*."

"I'm well aware of that."

"Then perhaps you could stop pretending to be so above it all."

He rose from his seat to loom over her, and she forced herself not to flinch away. "Are you determined to make me choose a side?"

"Sometimes you have to."

A muscle flicked in his cheek. "Ah, yes. Last time I chose *you,* and you ran away. Good morning, my lady."

He was almost at the door before she took a hasty step toward him.

"Benedict, I'm not asking you to choose between your father and me. I'm asking you to use all your considerable gifts to solve this case."

He turned around and stared down at her. "And then what?"

"Then we'll know the truth."

"That is all you require of me, is it, ma'am?"

She nodded.

"So that you can return to Alford Park and live out the rest of your days in peace."

"That has always been my aim."

"Of course, how could I have forgotten?" He swept her a low bow. "Then I'll do my very best to ensure that it happens."

He turned and left, shutting the door quietly behind him. Malinda stared down at the polished walnut table and told herself not to be stupid. He'd made it very clear that he didn't trust her, or anyone else for that matter. Despite everything, he still hoped his father would be innocent. Was he right? Was she too consumed in her need to make *his* father pay to be objective? Would it be better if both of them left the case to others?

She'd tried not to think about how he'd stood up for her in front of his father all those years ago. She'd never expected it, hadn't believed him, hadn't had enough faith in him to stay and fight for their marriage. Did that still rankle? Had he found it impossible to forgive her even after all this time? Perhaps he felt that defending his father now balanced out his earlier actions of mistakenly supporting her. He certainly seemed to have an issue trusting anyone.

It was lucky for him that she'd decided to tell him the truth, or else he wouldn't have known . . . she paused and thought back over the conversation. With a curse, she flung open the door and went into Benedict's office. Mr. Maclean looked up as she came in.

"His lordship went upstairs, my lady. I believe he was getting ready to go out."

"Thank you."

She ran up the stairs in a very unladylike fashion and stormed into his suite. He was in their bedroom collecting his outdoor coat, hat, and gloves. She shut the door and leaned against it, breathing hard.

"You already knew I'd gone with my father before I spoke to you."

"What makes you think that?" He continued to study his reflection in the mirror as he adjusted the set of the pin in his cravat.

"Adam said I was seen with the party on the coast."

"We were told that a young red-haired boy was with the soldiers. I guessed it might be you. You might recall that there weren't any redheaded boys in our regiment." He brushed the sleeve of his coat, his gaze fixed on the task.

"What would you have done if I hadn't volunteered that information to you?"

"I had faith that you would, eventually." He picked up his gloves and hat.

She stared at him. "Because if I hadn't, you might have believed I was part of the conspiracy? Do you really think I would be involved in a plot to kill my own *father?*"

He looked at her then. "I had to make sure." He walked toward her and she flinched out of his way. "If you insist I treat my father as a suspect, you can hardly expect me to treat you any differently."

She let him leave and waited until she heard the outer door of the apartment slam before she slid down the wall to the floor and allowed herself to cry. What was worse was that she could see the logic in his decision, could even applaud his resolution to be evenhanded. Wasn't that exactly what she'd just asked him to do?

But damn him, it hurt.

She wiped her eyes and loudly blew her nose. She'd challenged him to use his formidable intelligence to solve the case, and she should be grateful for his ability to put his personal desires to one side. With a groan she rubbed away all traces of her tears. If he could be unemotional about what had happened, then so could she. It was probably the only way either of them would survive.

"Benedict."

Adam stood at the bottom of the stairs right in his path, which meant unless Benedict was prepared to shove his friend out of the way, he'd have to speak to him. Part of him welcomed the notion of violence—of the chance to clear his head with something as pure as a fist in the face or a broken nose.

Adam put his hand on his arm. "What's wrong?"

"Oh, nothing, just that Malinda worked out that she was considered a suspect along with my father."

"Oh, dear." Adam winced. "She is a remarkably astute woman."

"I know."

"Where are you going?"

"Preferably somewhere without a female in sight."

Adam smiled. "Then wait a moment until I get my hat, and I'll come with you."

It was only when he stumbled as he walked up the stairs of the Sinners that Benedict wondered if he was drunk. Adam had taken him in hand, and they'd spent the rest of the day shooting pistols, boxing, and viewing horses at Tattersalls. They'd ended up watching a cock fight at a notorious London pub where a fight was usually guaranteed. Rather than leaving to avoid the inevitable, they'd stayed and both fought with abandon, resulting in a bloody nose for Adam and cracked knuckles for Benedict.

He flexed his fingers as he went into his apartment and winced. Apart from the red glint of the banked-up coal in the fireplace, the room was in darkness. He headed toward the closed door of his bedroom and then hesitated. Would Malinda welcome him into her bed? That was debatable at the best of times, and in his current state highly unlikely.

He gently belched and turned away, tripping over one of the chair legs and making a terrible racket that rang through the silence like a bell. Holding his breath, he waited for the inevitable appearance of his wife, but there was no sound. A waft of stale beer, sweat, and smoke came from his person and he wrinkled his nose. Perhaps he'd be better off having a bath before he allowed himself to fall asleep.

Moving more cautiously now, he crossed over to the door leading to the shared bathroom and let himself in there. It took him a few moments of fumbling around to light the fire and a set of candles. He touched the brass boiler, which was still warm. Had Malinda already bathed? He pictured her creamy skin, the pink of her nipples, and the freckles he loved to kiss.

While the bath filled, he stripped off his clothing, discovering quite a few bruises and bumps as he went. After testing the water, he stepped in and sank down with a sigh, the back of his head resting on the rim of the bath, his gaze fixed on the ceiling.

Peace . . .

He closed his eyes to savor it.

"Benedict."

He ignored the voice, persistent and familiar as it was.

"Benedict!"

He opened one eye, and Malinda's pale face swam in front of his vision and abruptly disappeared.

"God, *no.*" He suddenly slid beneath the surface, his mouth filling with water.

She hauled him up by his hair, coughing and spluttering.

"You nearly drowned! Now, get out of the bath. The water is freezing!"

He became aware of a coldness eating its way into his bones, making him shiver, and struggled to sit up. With an impatient sound, Malinda brought a large drying cloth over to him and wrapped it around his shoulders. He managed to step out of the bath without disgracing himself, and allowed her to lead him back into the apartment and tuck him into bed.

She smoothed his damp hair away from his face and lay down beside him, her nose practically touching his.

"Go to sleep, Benedict."

He nodded and closed his eyes again. If she wasn't going to

shout at him, he was simply going to appreciate the moment, and do as she suggested without any argument at all.

Malinda studied Benedict as he slept, his ridiculously long eyelashes and the stark curve of his jaw and slanted cheek-bones. Seeing him like this, she realized nothing much had changed from the boy she'd once known and loved. His expression was peaceful, his mouth curved up in a half smile as she stroked his damp, curling hair behind his ear.

But when he woke and directed his deceptively cool blue gaze on her, things were always more complicated. If she'd known there would still be a spark between them, would she even have begun this mad dance? She'd seen him as a means to get to his father, and that hadn't proved to be the case at all. He was still Benedict, *her* Benedict, the other half of her soul. Just because she tried to deny that connection didn't mean it didn't exist.

She sighed and kissed his nose. He stirred on his pillow, fighting against the constraints of the towel that was still wrapped around him. Hardly daring to move, Malinda slowly pulled the covers away and started to extricate him from his tangled cocoon. Eventually she had the towel laid flat beneath him and was ready to cover them both up again.

Except she paused to admire him in the soft dawn light, the muscled length of his legs, his narrow waist, and the way his hip bones jutted out in a distinctly masculine way that made her want to lick them. She leaned closer to examine the scar on his left arm, her hair trailing over his chest. He murmured her name, one hand catching in her hair, and brought her down to meet his mouth.

She kissed him because she wanted to, because in this half light maybe she could offer him something without words and recriminations and reach that boy inside him, the one she'd loved, the boy who'd been willing to risk everything for her.

She kissed him slowly and tenderly, aware that he wasn't quite awake, but almost glad of it. Reluctantly, she released his mouth and nuzzled his jaw, the rough stubble only adding spice to the caress.

Moving her way down, she continued to use her mouth on him, licking his nipples, counting off his ribs with her fingers and then with tiny nips until she reached his muscled stomach and the jut of his hips. She sighed as his cock stirred and bent her head to it, taking him gently into her mouth. She sucked him in long, slow pulls from tip to root until he was filling her mouth and moving with her.

"Mally."

He moved suddenly, and then she was beneath him and he was easing himself inside her tight passage. She arched her back and lifted her hips to help him surge into her and then wrapped her arms and legs around him as he started to thrust. Why did she always feel so safe with him when he pushed her to sexual extremes she'd never consider alone? They came together and he rolled them, still joined, onto their sides and instantly went back to sleep, leaving Malinda to bury her face against his chest and simply breathe him in.

They'd be fighting again soon enough, but maybe in this place, in this small corner of their complex world, they could truly be themselves. With that thought she finally managed to go back to sleep.

17

A knock on the door made Malinda put down the book she was pretending to read and look up. Faith's head appeared around the door.

"May I come in?"

"If you are looking for Benedict or Adam, you are out of luck. They've both gone out."

Faith came in, took off her bonnet, and patted her curls. "Actually I was looking for you. I've just been visiting with the Marquis and Marchioness of Alford."

Malinda put away her book. "And?"

"The marchioness is *extremely* annoying."

"Did she prevent you from speaking to the marquis alone?

"She tried, but he sent her away."

"Oh, good." She looked expectantly at Faith. "Well, what did he have to say for himself?"

"Firstly, he was extremely annoyed that we'd found out about the gold and who owned it."

"I'm not surprised." Malinda hesitated. "Are you sure you don't want to wait until Benedict is here to discuss this?"

"I'm not sure if he'll want to hear what I've discovered."
Faith frowned. "After a lot of blustering about not discussing
such important matters with a woman, the marquis told me
that he'd never seen the gold again, but that in return he *had*
kept back some of the promissory notes and coins the government had eventually sent on. He said it was only a token
amount to cover his expenses, but for all intents and purposes,
what he did was stealing and completely illegal."

"And he doesn't want Benedict to know about that."

"As his only son is employed by the government, he feels
Benedict might be honor bound to report the matter to his su-
periors."

"He might. He is a great one for the truth." Malinda sighed.
"How do we know the marquis isn't lying this time?"

"He offered me access to his accounting books from that
time period, which he says show the true state of affairs. Of
course, he could be lying about that as well. I got the sense that
his whole aim in this matter was to prevent his past mistakes
from being revealed to Benedict."

"I wish that didn't sound so plausible." Malinda grimaced.
"But it would be just like him. It would be so much easier if the
marquis would simply admit that everything is his fault."

"And what if it isn't?"

"Then we're still fumbling around in the dark." Malinda
stood up to add some more coal to the fire. "What are you
going to tell Benedict?"

"I rather hoped you would do that."

"Me? He won't believe a word I say about his father."

"But if I have to tell him or Adam, or my husband, it immediately becomes an official matter. Benedict might feel he has
no choice but to take the subject further."

"Don't you want him to do that?"

"Malinda, my love, the marquis is dying. He probably won't

last the year. I don't see the point of harassing him to his death with threatened legal action, do you?"

"It has its attractions."

"I can understand you thinking that. He's hardly been a good friend to your family, has he?"

"He did pay my mother a pension of sorts after my father died."

"It must have been fairly substantial if it allowed you and your sister to board at a nunnery."

"Well, apparently, Benedict sent money, so we were well provided for." She paused to gather her thoughts. "I suppose there isn't any point in forcing Benedict to turn in his own father."

"Which is why the information is better coming from you. You can tell him that if he chooses to deal privately with this matter, none of us will ever mention it again."

"You care about him, don't you?"

"Benedict? Yes, he's been very much alone these past few years."

"I thought we were divorced."

Faith widened her eyes. "Oh, my dear, I wasn't criticizing you."

"You don't need to. I feel guilty enough myself. I didn't know he'd . . ."

"Wait for you?" Faith smiled. "That was always the sense I got from him. That he'd found what he wanted long ago and nothing else had matched up to it ever since."

Malinda scowled at Faith. "Now you're going to make me cry. He's not the same boy I married. He deserves more."

"Isn't that up to him?" Faith rose and came around to drop a kiss on Malinda's bowed head. "Speak to Benedict when he gets back, and then make sure you are down in Adam's study by six o'clock to hear what Nicodemus has to tell us about our arsonist."

Malinda returned to her book, but found herself constantly rereading the same sentences. It was almost a relief to hear Benedict's firm tread on the stairs. She rose to her feet, the book clutched to her chest, and smiled at him as he came through the door.

He abruptly halted. "What's wrong?"

Her smile dimmed a trifle. "Benedict, would you like tea? I can ring for some to be brought up."

He remained by the door as he peeled off his gloves and took off his hat. "I repeat, what's wrong?"

"I just asked you if you'd like a cup of tea. What's 'wrong' with that?"

"Because normally you're not this nice to me."

"That's a horrible thing to say."

"But it's true, isn't it? Usually you barge into my office and *demand* things."

"I'm fairly certain you are exaggerating somewhat, Benedict. I am generally considered to be a very pleasant person."

"Not by me. The only time you're sweet to me is when you either want me to do something for you, or you have a confession to make about something you've done that you know will infuriate me. So which is it?"

She scowled at him as he placed his hat and gloves on the small table by the door.

"That's much better. Now, what's wrong?"

"Perhaps you'd like to sit down. Are you sure that you don't want some tea?"

He sat, crossed one long leg over the other, and looked at her inquiringly.

She sank down into the chair opposite. "It's about your father."

"Oh?" His smiling mask was in place and his gaze was guarded. "And what did he have to say for himself?"

"He denied ever seeing the gold again."

"As I expected. What else?"

"He said that when the pay did arrive from the government, and he dispersed it to the men, he kept back—a certain percentage to cover some of his losses."

His hand tightened on the arm of the chair. "His words, I assume."

"So I believe."

"You didn't go and see him yourself?"

"No. I promised you I wouldn't do that."

"Then how do you know about this?"

"Faith went as planned."

"Then why didn't she tell me this herself? She can hardly have thought it would sound more palatable coming from a woman who hates my father even more than I do."

There was a sharp edge to his voice that made her want to throw up her hands and walk away. But she'd promised Faith she'd tell him. It wasn't uncommon for the messenger to bear the brunt of the recipient's displeasure.

"Faith was concerned that if you received this information from a more 'formal' source that you might feel you had to act on it. She thought that if I told you—"

"I wouldn't believe it?"

She held his icily amused gaze. "No, that you would understand that if you choose not to act, no one would mention the matter again."

"Then my father would be allowed to get away with defrauding both his government and, worst of all, the men who served in that regiment?" His smile was a masterpiece of scorn. "Why aren't you ripping up at me? What in God's name made Faith think *you'd* agree with me dropping a potential prosecution against my father?"

She forced herself to remain calm. "Because I understand."

He simply stared at her, one eyebrow raised.

"He's your father, Benedict."

He sat back. "And you've all agreed amongst yourselves that I am too weak to act against him, have you?"

"You're not weak."

"But you've all decided to protect me from myself?"

"Yes."

"Even you?"

She nodded.

"For God's sake, *why?*"

"Because Faith is right. He's dying. It would be cruel to drag him and your family name through the courts."

"You were quite willing to do that when you accused him of killing your father."

"No, I was just going to kill him myself. The only person who would've stood trial would've been me." She tried again. "Despite everything, Benedict, I do understand that your father usually has your best interests at heart."

"Like when he forced us to part?"

"I didn't say they were *our* best interests. He is an arrogant man. He knows best for everyone, especially his only son."

"I can't believe you are defending him."

"I'm not, I'm—" She took a deep breath as her voice rose. "The only person who would suffer if all this came to light would be you, Benedict."

He slowly rose to his feet, his hands fisted at his side. "You think I'm not strong enough to cope with that kind of notoriety—with prosecuting my own father—with upholding the standards of the very government I work for?"

"That's not what I meant." She forced herself to hold his now hostile gaze.

He smiled. "Oh, I forgot, now that you've realized you're still married to me, are you perhaps afraid of me damaging *your* reputation?"

She held on to her temper. "No one doubts your courage, Benedict, or your ability to do the right thing."

"Then what?"

"I just don't want you to be hurt."

He froze. "Damn you to hell." He turned on his heel and headed for the door.

She closed her eyes as he slammed it shut behind him. Hadn't she learned anything about men? Suggesting that they might be too emotionally involved in something was tantamount to questioning their virility. Benedict hadn't changed in that respect at all.

She sank back down onto the seat. And now she didn't know what he was going to do and she couldn't report back to Faith. In this mood, Benedict could make things worse by demanding answers from his father and deliberately causing the kind of scandal they'd all been trying to avoid.

The clock on the mantelpiece struck six times, and she rose to her feet. Sitting here worrying wouldn't achieve anything. She would go downstairs, warn Faith that Benedict was not in the best of moods, and listen to what Nicodemus Theale had to say for himself.

"My lord?" Benedict glanced up as his new secretary came toward him with yet another pile of papers in his hand. "Are you intending to go out again? Mr. Fisher asked me to remind you that Mr. Theale is due to report in at six."

Benedict glanced at the open front door and then back at his secretary.

"I suppose I should attend that meeting." He turned away from his glimpse of freedom and went down the corridor toward his office. "Is there anything else you wished to discuss with me?"

"Nothing urgent, sir."

"Thank God," Benedict muttered. Sense was returning to

his brain and the urge to rush around to his father and shake him until his bones rattled was slowly subsiding. He *never* behaved like that. He was known for his coldness, his ability to stand back and not let his emotions become involved. Malinda would laugh if she could hear his thoughts. She thought he was an irrational, emotional, tempestuous bully, and to be fair, he felt like one when he was with her.

But that wasn't her fault, was it? He had the opportunity to prove to all of them that he could handle himself perfectly well even with regards to his father.

His father . . .

"Ah, Benedict, are you coming in?"

He looked up to see Adam approaching his study, Nicodemus behind him.

"Yes."

He followed them in and saw that the Countess of Westbrook and his wife were already sitting at the table. Nodding politely in their direction, he took the seat as far away from Malinda as possible and turned his attention to his colleague.

Nicodemus took a large leather-bound book from his capacious pocket, leafed through the pages, and stood up.

"Good evening, everyone. I'm pleased to tell you that I found the man I believe was responsible for setting fire to your house, Lord Keyes."

"And where is he now?"

"Awaiting the attention of the magistrates at Bow Street." Nicodemus paused. "Obviously, he wasn't acting for himself, but he could have killed any of the occupants of the house. When he protested at revealing his employer, I reminded him of that, and suggested his sentence could be lighter if he gave me the name of the person who paid him."

"I assume he accepted your generous offer."

"Oh yes, Edgar's no stranger to the criminal courts, my lord. He insisted he was told quite specifically not to stop anyone leaving the house, so that he could hardly be accused of murder. According to him, it was supposed to be a warning. He was offered the job by a man he'd met at the Red Dragon, a coaching inn near Bethnal Green just off the great road."

"Did he give you the man's name?"

"He insisted he didn't know it, sir. But he did describe him to me." Nicodemus turned a page of his book and scrutinized the tightly written script. "The man was pleasantly spoken, and neither a swell or a beggar. He was in his late fifties, about five and a half feet tall with black hair, graying at the temples, and blue eyes."

"That's hardly helpful," Benedict said. "What else?"

"From something that he let slip, Edgar thought the man worked at the Red Dragon. We might be able to locate him there."

"I wonder if he is another intermediary?" Adam said. "If he works at an inn, it hardly sounds as if he's living in luxury."

"True." Benedict considered the information. "Perhaps our real target thinks that one of us will recognize him, and is therefore being very cautious about revealing himself."

Adam nodded. "That would make sense."

"Which also means that it is probably someone Malinda and I knew from our days with the regiment."

"Unfortunately, yes."

"But it does help. Before word gets back to our man that his arsonist has been apprehended, I suggest that Malinda and I visit the Red Dragon." He glanced over at his wife for the first time. "Are you willing to accompany me, my lady?"

"Yes."

She looked as calm as he did, her normally expressive face reserved.

"Then we'd better make haste. We'll need to go in disguise."

"What do you want me to wear, my lord?"

He thought quickly about the clothes she had and dismissed them. "I want you to look like my mistress. There should be some items on the second floor that you can borrow. Consult with Maddon."

"I'll do that right now."

"And don't forget something to cover up your hair."

She nodded, curtsied to the room in general, and went out. He was about to follow when Faith touched his arm.

"Benedict, before you go, I wanted to share something else with you."

"Can't it wait?"

"It depends on whether you want to catch our ambushers or not."

Something in her tone made him sit down again. "What is it?"

"I've been reading Malinda's mother's journal, and it mentions the name of the nunnery where she left her daughter."

"So?"

"I asked Nicodemus if he could find out anything about it. He says it was an extremely well-protected and expensive place to stay."

"I gathered that from the way Malinda was transformed from a hoyden into a lady there."

"But how did Mrs. Rowland, or Mrs. Makethorpe as she became known, afford that?"

"I believe it was a combination of the pension my father sent her, and my contributions."

"From what Nico tells me, I still doubt she could've afforded the place."

Nicodemus nodded in agreement.

"Maybe they took pity on her and let her stay for a pittance?" Benedict suggested. "Or perhaps when the war engulfed them, they had no choice but to keep the girls until someone chose to return for them?"

Faith looked unconvinced.

"Why does it matter?"

"Because it doesn't quite fit with everything else."

He held her gaze. "No, you're right, it doesn't. Do you want me to give my permission to Nicodemus to investigate further?"

"If you would."

He turned to the investigator, who had been listening quietly to the conversation. "Please go ahead and find out anything you can."

Nicodemus bowed.

"Thank you, Benedict." Faith patted his hand.

"Now, is there anything else before I go and brave the delights of the Red Dragon?"

"Are you speaking about your wife or the inn?" Adam murmured.

Benedict smiled and went to the door. "To be honest, I'm not quite sure."

"Will this do?"

Benedict's face was enough to convince her that she'd perhaps gone too far in her efforts to look like a man's mistress. She attempted to pull up the low purple-striped satin bodice to a more decorous level.

"No, you look perfect. I almost didn't recognize you."

She touched her hair. "It's the blond wig, isn't it? I must confess that I hardly recognized myself when I first put it on."

"Let me just finish dressing and we can go."

He'd changed into a flashier suit of clothing that shouted new money and padded out his normally slender frame until he had a distinct potbelly. He was currently engaged in dousing his blond hair in white powder and pomade, making him look twenty years older. A pair of spectacles completed his disguise. He turned to her and bowed.

"Ma'am?"

Even his body seemed different, his posture less certain, his shoulders hunched over, and his demeanor that of an aging roué.

"What shall I call you?"

"Darling, sweetings? Mr. Ludlow?"

"I assume I'm not *Mrs.* Ludlow."

"No, she is a dour-faced churchgoing Methodist from up north. You, my dear, are Clarabelle Evans, my current mistress."

"Clarabelle?"

"It's your stage name and that's where I met you. You used to be a dancer in one of the musical shows."

"Oh." She took his arm and they proceeded down the backstairs. A hired carriage awaited them in the street. When Malinda stepped inside, she was greeted by the sound of excited yapping somewhere within a sea of parcels and bandboxes.

"What is that?"

Benedict groaned. "It's probably one of Faith's annoying little dogs."

Malinda found a small, white fluffy dog on one of the seats and held him in her arms. "He's adorable."

"He's a combination of a feather duster and a rat."

"And is just the sort of dog a woman of ill repute would love."

"You may bring him as long as you promise to be responsible for him."

"I will be." Malinda buried her face in the pup's soft fur. "I miss my dogs terribly."

He took the seat opposite her. "I've never owned a dog." He half-smiled. "I've never settled long enough anywhere to actually have one of my own. It didn't seem fair."

Malinda looked up at him and reminded herself not to be anything less than professional.

"What exactly are we looking for at the inn?"

"The man Nicodemus described and anyone else who looks

familiar." He hesitated. "I would appreciate it if you took your cues from me."

"I will."

"Thank you." He looked out of the small window. "We should be there fairly quickly."

"Good."

She repressed a sigh and turned to admire the view from her own window. They were being excruciatingly polite to each other and she hated it. The carriage started to slow and made a left turn. The line of modest town houses disappeared, leaving more irregular timber buildings along the sides of the narrowing road. A blaze of light and a red dragon of Wales sign heralded the appearance of the coaching inn.

Benedict took her hand as their carriage turned in to the coaching yard.

"Ready, love?"

She fixed a smile on her face and waited for him to open the door and help her down. Dodging the stable hands who were already dealing with the horses, they approached the main door of the inn. Before her eyes Benedict turned into an elderly roué strolling along with his latest ladybird proudly on his arm.

"I say, landlord!"

Even his voice was different, higher pitched, more anxious, and yet full of overbearing conceit.

"Yes, sir, how can I help you this fine evening?"

"Dinner for myself and the lady." Malinda giggled when the landlord looked at her. "In a private parlor."

"Of course, sir. If you'll just step this way."

"Oh, Mr. Ludlow, you are so fancy! A private parlor? I'd be quite happy to sit down and eat with all the common folk." She winked at the landlord.

"And have them ogling you all night, my love? I don't think so."

She pouted. "We must make sure that Mr. Feathers gets

something special to eat too. You know how sensitive his little tummy is."

"All too well, my dear. Landlord, my lady's little dog is in the carriage. Could you have someone bring him around to her?"

"Yes, sir." The landlord looked around and beckoned to one of the harassed-looking serving girls. "Joan, go and fetch this lady's dog, will you? And bring it back to parlor number three."

"Oh, three is my favorite number," breathed Malinda. "You know why, my little bunny, don't you?" She kissed Benedict's ear and whispered far too loudly, "Especially when I'm in the middle."

The landlord's ears went red as Benedict patted her bottom, and they followed him into one of the private parlors. When he'd left, Malinda sat down by the fire as Benedict closed the curtains and checked that the doors leading into the other parlors were firmly locked.

"We're not going to see much trapped in here."

"*You're* not going to see much. I, however, can wander around and chat with the common folk at will."

Why had he brought her if he didn't intend to let her help? She compressed her lips into a straight line and said nothing. There was a knock on the door, and Joan appeared clutching the squirming little dog to her bosom.

"Here you are, miss."

Malinda let out a shriek of joy and dropped to her knees. "Oh, look, it's my precious, my darling little boy." She scooped up the dog and kissed him. "Thank you, Joan."

"You're welcome, miss."

Benedict pressed a coin into her hand, and Joan curtsied before she turned and left.

"Are we really going to eat here?" Malinda asked.

"Yes, and we'll take our time doing so. I want to have a good look around."

She picked up the little dog and settled in a chair by the fire. Benedict seemed unable to settle. She suspected he was finding it equally difficult being trapped in a room being polite to her. The quicker he went off exploring, the quicker she could get on with her own agenda.

A knock on the door heralded the arrival of the landlord. "Dinner will be served in the next half hour, sir. I hope that is satisfactory."

Benedict looked resigned and Malinda pouted.

"My fluffy bunny will be hungry." She gazed at the landlord, but he was staring at her breasts. "Can't we give him something before he fades away?"

"Maybe a bone from the kitchen, my dear?" Benedict inquired.

Malinda screeched with laughter that made both the men wince and danced over to Benedict.

"Not the doggie, bunny, *you!*" She kissed his cheek, leaving the imprint of her lip stain. "I know you'll need your strength for later." She winked at the landlord, who practically swallowed his tongue. "My sweeting needs red meat to keep up with me."

"I'll be fine, my dear."

Malinda's face fell, and she whispered loudly in Benedict's ear, "But last time you only managed it three times, bunny, and you *know* that's not enough for me." She cast a sly glance at the landlord. "Unless you want to find reinforcements—isn't your valet here yet, my love?"

"He's—" Benedict suddenly turned to the landlord. "Be on your way, man! And bring me a jug of your best ale, and some ratafia for the lady."

"No champagne?" Malinda's lip wobbled. "Are you bored with me already?" Despite everything, she was beginning to enjoy herself.

Benedict patted her cheek. "Champagne if you have it, land-lord. All shall be as my lady desires."

Malinda gave another little squeal and wrapped her arms around Benedict. "Thank you, bunny. I *adore* you!"

"Yes, well." Benedict extricated himself from her embrace and waved a hand at the landlord. "Off with you."

The door had barely shut behind the landlord before Malinda collapsed laughing into the nearest chair. Benedict stared down at her, his expression inscrutable.

"I never realized you should've been on the stage."

"With Ben, perhaps? We make a remarkably amusing pair."

He finally smiled, and she grinned back at him.

"I'm going to wander out into the bar and see if I can find the man we're after."

"I'll be here." She cuddled the dog and kissed his adorable face.

He hesitated by the door. "You did agree to follow my lead in this situation."

"I know." She kept her tone light and nonconfrontational. "Good luck with your hunt."

When Benedict returned a quarter of an hour later, Malinda was still sitting by the fire petting the dog and drinking a glass of what appeared to be champagne. He paused, both to admire the sight of her glorious bosom swelling over the nonexistent bodice of her gown and to accustom himself to the sight of her actually doing what he'd asked.

"Did you find him?"

"No." Benedict sighed and dropped into the chair opposite hers. "I didn't see anyone I recognized either."

"Oh, dear." She moved the sleeping dog to one side. "Joan said dinner was about to be brought in."

He realized he was hungry. It was turning into yet another frustrating day. He couldn't even find the energy to provoke

Malinda into a fight, not that he intended to do that anyway. He was beyond such childish matters.

Malinda rose as the door opened and clapped her hands, waking up the dog, who jumped down on the floor and started barking.

"Dinner's here, bunny!"

"So it is." Benedict stayed out of the way as two serving men brought in a variety of dishes and set them on the table. At least the food looked edible. He held out a chair for Malinda and then sat himself. "May I help you to some lamb, my dear?"

Malinda ate well, throwing scraps to the little dog at every opportunity until he stopped looking for them and went and sat expectantly by the door.

"I think I need to take the dog outside."

"I can do that." Benedict was still eating, but he put his knife down.

"You'll look silly holding a little dog, and we don't want to draw attention to ourselves, do we?"

"I think you're the one who should be remembering that."

"I'll ask one of the serving maids to accompany me. Will that satisfy you?"

He glanced at the clock on the mantelpiece. "If you're not back in five minutes, I'm coming to find you."

She slid out of her chair and raced over to the door, picking the dog up in her arms.

"Be careful."

She went out into the corridor and walked toward the front of the inn, her gaze lingering on every face she encountered.

"May I help you, miss?"

It was Joan again. Malinda smiled at the girl. "Oh, yes please. I need to take my little doggie outside for a moment. Is there somewhere quiet where those big, beastly horses won't trample him to death?"

"There's a separate yard at the back. You can take him out there."

"Thank you."

"Follow me."

From the set of Joan's shoulders and the tone of her voice, Malinda guessed she didn't approve of scantily clad women who arrived at inns on the arms of elderly gentlemen.

"Do you enjoy your work here, Joan?"

"It's a respectable living, miss."

Malinda tittered. "I can hardly say that about myself."

"Each to their own. Our good Lord told us not to judge others."

"Oh yes, Mary Magdalene and all that. I wonder if bunny would like it if I dried his feet with my hair?"

Joan made a snorting sound and Malinda bit her lip.

"Do you live here too?"

"Yes, miss. My father's the landlord."

Ah, she'd guessed right. Joan's large nose was identical to her father's.

"He owns the inn?"

"No, that would be Mr. Castleton."

Malinda stroked the dog's head. "That name sounds familiar to me. I wonder why?" She flicked a glance at Joan. "Is Mr. Castleton in his fifth decade and does he have blue eyes and black hair graying at the temples?"

"That sounds like him, but—here you are, miss." Joan opened another door and Malinda peered into the darkness. She could smell the stables and other unsavory things, but it was at least quiet.

She had a name and it was vaguely familiar to her. Perhaps it was time to return to Benedict. The dog whined and scrabbled to be put down so she released him into the yard.

"What are you doing back here with that door open, lass?"

Malinda turned to see an older man approaching them and

immediately spun back 'round, crouched down on her heels, and called the dog.

"The lady needed to see to her dog, Mr. Castleton."

"Did she now, then ask her to be quick about it before we all freeze to death."

"Yes, sir."

A sharp bark announced the return of the dog. Malinda gathered him close in her arms and turned back to Joan.

"Thank you so much. I should be getting back to my bunny before he becomes anxious."

"You're welcome, miss."

They started back up the corridor. It was only at the last moment that Malinda realized the elusive Mr. Castleton had remained in the hall and was staring at her intently. She hurriedly buried her face in the dog's fur and hoped he hadn't gotten a good look at her. Hopefully, like most men, he was more concerned with ogling her bosom.

Just as she reached the door of the private parlor, it opened and Benedict appeared, his pocket watch in his hand.

"Oh, there you are, bunny!" Malinda cooed. "Did you miss me?"

She wrapped an arm around his neck to kiss him and whispered, "I have a name, but I think we should leave right now."

"I've already ordered the carriage to be made ready."

He stepped back into the room and she let go of him. To his credit, he didn't immediately start interrogating her. Instead, he left some coins on the table, wrapped her cloak around her, and picked up the dog.

"Let's go."

She tucked her hand in the crook of his arm and leaned against him, burying her face in his coat. He might not look like her Benedict, but he still smelled like him. The inn was busier now, and he had to force a passage through the incoming passengers who'd just alighted from one of the mail coaches. Malinda kept her head down and clung to him like a limpet.

She didn't take a proper breath until they were inside the carriage and moving away.

"What happened?"

Benedict's relaxed air had disappeared.

"It was unfortunate."

"What did you do?"

She raised her chin. "I merely took the dog out to piss. I asked Joan to come with me. She told me that her father was the landlord of the inn."

"So?"

"I asked if he owned it, and she said that was Mr. Castleton. I described our man and she agreed it sounded as though it could be him."

"And that didn't make her suspicious?"

"I implied that I knew him in a more intimate manner than she did. She didn't question me further." She sighed. "Unfortunately, the man himself chose to come and inquire why the blasted door was open and letting in the cold. I didn't realize until too late. I think he caught a clear glimpse of me."

"Is it likely that would matter?"

She met his gaze. "It might. Do you remember Fred Castleton from the regiment?"

"I do. He was a friend of your father's."

"Well, I think it was him."

18

Malinda hid a yawn as she glanced around the table in Adam's office. It was well past midnight and it felt as though she'd been sitting in the same spot for hours. Benedict, Adam, and Faith were locked in an argument about the importance of what had happened at the inn, and what they should do about it. She was still surprised that Benedict had taken the news so calmly. He was obviously determined to prove that he could conduct an investigation without emotion. It was quite disconcerting.

He looked over at her. "Are you all right, my lady?"

"Just a little tired." She summoned a calm smile. "Now that I think about it more rationally, I don't understand why we need to worry about Fred Castleton. It's unlikely he would remember me after eighteen years, and I *was* disguised."

"Surely that depends on whether he's involved in this business or not. I doubt it was a coincidence that we ended up at the very inn he owned, do you?"

"I wonder how he got the money to purchase the place?" Adam asked. "Was he an officer?"

"No."

"Then perhaps we need to find a way to talk to him about his finances."

Benedict stood up and held out his hand to Malinda. "We aren't going to come to a decision tonight, so maybe we should all go to bed and sleep on it?"

"An excellent idea." Faith rose too. "Ian will be furious at missing all this." She paused to kiss Malinda's cheek. "Sleep well, love."

Malinda followed Benedict up the stairs and into his apartment and allowed him to help her out of her elaborate gown. She sat down at the dressing table to unpin the blond wig and grimaced at the faint stirring of a headache. Even after taking off the wig, she still had to undo her tightly braided hair.

Benedict disappeared into the bathing room next door and returned with wet but powderless hair and climbed into bed, blowing out all but one of the candles. By the time Malinda eased the final braid apart, the candle had almost burned through. She brought it over to the bed, found her nightdress, and put it on. She knew immediately that Benedict was not asleep. Tension hummed through his frame and heat radiated from his extremities.

She turned onto her side away from him and resolutely closed her eyes, only to open them again as Benedict sighed.

"Do you wish to talk about it?" Malinda asked.

"No."

She persisted. "You told me that you do your best thinking last thing at night."

"That's true."

"I can hear your mind ticking like a carriage clock."

He touched her shoulder. "I'm sorry. I know that you're tired."

"I won't be able to sleep until you settle down, so you might as well say what you are thinking. I did my best to do as you asked me, Benedict. I wasn't sure if my questions to Joan would yield anything."

"Yet you had to ask them."

"When the opportunity arose, I took it—which was exactly what you would have done in my shoes."

"Fair enough." He rubbed his hand over his unshaven jaw. "I wasn't actually thinking about Fred."

"Then what?"

"Your performance this evening."

"I knew you wouldn't approve." She rolled onto her back. "It worked, didn't it? I got the information we needed. And to be honest, I suspect Fred Castleton was too busy looking at my décolletage to worry much about my face."

He shifted on the sheets. "As was every man there."

"I know. It's ridiculous." She cupped her breast. "I'm not even that well-endowed."

His hand covered hers. "You're perfect."

Her nipple pebbled against her palm. She tried not to think about it. "Every time I believe we are making progress, everything gets more complicated."

"Are you talking about the ambushers or about us?"

She sighed. "Both, I suppose."

"There is one certainty." His fingers slid underneath hers and took possession of her breast. "We are married."

"So you keep telling me."

"Which means that anything we do in this bed together is sanctified by both church and state."

She swallowed hard. "You don't have to justify your lust, Benedict."

His hand went still. "I apologize if I have insulted you."

"That's not what I meant. There's always been a spark between us. Lust is as convenient a name for it as anything else."

The candle finally spluttered and went out, leaving them in darkness.

"I can't stop wanting you."

He sounded as though the words were being dragged out of him.

"You don't have to." She tried to sound calm. "It's not as if I have the willpower to say no. And as you mentioned, we *are* married, so you don't even need my permission to exercise your conjugal rights."

He came up on one elbow and looked down at her. "That's not amusing. I would never—"

"Force me?" She forced herself to smile even though he probably couldn't see her face. "Shall I make it easier for you? Would you like me to seduce you? Then you can lie there and simply pretend to endure."

He stayed braced over her and she wished he would simply *move* or do something before she said something she might regret.

"You think I *endure* your touch?"

"If I answer you, will you go to sleep?"

"Surely that depends on what you say."

She set her jaw. "You endure me touching you, and being close to you, because you lust after me. Is that clear enough?"

"Even if it is just lust, I still like to be touched."

"No, you don't, Benedict. You put up with it to get what you want, which is use of my body because you *lust* after me. And you hate yourself because you want me."

"I do not—"

She reached up and put her trembling fingers over his mouth. "You've made it very clear that you don't want anyone in your nice, ordered life. You certainly don't want someone like me, who irritates you enormously."

He jerked out of her reach. "You're my wife."

"So you keep saying." She reached down and pulled her night-gown up to the waist, spreading her legs wide. "Then take me."

With a groan, he lowered his weight onto her, his cock a

hard, throbbing presence against her stomach. She wrapped a hand around his neck.

"It's all right to want, Benedict."

He bit her throat, her shoulder, his whole body shuddering as he entered her and started to thrust hard and fast. She turned her face to the side and contemplated the shadows thrown by the fire while he worked himself to a climax and came deep inside her.

After a long moment, he raised his head, his breathing uneven. "I thought I was the one who was supposed to lie back and endure."

"I believe this is how a wife is supposed to behave."

"So you denied yourself pleasure to prove a *point?*"

She bit down on her lip and steadily avoided his gaze. "Are you done? May I go to sleep now?"

"Damn you."

He moved, and she tried to turn away from him, but he was too quick, his hands spreading her thighs wide and his mouth descending on her sex. He had her coming around his tongue and fingers in less than a minute, and she shook with pleasure. He didn't stop there and rolled her onto her stomach, mounting her from behind, his fingers plucking at her clit, demanding her response as he fucked her again.

When he came, he collapsed over her and pinned her beneath him, one hand planted by her face, his head beside hers on the pillow.

"There's one other thing a wife does for her husband, Malinda. She gives him children. Have you thought about that?"

She kept her eyes closed to keep him out, but it didn't work.

"You've let me come inside you." His voice roughened. "Many times. If you are with child, Malinda, you *will* tell me."

So many words crowded her throat. She forced them all down. She couldn't fight him about this, she just couldn't.

He gave her shoulder a slight shake. "Malinda . . ."

She kept herself still and quiet, hoping he'd give up, knowing that had never been his style.

With an exasperated sound he moved away from her, but only to light a candle and return, scooping her up into his lap. She instantly buried her face in his shoulder.

"What's wrong?"

Dammit, what could she say? What would he like to hear? "If I'm carrying your child, I'll let you know."

He caught her chin in his hard fingers and made her look at him, his gaze steady.

"Are you already with child?"

God, she had to end this conversation for both their sakes. She forced a smile and patted his cheek.

"Don't worry, Benedict. If the worst happens, I'll remove myself and any offspring of yours to Alford Park. You can come and reclaim the boys when they are old enough to go away to school."

He blinked and she saw the mingled anger and hurt in his blue eyes.

"I'm not my father."

"Is that what he did to you?"

"That's what every aristocrat does."

She kissed his nose and wiggled off his lap. "Then, that being settled, may I go to sleep now? It's been an eventful day."

He didn't stop her getting away from him, but he didn't move either, his gaze fixed on his lap where she'd been sitting. He slowly exhaled.

"If the prospect of bearing my children alarms you so greatly, would you rather I didn't share your bed at all?"

She squeezed her eyes tightly shut. How had she ever thought she'd fool him into believing she didn't care? He knew her better than she knew herself.

"That's up to you and your inconvenient lust, isn't it?"

"Oh, don't worry about me. I'm sure I can find someone who's perfectly willing to help with that."

Without another word, he rose from the bed and walked out, shutting the door softly behind him. Malinda kept her eyes closed, but the tears still came and there was nothing she could do to stop them or control her anguish. Like a fool, she kept arguing with her conscience, that if they could just get through the current crisis, she could tell him *everything* and be strong enough to watch him walk away. She'd misjudged him. He obviously didn't know the whole story, and that was probably due to his father's machinations. She'd realized that almost immediately, and was simply being a coward. She was afraid to alienate him further because she needed his strength. She needed *him*. And that was as terrifying to her as his lust probably was to him.

"You're up early, Benedict."

"Good morning, Faith."

She waved him back into his seat and poured herself some tea. "Did you even go to bed?"

"I—" He stopped abruptly as he remembered exactly why he'd spent the night in his office sleeping uncomfortably on the couch. "I had a lot to do."

"Strange. You look exactly like Ian does when he's at odds with me and didn't sleep in his own bed."

"I'm always at odds with Malinda."

"She certainly challenges you."

His appetite deserted him. "She thinks I prefer my life to be barren and uncomplicated."

"And do you?"

He looked across the table at her. "I don't know. It's certainly more comfortable."

"I can understand that. Before I met Ian, I thought I'd be perfectly happy being the strange bluestocking maiden aunt to my sister's children. Marital relationships seemed either overtly

messy or downright miserable." She half-smiled. "And sometimes they are, but the overall experience of being married to
someone triumphs over those bad days."

"I haven't decided whether that's the case for me yet." Benedict used his napkin and rose from the table. "And now, if you
will forgive me, I have to get on."

"Are you still happy for me to take Malinda to the musical
afternoon at the Spensers?"

"Yes, as long as you take one of the guards with you."

"I will, and Benedict?"

He paused at the door. "Yes?"

"I've sent someone directly to the convent where Malinda
and her sister were lodged during the war. Do you have any ob-
jection?"

"Not at all."

"Thank you."

Malinda sighed and tried to refocus her attention on the
opera singer who was murdering a piece of Mozart's *Marriage
of Figaro*. She'd worn one of the new dresses Benedict had sup-
plied to replace the ones that had perished in the fire, but even
its peach beauty couldn't console her for the entertainment. Beside her, Faith was listening with a slight frown on her face and
her hands clasped tightly together in her lap.

"Don't look so horrified, Malinda," Faith whispered.

"But she is so off-key she's setting my teeth on edge."

Faith touched her arm. "Let's discreetly move along, shall
we? Thank goodness we sat near the back."

They escaped into the adjourning salon and helped themselves to a fresh cup of tea and some pastries until polite ap-
plause signaled the end of the performance.

Malinda shuddered. "We don't have to go back in there,
do we?"

"Not if you don't wish to, my dear."

"I already had a headache, and that didn't help."

"Didn't you sleep well either?"

Malinda narrowed her eyes. "I assume you've seen Benedict?"

"He was just finishing his breakfast when I arrived in the morning room." Faith paused. "He seemed rather upset."

"Upset? Benedict? I doubt it." Malinda put down her plate. "About what?"

"Presumably the same thing that you are upset about."

"I'm . . ." Malinda sighed. "I can't wait until this is all over and he allows me to go back to Alford Park."

"I'm sure that will make you very happy, dear."

"It will make Benedict even happier."

Faith considered her for a long moment. "I'm not sure about that. Benedict might *think* he wants everything to go back to how it was, but I doubt he means it."

"If that's what he said, I'm sure he meant it." Malinda tried to ignore the tight ball of pain around her heart. "I've caused him nothing but trouble."

"You've certainly shown the rest of us a side of him we never knew existed."

"And he doesn't like that at all." Malinda looked toward the door, where people were starting to come through from the music room. "Can we leave?"

"If you wish." Faith paused. "Your mother-in-law is staring at you."

"Let her stare." Malinda inclined her head an inch in the marchioness's direction, and moved toward the exit. She came down the stairs and smiled at the footman on duty.

"Can you call for our carriage, please?"

"Yes, my lady."

Faith paused to speak to an acquaintance, and Malinda walked outside to await the appearance of the Westbrook carriage. The wind had come up and the front door of the mansion suddenly slammed behind her, cutting her off from Faith. Almost at the same time, someone grabbed her elbow and pulled her off the steps and down into the dark basement entrance below. She kicked out as hard as she could and her captor cursed, but it was to no avail. Her head was covered with a filthy sack, and she was swept up and over someone's shoulder in a grip that bruised her ribs.

She tried to struggle but received a crashing blow to the side of her head, which left her dizzy and sick. Surely someone would notice she was being abducted in broad daylight? Seconds later, she was flung onto the back of a cart of some kind, and her captor followed her in. He rested one enormous foot on her torso while he tied her skirts around her ankles.

The cart started to move and they were away with no sounds of pursuit behind them. A light rain started to fall, dampening the sack and Malinda's clothing. Why was it that every time she wore one of her new gowns it was ruined? Where was the man Benedict had sent with them? Where was Faith?

It seemed to take forever for the cart to stop moving through the streets and for Malinda to be bodily picked up again and brought into what she assumed was some kind of shelter. She was carried down some steps into a place that echoed and smelled of ale, wooden barrels, and decay. Was she in the cellars of the Red Dragon? Surely that would be one of the first places Benedict would look for her.

"Here you are, Mr. C. She's a feisty bitch."

She was suddenly upended and dumped on a rickety chair. The blade of a knife nicked her throat as the burlap sacking was cut away.

Fred Castleton grinned and slapped his thigh. "Malinda Rowland, it is you, by all that's holy."

"Do I know you, sir?" Malinda glared at him.

"There's no need to be all high and mighty with me, lass. I

knew you when you had pigtails and were carried around on your father's shoulders."

"Then one might ask why you abducted me rather than simply asking me to meet you when it was convenient?"

His smile died. "I think you know why. What I want to know is what Patrick Rowland's daughter is doing hanging around with the likes of Lord Keyes and that bastard, the Marquis of Alford."

"What does it matter to you?"

He slowly rose to his feet, advanced toward her, and casually slapped her face. "Less of that cheek, lass. Answer the question."

She stared at him, ignoring the pain and the sting of her lip where his signet ring had cut into her flesh. "I came to London to find out if the Marquis of Alford killed my father."

He cocked his head to one side and studied her. "You thought he might confess such a crime to you?"

"I intended to force him to do so." She gathered her scattered wits. "I used Lord Keyes's old friendship with me to get access to his father."

"So why is the old bastard still alive?"

"Because . . . when it came down to it, I found I didn't have the guts to shoot an old man in his own bed."

"You're a woman." Fred returned to his seat and sat down. "You don't have the stomach for it."

"Do you want to kill him too?"

"I'm asking the questions, lass, not you."

She went still, aware of the threat of violence in his voice.

"Why did you come here to my inn with Lord Keyes, then, if you're at odds with him?"

"He forced me."

Fred nodded. "I can believe that. Keyes is a coldhearted sod like his father. But why this inn?"

"Someone set light to his property in Maddox Street, and he was told the suspect worked here as a waiter."

"By whom?"

"I don't know. I'm not in his confidence. He said he needed to come here in disguise to look for the man he sought, and that I was merely to act as a distraction. He made me stay in the parlor while he asked questions." She shivered. "I believe he has many enemies."

"Why do you think the Marquis of Alford killed your father?"

If she'd hoped to distract him into thinking the matter was all about Benedict, it hadn't worked.

"My mother left a journal. She suggested that my father and the marquis had some sort of secret involving the contents of the baggage train. She believed the marquis killed him to stop him talking about whatever that secret was."

Fred rose again and she tensed. He put his hands behind his back and walked a slow circle around the cellar. She tried not to crane her neck to see where he was, but it was so tempting.

"Where is that journal now?"

"In my room at the Sinners Club."

"Has Keyes seen it?"

"No."

He was right behind her now and all the hairs on the back of her neck bristled. She jumped when he touched the cut on her throat.

"Who has seen it?"

"No one, but me."

"I don't believe you." His fingers closed around her throat and tightened until her vision blurred and she started to choke. "Who else?"

"No one." She managed to gasp out the words. "I wouldn't share it with the family I believe killed my father."

"And what if I told you that you are both right and wrong about that?"

He released her throat and she gulped in some much-needed air.

"What if I told you that your father was part of a plot to deceive innocent soldiers of their hard-earned pay?"

"My *father?*" she whispered.

"Aye. I suppose he thought he was going to be rich, but you should never make a deal with the devil."

He poured himself a drink from the brandy bottle on the upturned barrel beside him. "The night before he left, Patrick had a drink with some of his old friends and told us the secret he shared with the marquis." He looked at her closely, but she kept her expression bewildered. "They were bringing in gold to pay the troops."

"Gold?"

"Aye, lass, and your father and the marquis decided between them that the gold would never get through."

She shook her head. "My father would never—"

"But your father was angry with the marquis because he'd been hauled before him and ordered to keep his filthy slut of a daughter away from the marquis's son and heir." Fred chuckled. "We all knew the boy lusted after you. In fact, we were taking bets as to when he'd tumble you. We didn't mention that to your father, obviously."

Malinda swallowed bile and forced herself to keep still.

"So Patrick asked us to help him instead. He would bring the gold back, and we'd arrange an ambush along the way and take care of it for him until the marquis stopped looking for it."

"But he died."

"That was unfortunate, lass. One of the men traveling with him realized they'd been betrayed, and shot your father in the back screaming at him for being a traitor and a coward." He shrugged. "By the time I reached him he was dead."

"And the gold?"

Fred looked around the well-stocked cellar. "As you see here. After the fuss died down, we shared the gold with our fellow soldiers—not quite all of it, obviously, because, well, we'd done the lion's share of the work to acquire it, hadn't we?"

Malinda stared at his smiling face, dug her fingernails into her palms, and risked another question.

"What is it that you want me to do?"

Fred finished his brandy and wiped his mouth. "It's like this, my beauty. If you stop poking your nose in where it doesn't belong and encourage your 'friend' Keyes to do the same, we'll keep mum about your father's part in this. If you don't, we'll ensure that your father and the marquis are publicly shamed."

She drew a painful breath. "My father and mother are dead."

"But the marquis and his son, your *husband,* my lady, are not. And if the marquis is finally brought to justice, don't you think suspicion will fall on the son too? A man who holds so many of the nation's secrets allied to a traitor like your father and a thief like his own?"

Malinda looked down at her shaking hands. Her father was beyond shame, but Benedict? He was the most honorable man she'd ever met. His reputation meant everything to him, and was vital in his line of work. She knew if scandal touched him, he'd resign and their country would lose a fierce defender.

"I don't believe I have enough influence with Lord Keyes to prevent him from carrying on this investigation."

Fred rose again and came toward her. "Then you'd better try harder to persuade him, hadn't you, lass?"

His gaze raked the neckline of her dress. "You looked better dressed as his tart with your titties hanging out." He reached out and ripped the front of her bodice away.

Forgetting her legs were tied, she leapt to her feet and went for him, nails clawing at his smiling face. He caught her in his arms as she toppled over.

"You're eager, aren't you?"

He squeezed her breast hard enough to make her gasp.
"Let me go."

He thrust his hand into her hair, forced her head up, and
brought his mouth down over hers. Dread shuddered through
her and she started to fight him again, but he was too strong for
her. She whimpered as his fingers closed over her wrist and
ground her bones together until something gave with an audible *snap*. Pain engulfed her and she stopped fighting him, going
limp in his arms, letting her knees collapse.

He struggled to contain her but she managed to fall to the
floor and curl up in a ball. She could see his booted feet but not
much else. She stiffened as he crouched down beside her and
caught her chin in his hands.

"I don't have the time to finish this now."

She licked her bleeding lips. "If you kill me, I can't help you,
and you will have to kill me before I'll let you rape me."

He laughed into her face. "I doubt it, lass. But you do have a
point. I don't intend to rape you. I still have some small fond-
ness for the daughter of my old friend. I just want your bastard
of a husband to know that I could've had you if I'd wanted to."
He looked up at the man still standing guard by the door.
"When it's dark, Nate, take her and drop her near the Sinners.
She'll find her way back." He patted her cheek. "I'll give you
three days to stop this witch hunt, and then I'll go to the news-
papers and the authorities. Do you understand?"

She nodded and he left her alone. She heard him walk over
to the man at the door and converse quietly with him before the
door shut behind him. She stayed where he'd left her, curled up
and defenseless, and tried to make sense of what he'd told her.
Benedict's father wasn't the only villain of the piece after all.
Her father was just as bad—worse maybe, because he'd chosen
to betray his own kind and the marquis.

She swallowed her own blood. Yet again it seemed that
Benedict would have to pay the price for caring about her and

her family. That wasn't fair, but how could she prevent it? A faint idea formed out of her desolation, and she concentrated on how to execute her plan. He'd already given her more than he'd ever know. It would mean the end of everything between them, but he'd survived her defection once and would do so again. Losing his career and reputation was another thing, and she was going to do everything in her power to stop that happening.

19

"Benedict, we've found her."

Faith's quiet voice had him spinning around to face the door. He'd been pacing Adam's study for hours, raging at himself and at the fates that had taken Malinda from him once again. Once more he'd let her down. Why was it that he couldn't protect those he cared about the most? She'd be better off without him.

"Where is she?"

"James found her in the square. He's bringing her in." Her voice broke. "I'm so sorry, Benedict. I don't know how I lost sight of her—"

For once he didn't stop to reassure Faith, his gaze on the front door of the Sinners, his attention all on the woman cradled in James's arms. Within seconds he was beside her, and he wanted to howl in anguish at the sight of her battered and bruised face. Her long auburn hair concealed her full expression, but pain radiated from her shaking form.

"Take her into my study, James, and get Dr. Finbar from the kitchen."

Adam's calm voice.

Benedict glared at him. "She needs to be in bed. I'll take her upstairs."

"As you wish, although I'll still send the doctor up." Adam waited until James carefully transferred Malinda over to Benedict. "Thank you, James. Where exactly did you find her?"

"She was clinging to the railings in the center of the square and she suddenly collapsed." James swallowed hard. "I recognized her hair."

"You did well." Adam thanked the footman. "Now go and find Dr. Finbar for me, would you?"

By the time Adam finished speaking, Benedict was already climbing the stairs with Malinda in his arms. He kicked open the door of his suite and took her through to the bedroom. With great care he eased her onto the bed. Her muddied cloak fell away, and his gaze registered the damage to her gown, to her face, to her throat. . . . Rage flooded his senses leaving him clenching his fists and shaking with the need to hurt someone, to damage something, to—

"Lord Keyes?"

"Yes." He couldn't tear his gaze away from her.

"I'm Dr. Finbar. With your permission, may I attend to your wife?"

His instinct was to say no, to cover her with his own body and stop anyone seeing the damage done to hers. His fault—all his damned fault. He should've let her go back to Alford Park.

"Benedict." Faith came up beside him and put her hand on his arm. "Let us help her, please?"

He nodded and took a reluctant step back, his gaze moving down from Malinda's ravaged face to the ring of black bruises that encircled her wrist like a heathen tattoo.

The doctor arranged the candlelight so that it fell fully on his patient. He removed his jacket and rolled up his sleeves before washing his hands. He took his time studying her, mentally cataloguing the extent of the injuries.

"Perhaps we could remove her clothes?"

The doctor's question was addressed to Benedict, but it was Faith who moved forward to offer her assistance while Benedict simply stood there and observed as if he didn't give a damn, as if this wasn't his wife lying bloody and bruised in his bed.

As they eased her out of her garments, she stirred and moaned something. Faith put her hand on her forehead.

"It's all right, Malinda. We have you safe now."

The extent of the damage revealed made him want to vomit. He'd seen death in all its grotesque forms, but somehow this was far worse. To his credit, Dr. Finbar was very gentle as he examined her and didn't seem to cause her any more pain. After a while he raised his head and addressed Benedict.

"From what I can tell, she has a lot of bruising, but almost no broken bones. I suspect her ribs are very sore." He pointed to what looked like a boot mark on her skin. "Unfortunately, her left wrist is broken. I'll bandage it and her ribs, dose her with laudanum, and let her sleep. That's probably the best we can do for her tonight."

"What about internal injuries?"

Benedict was surprised at how calm he sounded.

"Obviously, we will have to watch out for any signs of internal bleeding, or cramps or pain." He hesitated. "I don't detect any signs of rape."

"Apart from a ripped bodice, bruised breasts, and a bloodied mouth?"

Dr. Finbar grimaced. "I'm not trying to trivialize the extent of your wife's injuries, my lord, I'm just attempting to relay the physical facts to you."

"Of course, as her husband that should offend me most, shouldn't it? The fact that someone might have raped her, might have—"

"Benedict." He looked up and saw Adam at the doorway.

"Perhaps you should leave the good doctor and the countess to settle your wife and return when they are done?"

"I'm not bloody leaving her."

"You're not going to help her by losing your temper. If you can't control yourself, come away." Adam glanced back at the bed. "You're upsetting her."

"I am damn well not—"

Faith shushed him and leaned over Malinda, who was trying to speak.

"She wants you to leave, Benedict. Please."

Without another word he walked out. Of course she wanted him to leave, didn't she always? He went down the stairs and into his office and then just stopped and tried to breathe through the need to break something.

"Take this."

Alistair Maclean handed him a glass of brandy. Instead of drinking it, he hurled it at the fireplace, where it shattered into a thousand pieces.

Another glass was placed in his hand. "You have three more in this set, sir. Go ahead."

This time he drank the brandy.

"Will you sit down, my lord?"

He glared helplessly into his secretary's calm green gaze.

"Seeing your wife like that was a terrible shock, sir. Your reaction is perfectly natural."

"I should have let her go home."

"I'm not sure about that." Alistair's Scottish accent was curiously soothing. "If you couldn't fully protect her with all the resources of the Sinners, I doubt your staff at Alford Park could've done any better." He sighed. "I've learned to my cost that sometimes you can't protect those you love from harm."

Benedict sank into the nearest chair. Alistair refilled his brandy glass and set the decanter within easy reach.

"Whom did you fail to protect?" It was an insensitive question as well as an intrusive one, and quite unlike Benedict.

"My wife." Alistair held his gaze, the memories stark and still fresh.

"What happened to her?"

"She died." His smile was crooked. "At least your lady is alive."

Benedict nodded and sipped his brandy. His hand finally stopped shaking and his breathing slowed. "I want to go out, find who did this, and tear him limb from limb with my bare hands."

"Totally understandable, my lord. Luckily you have the ability to do so." He looked past Benedict's shoulder. "Mr. Fisher is at the door. Do you wish to speak to him?"

"I suppose I'd better." Benedict rose and handed the glass back to his secretary. "Thank you."

"For what, sir?"

"The brandy."

A smile flicked over Alistair's austere features. "You are most welcome."

Adam waited for him in the corridor. "She is sleeping now. Do you want to go up and see her?"

"Yes." He glanced across at Adam as they went toward the stairs. "I apologize if my behavior was inappropriate."

Adam stopped moving. "Benedict, your wife was savagely beaten. I'm not sure that any 'behavior' is appropriate in that situation other than howling with rage, which means you were remarkably restrained."

"I'll apologize to Dr. Finbar too."

They reached the top landing, and Adam patted his shoulder and left him there, going on to his own apartment. Benedict paused and slowly opened the door. The living room was in darkness, but candles illuminated the bedroom. Dr. Finbar was putting his coat back on.

"My lord. She is sleeping now. I'll call again in the morning. If anything untoward happens before then, please send for me."

Benedict held out his hand. "Thank you. I apologize if I was a little sharp with you earlier."

"There's no need, my lord. You were simply anxious about your wife."

He bowed, picked up his bag, and left the room. Benedict turned to Faith, who was sitting in a chair by the fireside, her hands folded on her lap. He went and sat opposite her.

"Thank you, Faith."

She looked up at him and he realized she'd been crying.

"I did very little except hold her hand and soothe her when she was in pain."

He swallowed hard. "Which was far more than I was capable of doing."

"Don't be so hard on yourself. Shock affects us in different ways."

"But this is my fault. I should have let her go home."

"Benedict, I'm the one who let her out of my sight." She sighed. "I'll never forgive myself."

He reached across and took her hand. "Take your own advice, my lady, and please don't blame yourself."

"We are a terrible pair, aren't we?" Fresh tears glinted in her blue eyes as she squeezed his fingers. "Now, do you want me to stay with Malinda for a few hours while you sleep, and then you can take over later?"

"You go to bed. You've done more than enough. I'll be fine." He helped her rise and kissed her cheek. "Good night, Faith."

"Do not hesitate to come and find me if you are in need."

"I'll do that."

She smiled and walked quietly away, leaving him alone with his wife for the first time. He went over to the bed and stared down at her. She looked more peaceful now, but nothing could disguise the ugliness of her injuries. He wanted to kiss every bruise and cut and hold her in his arms until she felt well enough to return to the world.

He wanted . . .

With a soft curse, he went and sat down by the fire. He forced himself to detach from his emotions, and think logically about what had happened and how he was going to discover who'd done this and destroy them.

Her anguished moan woke him from a troubled doze and he jerked awake and went over to the bed.

"Malinda?"

She opened her eyes and studied him carefully as though he might hurt her. He forced a smile. "It's all right. You're quite safe." She blinked at him, and he gently cupped the uninjured side of her face. "Do you want anything?"

She shook her head and then winced.

"Then go back to sleep. I'll be here when you wake up properly." He waited another minute, barely breathing, until she settled back down, and then he resumed his vigil in his chair.

Adam tapped on the door at dawn and brought hot water for Benedict to shave with and a pot of coffee. Leaving the bedroom door ajar, Benedict went into the living room with him.

"Do we have any idea who took her?"

"Faith said that Malinda's clothes and cloak stunk of ale. I'm betting we'll find our man at the Red Dragon. I've already sent two men over there to investigate the cellars whether Mr. Castleton is agreeable or not."

"Good." He glanced back at the bedroom. "She hasn't said anything about what happened yet. She's still sleeping."

"She might not even remember what happened. Blows to the head can have that effect sometimes."

"I know." Benedict's smile quickly faded.

"Dr. Finbar will be here in an hour or so." Adam patted his shoulder. "I'll have some breakfast sent up to you."

"Thank you."

Benedict shaved himself while the water was still hot and drank his way through the entire pot of coffee. When his breakfast arrived, he ate it on a tray with one eye on the bedroom door in case Malinda woke up.

Eventually, he went back into the bedroom and, working as quietly as he could, piled coal on the dwindling fire.

"Benedict?"

He turned to see her looking down at him. With great care, he dusted off his hands and went over to her. Between the purple bruises her skin was paper white and her hazel eyes were huge pools of pain.

"How are you feeling?"

"Not my best. Can you help me sit up a little?"

"Are you sure?"

"Yes."

He slid an arm around her back and gently eased her up on her pillows. "How's that?"

"I'm fine."

He doubted it, but he wasn't going to argue. He also wasn't going to interrogate her. If she wanted to talk about what had happened he would, of course, listen, but he was not going to ask the first question. He poured her a cup of water and helped her sip from it.

"Better?"

She reached for his hand. "I need to speak to you about something."

"Whatever you wish."

"I want Adam and Faith to hear too."

"Are you sure?"

She swallowed. "I don't want them thinking you misheard."

"Then I'll go and see if they are available."

* * *

It took only a few minutes to find Adam and Faith and bring them to Malinda's bedside, but it was long enough for a ball of apprehension to lodge itself deep in Benedict's chest. She wouldn't even look at him. It was as if he didn't exist. Was she angry because he'd failed to protect her, or was it something worse? The fact that she required witnesses before speaking to him didn't bode well either. He set chairs by the bedside for Adam and Faith, but preferred to stand himself.

"Thank you, Benedict." Malinda's voice was husky, but that was hardly surprising seeing as someone had tried to strangle her. "Firstly. I want to apologize for bringing so much trouble down on you all. I never meant for things to get this far."

Adam patted her hand. "Malinda, we all care about you. Nothing is too much trouble."

She lowered her gaze to his hand. "I don't deserve such regard. I lied to you all about my involvement with the ambushers. I want to tell you the truth." She drew an unsteady breath. "My father and I planned the whole thing."

"That's ridiculous," Benedict snapped.

Adam gave him a pointed look and turned back to Malinda. "What exactly do you mean by 'planned'?"

"The marquis threatened to trump up a charge and court-martial my father because of my involvement with Benedict. He called me several uncomplimentary names, which didn't sit well with my father. He was very proud of his reputation in the regiment and furious that after all his years of loyal service he might be disgraced over nothing. When the opportunity arose to steal the marquis's gold, he decided to take it. The plan was that some of his friends from the regiment would ambush the mule train, steal the gold, and he'd share the proceeds with them."

"And why did that necessitate your involvement?" Benedict asked.

She still wouldn't look at him. "Because I was the one who was supposed to show the men where to hide the gold after the raid."

He stared at her, one hand gripping the bedpost so hard it hurt. "Your father died in that ambush. Have you forgotten that?"

"He wasn't supposed to die. One of the men in his party suddenly realized what was happening." She swallowed hard. "He shot my father in the back before he could get away with the others."

"And what happened to the gold?"

She raised her gaze to his. "How do you think I managed to live once I'd left you?"

He shook his head, his throat tight. "This is nonsense!" He gestured at her face. "Whoever beat you frightened you enough to make you say this."

"No, he beat me because I took most of the gold and didn't share it in what he considered to be a fair fashion. When I told him that there was nothing left, he became enraged and decided to teach me a lesson."

Benedict had to turn his back on her and walk away to the window. Outside, he saw Dr. Finbar emerging from a hackney cab through the fog, his bag in his hand and his gaze on the frontage of the Sinners.

"You should be pleased, Benedict," Malinda said. "This exonerates your father."

He didn't turn around. He couldn't. "Why did you pursue my father so relentlessly if you knew he was innocent?"

She sighed. "Because I thought I'd gotten away with everything and that it was safe to return to England. On my return, certain people threatened me and I needed your help to protect me. That part at least is true, Benedict. I also assumed your father had finally found out what happened. I needed to get to him through you and stop him from speaking out."

He shook his head and stared blindly out of the window into the shrouded square below.

"I didn't know that we were still married." She hesitated and her voice cracked even more. "I would never have involved you if I'd known that."

"So you are saying the ambush was a plot by your father to punish mine for daring to criticize our relationship. That the ambush went badly wrong, and your father was killed, but you still managed to steal the gold and live off it when you ran away."

He turned to face the bed, saw Faith's horrified expression and that Adam remained his usual calm self. He concentrated his gaze on Malinda's clenched hands.

"Recently, your father's coconspirators decided they needed more gold, and were enraged when you declared it was all gone. In retaliation, they kidnapped you and beat you severely. Do I have that right so far?"

"Yes."

He nodded. "And what do you think should happen to you next, love?"

Adam stirred. "Benedict . . ."

"It's a reasonable question, isn't it? After all, she attempted to drag my family's name in the mud to cover up her father's guilt—and her complicity. What exactly do you want me to do, Malinda?"

"I want it to stop. I want *you* to stop. Punish me, and let it end here."

"You don't think you've been punished enough?"

She licked her lips. "I deserved what happened to me, Benedict. I also accept that as a representative of my father, you or the marquis might wish to formally charge me for stealing the gold."

He advanced toward her, clapping his hands.

"What an outstanding performance, my dear." He smiled at Adam, who rose to his feet, his hand outstretched. "Don't worry, I'm not going to touch her. She's suffered quite enough, hasn't she? And she damn well knows it. Here's another thing she knows. She's my wife, and if I wish to preserve a shred of my reputation I have no ability to bring her to trial for *any- thing*.

"Well played, Malinda. If you wanted revenge on my family, you've certainly achieved your aim." He locked gazes with her. "As requested, I shall do *nothing* except what you've wanted all along. I give you permission to leave for Alford Park, where I hope you'll live out your days in peace and prosperity."

He bowed low. "Have a safe journey, my dear. I'm sure Adam can be relied upon to sort out the details for you."

"Benedict—"

Ignoring Faith's plea, he walked out of the bedroom and down the stairs. He didn't make the mistake of going into his study and finding the compassionate Alistair Maclean this time; he just kept walking until he was out on the street. Eventually, he reached a white-stucco mansion backing onto Barrington Square and took the private route into the Delornay House of Pleasure.

He was welcomed by Christian Delornay, who took one look at him and got out of his way. Benedict found himself a seat in the far corner of the main salon, ordered a bottle of brandy, and set about drinking himself into oblivion.

"For what it's worth, my lady, I don't believe a word of your story either."

Adam's cold words stung, but Malinda could do nothing to defend herself. "I wish I had time to chat, but my priority is to stop Benedict from doing something stupid, like going in search of the man who beat you and tearing him apart."

"I don't want him to do that, I just—"

"Whatever you may think about him, Benedict is hardly the man to sit back when his wife has been violently hurt."

"Please . . ." Malinda's voice wobbled. "*Please*, don't let him. He *promised* me, he wouldn't . . ."

"Why do you care when you just ripped out his heart?" Adam stared down at her. "I don't understand you at all."

"That isn't important. As you said, Benedict is the one you have to protect. Please keep him safe, and keep him away from the Red Dragon."

"I'll do my best." Adam bowed and went out, leaving Malinda alone with Faith.

"Why did you lie, Malinda?"

Unlike Adam, Faith's expression was full of concern as she took Malinda's hand.

"Please don't be kind to me. I don't deserve it."

"Even if I believed what you'd just told us, I still would be kind to you." Faith hesitated. "You were only seventeen when you became involved in this horrible mess. Everyone deserves a second chance. What I want to know is why you are determined to destroy yours?"

"I have no *choice*."

"There is always a choice, my dear."

"Not always." She couldn't confide in Faith, she couldn't afford to trust anyone. "Will you help me get back to Alford Park?"

"If that is truly what you wish, but oh, my dear, I think you're making a terrible mistake."

Malinda forced a smile. "Benedict gave me his permission."

"Are you sure that you don't want to trust him with the truth?"

"This is the truth. My father was a traitor who stole from his own companions."

"Then surely the shame is his and stays with him in his grave?"

"But I benefited from that." Malinda met Faith's steady gaze. "I have to go home."

Faith stood up. "Then I will arrange for you to leave as soon as you are able to travel." She glanced at the clock on the mantelpiece. "I believe Dr. Finbar is waiting to see you. I'll consult with him as to whether you can be moved today."

Benedict glanced up as Adam took the seat beside him in the busy salon, and poured himself a large glass of brandy from Benedict's bottle.

"Go away, Adam. I don't need a nursemaid."

"I'm not going anywhere. I promised your wife I'd keep you safe."

Benedict belched. "What wife?"

"It's obvious that she's lying, Benedict. I just don't understand why."

"I don't understand why you are pursuing the subject when I've come here to obliterate her presence from my mind."

"Your mind, or your heart?"

He turned slowly toward Adam, grabbed a handful of his waistcoat, and yanked him off his chair and almost on top of him. "Be silent."

"Or what?" Adam put his hands on Benedict's shoulders and stayed put. "She obviously cares about you."

"She likes to fuck me, but she doesn't trust me. It's an arrangement that suited us both perfectly."

"Because you don't trust her either?"

"I don't trust anyone." Benedict stared into Adam's calm gray eyes. "Shut your mouth, my friend, or I'll find some other use for it."

Adam shoved at his chest and Benedict let him stand up.

"Now get the hell away from me." Benedict stood, too, swaying slightly from the effects of the brandy. "I'm going upstairs to find someone to fuck."

"No, you are not." Adam blocked his path. Benedict tried to move past him, but Adam resisted. "If you want to fuck, use me, use my mouth, push me down on my knees and make me suck your cock."

Benedict cupped Adam's chin. "I'm going to the top floor."

"So you can take out your anger on some poor submissive man? That's not what you want." Adam leaned in and bit Benedict's lip. "I'll fight you. I'll make it plain to you that I think you're a fool for walking away from your wife when she needs you most."

"Shut up," Benedict snarled.

"Make me."

Benedict wrapped his hand around Adam's neck and tried to shove his tongue into the other man's mouth, but his friend was not making it easy for him. He pushed harder, and with a groan Adam opened his mouth and kissed him back, although it was more like they savaged each other. But it was what he needed, what he craved . . .

He pushed down on Adam's shoulder until his knees buckled and he knelt on the floor in front of Benedict.

"Suck me."

"Damn you."

Adam rammed his shoulder into Benedict's stomach, and he fell backward, barely missing one of the chairs and upending the small table where the brandy bottle sat. Adam was on him in a trice, his forearm wedged beneath Benedict's chin, forcing his head up.

"You're a damn coward, Benedict."

"She doesn't want me, she doesn't trust me—how in God's name am I supposed to help her?"

He lashed out at Adam's braced shoulder and managed to roll him beneath him. Using his superior weight to hold the other man down, he slid his hand between their bodies and squeezed Adam's half-erect cock until he bucked against him.

"So you're going to let her go?"

"That's what she damn well wants!"

He ripped the button off Adam's trousers and shoved his hand inside, rubbing Adam's cock in rough, needy jerks. His companion moaned and grabbed Benedict's hair, bringing his mouth down to his, but he didn't want to kiss, didn't want to enjoy any tenderness.

He rolled Adam onto his front and pressed his hard cock against the other man's arse. Capturing Adam's wrists, he drew them over his head until his back arched and kicked his feet apart. It was an easy matter to pull down his lover's trousers and underthings and unbutton himself. He returned his hand to Adam's cock and jerked him off until he came all over Benedict's demanding fist.

"Keyes, I hesitate to interrupt, but do you perhaps wish to retire to a more private room?"

Benedict looked up to find Delornay, the blond-haired owner of the pleasure house, smiling politely down at him. A crowd of guests whose attention was riveted on the two men and the overturned chairs and table surrounded Christian. He moved closer, his appreciative gaze on the swell of Benedict's cock, and lowered his voice.

"You are known as a man of many appetites, my lord, but Mr. Fisher is not. He might not wish to be . . . exposed in this fashion."

"It's too late for that. Mr. Fisher will take whatever I damn well choose to give him." Benedict panted. "He wanted this."

Adam groaned what sounded like an assent.

Benedict smiled at Christian. "Are you satisfied now?"

"Not half as satisfied as I suspect Mr. Fisher is. If you do change your mind, the third room on the right is unoccupied." He half-turned away and then stopped and took something out of his pocket. "You might need this." He dropped the bottle of oil and Benedict reflexively caught it. "Your cock *is* rather large."

He turned away and managed to persuade the vast majority of the watchers to move away with him, leaving Benedict still straddling Adam, his cock throbbing right alongside his anger.

"Get up." He moved off Adam and hauled him to his feet.

"This is pointless. Let me go upstairs."

"No." His lover's gaze fell to Benedict's exposed cock and he licked his lips.

"Adam, stop this."

"Why not fuck me here in front of everyone?"

"Because I'm *trying* to preserve your reputation," Benedict said through his teeth.

"Perhaps Malinda had a point, and you are more concerned with upholding your bloody aristocratic *name* than dealing with those who love you."

"She doesn't love me. She—"

"I wasn't just talking about her." Adam shook his head and started to walk away from him. He had to follow, had to slam his best friend against the wall to stop him from leaving.

"Goddamn you, don't do this!"

"Love you? Devil take it, I wouldn't dare!" Adam shoved him away. "The high and mighty Benedict Keyes doesn't need anyone, does he?"

Benedict struggled to breathe as his gaze clashed with Adam's. "I can't . . ."

"You can't love anyone? God almighty, Benedict, we all know that."

Benedict pushed past him and went into the room Christian had pointed out. With a curse, he started to pull off his clothes.

"What are you doing?" Adam wasn't shouting anymore. He leaned up against the closed door of the bedroom, his expression a mixture of fury and concern.

"What do you think? You wanted me to fuck you."

"Because it's easier to do that than deal with Malinda?"

"*Yes!*"

Adam raised an eyebrow. "Because you don't believe that she loves you?"

"Did you *hear* what she said?"

"*Yes,* and like you, I didn't believe a word of it."

"Then why are you determined to make this all my fault?"

"Because you're being stupid, Benedict."

He clenched his fists in an effort not to use them and Adam smiled.

"It's obvious. She lied *because* she loves you. She begged me to protect you. She's desperate to stop you going anywhere near Fred Castleton at the Red Dragon. Now, if you can calm down and apply your usual good sense and impeccable logic to this matter, all we have to do is find out why."

20

"She's gone, Benedict."

On some level he'd already known that the moment he opened the door. He turned around in his empty bedroom and stared at Faith.

"Dr. Finbar said she could travel in slow stages, and she insisted on leaving immediately." She leaned against the door frame. "I made sure she took several of our guards with her and sent another less obvious team to follow her home."

"Thank you for that." He forced a smile past the sick emptiness ringing through his mind. "It's all right. I've calmed down now. Maybe with her in a safe place I can focus my energy on sorting out this tangle of lies."

"That's always been your strength, Benedict." She blew him a kiss. "Keep me informed of your progress, won't you?"

He took a moment to walk around the apartment, but there were no traces of his wife. She'd taken everything and left the place just as it had been before, sterile and empty, just how he liked it. But he missed her presence so much it was hard to breathe.

"Benedict, are you ready to face Mr. Castleton?"

He turned to find Adam behind him, his cheek still bearing a bruise from where Benedict had shoved him down onto the floor.

"You have him?"

"I sent two men to investigate the cellars of the Red Dragon and Mr. Castleton took exception to that. Apparently, he's downstairs waiting to voice a protest."

"Excellent." Benedict met Adam's slightly worried gaze. "Don't worry, I won't kill him."

"Good man, let's make use of him first. You can consider your other options later."

Adam followed him down the stairs and into Benedict's office and took a chair to one side of his desk. Mr. Maclean went to fetch Castleton from the hall where he'd been left to kick his heels.

Mr. Castleton was announced and strode into the room, color high and fists already clenched. Benedict didn't rise to his feet.

"What's the meaning of this, Keyes?"

Benedict finished what he was writing before he looked up. "I beg your pardon?"

"I found two of your men messing about in my cellars this morning. What right do you have to invade my premises?"

"As I don't even know who you are, that is a difficult question to answer."

"I'm Fred Castleton, owner of the Red Dragon in Mile End. You damn well know that."

"I once knew a Fred Castleton who was a private in my father's regiment." Benedict pretended to scrutinize Fred's fleshy red face. "Are you the same man?"

"Enough of these games, my lord. What were your men doing in my cellars?"

"They weren't my men."

Fred visibly swelled. "Who else would concern himself with me? It's not the first time you've been in my inn, now is it?"

"Firstly, those men were probably employed by our government, so I suggest you take up your concerns with the appropriate agency you have offended. Secondly, I was in your establishment because I received information that the man who tried to set fire to my house worked there." He raised his eyebrows. "Anything else?"

"He might care to explain why this was in his cellar." Adam came over to Benedict's desk and dropped a cheap, tarnished gold locket on the white blotter.

Benedict went still and used his fingertip to turn the locket over.

"The 'government officials' brought it to me because it has the name *Keyes* engraved on the back." Adam said.

"I have no idea what you're talking about, Mr. Fisher." Fred snorted. "Knowing you, one of your men probably planted it there to incriminate me."

"Incriminate you of what?" Benedict said softly.

Fred met his gaze. "Of stealing from your house before setting fire to it."

"But I don't own this particular piece of jewelry."

"Then, as I said, one of your men is trying to ruin me."

"It belongs to my wife. I gave it to her when we got married." Benedict rubbed his thumb over the worn engraving. It was a cheap little thing, the best he'd been able to afford at eighteen, but Malinda had loved it. "She was wearing it the last time I saw her." He paused. "Where is she, Mr. Castleton?"

Something flickered in the other man's eyes. "How should I know? Maybe she dropped it when she was impersonating your doxy the other night."

"No, she wasn't wearing it then. She's been missing since

yesterday afternoon. If you have her, Castleton, you'd better tell me where she is, or I'll arrange to have your entire premises reduced to rubble." He raised his head. "And I can do it, don't doubt me on that."

"I don't know where she is."

Benedict sighed and turned to Adam. "Can you ask Mr. Maclean to come in? I need to send an urgent message to the Excise Department."

"You wouldn't bloody dare."

"I damn well would. Where's my wife?"

Fred abruptly sat down and adopted a more conciliatory tone. "She's run off, has she? Well, it isn't surprising, is it? No one likes to hear that their father is a traitor and a thief."

"So, you have seen her?"

"She came to the inn yesterday afternoon, asking to see me. I didn't feel it was right not to speak to the girl. She had some wild idea that your father had stolen his own gold and was seeking my help to kill him." He shrugged. "Of course, I couldn't allow the poor, deluded lass to do that, so I told her the truth."

"Which was?"

"That her father conspired against the marquis to steal the gold."

"And what else?"

"Nothing. But that's probably why she ran out of my inn like a fox before a hunt." He frowned. "She didn't come home, then?"

"No." Benedict took refuge in the cold fury vibrating through him. "Do you really believe Patrick Rowland was capable of such villainy?"

"He was shot in the back by one of his own soldiers. That doesn't sound like a loyal man to me."

"How do you know how he died?"

"Your father received compensation for the gold from the government. Why do you care about this matter?"

"I don't. I'm trying to locate my wife, not delve into ancient history."

Fred considered him for a long moment. "And if I told you that I knew what happened because I was an innocent by-stander?"

"Who left his friends to die or steal as they wished?"

Fred scowled and crossed his arms over his chest. "Perhaps I wasn't there after all, then."

"Come now, Mr. Castleton, do you want your place of business to survive or not?" Adam interrupted, his voice calm. "If you wish to tell us the truth, we would appreciate it."

"By leaving my business unharmed?"

Adam glanced at Benedict and raised an eyebrow. "Do we agree to leave the Red Dragon intact?"

"Yes." Benedict nodded. He was more than happy to leave the building alone if he could obliterate the owner. . . . "As I said, my prime objective at the moment is to locate my wife. If you saw what happened, we'd like to hear about it."

Fred settled into his chair. "Well, it was like this, see. Three of us arranged the ambush in the place Patrick suggested. It was where the mountain pass narrowed, which meant it was almost impossible for his party to turn around, or see who or what was shooting at them. When the smoke cleared, Patrick, all his men, and one of ours were dead." He shrugged. "There was nothing we could do about that. We took what we needed as quickly as possible and made off with it."

"Where did you hide the gold?"

"We didn't need to hide it. We'd come prepared. We split it between the two of us and went back down to camp."

"Patrick Rowland's family received nothing?" Benedict asked.

"Not directly, but they did all right in the end."

Benedict let that avenue of inquiry alone until he had time to think. "When you informed my wife that her father was the traitor, and not mine, did she not question you about where the gold ended up?"

"No, the silly lass was too worried about you to think straight." Fred sighed. "It's no wonder she ran off. I wonder if she's gone back to France? Perhaps it's for the best. She had the sense to realize that you wouldn't want her near you—what with your reputation for integrity and all that."

"That's possible, although I will do my best to find her and ensure that she hasn't been harmed in any way." He fastened his gaze on the ruby signet ring Fred wore on his index finger and saw instead Malinda's bloodied mouth. He rose from his seat. "Thank you for your help. If I require further information, I assume you'll be at the Red Dragon?"

"Aye." Fred stood, too, his gaze sharpening. "I've got to make sure it remains standing as you promised."

"It will as long as you are there to protect it," Adam added, and went to open the door. "Good morning, Mr. Castleton."

Benedict waited until Adam returned and closed the door behind him.

"I'm impressed that you didn't leap over your desk and kill him with your bare hands. What an extremely unpleasant individual."

"But he did give us some very interesting information." Benedict studied his clasped hands. "He neglected to mention that Malinda was also present at the ambush."

"Which makes sense if he thinks we don't know that." Adam frowned. "I assume he'd be quite pleased if Malinda hadn't made it back to the Sinners last night."

"One must assume so because he was willing to reveal himself as one of the ambushers. If my wife is dead, there is no one else who can divulge his part in the crime. He probably thinks he's safe now, the bastard."

"He also suggested they took all the gold themselves."

"And Malinda told us she showed them where to hide it, and then stole most of it when she ran off and he took the gold."

Adam whistled. "If Castleton is right, it still doesn't explain how she and her mother had the money to survive for all those years in France."

"No, it doesn't. But it does confirm our suspicion that she lied." Benedict searched Adam's face. "But why?"

"Perhaps Castleton had something right. If Malinda truly thought her father was responsible for plotting that ambush, would she want to transfer that shame onto you? It wouldn't be the first time she's put your standing before her own, would it?"

"Am I really considered so wedded to maintaining my reputation that I'm not allowed to have feelings too?" Benedict demanded.

Adam's expression sobered. "Unfortunately, your unblemished reputation is the backbone of our government and our nation. It makes the unpleasant decisions we occasionally have to adopt in our underworld acceptable to those in power who have to condone them. If you were revealed to be a worthless man allied to a father and a father-in-law who plotted to deceive honest soldiers of their pay, there would be hell to pay."

"So Castleton didn't need to threaten her. He probably threatened me." Benedict groaned and rubbed his hand over his face. "Which is what made Malinda concoct her absurd story. Why didn't she *tell* me?"

"Well, that, and Fred telling her that her father wasn't an innocent man after all."

"Oh, Christ, yes." Benedict closed his eyes and tried to think through the tangle of lies. "No one's telling the truth, are they?"

"Obviously not, and I suspect there's more to it than we realize."

"Why?"

"Because if your wife didn't take any gold, we still don't know how Malinda's mother managed to pay for that damned nunnery."

"Castleton said something about 'They did all right in the end,' didn't he?" Benedict slowly raised his head. "What the devil did he mean?"

Adam was already on his feet. "Let's see if we can find Faith."

Faith was finally located coming in the door of the Sinners deep in conversation with Nicodemus Theale, and both of them were ushered by Adam into Benedict's study with all possible haste. Alistair made himself quietly useful, bringing food for the ever-hungry Nicodemus and tea for the countess before settling down with a pen and paper at the desk while Benedict paced the hearthrug.

"We have news," Faith said, exchanging a glance with Nicodemus. "You go first, Mr. Theale."

"Our arsonist confessed to being hired by a Mr. Fred Castleton, the owner of the Red Dragon Inn just off the Mile End Road."

Benedict nodded. "Go on."

"We convinced the magistrate to reduce his sentence and allow him to take his money and leave the country." Nicodemus looked up from his notes. "Do we wish to start proceedings against Mr. Castleton?"

"We might. Do you have anything else?"

"No, my lord." Nicodemus's glow of quiet triumph dissipated. "Did I not do as you wanted?"

"You did very well. In fact, prosecuting Mr. Castleton for arson might be our last resort."

"Or a way to encourage him to confess even more of his sins," Adam agreed.

Benedict turned to Faith. "Have you heard back from your man in France yet?"

"Actually, that's why I went out. I met him down at the docks this morning after seeing Malinda off. Such a charming man." She took Malinda's mother's journal out of her reticule and placed it on her knee. "He confirmed that the nunnery only took in the wealthiest of orphans and children and that their fees for doing so were extremely high."

"Was your man able to get inside the place?"

"He was. I didn't ask how. He even got into the library and made copies of all the entries regarding Malinda and Doris during their stay there." She hesitated. "You might wish to read them through yourself, Benedict, in *private*."

He took the papers she handed him and put them on his desk before returning to the subject that concerned him most.

"Did he mention who paid the bills?"

"That's the interesting part. *Apparently,* they were paid by George Makethorpe."

"Mrs. Rowland's *second* husband?"

"And wait, there is more." Faith opened Mrs. Rowland's journal. "Do you remember Malinda telling us that George came into money and bought a promotion into another regiment?"

"Yes. He married Malinda's mother less than a week after Patrick's death, and took her away with him." Benedict slammed his hand down on the desk. "*Damnation,* why didn't we think of him when we were trying to find out which of Patrick's fellow soldiers came out of the conflict with money?"

"Because he was no longer part of the regiment." Faith consulted a page in the book. "One has to wonder if he is the other surviving ambusher."

"Who took care of Malinda and her mother with the money he received as his share?" Benedict stared at Adam. "It all makes a horrible kind of sense."

"I'm afraid it does. And now for an even more worrying question. Do we know if George Makethorpe is still alive?"

21

"This was a mistake."

Malinda muttered as the carriage slowed yet again to pass through a tollbooth. Being shut in a carriage in luxurious solitude had given her far too much time to think. It was dusk, and they'd been traveling for most of the day. At the last halt, Jon Snow, the man who was in charge of the trip, had told her they would stop for the night at the next inn they encountered.

She shouldn't have left.

That thought kept drumming through her head, and nothing she could tell herself made any difference. She'd walked away from Benedict once when she was seventeen and now she'd done it again. Even if he didn't trust her, she should have shown him that she at least had matured enough to trust *him*. . . .

She was a fool. He'd tried to tell her that her sense of being worth less than him and his aristocratic family was nonsense, but she'd pretended not to understand. And then there was the other thing that she hadn't told him. The even bigger thing.

The carriage slowed and turned down a smaller track toward the lights of a low building with the sign of a blue boar.

She barely waited for Jon to open the door before she was speaking.

"We need to go back."

He clutched her elbow in a gentle grasp. "My lady?"

"I have to go back and tell Benedict something important."

"My orders were to escort you home, my lady. I'm afraid I can't deviate from them."

His voice was firm as he maneuvered her into the inn.

"But you don't understand."

He greeted the landlord, who showed them into a private parlor. Jon shut the door and stood with his back to it, his stance and his expression unmoving.

"Lord Keyes was most specific, my lady. He said you might try to challenge my orders, but that I was not to give in to you unless you were on your deathbed, and even then I was to take care." He gestured at the desk in the corner. "If you wish to write him a letter, I can guarantee that one of my men will take it back to Lord Keyes as quickly as possible."

"That's not good enough. I need to see him. If you will not take me, I'll hire a horse and go myself."

"My lady, you are still unwell. Attempting such a journey would be ruinous to your health." He sighed. "Please don't make me have to resort to drugging you."

"Lord Keyes condoned *that?*"

Jon retrieved a letter from his pocket. "He said to show you this if you started arguing with me."

She took the single sheet of paper that was covered in Benedict's distinctive handwriting and read it out loud. "Jon, my wife is used to getting her own way. On no account allow her access to any guns, knives, or heavy objects. If she refuses to continue her journey at any point, you have my authority to drug her so that she sleeps though the rest of the trip."

She handed the letter back. "My husband is a *horrible* man."

"And my employer, my lady." John looked wretched. "Please

don't make this hard on us both. Write him a letter, continue on to Alford Park, and by the time we get there, he'll probably have answered you, and everything will be all right again. If it isn't and he instructs me to accompany you back to London, I'll do so most willingly." He swallowed hard. "I have a young family, my lady. I can't afford to be turned off."

"Oh, all *right*."

She walked over to the desk, pulled out a sheet of paper, and sat down with a thump.

"Thank you, my lady. I'll just go and see about your dinner."

She heard the key turn and realized he'd locked her in. That had probably been Benedict's idea too. He really did know her rather too well. Her head was aching and she was shivering. In her present battered condition, the thought of leaping on a horse and charging hell for leather down to London was surprisingly unattractive. But how could she convey how she felt to Benedict in a letter?

She couldn't. And she certainly couldn't mention the other matter. She pondered the blank page in front of her and finally settled on an apology for insisting on leaving and a request to be allowed to see him at his earliest convenience. It was galling to have to ask, but she deserved it.

When the door opened and Jon appeared with a tray containing her dinner, she was fairly resigned to eating her food and taking herself off to bed. His relief at her apparent docile behavior was evident and he promised to get the letter to Benedict as soon as humanly possible.

After her dinner, he escorted her and one of the maids from the inn up to the best bedchamber.

"Good night, my lady." He bowed. "I'll be outside guarding the door all night and Daisy is going to sleep in there with you. If there is anything you need, just call out to me."

"Thank you, Jon."

She went into the bedchamber and allowed the maid to help

her out of her gown and into her nightdress. Daisy settled herself on one of the chairs by the fire, and Malinda fell into a dreamless sleep.

"And to what do I owe the pleasure of your visit this time, Mr. Fisher, Lord Keyes?"

Fred Castleton appeared at the foot of the stairs that divided the tavern from the private rooms at the back and stared at Benedict. The hostelry was quieter than it had been during his last visit and the number of occupants less due to the lack of mail coach passengers hurrying through.

"We have some more questions for you."

"And what if I don't choose to answer them?"

"That's up to you." Benedict paused. "I heard the magistrate's court at Bow Street was about to start proceedings against you, but if you are already aware of that, we'll wish you good night."

He started back toward the door.

"Wait."

Benedict looked over his shoulder.

"What have you done, Keyes?"

"I've done nothing. I understand that the proceedings were brought by the occupants of the ground floor apartment in my town house."

Fred Castleton pushed open the nearest door. "Come in here."

Benedict and Adam followed him through into the room, which lacked a fire and had undrawn curtains and a grimy window that looked out into the stable yard.

"What's going on?"

"You're about to be prosecuted for setting a fire at my property in Maddox Street."

"On whose say-so?"

"The man you hired to do your dirty work. Apparently in

an effort to avoid his fate, he told the magistrate who paid him to set the fire. It's all in the court record if you choose to read it."

"You bloody bastard!"

Fred went for Benedict, but Adam was quicker. He stepped in between the two men, his pistol at the ready.

"Do you wish to die, Castleton? I'm quite willing to oblige you. But perhaps you might care to listen to what Lord Keyes has to say to you first." He gestured at the nearest chair. "Sit down."

Fred slumped into the chair, his chest heaving, and his expression thunderous.

Benedict took the seat opposite him. "There are always opportunities to avoid the full magnitude of the law."

"If you're a rich nob."

"Or if you happen to know one. I'm fairly certain that I could extricate you from this charge if you provided me with the information I require."

"What exactly do you want to know?"

"The name of the other surviving ambusher."

Fred chewed his lip.

Benedict continued. "I'm fairly sure I know who it is, but I'd like you to confirm it."

"Then tell me yourself and I'll tell you if you're right."

"That won't work. I need the name."

"And if I tell you, you'll have the charges against me at Bow Street dropped?"

"If your answer turns out to be correct, yes."

"It was George Makethorpe."

Benedict couldn't allow himself to relax or show anything in his face. "Thank you. Do you happen to know if he is still alive?"

"I'd bloody like to know that myself. From what I can tell, he wasted his blunt on Patrick Rowland's widow and her children."

"You knew about that, did you? Perhaps, unlike you, he felt some responsibility toward the wife and child of the originator of the plan."

He wondered if Fred would rise to the bait and claim ownership of the scheme, but wasn't very surprised when he remained mute. Benedict rose from his seat and nodded at Adam, who stepped out into the hallway to safeguard the door. He turned back to Fred and picked him up by the throat.

"I believe we have a score to settle, Castleton. No man lays hands on my wife and gets away with it."

He drew back his fist and had the immense satisfaction of seeing it smash into Fred's startled face and break his nose. Within a second the other man was on him, but Benedict was younger and fitter, and fueled by a rage that demanded satisfaction at any cost. Each blow he landed was for Malinda, each grunt of pain and gasping cry canceled out one of hers. Within a very short space of time, Fred was on his knees and then on the floor, blood streaming from his nose and mouth, his pleas garbled.

With a final, well-aimed kick at Fred's ribs, Benedict stepped over his opponent's writhing form and headed for the door.

"Good night, Mr. Castleton. If you dare to come near me or any member of my family again, I'll kill you. Don't ever doubt it."

Rubbing his bruised knuckles, he went through the door and found Adam, who raised an eyebrow.

"Is he still alive?"

"Unfortunately he is. I am a man of my word, after all."

They exited the inn as quickly as possible and headed back to the Sinners. As they neared the entrance, Benedict slowed.

"What's wrong?" Adam asked.

"I'm trying to remember what George Makethorpe looked like."

"Why?"

"Because I have a horrible feeling that I've seen him recently." He turned to Adam. "Order a horse saddled for me. I'm going after Malinda."

A squeak and a rustle of movement woke Malinda from a troubled sleep. She opened one eye to see Daisy, the maid, leaning over her making frantic circles with her hands.

"That's right, missy, wake her gently."

The barrel of a pistol glinted against Daisy's head. Malinda's gaze traveled along the serviceable pistol and up the arm and shoulder of the man who held it. She slowly sat up.

"Evening, Mally, love."

"What are you doing here?" she whispered.

"Just tying up a few loose ends." He motioned at the terrified Daisy. "I'm going to tie her up while we talk so that we don't rouse the man on guard."

Malinda nodded and watched as her stepfather efficiently gagged and bound Daisy to a chair close to the fire. He came back to sit on the side of her bed, and she got her first good look at him.

"Where have you been? After Mother's death you told me you had business to attend to and disappeared!"

He shrugged. "I had a few things to settle."

"Your hair is black."

"Boot polish. I didn't want you seeing me too soon, and making trouble."

"About what?"

He sighed. "About the gold, Mally."

"I don't understand."

He patted her hand. "If you've been talking to Fred Castleton about it, you probably don't. Did he tell you about me?"

"No." She covered her mouth. "Don't tell me you were one of the ambushers? Oh, God, no."

He looked wretched. "I'm sorry, lass."

"*Why?*"

"It was like this. The night before he left to pick up the supplies, Patrick got very drunk. He was angry about the way the marquis had treated you. The more he drank, the more indiscreet he became, until we all knew about the gold. The marquis happened upon us and took Patrick back to his tent. He was furious with him."

George hesitated. "When they'd gone, Fred Castleton made a suggestion that the three of us should steal the gold ourselves, share it with the men, and have the last laugh on the Marquis of Alford."

"So my father didn't know?"

"Not until it was too late and he recognized Fred." He swallowed hard. "I never meant for it to go that far, lass. I was sickened by both your father's death and the fact that you witnessed it."

"You saw me?"

"Aye, but I thought I was the only one." He took her hand in his. "I couldn't bring your father back to life, but I did everything I could to make it up to your mother and you."

"You bought your commission, married my mother, and paid for me to go to the nunnery."

"Yes, lass."

"With the rest of your gold."

"Yes. I was a fool. I knew nothing I did would ever make up for Patrick's loss, but I had to try."

Malinda's breath shuddered out. "Then why are you here now?"

He grimaced. "I've been keeping an eye on you since you set foot in England. Knowing you and your belief that the Marquis of Alford was responsible for all the ills in the world, I had a sense the past wouldn't stay buried for long."

"You were right."

"And I also knew that the real source of the trouble wasn't

the marquis, but Fred Castleton." His face twisted. "Damn him to hell."

"He certainly seems determined to do away with me."

He touched her bruised cheek. "You don't have to worry about him anymore. He really wants me. I'm prepared to go and see him if it means he leaves you alone."

"I think Lord Keyes is already dealing with that."

It was George's turn to look surprised. "The marquis's son?"

"It turns out that we are still married after all. He feels a sense of 'responsibility' for me."

For the first time George smiled. "Then I'll be leaving you in very capable hands."

"You're leaving? I thought you were planning on coming and living with me at Alford Park."

"Yes, but I have to meet with Fred Castleton and get him to leave you alone first."

"Benedict has that in hand, I swear it."

He squeezed her fingers. "I have to do this myself, lass. He needs to forget that he ever saw you."

"But you will come back?"

He leaned in and kissed her on the nose. "I'm glad you've found Lord Keyes again. You always loved him, didn't you?"

"Yes, but—"

He stood up and put his pistol away. Despite being in his early fifties, he was still lean and fit and bore himself like a soldier. She had a terrible feeling that she was never going to see him again.

"God bless, Mally. Please try and forgive me."

"There's nothing to forgive. Without your support, my mother and I would've starved to death."

His smile was crooked as he blew her a kiss. "Once I've been gone awhile, free the poor maid and give her that bag of coin. If you can convince her not to say anything about my presence here, that would be even better."

"I'll do my best."

He strode over to the narrow window and climbed out onto the steeply angled roof. Malinda waited until she heard the sound of a horse moving off below before she turned her attention to Daisy, who was sitting patiently in the chair, her eyes huge above the gag.

Malinda removed the gag and held up the bag of coins.

"Please don't scream, Daisy. He didn't want to hurt you and this money is yours." She smiled beguilingly. "Can we pretend that nothing happened and go back to sleep?"

22

Benedict finally spotted the carriage on the road ahead of him and breathed a prayer of thankfulness. He'd used all the resources of the Sinners to demand fast horses and the quickest changes of mount along the road, and yet he still hadn't been sure he'd find her in time.

A horse came out of the forest and the rider drew alongside him. He recognized one of the men he'd sent to guard the rear.

"Jarvis. It's me."

"My lord, is something wrong?"

"You tell me. Is her ladyship in good health?"

"I believe so, sir." He cast a quick glance at Benedict's mount. "Your horse looks done for. Do you want me to ride ahead and stop the carriage?"

"There's no point in alarming them. I'll catch up. Please remain in place and keep watch."

"Are you expecting trouble, sir?"

"I'm not sure. Just keep your wits about you."

Jarvis touched his hat and fell back, leaving Benedict to urge his tired mount closer to the much slower carriage. There was a tollbooth on the road ahead. If he was lucky, he'd catch them there.

As he approached, Jon Snow, who was sitting on the box with the coachman, swiveled around and pointed his pistol at him. Benedict waved and Jon's face relaxed.

"My lord."

The coach slowed to a stop. Benedict dismounted and tied the reins of his horse to the back of the conveyance. He opened the door and pulled himself up into the interior of the carriage, his legs aching from his hard ride.

"Benedict?"

Malinda's pale, bruised face appeared, and he took the seat opposite her and nodded.

"My lady."

She regarded him suspiciously. "Did you get my note?"

"What note?"

"The one I sent you from the inn yesterday evening."

"No."

"Then why are you here?"

He stared at her for a long time as he tried to collect his scattered thoughts. "How has your journey been?"

"You came all the way to ask me *that*?"

"I thought you might have encountered some trouble along the way."

"With six men guarding me?"

"Malinda, I could enlist a whole regiment to guard you and you'd still do exactly what you wanted anyway." He narrowed his eyes. "What *did* you do?"

"For goodness' sake, Benedict, I have done nothing but sit in this carriage, go into the inn Jon Snow ordered me to last night, eat my dinner, and go to bed."

"You also asked Jon if you could return to London."

A slight flush gathered on her cheeks. "Which was a mistake I soon rectified."

"You wrote to me and assumed that I'd come after you because of that note. What did you say that was so important?"

"I'm not stupid enough to put all my secrets in a letter."

"Then why weren't you surprised to see me?"

"Because—" She sniffed. "In my note I apologized and asked you to visit me when you had time."

"You apologized to me. For what?"

"For running away again."

He leaned back against the cushioned seat and studied her closely. "What were you going to say before you decided to distract me with your apology?"

"Benedict, you are *impossible!*"

"Would your attempts to divert my attention away from your behavior at the inn last night have anything to do with your unexpected nocturnal visitor?"

She opened her mouth and then closed it again.

"I stopped briefly at the inn to change horses and spoke to a very charming young lady named Daisy. Do you remember her?" He paused. "I'm sure you do. She's the poor woman your visitor tied up so that he could speak to you. She was under the mistaken impression that your companion was in love with you and that she was aiding in a proposed elopement."

She snorted. "If she described my visitor thusly, you must know that she was mistaken."

"Who was he?"

She stared back at him, her hazel eyes bright within the dark confines of the carriage.

"It was my stepfather."

"George Makethorpe."

"I suppose you think you know all about him, don't you?"

"Obviously not, because in your shoes I would've shot him."

"He was stupid enough to agree to take part in the raid, thinking it would only hurt your father. He didn't realize that Fred Castleton had other plans both for my father and for the money. When my mother and I were in danger, he did the best he could and took us away from the regiment."

"He told you all this?"

"Last night." She sighed. "I thought my father was the one responsible for planning the ambush. But George said he'd been taken away by the marquis before Fred brought the idea up."

"So George reckoned Fred had to silence your father in case he remembered anything, and betrayed them."

"I suspect Fred would have preferred to be the only one who emerged from that ambush alive." She drew an audible breath. "It seems that both of our fathers were taken advantage of."

"Indeed. Is that why you wrote to me and apologized?"

"No."

"*No?*"

"I wrote that letter before I saw George."

"How interesting."

She glared at him. "I realized that even if you didn't trust me, I should try to trust you."

"Trust that I would find a way out of your difficulties with Castleton? I assume he used me as a lever to spur you on to tell that ridiculous story about your part in the ambush?"

"Benedict, he said my father had come up with the scheme because the marquis had threatened to drum him out of the army if I didn't stop consorting with his son. He *said* that if I didn't persuade you to drop the matter, he would inform against my father *and* yours, and destroy your career."

"And you thought that was important?"

"Of *course* I did." She pressed her hand to her heart. "You laugh at the notion, but you truly are the most honorable man I've ever met. I couldn't allow myself to be the architect of your downfall."

"But I'm not eighteen anymore." He hesitated trying to find the right words, words that wouldn't hurt her. "I've learned that honor comes at a cost, and that I'm willing to use every dirty trick I know to safeguard my country and those I care for." He met her gaze. "I'm not that boy you loved anymore. I don't need you to fight my battles for me."

She looked away from him, and he felt the loss of connection like a punch in the gut.

"I know you've grown up and lost the ability to trust anyone. It doesn't mean that I can't trust you to make things right. That's exactly why I came to you in the first place and why I decided to return to London."

She was slipping away from him again; he could feel it in his bones.

"I trust you."

She shook her head. "Benedict . . ."

"I trust you with my heart. I always have." He took a deep breath. "That's why I'm here. That's why I came after you. I don't ever want to have to choose between my career and the woman I love, but if it came down to it?" He forced a smile. "I'd resign in a heartbeat."

He moved across to her seat, picked her up, and settled her gently in his lap. "Please don't argue with me about this. I don't think I can bear it."

Her hand crept up to rest on the curve of her jaw. "Are you feeling quite well?"

"Never better."

She examined his face closely. "You've been fighting."

"I damned near killed Fred Castleton."

"Good." She held his gaze. "There was another reason why I wanted to see you."

"Apart from apologizing?"

"Yes, and this part had to be said to your face. I agreed to go to the convent because I had no choice." She squirmed uneasily on his lap. "I was pregnant."

Surprise slammed through him. "Why didn't you tell me at the time?"

"For a long time, I didn't realize what was wrong with me, and then I thought our marriage had been dissolved, and . . ." She swallowed hard. "I couldn't bear to ask your father to provide for his son *and* daughter's bastard."

He thought about the papers Faith had told him to read in private that he'd left behind on his desk. Had she hoped to prepare him for this?

"So Doris isn't your sister; she's your daughter? *My* daughter? Good God, no wonder she reminded me of someone. She is very like my mother, isn't she?"

"Just in looks." She cupped his chin. "Aren't you angry with me?"

"When it was my father who ran you off, and I let him?" He shook his head. "We were too young to know any better, and we were exploited by those who should have had our best interests at heart. I'm glad that George used his money to save you, your mother, and our child. My father certainly has a lot to answer for."

He rested his chin on the top of her head, and she leaned in against his shoulder. "Is that everything now, Benedict?"

"Unless you have any other dark secrets you'd like to share with me, my lady, then, yes."

"I'm glad. Despite what you might think, I hate being at odds with you." She kissed his throat and then suddenly stiffened. "I am worried that my stepfather intends to seek out Fred Castleton, though."

"If he does and he kills the man, I'll be damn grateful to him." He tightened his arm around her. "I wanted to kill Fred so badly for hurting you, and yet I had to keep him alive to find out the truth."

"Which you did."

"Which is why you should've trusted me right from the start."

"Benedict . . ."

He stopped her mouth with his own, kissing her gently until she responded and then neither of them retained the ability to voice anything for quite a while.

Benedict stirred. "I just had a terrible thought."

"What?"

"Doris."

"What about her?"

"She saw me chained and naked in your bed."

"Not *naked*. I always made sure you were decently covered when she was around."

"Thank goodness for that. Does she know?"

"That I'm her mother, or that you are her father? Neither. I planned on telling her on her eighteenth birthday."

He calculated rapidly in his head. "Which must be soon."

"Yes."

He claimed her hand. "Might I suggest that we reveal we are married first, and then tell her together?"

She smiled up at him. "I knew you would come in useful at some point."

"I'm glad to be of service." He kissed her hand. "We're just coming through the gates of Alford Park. Perhaps you might care to alight first in case anyone tries to shoot me?"

She smiled at him. "I'd be delighted."

23

Malinda opened the door into the crimson bedchamber and spied Benedict stretched out on the covers. He was a glorious sight, his long naked limbs, tight stomach, and muscled chest gleaming in the candlelight.

"Ah, there you are, Malinda. I was beginning to think you weren't coming to bed."

She advanced slowly toward him, enjoying staring at him too much to hurry. Not only was he her legal husband, but she had a perfect right to live in Alford Park. Everything had turned out far better than she had anticipated.

"I had a lot to catch up on. Apparently Jenny has taken on the role of housekeeper and seems quite willing to settle here with her boys. Would you mind if she stayed?"

"Not at all. As long as you don't mind." He patted the sheets. "Come to bed."

She climbed onto the bed, sank down beside him, and he gathered her close.

"You still don't have a competent ladies' maid and you have

too many clothes on to sleep comfortably. May I help relieve you of some of them?"

She surrendered herself into his hands as he slowly and competently undressed her down to her shift. With a sigh she lay down and pressed her cheek against his chest. He stroked his fingers through her hair, withdrawing the pins, and put them in a neat pile on the bedside table.

"Why does this feel so comfortable?" she whispered.

"Because it is."

"That's hardly helpful."

"I like lying next to you. I always have. Do you remember when we were children, we'd lie on our backs and stare at the stars and imagine how we might travel there?"

"I remember. Such foolish dreams."

He kissed the top of her head. "Not so foolish, love, because here we are, together at last. That was my favorite dream of all."

She came up on one elbow to stare down at him. "Now you are just being silly."

He held her gaze, his blue eyes clear. "I always knew I wanted you, Malinda, and I very rarely fail to achieve my goals."

"Is that why you agreed to help me?"

He slowly blinked at her. "Naturally. I hate to lose."

"So I'm some kind of prize?"

His smile was a delight. "I suppose you are."

"And having achieved this prize, what happens now? You move on to your next conquest?"

He slid his hand into her hair and brought her mouth down to within an inch of his. "Not unless I want to get shot again." He kissed her very thoroughly until she had to kiss him back. "I'm not a fool, Malinda. Having been lucky enough to be given a second chance, I'm not going to ruin it."

"A second chance at what?"

He frowned at her, one hand stroking her back. "Why are

you interrogating me right now? Can we not spend one quiet night enjoying each other in this bed before you launch your next campaign to infuriate me?"

"What?" she repeated softly. "You said that you trust me with your heart. What exactly does that mean?"

"You are determined to make things difficult, aren't you?"

"No, I'm just trying to make sure I understand you correctly."

"Before you decide to tell me how *you* feel about me?"

She nodded, too scared to speak.

His gaze softened. "I love you. I always have. Everything I've done has been because of that."

"Oh."

"Is that all you have to say?" he demanded. Reaching up, he carefully rolled her underneath him and straddled her, keeping his weight off her. "I spill my heart out to you, and all you can say is, 'oh'?" He kissed her. "You knew, dammit. You came to me for help because deep down you knew I loved you and that I always would."

She studied his handsome face and considered the note of uncertainty in his voice and the slight trembling of his body. Had she known?

"Mally . . ."

She drew him down over her and licked at his lips until, with a helpless sound, he opened his mouth to her. She kissed him slowly, savoring the taste and texture of his mouth as if for the first time. He didn't stop her or try to take control of the kiss. Pushing on his shoulders, she made him go onto his back. His cock jutted out from the fair hair at his groin, straining for her touch.

She hadn't needed to chain him to her bed. He would've done what she'd wanted. He always had caved in to her eventually. . . .

Wrapping her hand around his shaft, she played with the

wetness streaming down until she could easily slide his slick flesh between her fingers. His hips bucked and his back arched off the bed as he caught her rhythm and responded to it. She straddled him and rubbed the crown of his cock against her clit until she was as wet and slippery as he was, and could slide easily inside her.

She took him deep and held him there, her gaze fixed on his.

"Are you sure it isn't just about this?"

"The sex?"

She squeezed her inner muscles around his shaft, enjoying the heightening of her own pleasure and the throbbing she'd set off in his flesh.

"It is rather remarkable, isn't it?" she murmured, bringing one of his hands to her clit. "Make me come."

He kept hold of her wrist. "If it had just been about this, we wouldn't have found each other again. You're my best friend and my lover." His grip tightened. "Tell me that you feel the same."

There was an edge of uncertainty in his voice that she'd never heard before.

"Is the great Benedict Keyes asking me if I love him?"

"Yes." The stark need in his eyes made her want to cry.

"I thought you knew everything."

"Not this."

"Of course I love you. How could you ever doubt it? I always shoot men that I love."

His smile wobbled. "Mally, I—"

She bent to kiss him and let him start thrusting upward as she rose above him. She came hard and he joined her a moment later, his cock holding deep as he climaxed inside her. With a sigh, she lowered herself over him, her face buried against his shoulder. Reaching up, she touched his cheek.

"It's all right, Benedict."

"I know."

She brought her fingers to her mouth, tasted the salt of his tears, and almost wept herself. There were some limits to teasing him that even she must adhere to.

"There *is* one more thing I should tell you."

"God, *no*."

Beneath her his muscles stiffened. She found herself grinning with anticipation as he braced himself for yet another battle. Fighting with Benedict was always glorious because they could always make up in bed.

"I think Doris is going to have a baby brother or sister before the year is out."

He clapped his hands over his face and his shoulders started to shake. Alarmed, Malinda sat up and smacked him on the chest.

"It's not that surprising, is it? Considering—"

He removed his hands to reveal his laughing face and shook his head. "Oh, Malinda, my dearest, darling love. Never change, will you?"

Please turn the page for an exciting sneak peek of
Kate Pearce's newest novel in her Sinners Club series

MASTERING A SINNER

coming in January 2015!

1

London, 1827

Alistair Maclean glanced at the clock on the mantelpiece and realized it wasn't working. With an exasperated sigh he drew out his battered pocket watch and studied the scratched glass face. Stepping over the accumulated odds and ends on the floor, he picked up the clock, rewound it, and set the correct time. It was almost three in the morning. He was due at his desk at the Sinners at eight sharp.

Where was Harry? He went over to the window, pulled aside the dirty lace curtain, and studied the empty cobbled street. If he hadn't been nursing an old injury, he'd be pacing the tattered hearthrug, worrying about what scrape his younger brother had gotten himself into now. And why *was* he still worrying? At twenty-five, Harry wasn't a child, even though sometimes he behaved like one.

Alistair built up the fire again using the few remaining lumps of coal in the scuttle and sat back down in one of the wing chairs. A faint sound echoed down the street and grew louder, a chorus of yells and shouts that evolved into hunting cries and catcalls that eventually burst through the door of the house.

One of the revelers almost fell into Alistair's lap. He recognized most of the men—bored younger sons of the aristocracy, accompanied by the upcoming sprigs of new wealth that clung on like a particularly thorny rose.

He rose slowly to his feet and stood amid the shouting and sway of inebriated flesh, which reminded him all too forcibly of being stuck in a field full of Scottish cattle.

"Good evening, gentlemen. Or should I say good morning?" He registered the blaze of his brother's red hair among the melee and bowed. "May I speak to you alone, Harry?"

With a groan, his brother staggered away from his companions. "Devil take it, Alistair, who let you in here?"

One of the other men belched loudly. "Want us to toss him out for you, Harry?"

Alistair turned to the leering drunken fool who'd just spoken. "I beg your pardon?" He'd faced Napoleon's armies in Spain. A few wild aristocrats didn't frighten him at all.

"No, when he looks like this, he means business, and as he pays my bills, I suppose I'd better listen to him." Harry grinned at his companions and started to herd them toward the door. "I'll see you all tomorrow."

"Night, Harry."

For once the men were willing to behave themselves and leave quietly. Alistair slowly let out his breath. He hadn't expected it to be so easy to disengage his brother from his drinking cronies. In truth it was becoming harder and harder to have any kind of conversation with Harry at all.

As soon as the door shut, Harry's easy smile disappeared and he swung around to glare at Alistair.

"What's wrong with you? Skulking in here, acting like my bloody father, and sending my friends away."

"They're hardly your friends, and in certain respects I do stand in place of your father."

Harry flung himself down into the nearest chair and unbuttoned his waistcoat. "You certainly do your best to control me just like he did."

Alistair took the seat opposite. "I came to tell you about a change in my circumstances."

"Let me guess, you've decided to petition Parliament to restore our ancient family title and see if they're willing to offer us a large annuity to go with it."

"Hardly."

"I was jesting. I know you wouldn't do anything to draw attention to our family."

"Why would I bother when you do a perfectly good job of that yourself?" Alistair snapped.

"Oh, for God's sake, leave me alone." Harry shoved a hand through his unruly red hair. "You nag like a fishwife."

Alistair reminded himself that he was too old to rise so easily to his brother's taunts. "I've taken a new position. I thought you should know about it."

"Why?"

"It's at the Sinners Club."

Harry went still. "So what?"

"I'll be working as the private secretary of Benedict Lord Keyes and Mr. Adam Fisher."

"As I said, so bloody what?"

"You were . . . friends with Adam Fisher once."

"Not anymore." Harry scowled and ripped off his cravat. "You should do well there. Adam's almost as prosy an old bore as you are."

Alistair set his jaw. "I just wanted you to know that if you come looking for me, or take part in any of the activities on the second floor, that you might encounter one of my employers."

"And *I* said that Adam Fisher means nothing to me and I'm extremely unlikely to come chasing after you at your place of business. I'm not that indiscreet."

Alistair studied his brother. "Are you quite sure about that?

Your current bout of drunkenness and irresponsible behavior began just after you parted company with Mr. Fisher."

Harry shrugged. "He wanted me to settle down and behave myself, wanted me to—" He stopped speaking and flashed his most charming smile. "It's none of your business, anyway, is it? Don't worry, I won't spoil your precious new job by turning up and starting a fight with Adam. I know how much you like the salary it brings you." He paused. "Adam doesn't want to see me again, anyway."

"I'm quite happy to visit you here if you need me, Harry." Alistair rose to his feet. "And your scorn for my having an occupation is hardly merited, seeing as it is my income that puts a roof over your head and supports our mother and sisters."

"And damn you for having to remind me of that every time I see you!"

Alistair met his brother's furious blue gaze. "Why does it offend you to be reminded of your current lifestyle, brother? From all accounts you don't just live off me, but off your aristocratic friends. Does it truly make you happy to be a parasite?"

"Go to the devil. What I do is no concern of yours."

Beneath Harry's hard-edged scorn lurked that touch of pain and self-derision that stopped Alistair from washing his hands of his brother and walking away. He took a steadying breath and unclenched his hands.

"Believe it or not, I didn't come here to fight with you. I simply wanted you to be aware of my new position before someone else told you about it and that became my fault, too." He bowed and turned to the door, kicking Harry's discarded boots out of his way.

"You're the one who should be worried."

"And why is that?"

"Because when Adam discovers you are my brother, he'll kick you out on your arse in an instant."

Alistair opened the door and looked back over at Harry, who remained sprawled in the chair, his eyes already half closed. "Actually, you are completely wrong on all accounts. Who do you think recommended me to Lord Keyes for the position in the first place?"

He had the momentary joy of seeing Harry's face frozen in shock before he closed the door and let himself out into the street. His brother wasn't the only person who'd been surprised at the recommendation. After a great deal of thought, Alistair had ended up asking both his new employers if they knew his brother. Both of them had confirmed that they did and that it didn't affect their decision to employ him in the slightest.

A cold wind hurried down the center of the street and Alistair picked up his pace, his slightly uneven gait making his right leg drag slightly. He doubted Adam Fisher had meant what he'd said. There had been too much pain and sadness in the man's eyes to believe he hadn't been affected by Harry's desertion and subsequent relationship with a man old enough to be his father . . . but then perhaps that's what Harry thought he needed—a father.

Sometimes he hated his brother's ability to breeze through life with his good looks and charm leaving devastation in his wake. He seemed incapable of deciding who to love, and left broken hearts everywhere. Alistair had wanted to tell Adam he'd had a lucky escape and that he should be thankful Harry's roving eye had moved on to someone else. Except this time, it felt different. Harry seemed more out of control than ever, as if he was trying to prove he was the wildest, most sexually provocative being in the whole of London.

And he needed to be careful. By law a man who was accused of sodomy could still be flogged and put in the stocks or, even worse, imprisoned, tried, and executed. He might find Harry exasperating, but he wouldn't wish that fate on someone he loved. It was a shame that every time they talked, Harry tried to shock him and *he* ended up acting like the prosy old bore his brother insisted he'd become. They'd been close once, back in Scotland, when their father was alive. They'd roamed the country-side together pretending to be border lords who vanquished the English in every battle. . . .

Alistair turned onto the main thoroughfare and saw an empty hackney cab standing at the corner. Waving a hand at the driver he gave in to the temptation to get back to the Sinners as fast as possible and at least attempt to get some sleep before his day started. As he reached the cab, a woman came around the opposite corner and almost knocked him over. He instinctively grabbed for her elbows to steady them both.

"Oh my goodness! Thank you, sir."

Her voice was low and far too cultivated to be out alone at this time of night in this sort of neighborhood. She wore a bonnet with a veil and such a deep brim that he could barely make out the outline of her pale face.

"Ma'am." He bowed. "I must apologize. I almost knocked you down."

"I'm so sorry, I didn't see you there, sir." She kept her hand on his arm. "I was too busy trying to attract the hackney driver's attention before he left me stranded here."

With a mental sigh, Alistair stepped back. "It seems as if we were on the same errand, but please, be my guest."

"Thank you."

She accepted his help and went up into the body of the vehicle and then turned back to him. "Perhaps we could share the ride, sir? In which direction are you headed?"

"To Mayfair, ma'am."

"I am going to Barrington Square, myself."

"Then our destinations are quite close."

She held out her gloved hand. "Please, join me."

Ordinarily, Alistair wouldn't have complied with her polite

request, but his hip was paining him, and he really couldn't see the harm in accepting her offer. "That's very kind of you, ma'am."

He managed to lever himself up into the small interior and settled on the seat opposite her. He'd damaged his hip thirteen years earlier fighting the French. Most of the time it behaved itself, but occasionally, when it was damp and cold, or he was stupid enough to fall off his horse, it caused him some pain.

The cab driver clicked to his horse and they set off, the only sound the *clip clop* of the horse's hooves on the cobblestones. Alistair leaned back against the seat and briefly closed his eyes. Dealing with Harry always sapped his energy, and he already had a busy day ahead of him. Both of his employers were present at the Sinners, which meant twice as much work for him. It was also rumored that Lady Benedict Keyes had accompanied her husband to London this time. She might have social arrangements he would need to see to as well. . . .

He liked his new job, but the unconventional nature of his employers' occupations wasn't quite what he was used to. Stately judges and government officials in Whitehall never behaved quite so *spontaneously*. He constantly struggled to impose order on the chaos of their irregular working lives and on the inner mechanisms of the club itself. The place wasn't quite as he'd envisioned it. The Sinners was not simply a gentlemen's club. It allowed female members, which was shocking enough, and *other* activities within its walls, more reminiscent of the Delornay pleasure house than a private club.

But while he might be expected to *arrange* some of those salacious activities on the second floor, he would never take part in them. It wouldn't be fitting. He had a reputation to maintain. Even as he framed the thought he imagined Harry laughing at him.

He caught a yawn discreetly behind his gloved hand and

stared out into the night as the ramshackle streets became wider and more prosperous. He desperately needed to down a large glass of whiskey and go to sleep. At least his small apartment in the Sinners came rent-free and had a door he could lock. He raised his voice so that the hackney driver could hear him. "Please stop in Barrington Square and let the lady out first."

"Right you are, sir."

He turned his attention to his silent companion, who had her head down and was searching for something in her reticule. A hint of lavender soap teased his senses as she snapped the bag shut.

"We're almost there, ma'am."

"I realize that, Mr. Maclean." She looked up. He blinked as the newly installed gas lamp on the corner of Barrington Square illuminated the barrel of the small dueling pistol she held in her hand. "Please don't move."

Alistair slowly raised his hands and considered his options. "I don't have any money to give you."

"This isn't a robbery."

"Then why are you holding a pistol on me?"

"To get your attention. I have a message for you from a client of mine."

"And what might that be?"

"My client wishes you to know that if you do not control your brother, my client will."

"That's a rather ridiculous statement. My brother is an adult. I am not responsible for his actions."

"My client doesn't believe that's true. If you don't rein him in, the consequences will be dire for your brother, and possibly ruinous for your career."

Alistair smiled as anger pushed aside his surprise and shock. "Indeed. Perhaps you might care to tell your client that unless he is willing to speak to me *directly*, I will take no heed of his words." He leaned forward and she jerked the pistol up until it was an inch from his face. "And you, ma'am, are a fool to allow yourself to be part of such a cowardly attempt at intimidation."

She laughed. "I've been paid well to deliver this message. That's all I care about." The carriage stopped, and she drew back from him. "Good night, Mr. Maclean."

He waited until she got out of the carriage and then asked the driver to move on until they'd cleared the corner of the square again. Stepping out of the cab, he paid the fee and turned back to the large houses. There were few lights on in any of them, and all was quiet. In less than an hour the maids would be up lighting fires and boiling cans of hot water for the household. He retraced his steps to where the woman had alighted and considered the steps up to the two front doors of the large, stone-terraced mansions.

As far as he remembered, one of the houses was vacant. The other, he recognized immediately. He'd wager his weekly stipend that the woman had entered into a world he knew all too well. Not many of the patrons of the house of pleasure realized that the mansion they visited extended into the building behind it. Which happened to be the very one he was standing in front of now on Barrington Square.

Not only did he know how to get into the house, but he also, courtesy of Jack Lennox, another Sinner, had a key. Sleep forgotten, he strode forward, went down the basement steps, and unlocked the door. The scent of lavender lured him on as he passed through the deserted scullery, out into the passageway that connected the two houses underground, and into the main kitchens of the pleasure house.

A passing footman stopped to wish him a pleasant evening, and Alistair paused. "Did you see a woman pass through here about a minute ago? She was dressed in black and wearing a bonnet."

"No, sir. I haven't seen anyone in the last half hour, but then

I've just come up from the cellars, so I might have missed them."

"Thank you."

"Mr. Delornay is in the kitchen, if you want to ask him, sir. I'll also inquire of the other staff."

"Thank you." Alistair forced a smile and went through into the homely kitchen, where several members of the staff sat eating and drinking around the large pine table.

"Mr. Maclean." An elegantly dressed blond man stood up and inclined his head. "Were you looking for me?"

"Good morning, Mr. Delornay." Alistair bowed. "I was looking for a woman who just came in through the Barrington Square entrance."

Christian Delornay frowned. "Through the Barrington house? That shouldn't be possible." He came around the table to Alistair's side. "Do you know who it was?"

"It was not someone I recognized." He hesitated, but Christian Delornay, the owner of the pleasure house, was the soul of discretion. "Actually she held a gun to my head and threatened my family."

"Obviously an enterprising female. Come and speak to my wife, Elizabeth. She knows everyone who comes here and works here."

Alistair followed Christian out of the kitchen and into the offices on the ground floor. He was quite familiar with the layout of the more practical areas of the house, having learned that if he wanted to fulfill his duties to provide entertainment at the Sinners, the Delornay family could offer him everything he needed.

As they walked, Christian spoke to every member of staff they encountered, asking after the woman in black, but to no avail. He knocked on a door at the end of the corridor and went in. "Elizabeth, we have a mystery on our hands."

His wife looked up from her perusal of the account books. She was one of the most beautiful and serene women Alistair had ever met. "Good morning, Mr. Maclean. And whatever do you mean, Christian?"

The smile Christian gave his wife was almost too intimate for Alistair to bear. It reminded him of how he'd felt about Gelis when he'd persuaded her to marry him.

"A mysterious woman in black gained entrance into the premises through Barrington Square. Mr. Maclean followed her inside, but there's no sign of her now."

"What did she look like?"

Alistair sighed. "I don't really know. She wore black, and her bonnet shielded her face from me. Whoever she is could simply take off her pelisse and hat and I'd never recognize her again."

"What did she want?"

Alistair hesitated for a second and then reconsidered. Anything he said to Christian and Elizabeth Delornay would remain between them, and they already knew the worst about his brother. "She'd been paid to give me a message concerning Harry. That I need to bring him under control." He met Christian's amused gaze. "As if I could."

"Oh dear," Elizabeth said. "I must confess to being worried about your brother. Christian and I were speaking of him only the other day."

"He seems intent on finding his way to the devil's very door," Alistair agreed. "And I don't know how to stop him."

Christian sat on the edge of the desk and took his wife's hand in his. "Perhaps you could ask Adam Fisher to speak to him."

"I wish I could. He was the only man that Harry ever *did* listen to. But he wants nothing to do with my brother anymore, and as he is my employer, I can hardly start meddling."

"Agreed. Perhaps it is time to let your brother face up to his responsibilities."

"But he'll fail and . . ." Alistair tried to swallow. "I'm afraid he'll end up dead and I'll never forgive myself."

Silence followed his confession and was interrupted by a knock on the door.

"Come in," Christian called.

A footman entered and bowed. "Mr. Delornay, the door-keeper reports that about five minutes ago, a woman dressed in black came through from the back of the house and went straight out the front door without acknowledging him at all."

"Why on earth would she do that?" Alistair asked. "Why come in here and leave straightaway?"

"Well, perhaps she did it to show she had the ability to get into the pleasure house, which I don't appreciate at all, *and* she found out something about you."

"And what might that be?"

"That you had the ability to get in here, too." Christian raised an eyebrow. "Now why do you think she wanted to know that?"